# THE STORIES OF THE LOTUS SUTRA

# PUBLISHER'S ACKNOWLEDGMENT

THE PUBLISHER gratefully acknowledges the generous help of the Hershey Family Foundation in sponsoring the publication of this book.

# THE STORIES OF THE
# LOTUS SUTRA

Gene Reeves

foreword by Rafe Martin

WISDOM PUBLICATIONS • BOSTON

Wisdom Publications
199 Elm Street
Somerville MA 02144 USA
www.wisdompubs.org

*Library of Congress Cataloging-in-Publication Data*

Reeves, Gene.
The stories of the Lotus sutra / Gene Reeves.
  p. cm.
Includes bibliographical references and index.
ISBN 0-86171-646-9 (pbk. : alk. paper)
1. Tripitaka. Sutrapitaka. Saddharmapundarikasutra—Criticism, interpretation, etc. I. Title.
BQ2057.R44 2010
294.3'823—dc22

                        2010025650


15 14 13 12 11 10
 6  5  4  3  2  1
eBook ISBN 978-0-86171-923-5

Cover and interior design by Gopa & Ted2, Inc. Cover illustration from The Illuminated Lotus Project (detail) © Roberta Mansell. Interior illustration © Robert Beer.

Wisdom Publications' books are printed on acid-free paper and meet the guidelines for permanence and durability of the Production Guidelines for Book Longevity of the Council on Library Resources.

Printed in the United States of America.

This book was produced with environmental mindfulness. We have elected to print this title on 30 percent PCW recycled paper. As a result, we have saved the following resources: 18 trees, 6 million BTUs of energy, 1,693 pounds of greenhouse gases, 8.153 gallons of water, and 495 pounds of solid waste. For more information, please visit our website, www.wisdompubs.org. This paper is also FSC certified. For more information, please visit www.fscus.org.

# TABLE OF CONTENTS

# FOREWORD BY RAFE MARTIN

A S A YOUNG MAN the great Japanese Zen Master Hakuin was terrified of falling into hell. He'd heard that salvation lay in the Lotus Sutra and so eagerly got hold of a copy and read it. He found—to his great disappointment—that it was just stories. He'd been so hopeful. And so now he put it aside. Years later, after much strong practice/realization, Hakuin happened to be looking at the Sutra again. As he read, a cricket chirruped nearby from within the foundations of the temple—and with that, Hakuin experienced deep enlightenment. Tears streaming down his face, he felt he now finally understood why the Lotus Sutra was called the "King of Sutras"—and he found himself overwhelmed by its depth, relevance, and profundity.

My old teacher Roshi Philip Kapleau used to say, quoting Hakuin, "The ancient teachings illumine the mind, and the mind illumines the ancient teachings." In other words, we ourselves have to bring the Lotus Sutra to life, even as it works skillfully on bringing us into our own real life. The relationship is dynamic and mutual, never static.

Actually, the Lotus Sutra (or the Dharma Flower Sutra, as Dr. Reeves beautifully terms it) is cosmic in scope and setting, vast in its imagination. And we, here on Planet Earth, have been literally dying for lack of such deep imagination. The corporation that pollutes the stream behind the nursery school is suffering, and causing suffering, too, from lack of imagination, lack of seeing how productivity, profit, community, and the communal resources of clean air and pure water are completely interconnected. War and hatred stem from similar failures of imagination, as does the rampant consumerism that literally melts icecaps and leaves polar bears to starve and die. We can see the shriveled fruits of failed imagination all around us. We live within it. But what would fulfilled imagination look like?

The Lotus Sutra tells us. It shows us that to the awakened imagination in reality we live in a buddha land. And that we ourselves, and all living beings, are buddhas! Talk about minds-eye-opening! Talk about revolutionary!

Imagination is a Way, and it is food and nourishment and a bed to rest upon while we're on the Way. Gene Reeves' stories from the Lotus Sutra *are* the Lotus Sutra, are Mind, are food and bed and shelter and hiking boots and a staff in our hands. For, wherever we're at, we can always go farther toward realizing the actualities that the Sutra embodies. As Hakuin also said, "Buddhism is like a mountain. The more you climb it the higher it gets. It's like an ocean. The further you go into it the deeper it gets."

To vow the vows to save all beings, to realize buddha-nature, and then to not just take a shortcut to personal peace but go through all the stages of bodhisattva development is to dream a big dream. What the Lotus Sutra through its stories reveals is that all beings are actually right now, *in reality*, already on that Great Way, that endless Path—whether they know it or not, whether they call it that or not. Great wisdom, great compassion, selflessness, skillful liberative technique, determined resolve, vigorous application are the heart of our common humanity. We all already have these in full. They are our nature. And yet, at the same time it remains up to each of us to actualize them. And to do that we first need to begin to see the possibility of such awakening and of making such effort. We have to be able to *imagine* it. Only then we can work at it for real. The Lotus Sutra is a skillful device left by the great teacher Shakyamuni Buddha to do just that—to open a gateway to ourselves, and what we actually are and so might be; a great engine of awakened activity to benefit all beings.

Gene Reeves skillfully props open the door to that deep imagination in our time, and by wisely focusing in this book on *stories* themselves, consistently gets us to the heart of the matter. If not for him, many of us would just be hopefully hanging on to an old text, lugging it around, gazing at it up on our bookshelves wondering how to get it to speak. Is there a button? Should I shake it? What?

For Gene knows that stories are not just make-believe, and not just bunches of words skillfully strung together, either. They are a technology, maybe the oldest and most powerful on the planet, real tools for inner change that can help us see with our minds and hearts, awaken deep aspirations, enhance our skills, revive the will to leave old and self-centered paths behind as we keep on working to accomplish the way of the real, fully flowered human being. Stories are not dogmas, or what Gene calls "doctrines." Nor do they address our somewhat lazy tendency of relying on belief. Stories are themselves *experiences* and here lies their power, a power that athletes today may understand better than scholars. If swimmers, for instance, want to swim better, they visualize doing it. They imagine a pool, feel the water temperature, see the color, draw in the salt or chlorine smell. Then they swim perfectly, feeling the water flowing smoothly past, feeling the muscles of the arms, shoulders, legs working perfectly, effortlessly, hearing the gurgling chime of water on the move. Then, getting into a real pool, in this actual world, they actually swim better. Experiences in stories get us or allow us to see with our minds, to experience realities of a different than physical sort. Yet what we experience in the imagination can affect us as deeply as actual experiences, ones we may draw on in memory. Their effect may be subtle, but it is not trivial.

As a storyteller I've experienced this myself in the act of telling stories, and I've seen it happen, too, with all sorts of audiences. When a story is told another, older kind of attention emerges. You can see it in people's eyes and faces, see it in the way they hold their bodies at "Once upon a time." Then this place we're in, where we're hearing the story told, whether it's a small room, a theater, a gymnasium, a cafeteria, a tent, or a hillside under the dark open sky, fades. That literal place becomes secondary, as in a figure/ground reversal, and the so-called "inner world," the world of the imagination, becomes primary. The world we *create* comes to the fore. We temporarily touch base with our innate power to participate in and co-create reality, and find again the original bonds of community and self. Though this happens often and naturally, it is never less than a thrilling moment. I've seen audiences shiver with cold on hot summer nights when stories are told set in ice and snow. I've seen alienated teenagers come to life, and seen them, after the story, share a newfound excitement with their own imaginative power.

Words create pictures in the mind. And each listener creates his or her own way of seeing, his or her own unique version of the tale. No one today knows how we do it—take sounds on the air, or squiggles on a page, and create realms that may never be seen with our physical eyes, uncover vast internal mandalas of good and evil, forests, mountains, and seas. Where are these scenes? Not in our heads. In our heads are bone, blood, and brain. So where is the realm of vision? This mysterious power to *see* seems to be hard-wired into our human being, for it happens naturally pretty much anywhere a story is well-told. Stories of bravery rouse our own courage. Stories of compassion awaken our own kindness and generosity. Stories of cause and effect make us wiser. Stories that change our perception of our own deep purposes on this earth can change the way we actually live and interact with ourselves and with our fellow beings. Stories in words may open doors unreachable by other technologies. Like the swimmer visualizing and practicing in a visionary pool, they help us develop our skills to first imagine, and then live, well. Unlike mere dogmas that can so easily put us to sleep, stories bring us to life.

I'd read the Lotus Sutra long ago and found it to be cosmic and full of wonders, just like Gene Reeves says. In fact, I'd found it to be a treasure house of stories, core stories of Buddhist vision and imagination, which is, in effect, Reality. In the Lotus Sutra or, maybe more accurately *as the Lotus Sutra*, are the stories/parables of the burning house and of the oxcart of the Great Way already carrying all beings; the story of the poor son of the rich man; the story of the jewel sewn into the robe; the stories of assurance of all eventually becoming buddhas—even us!— and the short sutra/chapter on the power of the Bodhisattva Kannon, the bodhisattva of great, limitless compassion. I read them all long ago and was indeed moved by this tremendous sense of vision. But then I'd set the sutra aside, looking into pithier texts like the Diamond Sutra, more down-to-earth ones like the Platform Sutra, and funnier, more iconoclastic ones like the Vimalakirti Sutra.

Now I'm going to have to put the Dharma Flower Sutra back on my essential reading list. I'll have lots more to look at and work with this time around, thanks to Gene Reeves and his dedicated work. Hands palm to palm. I'm deeply grateful for this offering. I think you will be too.

Rafe Martin

RAFE MARTIN is an award-winning, internationally known author and storyteller who has been a featured teller at the prestigious National Storytelling Festival, the International Storytelling Center, and the Joseph Campbell Festival of Myth and Story. He is also a fully ordained lay Zen practitioner with many years of formal Zen practice and study, and the author most recently of *The Banyan Deer: A Parable of Courage and Compassion*.

# INTRODUCTION

B
E FOREWARNED! This book might transform you into the kind of Buddhist who loves the Lotus Sutra and therefore deeply cares about this world. It is a commentary on the stories of the Lotus Sutra, a sutra that more than any other has been both loved and reviled. Though intended to be a companion volume to my translation of the Lotus Sutra,[1] this does not mean that it cannot be read without the translation at hand. I think everything in this book can be understood on its own. Still, one's understanding of the Dharma Flower Sutra will be greatly enhanced by reading the translation—or better yet by reading a Chinese version!

In this book I try to avoid use of non-English terms, including Sanskrit terms. Yet to some extent they cannot be avoided. I frequently use such terms as *buddha, dharma, bodhisattva, shravaka, pratyekabuddha*, and so on, all of which are Sanskrit terms, though some have been brought into the English language. In my view at least, good translations of these terms are not to be found. On the other hand, there are Sanskrit terms often used in English by Buddhist scholars and others that I believe can indeed better be understood in translation.

Chinese Buddhist terms, both proper names and common nouns, can be and often are translated in various ways. In fact, a great many

Sanskrit Buddhist terms have been translated in various ways into Chinese. The Buddhist names and terms used in this book are all from my translation, *The Lotus Sutra*. In the back of that volume, you can find two large glossaries in which are shown Sanskrit, Chinese, and Japanese versions of all of the proper names and Buddhist terms found in this book.

Though originally given as a series of lectures, versions of most of the chapters in this book were previously published in the magazine *Dharma World* over a period of several years. All have been revised for this volume, and some new material has been added. I have tried to have the vocabulary of this work be consistent, from beginning to end of the book itself, and also with that of my translation.

During most of my adult life I have been both a teacher and a preacher, roles which I understand to be different, though, of course, teaching can be included within preaching and sometimes a little preaching may show up in a teacher. And that is what this book does, at least that is what I hope it does. I hope it will inspire at least some readers not only to understand the Lotus Sutra better but also to embrace it, at least some part of its core teaching. I hope some will be moved by it to improve their lives in some significant way. But where it has seemed relevant to do so, I have included factual information both about the text and about the subjects of the stories in the text.

I hope it will shed some light on and even open up the profound meaning of that text—which is normally known in East Asia as the Dharma Flower Sutra.[2] (In this book I will use "Lotus Sutra" and "Dharma Flower Sutra" interchangeably.) Though any text, including the Dharma Flower Sutra, can be interpreted and understood in various ways, I believe that this text is first of all a religious text, intended primarily not to settle some dispute among monks in ancient India, or to expound philosophical doctrines, but rather to influence the lives of its hearers or readers in highly significant ways. In an important way, we might say that the text wants to teach and transform you! For that purpose to be fulfilled or even appreciated widely, it is important that the meaning and thrust of the Sutra be readily available to ordinary English-language readers. This attempt to interpret the Lotus Sutra in plain words is an attempt to have its rich meanings and significance available to a wider and widening audience.

The Lotus Sutra uses a variety of stories, including its famous parables, to draw us into its world, a world in which, if we truly enter it, we are likely to be transformed. It is thus a book of enchantment, a story book.

Emphasis on stories can be contrasted with emphasis on *doctrines*, or, as we tend to prefer these days, "teachings." The Lotus Sutra does have teachings. Indeed, one meaning of "dharma" is "teachings." Most important perhaps of its teachings are the doctrines of skillful means, of the One Buddha Vehicle, of the long life of the Buddha and many embodiments of Buddha, and of universal buddha-nature. An outline of the main teachings can be found in my "Translators Introduction" to *The Lotus Sutra*. Stories, perhaps parables especially, can be seen as illustrations of such teachings, and often they are. This is one way to understand and interpret the Lotus Sutra—but to understand its teachings and stories only in this way may be to miss what the Lotus Sutra is really about.

I believe that nearly everything taught in the Lotus Sutra is for the purpose of reorienting the lives of its hearers and readers. Its teachings, I believe, are not—at least not primarily—for giving us interesting ideas, or for adding to our store of knowledge, or for teaching us doctrines to believe or affirm. The teachings of the Dharma Flower Sutra are aimed at changing people's lives.

In this sense, the Dharma Flower Sutra is as much, or more, an earthly, bodily, "physical" text as it is a spiritual one. It aims not merely for spiritual experiences, but change in behavior. In Chapter 12, the

Bodhisattva Accumulated Wisdom says, "I have observed that in the [whole] world there is not even a spot as small as a mustard seed where [the Buddha] has not laid down body and life as a bodhisattva for the sake of the living." (LS 252) The Lotus Sutra has to do with laying down one's body and life.

It may be that both the teachings and the stories are not so much ends as they are means to something else. The "something else" is not easy to describe, or to believe, as the text tells us over and over again. It is nothing less than a radical transformation of the hearer or reader of the Sutra.

Take, for example, the doctrine of universal buddha-nature, which can also be said to be a doctrine of universal liberation or salvation. It has been said that this doctrine of universal salvation is the core teaching of the Lotus Sutra, and in a sense it is. But universal salvation is not something anyone can experience for themselves. In the text it approaches being something of a metaphysical doctrine, asserted implicitly over and over again, without argument. As universal, it cannot, of course, be illustrated or demonstrated. But stories can be told that reinforce the idea.

Thus stories are told of shravakas (those who hear the Buddha) who, despite having previously bought into the arhat ideal, an ideal which assumes that they are incapable of reaching the highest goal of becoming buddhas, become instead bodhisattvas—beings on the way to becoming buddhas. A story is told of Devadatta, infamous everywhere as a kind of epitome of evil due to his efforts to harm or kill the Buddha or to split the sangha, the community of monks—Devadatta is assured by the Buddha that he too is to become a buddha. And a story is told of a young dragon princess who, despite being both young and female (traditionally regarded as handicaps), is able to become a buddha extremely quickly.

All of these stories essentially say to the hearer or reader, "you too." If shravakas and evil monks and little girls can become buddhas, so can you. And the teaching that buddha-nature is universal, a teaching not explicitly presented but strongly implied in the Lotus Sutra, does the same thing. It basically says that there are no exceptions to having buddha-nature; therefore you cannot make an exception of yourself.

That, I think, is the core purpose of the Lotus Sutra, not merely the abstract notion of universal awakening, but the always-present possibility and power of awakening, which is a kind of flowering, in each one of us.

The Buddha says to Shariputra in Chapter 3 of the Lotus Sutra, "Did I not tell you before that when the buddhas, the world-honored ones, by using causal explanations, parables, and other kinds of expression, teach the Dharma by skillful means, it is all for the purpose of supreme awakening? All these teachings are for the purpose of transforming people into bodhisattvas." (LS 112)

These stories, then, are instruments, skillful means, to help us see and embrace what we might not otherwise see or appreciate—the potential and power in each of us to take up the way of the bodhisattva, which is to become supremely awakened, which is to become a buddha.

Such stories should be taken seriously but not too seriously. Taken too seriously, too literally, too doctrinally, they can mislead. Take, for example, what is probably the most famous parable in the Dharma Flower Sutra, the parable of the burning house, found in Chapter 3. In that story, in order to get his children to flee their burning house their father promises them a variety of carriages, goat-drawn carriages, deer-drawn carriages, and carriages drawn by oxen. That promise works to get the children out of the house to safety. But, after everyone is safely out of the burning house, the father has some second thoughts about the carriages. Realizing his own great wealth, he decides to give each of the children something even greater than he had promised, namely a carriage drawn by a great white ox—a carriage called the "Great Vehicle."

In the text itself, the three original carriages are called the shravaka, pratyekabuddha, and buddha vehicles. And it is said that the third is the "Great Vehicle," the vehicle pursued by bodhisattvas. What is the relation of this third vehicle and the "Great Vehicle" that is given in place of the three? Are there four vehicles in total, or only three? This question and questions related to it have been pondered over, discussed, and debated for centuries. Several different solutions to the seeming puzzle have been offered. And the question raised is not a trivial one; it has to do with the relation of the Great Vehicle, the Mahayana, and the bodhisattva path to the paths of the shravakas and pratyekabuddhas.

But perhaps the problem only arises from taking the numbers too seriously. The point of the story has nothing at all to do with the number of kinds of carriages. Basically the story is to have us understand that, while any number of kinds of teachings can lead to entering the way, the path of the bodhisattva is what eventually leads to being a buddha. The number of kinds of vehicles is irrelevant! Concern over it can be a distraction from the core message—that no matter what kind of carriage you pursue, you are always also pursuing supreme awakening and will become a buddha!

The emphasis here on stories means that some things are left out, from the Dharma Flower Sutra itself most prominently perhaps discussion of Chapters 17, 18, and 19, Chapter 26, "Incantations," and of the so-called "opening" and "closing" sutras. There are also discursive sections in several chapters that are not treated in the present story-centered book.

Chapters 17, 18, and 19 are entitled "The Variety of Blessings," "Blessings of Responding with Joy," and "The Blessings of the Dharma Teacher." All three have to do with the many blessings that can come to one who truly understands the meaning of the long life of the Buddha or who follows the Sutra. Chapter 17 emphasizes the importance of believing and acting on the belief that the Buddha's life is extremely long, which amounts to following the way of the bodhi-sattva. This, it says, is even more important than following the transcendental practices or building stupas or temples. Chapter 18 emphasizes, as the title indicates, the importance of responding to the Sutra in joy. But here responding with joy entails spreading the teaching of the Sutra to others, either by teaching the Dharma oneself of by encouraging others to hear it from someone else. This is not unrelated to the previous chapter in that it is by spreading the Dharma from one person to another that the Buddha's life becomes longer and longer. Chapter 19 describes supernatural powers that may come to someone who embraces and teaches the Dharma Flower Sutra: powers of the senses, the eyes, ears, nose, tongue, and body, as well as powers of the mind. These powers are fantastic and interesting to read about, but I don't know that discussing them at length would add appreciably to this book.

Incantations, *dharanis* in Sanskrit, have played and continue to play an important role in East Asian Buddhism. Recitation and repetition of them, including but not only those in the Dharma Flower Sutra, is widely believed to be an important, especially auspicious Buddhist practice. And this is so whether the language be Chinese or Japanese, English or even Sanskrit. Today, each of several Japanese Buddhist organizations based on the Lotus Sutra has its own slightly different way of pronouncing the incantations found in the text. In any case, it is the sound that is efficacious, as no intellectual content is to be found in them. It may well be that this emphasis on sound in the absence of intellectual content in some ways serves a purpose not unlike that of stories. Without denying the importance of Buddhist teachings, they direct our attention away from doctrinal interpretation of the text and of the larger traditions of which it is a part toward an appreciation of *dharanis* that elicits a kind of mystical empowerment of those who are in their presence.

The main reason a chapter on incantations is not included in this book is that I am not ready to explain or interpret them—and suspect that I never will be. Like music, they are best enjoyed in the doing or hearing of them. I don't think I can add anything about them that would be helpful, and I might, as it were, destroy their spell, for they are spells, and spells can be broken.

The Sutra of Innumerable Meanings has long been taken to be a kind of "opening" to the Dharma Flower Sutra itself, where it is mentioned. But there is not a story in it. At a doctrinal level it can be taken to be a supplement, even a kind of explanation of an important emphasis within the Dharma Flower Sutra, an emphasis which is embodied in the title of Chapter 2 of the Dharma Flower Sutra, "Skillful Means." It can be seen as providing an interpretation of skillful means before that term is given the kind of prominence it has in the Dharma Flower Sutra. Thus, to begin with a discussion of the Sutra of Innumerable Meanings would be to give a kind of emphasis to doctrine, especially to the great powers of bodhisattvas and to the characteristics of the body of a buddha. This is not what I think the Lotus Sutra wants to emphasize. Thus, after some discussion of the role of stories, we begin with a story about the Buddha and his great assembly rather than with this "opening sutra."

In the Sutra of Contemplation of the Dharma Practice of Universal Sage Bodhisattva, the so-called "closing sutra" of the threefold Lotus Sutra, the Lotus Sutra is mentioned. This is also a different genre of text. It is a guided meditation, especially intended, at least as the tradition has taken it, to be a guide to repentance. Here, too, the emphasis is hardly on doctrine or teachings. It provides a visualization sequence that is probably impossible to follow, at least intellectually, thus eliciting a kind of experience in the reader which can lead to the practice, both internally and ritually, of confession and repentance. Again, this may have some of the same effect as the Dharma Flower Sutra itself, but it lives, so to speak, in a different kind of environment.

The Dharma Flower Sutra is not a Chinese or Japanese text, at least not *only* a Chinese or Japanese text. It is a text originating in India some twenty-two centuries or more ago. A Sanskrit version, or versions, which themselves would have been translations or adaptations from some more common language or languages, were translated into Chinese several times during the first few centuries of the common era. One of those Chinese translations, that of Kumarajiva, became enormously popular and influential in Chinese culture and thence in all of East Asia, including China, Korea, Japan, and Vietnam. And this Chinese version has now been translated into many European languages, several times into English, and also in recent years into French, Italian, German, Russian, and other languages.

While Kumarajiva's Chinese version has been adapted into Japanese, no one imagines that this Japanese version, or the Chinese version, or any other version is by itself the Dharma Flower Sutra, the Sutra of the Lotus Flower of the Wonderful Dharma, to use the full title. The precise meaning of the term "The Dharma Flower Sutra" and its equivalents in other languages has to remain somewhat imprecise, as there is no single text which is "The Lotus Sutra," no one original from which others are derived. Even in the Sutra itself, there is no consistently maintained distinction between the Dharma Flower Sutra and Buddha Dharma. In a sense, we can say that the Sutra understands itself to be the most inclusive and important expression of the teachings of the Buddha.

1

# THE ENCHANTING WORLD
# OF THE LOTUS SUTRA

Chinese/Japanese term often used for "introduction" is more literally "entrance gateway." And while that is not what the first chapter of the Lotus Sutra is called, that is exactly what it is. It is a gateway through which one can enter a new and mysterious world, an enchanting world—a world of the imagination.

The setting, the opening scene, is on Holy Eagle Peak. This Holy Eagle Peak is not off somewhere in another world. It is a real place on a mountain in northeast India. I was there a few years ago. But as well as being an actual, physical, and historical place, the Holy Eagle Peak of the Dharma Flower Sutra is a mythical place.

The place we visited, the geographical place, is like a ledge set on a steep mountainside, perhaps three-fourths of the way up the mountain. Above and below it, the mountain is both steep and rough, not the kind of place where anyone could sit and listen to a sermon or lecture. And the ledge itself would not hold more than three dozen or so people at a time.

In the Sutra this little place is populated by a huge assembly, with thousands of monks and nuns and laypeople, eighty thousand bodhisattvas, and a large number of gods, god-kings (including Indra, King of the Gods), dragon kings, chimera kings, centaur kings, ashura kings, griffin kings, satyrs, pythons, minor kings, and holy wheel-rolling kings. Already, just from the listing of such a population, and there is more, we know we have entered a realm that is special, even magical.

We do not know much about the Indian origins of the Lotus Sutra, but we can be reasonably confident that it was produced in northern India by monks, and it is very likely that many of its first hearers and readers would have known perfectly well that Holy Eagle Peak was in actuality much too small for the kind of assembly described at the beginning of Chapter 1. We are to understand from the very beginning, in other words, that this is a story, not a precise description of historical events, but a mythical account of historical events. It is meant not just for our knowledge, but for our participation. It invites us to use our own imagination to participate in the Sutra's world of enchantment.

Some years ago when I wrote to a friend that I had moved to Japan to work on the Lotus Sutra, he responded that he had read the Sutra a long time ago and could not remember much about it, except for the fact that it contained a lot of "miracle stories." There is, of course, a sense in which that is correct. The Sutra does have a great many stories of fantastic, supernormal, or supernatural events, and of the Buddha's and various bodhisattvas' holy or supernatural powers. But one thing these stories do not and cannot do is to function as "miracle stories" in the Christian sense of that term, that is, as stories that can be used to "prove" something about the intervention in history of a supernatural power.

The stories in the Dharma Flower Sutra, or at least many of them, are so fantastic, so imaginative, so unlike anything we have experienced, that they cannot possibly be taken for history or descriptions of factual matters, or stories about actual historical events. The reader of the Dharma Flower Sutra knows from the very first chapter that he or she has entered an imaginary world quite different from what we ordinarily perceive. And if the stories are successful, the reader will come to understand that he or she is empowered to perform miracles by them.

That this setting is in the actual world, on earth, is very important for the Lotus Sutra. In it there is explicit rejection of forms of idealism—exemplified for instance by Platonism—in which actual things are only poor reflections of some other, ideal reality. In Buddhism, idealism sometimes takes the form of a "two-truth theory" according to which there is a conventional world of appearance or phenomena and an absolute world of reality or truth. For the Dharma Flower Sutra, however, this world, the world of things, is an ultimately real world. This is the world in which Shakyamuni Buddha lives, both historically and in the present. This is the world in which countless bodhisattvas emerge from below to indicate the importance of bodhisattvas of this world taking care of this world. This is the world to which buddhas and bodhisattvas from all over the universe come to witness the teaching of Shakyamuni Buddha. This is the world in which all human beings are offered a special opportunity to be bodhisattvas and practice the Buddha Way, the way by which we too can be buddhas, buddhas right here on earth in the midst of the world's suffering, including our own.

## AFFIRMATION OF THE CONCRETE

William LaFleur[3] describes how Tendai thought, especially Chih-i's *Mo-ho-chih-kuan* and the Lotus Sutra, influenced a transformation of Japanese poetry in the twelfth century. He points out that in the Lotus Sutra there is a philosophical move that is the opposite of what predominated in the West under the influence of Platonism. In the Sutra, "the illustration is in no way subordinate to what it illustrates." Not a shadow of something else more real, "the narratives of the Lotus are not a means to an end beyond themselves. Their concrete mode of expression is not 'chaff' to be dispensed with in order to attain a more abstract, rational, or spiritual truth."

The Sutra itself says:

> Even if you search in all directions,
> You will find no other vehicles—
> Except the skillful means of the Buddha. (LS 128)

In other words, apart from concrete events, apart from stories, teachings, actions, and so on, there is no Buddhism.

Thus, LaFleur explains, Chih-i's contemplation is a kind of mindfulness directed toward objects of ordinary perception in which there is an implied rejection of the kind of ontological dualism in which essences are more real than concrete things. Thus what was important in the *Mo-ho-chih-kuan* for the poets Fujiwara no Shunzei (1114–1204) and Fujiwara no Teika (1162–1241) was the teaching of *gensho soku jisso*—the identity of the phenomenal and the real, held together in a dynamic tension by Chih-i's notion of the middle.

In LaFleur's words, this constitutes a kind of "ontological egalitarianism" in which the abstract is no more real than the concrete. As the philosopher of religion Shin'ichi Hisamatsu (1889–1980) suggested, "to dig to the core of the core is to discover the invalidity of such distinctions and also to discover that, seen from the inside, the surface is deep."

A famous poem of Teika is analyzed by LaFleur.

> Gaze out far enough,
> beyond all cherry blossoms
> and scarlet maples,
> to those huts by the harbor
> fading in the autumn dusk.[4]

This is no ordinary evocation of impermanence, but an invitation to see that by attempting to look over and beyond the ordinary and transient we discover that the huts in the distance have also begun to disappear, signifying a collapse of the distance between them and the cherries and maples.

LaFleur concludes:

> The world of such poetry and such drama was one in which determinate emotions or ideas were no longer fixed to determinate images or actions. Simple symbols no longer seemed adequate; their portrait was deemed naive because it had too severely limited the relationship among phenomena. The Buddhists of medieval Japan, nurtured as they were in Tendai, held that the universe was such that even "in one thought there are three thousand worlds" (*ichinen sanzen*). This implied the boundlessness of the interpenetration of phenomena with one another. To the dimension of depth in the universe itself these Buddhists reacted with a sense of awe.... And, to poets such as Shunzei, a universe of this depth deserved a degree and a mode of appreciation beyond that given to it by the traditional aesthetic.[5]

In Chapter 1 of the Sutra, before the vast assembly, having already preached the Sutra of Innumerable Meanings, the Buddha entered deeply into meditative concentration. Then, to prepare the assembly to hear the Buddha preach, various omens suddenly appeared—flowers rained down from the heavens on everyone, the earth trembled and shook, and the Buddha emitted a ray of light from between his eyebrows, lighting up eighteen thousand worlds to the east, so that the whole assembly could see these worlds in great detail, including their heavens and purgatories, all their living beings, and even their past and present buddhas. Surely we are being advised here that we are entering a different world, and a different kind of world, a world that is at once rich in fantasy and at the same time anchored in this world.

Thus the Dharma Flower Sutra opens up and reveals this world as a magical world, a world in which flowers rain down from the heavens, drums sound by themselves, and Shakyamuni Buddha lights up all the worlds with beams of light streaming from between his eyebrows. It is a world in which an illusory castle-city provides a resting place for weary travelers, in which a stupa emerges from the ground so that an extinct buddha from long ago can praise Shakyamuni for teaching the Dharma Flower Sutra, where the Bodhisattva Wonderful Voice, with his nearly perfect, giant, and radiant body, from another world makes flowers appear on Holy Eagle Peak and then comes through count- less millions of worlds with eighty-four thousand other bodhisattvas to visit Shakyamuni Buddha and others, and where the Bodhisattva Universal Sage comes flying through the sky on his white elephant with six tusks to visit and help those in this world.

I call this a world of enchantment. And *enchantment*, here, means a certain kind of fascination with the ordinary world. It means finding the special, even the supernatural, within the ordinary world of our existence. It means seeing this world itself as different, as special—as important and valuable. And this means that our lives—how we live and what we do—are important, not only for ourselves, but also for the Buddha and for the entire cosmos.

One person who understood well the importance of enchantment was Kenji Miyazawa, the poet, storyteller, science-fiction writer, scien- tist, and lover of the Lotus Sutra. Chanting *Namu Myoho Renge-kyo*, he imagined his spirit in boundless space, where he was filled with joy in the great cosmos, and from which he returned to earth, having acquired strength and courage to endure a life of suffering.

Known throughout the Tohoku area of Japan as "Kenji *bosatsu*" (Kenji the bodhisattva), Miyazawa devoted his whole life to the Dharma Flower Sutra—to practicing the Lotus Sutra, to embodying the Lotus Sutra, to living the Lotus Sutra—for example by helping struggling farmers of Iwate Prefecture with modern agricultural science.

One of his most ambitious works, *A Night on the Milky Way Railroad*, was turned into a popular animated film and used in various Japanese *manga* comic books. It is a story about a young boy, Giovanni, and his friend Campanella, who ride a train to the stars together—a celestial railroad, soaring through deep space—experiencing numerous adventures and encountering unusual characters. In the final passages of the story it becomes clear that this night train to the stars that Giovanni and his friend Campanella are riding is actually a ferry for souls traveling to life after death!

In a chapter called "Giovanni's Ticket," the conductor asks the passengers for their tickets. Campanella, who is dead from drowning, like the other passengers has a small gray, one-way ticket. Giovanni, who at first is very nervous because he thinks he has no ticket at all, discovers in a pocket a larger folded piece of green paper with mysterious characters written down the center. Examining this ticket, the conductor is astonished, and asks: "Did you get this ticket from three-dimensional space?" Bird-catcher, another passenger, then exclaims:

> Wow, this is really something. This ticket will even let you go up to the real heaven. And not just to heaven, it is a pass that enables you to travel anywhere you want. If you have this, in fact, you can travel anywhere on this Milky Way Railway of the imperfect fourth-dimension of fantasy.[6]

Giovanni alone on that train has a magical round-trip pass that enables him to freely travel from the "three-dimensional space" of ordinary reality to anywhere in the "fourth-dimensional space" of the invisible, spiritual, imaginative, and enchanting world that is the Milky Way Railroad.

What is this extraordinary railway ticket that enables one to enter the fourth-dimensional world and then return to the ordinary world? Giovanni's ticket is the *gohonzon* (object of worship), or mandala, of Nichiren, with its inscription of the *daimoku*, the sacred title of the Lotus Flower of the Wonderful Dharma Sutra: "*Namu Myoho Renge-kyo.*" The *daimoku*, as it represents and embodies the Dharma Flower Sutra, provides a connection, a passage as it were, between earth and heaven, between earthly and cosmic perspectives, between science and imagination.

Like poets before him, Miyazawa understood the deepest meaning of the Lotus Sutra—an affirmation of the reality and importance of this world, the world in which suffering has to be endured, and can be, combined with an imaginative cosmic perspective engendered by devotion to the Lotus Sutra. And with his imaginative power and skill as a writer, Miyazawa offers Giovanni's ticket to each of us. Like the Sutra itself, he uses his own imagination to invite us into an imaginary other world in order to have us become more this-worldly.

In other words, the imagination, which makes it possible to soar above the realities of everyday existence, also makes it possible to function more effectively in this world.

When Giovanni wakes from his dream of adventures on that very strange and special railroad, he learns that his friend has indeed died, drowned in the river which is at that time the center of a festival. And Giovanni sees reflected in the water of the earthly river the river which is the Milky Way (named a river in Japanese). It is a kind of epiphany, a moment in which the vast cosmic reality and the right here on the ground are united in the imagination.

Having experienced the fantastic cosmic world, having experienced a unity of heavens and earth, Giovanni then finishes what he started out to do that day. He walks to the dairy and brings a bottle of milk home to his mother.

# 2

# STORIES OF THE LOTUS SUTRA

T HE CHIEF WAY in which the Lotus Sutra enchants is by telling stories—parables and similes, accounts of previous lives, stories of mythical events, and so forth.

Though there are various ways of counting, it contains well over two dozen different stories. In the Sutra, a great many traditional Buddhist doctrines are mentioned, such as the four noble truths, the eightfold path, the three marks of the Dharma, interdependent origination, the twelve-link chain of causation, the six perfections, and more. Even one of the Sutra's most emphasized teachings, that of the one vehicle of many skillful means, is initially presented as an explanation of why there is such a variety of teachings within Buddhism. There are plenty of teachings or doctrines in it, but if we want to approach a fuller understanding of what the Dharma Flower Sutra teaches, we had better pay attention to its stories, and not merely to propositions within them or to sentences that explain them, but also to the overall thrust and function of the stories within this very unusual Sutra.

It is not incidental that the original Lotus Sutra probably began with the chapter on skillful means, Chapter 2, and then in Chapter 3 told a story, the parable of the burning house, to illustrate and explain skillful means. And this "parable" chapter is immediately followed by the "attitude" (*adhimukti*) chapter, which is built around another story—the parable of the rich father and the poor son.

As we have it now, the first twenty-two chapters of the Sutra, except for Chapter 12, constitute a single story, a story about a time when the Buddha was at the place called Holy Eagle Peak and preached the Dharma Flower Sutra. In other words, about 85 percent of the Sutra falls within a single story.

Thus while there are many stories in the Lotus Sutra, many of them are actually episodes within a larger story that begins with Chapter 1 as a kind of introduction and continues through Chapter 22, which provides a natural end for the Sutra, as well as to the story that begins in the first chapter. Chapter 12 is inserted in order to emphasize the universality of the buddha-nature, and Chapters 23 through 28 are added, for the most part, as illustrations of bodhisattva practice. Thus, chapters 12 and 23 through 28 are regarded by some scholars as a third group of chapters in terms of the order of their inclusion into the larger text. In these chapters there are almost no references to the main ingredients of the story found in Chapters 1 through 22: the stupa in the air, the buddhas and bodhisattvas who have come from all over the universe, or the bodhisattvas who have emerged from the ground. Some of these appended chapters no doubt circulated as independent sutras, as does Chapter 25, known as the "Kwan-yin Sutra," to this day.

Within the longer story that ends with Chapter 22, there are many other stories and parables, which in this book we will look at separately, while trying not to lose sight of the context, the larger story, in which they occur.

These stories are the primary skillful means through which the Dharma Flower Sutra invites us into its world, which is indeed our own world, albeit seen and experienced differently. But it goes without saying that not everyone will welcome such an invitation or read the stories in this way. Some will reject them as supernaturalistic miracle stories. Others will see them as nothing more than the intra-Buddhist polemics of more than twenty centuries ago. Some will judge them to be nothing more than quaint filler for a text that only seeks to promote itself, as if it were a panacea for all things, a spiritual "miracle cure."

Yet an invitation into an imaginative world can always be turned down or rejected. A religious text will not function as a religious text for everyone. There is no compelling science or logic to lead one into the world of the Dharma Flower Sutra. There are even good reasons to stay away. But there is an enchanting and fascinating dimension to the book, perhaps even a kind of benevolent seduction to be found in its stories.

## AFFIRMATION OF LANGUAGE

There is no shortage in Buddhism of words expressing distrust of words. There is some of that in the Lotus Sutra as well—but not a lot.

Words are never quite up to the tasks we give to them. We can never put into language just what it is that we see or feel or think. Our experience is always vastly richer than we can express. Yet words are what we have; they are part of the rich world that is given to us. Though always inadequate, they are probably the most important way in which human beings communicate—though not, of course, the only way. Like nothing else, they make it possible for us to travel across vast distances of both space and time. And, as we have seen, they can invoke a certain kind of concreteness.

It is not very clear to me just how it is that stories function to affirm the concrete. Is it merely that they are less abstract in some way than doctrines? "Everything is impermanent" is, after all, about as abstract (and as metaphysical) as one can get. Stories do have a kind of concreteness about them, more, as it were, flesh and blood in them. But I do not think that is the complete account of how they can function to elicit the concrete.

Perhaps it is that to tell a story is to trust words, despite the fact that they are unreliable both in the sense that they are inadequate to the tasks of expressing or describing and in the sense that a speaker or writer can never know what kinds of associations or connotations will be suggested to the reader or hearer.

But, so far at least, words are, for many purposes, the best communication tool we have. Sometimes there is communication: questions get answered, feelings shared, descriptions used, images aroused, moral and practical purposes served.

Of course, storytelling is not the only or even primary function of words. So this does not tell us very much about the power of stories to express the concrete. I think that what is special about stories in this regard is that they use concrete images. The images of a burning house that each of us has when reading that parable may all be different from each other, but each is concrete in that it is an image of a particular house, and not at all like the abstract notion of "house."

Yet concrete images are, of course, in our minds. There is no need for me to have seen any burning house, much less any particular burning house, for a house to burn in my mind, as a kind of reality created in part by the words on the page. The image, in a sense, testifies to the efficacy of words—it provides evidence that words can make things live, at least in our imaginations.

If words can evoke images of concrete imaginary realities, can they not evoke images of concrete, non-imaginary realities as well? Can they not, in other words, help us to be in touch with the concrete world that always envelops us? If so, might it not be the case that stories, by being concrete themselves, function to draw our attention to the concrete, to the world of everyday plants and people, houses and vehicles?

It is quite possible to study the Dharma Flower Sutra by focusing on its teachings, perhaps using its parables and stories to illustrate those teachings. But by focusing on the stories, we will discover some things that we could not see by focusing on teachings.

In many ways the Dharma Flower Sutra is a difficult book that stretches beyond, and sometimes even makes fun of, the tradition in which it lives. It surprises. But it does so primarily in its stories, which force us to think, for example, about what it means to tell the truth, or what it means to be a bodhisattva or a buddha. And its stories call for, elicit, a creative response from the hearer or reader.

## INVITATION TO CREATIVE WISDOM

What is the purpose of all this enchantment and magic? Entertainment? In one sense, yes! It is to bring joy to the world. Stories are for enjoyment. But not only for enjoyment. Not in all of them, but in a great many of the stories in the Lotus Sutra, especially in those that are used to demonstrate practice of skillful means, it is important to recognize that what is being demanded of the reader is not obedience to any formula or code or book, not even to the Lotus Sutra, but imaginative and creative approaches to concrete problems. A father gets his children out of a burning house, another helps his long-lost adult son gain self-respect and confidence through skillful use of psychology, still another father pretends to be dead as a way of shocking his children into taking a good medicine he had prepared for them, and a rich man tries to relieve his friend's poverty. These stories all involve finding creative solutions to quite ordinary problems.

Creativity requires imagination, the ability to see possibilities where others see only what is. It is, in a sense, an ability to see beyond the facts, to see beyond the way things are, to envision something new. Of course, it is not only imagination that is required to overcome problems. Wisdom, or intelligence, and compassion are also needed. But it is very interesting that the problems encountered by the buddha figures in the parables of the Lotus Sutra are never solved by the book. They do not pull out a sutra to find a solution to the problem confronting them. In every case, something new, something creative, is attempted; something from the creative imagination.

Of course, creativity is not always successful. In the first parable of the Dharma Flower Sutra, the parable of the burning house, before the father comes up with an effective way to get his children out of the burning house, he tries some things that do not work. He shouts at his children, telling them to "Get out!" He considers forcing them out by wrapping them in robes or putting them on a tablet and carrying them out. And when one approach does not work, he tries another. Or consider, perhaps as a better example, the parable of the hidden treasure, the gem in the hem, in Chapter 8. Here a rich friend tries to help out his poor friend by sewing an extremely valuable gem into his robe. And this does not work. The poor man does not realize that he has this great treasure until he is told so in a subsequent encounter with his rich friend. The possibility of failure is always a part of any creative effort, requiring additional creativity.

We do not find mistakes in all the stories by any means, but in many there is still an element of surprise, creativity, and inventiveness. The guide along the difficult way conjures up an illusion, a castle in which the weary travelers can rest. The dragon princess does her little thing with the jewel. Even the Buddha Excellent in Great Penetrating Wisdom of Chapter 7, after achieving supreme awakening only with the help of many gods and promising to preach, surprises everyone by waiting twenty thousand eons before preaching the Dharma Flower Sutra, which he then proceeds to do without resting for eight thousand eons, then (exhausted?) retreats into deep meditation for eighty-four thousand eons, forcing sixteen bodhisattva novices to teach and explain the Sutra for eighty-four thousand eons. Clearly there is a lot of imagination at work in the creation of these stories.

In a certain way, creativity involves being free from karma, from fate due to past actions. In the Indian context in which Buddhism arose and the Dharma Flower Sutra was compiled, this was especially important. A religiously based, rigid caste system apparently forced many to despair. Many became resigned to a Hindu fatalism that taught that everything is as it should be and that if you follow the rules you may be able to be born in better circumstances in your next life. Buddhism offered a way out of this system of thought and social structures, a new world in which one could exercise the imagination, in part at least to gain control of one's life.

But fatalism is by no means unique to India. In the West it could take the form of debilitating doctrines of divine omnipotence and providence. Liberation from such fatalism is important. But creativity is needed not only for breaking the bonds of such karma. People can be victims of other kinds of karma, of dull habits, or of lack of self-confidence and shyness, or of terrible mental states. People can also be victims of abusive parents or siblings. And people can be held in bondage by unjust political or social systems.

Through the very act of creating a community of monks, which became the Buddhist Sangha, the Buddha recognized, and enabled others to recognize, that social structures do not have to be as they are. This was recognized as well, I think, by some Japanese followers of the Lotus Sutra in the nineteenth century, long before anyone in Japan was influenced by modern Western sociological ideas. Poor people would have something like a parade in which there was too much drinking perhaps, and cross-dressing, and other forms of unusual, custom-breaking, behavior. Even the homes of rich people were invaded and people took whatever they wanted, asking, "Why not?"

Creativity is a path to liberation, and imagination is a path to liberation. That is why the Dharma Flower Sutra invites us into a world of enchantment—to enable us to enter the path of liberation, a liberation that is always both for ourselves and for others. Notice, please, that this first chapter of the Lotus Sutra does not come to us as an order; it is an invitation to enter a new world and thereby take up a new life, but it is only an invitation.

But this invitation also carries a warning—enter this world and your life may be changed. It may be changed in ways you never expected.

The Dharma Flower Sutra comes with a warning label. Instead of saying "Dangerous to your health," it says, "Dangerous to your comfort." The worst sin in the Lotus Sutra is complacency and the arrogance of thinking one has arrived and has no more to do. The Sutra challenges such comfort and comfortable ideas. Danger can be exciting. It can also be frightening. We do not know if we can make it. We do not know whether we even have the power to enter the path, the Buddha Way.

## EMPOWERMENT

This is why, while the Dharma Flower Sutra begins with enchantment, it does not end there. It goes further to announce that each and every one of us has within us a great and marvelous power, later called "buddha-nature." The term "buddha-nature" does not appear in the Lotus Sutra, probably because it had not yet been invented, but the idea that would later be called "buddha-nature" runs through these stories not as a mere thread, but as a central pillar—albeit a very flexible one.

Stories can be understood, of course, as illustrating teachings, which in a sense they do. But to see them only in that way, as something designed to improve our understanding, is, I believe, to miss their meaning. These little gems of stories have within them the power to persuade readers that they have the potential and power not only to make more of their own lives but also to make a contribution to the good of others.

And since according to the stories the Buddha—now no longer existing in this world in the way he once was—needs others to do his work in this world, what readers do with their own potential to be buddhas makes a cosmic difference, that is, what we do determines to what degree the work of Shakyamuni Buddha gets done in this world. Using that power can cause the whole universe to shake in six different ways! It can even cause a magnificent stupa to come flying to where we are.

The fireworks in the Sutra are not mere entertainment. They are, I believe, to stress the reality and importance of this world, which is the world of Shakyamuni Buddha, the world in which he preached the Dharma Flower Sutra, bringing joy to countless millions.

Stories of such cosmic events—drums rolling in the heavens; flowers raining down from the skies; beams of light, or even long tongues, streaming from a buddha; dark places becoming illuminated; things and bodhisattvas flying through space—all such things are an invitation to exercise the imagination.

Perhaps the most important of the stories in this connection is the one about the great horde of bodhisattvas who spring up from below the earth in Chapter 15. The chapter begins with some of the bodhisattvas who have come from other worlds asking the Buddha to allow them to stay and help him out by preaching the Sutra in this world. But the Buddha promptly declines on the ground that there are many bodhisattvas already in this world who can protect, read, recite, and teach the Dharma Flower Sutra. Whereupon the ground quakes and a fantastically enormous number of bodhisattvas and their attendants emerge from below the earth, where they had been living. Maitreya and the others almost go into shock from unbelief when told by the Buddha that these bodhisattvas are his own disciples, whom he has been training for countless millions of eons. Why, it is as impossible to believe as a twenty-five-year-old man claiming to have a hundred-year-old son! But the point has been made—it is not by bodhisattvas from other worlds that we are to be saved, but by those who belong to this world.

These kinds of stories are like invitations to unfreeze our imagination, our creativity, so that we too might be empowered through them to make use of the power that is within us to be the Buddha, which means nothing more or less than being representatives of Shakyamuni Buddha in this world by practicing, like him, the bodhisattva way.

The purpose of the enchantment is in part to have us know not only intellectually that we have buddha-nature, but also to have us know it physically, in our very muscles and bones. Then we can become the hands and feet of, the very body of, the Buddha. We are empowered by the Lotus Sutra to take charge of our lives, so that the world will be a better place because of our choices and our actions. In this way, the Dharma Flower Sutra, chanted and studied and embraced, can give us fantastic power, helping us to realize that we too have this fantastic ability to be creative, to use our imaginations and our energy to make ourselves and those around us, that is the entire world, a bit better than it would be otherwise.

Right now in this year, right now in Tokyo or New York or Colombo or wherever you are, let the flowers rain, let the drums sound, let the world shake, and let the Dharma-wheel roll on!

# 3

## THE DHARMA FLOWER ASSEMBLY

THE FIRST PART of Chapter 1 of the Lotus Sutra, "Introduction," is devoted to setting the scene for what is to follow in the Sutra. It is, in a sense, the first chapter of a story that ends with Chapter 22, "Entrustment." It truly is an introduction, in that it both introduces the overarching story and creates a setting for this story, as well as introducing the reader to the special, even magical, world of Dharma Flower Sutra stories.

## THE STORY

The Buddha, we are told, once lived on Holy Eagle Peak, near Rajagriha the capital of Magadha, where he was accompanied by a vast assembly—a great variety of twelve thousand monks, nuns, lay devotees, kings, arhats, eighty thousand bodhisattvas, gods, god kings, dragon kings, ashura kings, griffin kings, chimera kings, centaur kings, and many other kinds of fantastic supernatural mythical beings.

Having preached the Sutra of Innumerable Meanings, the Buddha entered deeply into meditative concentration (*samadhi*). Then, to prepare the assembly to hear the Buddha preach, various omens suddenly appeared—extremely rare flowers rained down from the heavens on everyone, the earth trembled in the six different ways that an earth can tremble, and the Buddha emitted a ray of light from the tuft of white hair between his eyebrows, lighting up eighteen thousand worlds to the east, so that the whole assembly could see these worlds in great detail, including their heavens and purgatories, all their living beings, and even their past and present buddhas.

Then Maitreya Bodhisattva asked Manjushri Bodhisattva why the Buddha was displaying such a wonder. Manjushri's response provides a brief summary of all of the major teachings of the Sutra. The Buddha, he says, intends to teach the great Dharma, send down the rain of the great Dharma, blow the conch of the great Dharma, beat the drum of the great Dharma, and explain the meaning of the great Dharma. He explains that in the past he has seen many other buddhas do the same thing in preparation for delivering a very great and difficult teaching, including Sun and Moon Light Buddha, who also displayed such a wonder before preaching the Dharma Flower Sutra.

## COMMENTARY

The Sutra begins: "This is what I heard." This phrase occurs at the beginning of most Buddhist sutras to indicate that the sutra has come from the mouth of the Buddha. At the time the Buddha was alive, apparently writing had not yet been invented in India. The sutras are said to have been memorized and recited orally, originally by the Buddha's disciple Ananda. None were actually written down until four or more centuries after the death of the Buddha.

We know that a written version of the Lotus Sutra was not completed until several centuries after the death of the Buddha. Nevertheless, it begins with "This is what I heard" in order to signify that it is an authentic embodiment of the Buddha's teachings, of Buddha Dharma.

While the Sanskrit term *dharma* is sometimes translated as "law," I believe that for many readers this creates a false impression of how the term is used in the Dharma Flower Sutra and in Buddhism in general. It is translated as "law" because it was translated by Kumarajiva into Chinese as *fa* (pronounced *hō* in Japanese), a term that can reasonably be translated into English as "law." But to many, the term "law" has negative connotations, reminding us of courts, police, and punishment. More important, the term "law" simply does not convey the rich meaning and significance of Buddha Dharma. That is why, like some other Buddhist terms, such as "nirvana," "sutra," or even "Buddha," it has become a term in the English language. And this is why the Rev. Senchu Murano, of Nichiren-shu, while originally using "Law," decided to use "Dharma" for the revised version of his very fine translation of the Lotus Sutra into English.[7]

While it can mean other things such as "way" or "method," there are four chief ways in which "dharma" is used in Buddhism:

(1) things—all the objects of experience that we can see, feel, hear, and touch, often translated as "phenomenon";

(2) the Buddha's teaching, a use which is often extended to include Buddhist teachings and practices generally, and thus can mean Buddhism itself;

(3) the truth that is taught in the Buddha's teachings, especially the highest truth disclosed in the awakening of the Buddha; and

(4) the reality that the truth reveals, that which enables and sustains all things in accord with interdependence.

## THE LOTUS SUTRA AS IMAGINATIVE VISION

As indicated in the first chapter, what the Dharma Flower Sutra offers is what we might call an imaginative vision. It not only does not ask us to accept its stories as though they were reports of historical facts; it invites us, from the very outset, to enter into a world that is very different from our ordinary world of historical facts, a world of stories in which strange things sometimes happen. In part, stories are used in the Dharma Flower Sutra to persuade and convince us, first of all, that we ourselves can take up the life of the bodhisattva.

## THE LOTUS SUTRA IS FOR ALL THE LIVING

Monks and nuns, laymen and laywomen, gods, dragons, satyrs, centaurs, ashuras, griffins, chimeras, pythons, humans and nonhumans, minor kings, and holy wheel-rolling kings, and others are all addressed by the Buddha in Chapter 1. What we should understand from this is that Buddha Dharma is not only for Buddhists, not only for those people who are good, and not only for human beings. Even gods and other heavenly creatures come to hear the Buddha's teaching.

There is an important truth here. While the Lotus Sutra, like any book, is very much a human creation, its significance goes beyond the human. The range of concern, in other words, is not limited to the human species, but extends to all the living. In part, this sense of cosmic importance is a reflection of the rich Indian imagination at the time the sutras were being compiled. People simply assumed that the world was populated with a rich variety of what we regard as mythical beings.

This imaginative vision urges us to reach out beyond what our eyes can see and our hands can touch, to understand ourselves as being significantly related to a much larger universe that is located in and transcends ourselves, our families, countries, and even species. It is a vision that urges us to imagine ourselves as part of a vast cosmos in which our own lives are important.

## SHARING THE DHARMA

In this story, the Buddha says he intends "to teach the great Dharma, to send down the rain of the great Dharma, to blow the conch of the great Dharma, to beat the drum of the great Dharma, and to explain the meaning of the great Dharma."

This represents an interesting mix of emotional and intellectual practices. The meaning of Dharma rain will be discussed at length later in this book. For now it is enough to say that it is a symbol of equality among the living, in that all the living equally receive the Dharma without discrimination or distinction.

The meaning of the conch and the drum is not so obvious. Almost certainly they are instruments used to lead an army in battle, to inspire and motivate soldiers to move forward. Similarly, those who receive the Dharma Flower Sutra in their hearts are not merely comforted by it; they are motivated to practice it passionately and to share it with others. Buddhism is in this sense a missionary religion. Here in Chapter 1 of the Lotus Sutra we can see that the Dharma is intended for all the living and that those who share it should enthusiastically share it with others. We can also think of the sound of the conch as representing the beauty of the Dharma, while the sound of the drums represents the power of the Dharma.

It is important to notice, also, that even enthusiastic teaching is to be accompanied by explanation of the Dharma. This suggests that we should not attempt to make only emotional appeals on behalf of the Dharma or treat it only as an object of faith. It is equally important that the Dharma be understood. What is both embraced and understood will have a more lasting value than what is embraced merely on an emotional basis. This is probably truer now than it was when the Sutra was composed. Today people are trained to think scientifically, rationally, and critically. For the Dharma Flower Sutra to be accepted by modern people, it has to be carefully taught and explained, and even criticized, in terms that people can understand.

## HEAVENLY FLOWERS

That heavenly flowers rain both on the Buddha and on the whole assembly is very important. It means that it is not only beautiful and rewarding to preach the Dharma; it is also beautiful and rewarding to hear it. It is, in other words, one of the ways in which there is equality among all of those in the congregation, including the Buddha. This shows that there should be no sharp distinction between teachers and learners. While many forms of Buddhism have adopted a kind of system in which some are authorized to be permanent teachers and others to be students, the Dharma Flower Sutra teaches that we should all be both teachers and learners. Nonetheless there will be times when some are in special positions as teachers or as learners—but this should always be understood as temporary and relative. All can and need to be teachers, and all can and need to be learners.

As any good teacher knows, what makes students good is not the ability to repeat what the teachers have said, but the ability to think critically and creatively about what has been said, thereby helping the teacher to be a learner. It is a remarkable feature of many of the stories in the Dharma Flower Sutra that the person who represents the Buddha is a learner, one who tries things, makes mistakes, and learns from experience.

## OTHER OMENS

In the first chapter we are introduced to the kinds of omens that occur in various stories in the Sutra—flowers rain from heaven, the earth shakes in the six ways it can shake,[8] drums can be heard in the heavens, the Buddha emits rays of light, etc.—which indicate that nature itself is moved by the Buddha. Buddha Dharma is not merely about something in our heads; it is about the whole world. Note also that these omens appeal to different senses—we see light, we see and smell flowers, we feel the earth shake, and we hear drums beating. This means that we are to embrace the Dharma not only with our minds, but with our senses as well, with our whole being.

## THE BUDDHA'S LIGHT LIGHTS UP ALL THE WORLDS

The Buddha is the Buddha not only of this *saha* world, in which suffering has to be endured and can be, but of all worlds, past and future, here and elsewhere. This is the major teaching of the second half of the Dharma Flower Sutra and will be discussed later at length. For now it may be enough to note that the vision enabled by the light from the Buddha is *four-dimensional*—it involves seeing not only other worlds, but also the past and anticipated futures of those worlds.

## THE WORLDS OF THE DHARMA

In the Lotus Sutra there are worlds, heavens, purgatories, and so on, making up a very rich imaginary cosmos. Much has been written about Indian and Buddhist cosmology, but none of it is very helpful in facilitating better understanding of the Dharma Flower Sutra. In this Sutra, cosmology is used, not as quasi-scientific description of the universe, but to enhance the place and importance of Shakyamuni Buddha, the Dharma Flower Sutra preached by him, and the world of Shakyamuni Buddha, this "*saha* world." It is important to realize from the outset that the cosmological episodes—the mysterious and even magical events that occur in the Dharma Flower Sutra—are imaginative stories, used for the practical purpose of transforming the minds and hearts and lives of the readers or hearers of the Sutra. They are used for the purpose of having us understand—not only in our heads, but also spiritually, in the depths of our beings—that how we live our lives is important, not only for ourselves and those close to us, but for the whole cosmos as well.

We should also recognize that each preacher or teacher of the Dharma must be so in his or her own smaller world, be it a university, a business, a playground, a home, or whatever. There are buddhas in temples to inspire us, but what the Dharma demands of us is that it be shared, taught, and embodied everywhere, that is, wherever we are.

In other words, from the perspective of the Dharma Flower Sutra what is most important is not finally the miraculous actions of the gods and heavenly bodhisattvas and buddhas, but the everyday actions of the people of this world.

### THE BUDDHA NEEDS AN ASSEMBLY

The Bible begins with the book of Genesis and a creation story in which God is initially all by himself. Then he decides to create the world. Later Christian theologians would develop the idea that this creator God is radically independent. Already perfect and complete in every way, he is in need of nothing and no one.

The perspective of the Dharma Flower Sutra and Buddhist views in general are vastly different. Here, and it should become increasingly apparent as we go through the stories in this text, the Buddha begins with an assembly. Surely he does not need this particular assembly, this particular set of individuals, but he cannot do what he vows to do without the help of others, especially bodhisattvas and Dharma teachers.

We might even say that the Buddha could not be the Buddha without the great assembly. The Buddha, after all, is primarily a teacher and preacher. And a teacher is not really a teacher unless there is at least one learner. Even more important in the Dharma Flower Sutra, the Buddha needs others to carry on his teaching practice after he is no longer active in this world. So the Buddha is doubly dependent on the assembly: he needs others both to receive his teachings and to share them with others.

This is why, in a sense, the unmentioned main focus throughout these stories is the *hearer or reader* of them. When contemplating any of the stories of the Dharma Flower Sutra, we would do well to ask oneself where we ourselves fit into the story—to remember in this case that I myself am a member of the great assembly gathered before the Buddha. That is what it means to be a hearer or reader of the Dharma Flower Sutra.

### THE THREE VEHICLES

Manjushri indicates that all buddhas have taught the four truths and nirvana for those who sought to be shravakas (monks who hear the Buddha's teachings), the teaching of the twelve causes and conditions for those who sought to be pratyekabuddhas (self-enlightened ones), and the six transcendental practices (perfections) for the sake of bodhisattvas.

These three sets of teachings represent the variety of different teachings and emphases within Buddhism. Here "three" is used to represent variety and multiplicity in general, but most often what is discussed and contrasted are two ways of encountering the Dharma, that of the shravaka and that of the bodhisattva. The three teachings are also presented as particularly important teachings, important in the sense that they have been effective. The point is not only that there are various teachings, though that is important, but an emphatic presentation that these various teachings actually work, that they are skillful and appropriate in that they can lead to following the bodhisattva way of helping others and becoming a buddha.

The chapter ends in this way:

> The time has come for people to understand.
> With your palms together, wait single-mindedly!
> The Buddha will pour the rain of the Dharma
> To satisfy those who seek the Way.
>
> If those who seek after the three vehicles
> Have any doubts or regrets,
> The Buddha will remove them
> So that none whatever remain. (LS 74)

In effect, the first chapter is a warning—a warning that you are entering an imaginative territory, a world that can change your life, and that such a change in you can be significant for the entire cosmos. The world of the imagination can be a frightening and even dangerous place, precisely because it invites us into a world that is new and unfamiliar and therefore difficult to understand.

It may place demands on us by assuring us that we can be and do much more than we ever believed possible—yet if we respond to it in joy, our entry into this transformative world can be very rewarding.

4

# SUN AND MOON LIGHT BUDDHA

WHEN MAITREYA BODHISATTVA asks Manjushri Bodhisattva why the Buddha was displaying such a wondrous beam of light, a large part of Manjushri's response is in the form of a story about Sun and Moon Light Buddha and others, especially the bodhisattvas Wonderful Light and Fame Seeker.

## THE STORY

Manjushri begins by explaining that in the past he has seen many other buddhas emit light just as Shakyamuni has, always in preparation for delivering a very great and difficult teaching. One such buddha was Sun and Moon Light, living many, many ages ago and preceded by twenty thousand buddhas of the same name all of whom taught a dharma that was thoroughly good—good in the beginning, good in the middle, and good at the end.

When the last of these Sun and Moon Light Buddhas was still a prince living in the palace of his father, he had eight sons. When these sons learned that their father had left home and become supremely awakened, they left their princely positions to follow their father, all of them becoming Dharma teachers.

This Sun and Moon Light Buddha taught the sutra called "Innumerable Meanings," a "dharma by which bodhisattvas are taught and which buddhas watch over and keep in mind." Then he sat cross-legged before the great assembly and entered into the concentration called "The Place of Innumerable Meanings," in which both his body and his mind were completely still. Here too, extremely rare flowers rained down from the heavens over the Buddha and the entire assembly, while the world trembled in the six different ways.

Enchanted, the whole assembly put their hands together, and in joy looked up at the Buddha with complete attention. Then, from the tuft of white hair between his eyebrows, Sun and Moon Light Buddha emitted a beam of light that illuminated the lands to the east, extending through them just as in the present the light from Shakyamuni Buddha illuminated the lands to the east.

Present at that time was a bodhisattva named Wonderful Light, who was actually Manjushri Bodhisattva in a previous life, along with eight hundred disciples. Because of Wonderful Light Bodhisattva, or perhaps especially for his sake, the Buddha preached the Sutra of the Lotus Flower of the Wonderful Dharma for sixty small eons, sixty small eons in which neither the Buddha nor anyone in the congregation moved from their seats.

At the end of this time, the Buddha announced that a bodhisattva named Good Treasury would be the next buddha and that he, Sun and Moon Light, would enter final nirvana that night at midnight.

Following the Buddha's extinction, Wonderful Light Bodhisattva taught the Dharma Flower Sutra for eight small eons. During this time, the eight sons of Sun and Moon Light Buddha took Wonderful Light Bodhisattva as their teacher, and he helped them strengthen their vow to become supremely awakened. Making offerings to thousands of billions of buddhas, all of them gradually became buddhas themselves.

Among the eight hundred disciples of Wonderful Light Bodhi-

sattva was one named Fame Seeker, who was Maitreya Bodhisattva
in a previous life.

> Wonderful Light, Dharma teacher,
> At that time had a disciple
> Who was always lazy,
> Greedily craving fame and gain.
>
> Always seeking fame and gain,
> He often visited homes of noble families,
> Casting aside what he had repeated and memorized,
> Forgetting everything and gaining nothing from it.
>
> Because of these things
> He was called Fame Seeker.
> Yet by doing good works
> He too was able to see innumerable buddhas.
>
> He made offerings to buddhas,
> Followed them in walking the great way
> And carrying out the six transcendental practices.
> And now he has seen the Lion of the Shakyas.
>
> Later he will become a buddha
> Whose name will be Maitreya.
> He will save
> Living beings everywhere. (LS 73)

As it was at the time of this story, the wonderful omen, explained
Manjushri, is a sign that the Buddha is about the preach the Sutra of
the Lotus Flower of the Wonderful Dharma. It is a device for revealing
the principle of the true character of all things.

## COMMENTARY

Manjushri Bodhisattva's story about Sun and Moon Light Buddha indicates not only that the Buddha is the Buddha of all worlds, but also that the Dharma Flower Sutra itself is not something devised a few centuries ago. It too is in all time, at least in the sense that it teaches timeless truths. Thus the books we have called "The Lotus Sutra" and the like, whether in Sanskrit, Chinese, Japanese, French, or English, are at best representations or exhibits of the Sutra itself. Such pages of text, on wood or palm leaf or paper, are embodiments of the Sutra. This does not mean, however, that the Lotus Sutra itself is in any way more real than the concrete embodiments. Rather, it is only in such concrete embodiments—not only in printed texts, but also in recitation, in teaching, and in practicing it—that the Sutra lives.

### PRINCE SUN AND MOON LIGHT

The fact that before becoming a fully awakened buddha Sun and Moon Light was a prince living in a palace with eight sons reveals a recurrent theme of the Sutra: the idea that what is happening now is both new and unprecedented, and has happened many times before. Here, that Sun and Moon Light Buddha was a prince living in a palace shows a biographical connection to Shakyamuni Buddha. Most buddhas, perhaps all buddhas in the Dharma Flower Sutra, anticipate or replicate the life of Shakyamuni at least to a large extent. Their life stories are similar. That Sun and Moon Light had eight sons while Shakyamuni had only one indicates, however, that their lives were not the same in all respects.

So when Manjushri, talking about the light with which the Buddha has illuminated other worlds, indicates that he has seen many buddhas in the past do the same thing as Shakyamuni, he does not indicate that what they do is exactly the same. In the Dharma Flower Sutra, the present is always emerging from the past, never completely discontinuous from it. Patterns are repeated, sometimes over and over. The first of the buddhas named Sun and Moon Light taught the four truths and nirvana for those who wanted to be shravakas,[9] the teaching of twelve causes and conditions for those who wanted to become pratyekabuddhas,[10] and to lead them to supreme awakening and all-inclusive wisdom he taught the six transcendental practices to bodhisattvas. This threefold structure and division of three teachings is precisely what will be ascribed to Shakyamuni Buddha in the Sutra. Yet in this story there are twenty thousand buddhas, one after the other, all with the name Sun and Moon Light. That is very different from Shakyamuni. In this sutra we are not given the name of his predecessor, but we are told that his successor is to be Maitreya. There is only one Shakyamuni Buddha.

Perhaps the most important point here is that in this, as in many other things, the Dharma Flower Sutra does not subscribe to a rigid structure. As in our own experience, here the present both repeats the past and is different from it. History is always bound to the past, enormously influenced by it, but never completely so.

## THE DHARMA TEACHER

Wonderful Light Bodhisattva is referred to in both the prose and verse sections as a "Dharma teacher."

It's significant though seldom recognized that the eight princes themselves were Dharma teachers under their father, the last of the Sun and Moon Light buddhas. Later, as disciples of this Dharma teacher Wonderful Light Bodhisattva, all of them became buddhas. They were, in other words, Dharma teachers before they became buddhas. This may be a hint of the theme of chapter 10, "Dharma Teachers," that not only bodhisattvas or especially gifted people but anyone can be a Dharma teacher, effectively bringing the Dharma to others.

## FAME SEEKER

To some extent this very brief account of Fame Seeker Bodhisattva anticipates the story of Never Disrespectful Bodhisattva found in Chapter 21 of the Sutra. Here we are only told that this Fame Seeker Bodhisattva, despite seeking fame and gain and forgetting what he had learned from sutras, by doing good was able to see countless buddhas and eventually become Maitreya Bodhisattva, the future buddha.

Two themes are worth noticing here: doing good and seeing countless buddhas.

"Doing good" occurs quite frequently in the Dharma Flower Sutra, yet it is a very abstract notion. What does it mean to do good? While some may have a formula for determining what constitutes doing good, in the Dharma Flower Sutra doing good is highly relative, relative both to the needs and capacities of those for whom good is being done, and relative to the insight and abilities of the one doing good. The Sutra includes many stories of doing good in different ways—saving children from a burning house or from poison, encouraging someone to live up to their potential, teaching Buddha Dharma and so on. There can be no formula for doing good; it depends and must depend on the situation, indeed on all aspects of the situation.

Yet there are some things that can be said about doing good in general. One is that for any act to be good it must be skillful, effective. Doing good has to be made real in one's everyday life. It has to be embodied skillfully and effectively in concrete activity. Thus it requires a kind of practical wisdom. Very often it involves being clever or creative, using one's intelligence to find new solutions that will actually work. And doing good is what bodhisattvas do. This means that doing good can never be a matter of complete selflessness. The Dharma Flower Sutra, and Buddhism in general, do not teach that complete selflessness is either possible or desirable. Rather, the bodhisattva is one who deeply understands that he or she cannot be saved unless others are—one who realizes, in other words, that the good he or she does for others is also good for oneself.

Of course one should never be focused only on one's own narrow interests or desires, and there will be times when it is good to sacrifice one's short term gain for the good of others, but this can never be a matter of completely rejecting one's own good. Doing good in the Dharma Flower Sutra means doing the good of all, *including oneself.*

Just as "doing good" appears often in the Dharma Flower Sutra, so too does the expression "to see countless buddhas" and the like. By doing good, we are told, Fame Seeker was able to see countless buddhas. What could this possibly mean?

Perhaps it means seeing the buddhas who are in the buddha lands in every direction. Or perhaps it means seeing countless buddhas of the past. But I do not think so. Though the idea was not formalized until much later, I believe the Dharma Flower Sutra would have us understand that the Buddha is to be found, is to be seen, in every living being. Thus to see countless buddhas is to see the buddha in others, in everyone one meets, just like Never Disrespectful Bodhisattva.

Thus doing good and seeing countless buddhas are truly connected. One does good because one sees the buddha both in oneself and in others, and seeing the buddha in others gives one a motivation for doing good, helping them in whatever ways are appropriate.

## THE TRUE NATURE OF THINGS

There are two versions of the story, one in prose, the other in verse. Except for the fact that the verse version gives much more detail about what can be seen by the Buddha's beam of light, the two versions are basically the same. Yet there are some interesting small differences. For example, in the prose version Manjushri Bodhisattva explains that the purpose of the beam of light is to announce that the Dharma Flower Sutra is about to be taught, while at the end of the verse version he says that its purpose is "to help reveal the principle of the true nature of all things."

This phrase, "the true nature of all things," has been variously translated and interpreted. There are two major possibilities: One is that it is an affirmation of the reality of the everyday world of concrete realities, as opposed to views that understand this world to be a product of our minds or an illusion. The other possibility is that it is a claim that the Buddha's teachings reveal the nature of all things, namely, that all things are interrelated and interdependent, ultimately empty of independent nature. The fact that a kind of equivalence of *announcing* the teaching of the Dharma Flower Sutra and *revealing* the principle of the true nature of things suggest this latter interpretation. That is: the Dharma Flower Sutra itself reveals the true nature of things.

5

# A BURNING HOUSE AND THREE VEHICLES

T HE SECOND CHAPTER of the Sutra, often called the key
to understanding the first half of the Lotus Sutra, teaches
in some detail the idea of *skillful means*,[11] certainly one of
the central teachings of the Lotus Sutra, and perhaps even the most
important one.

## THE STORY

The chapter begins with the Buddha emerging from contemplation
to explain to his disciple Shariputra why it is that the wisdom of the
buddhas is so difficult, so nearly impossible, to comprehend. This is
basically because, in order to save various living beings, all the buddhas have made use of an enormous variety of methods and teaching
devices appropriate to different situations in order to teach Buddha
Dharma. Thus the three ways—the way of the shravaka, the way of
the pratyekabuddha, and the way of the bodhisattva—are teaching
devices to enable different kinds of people to enter the One Buddha
Way. Shariputra, speaking on behalf both of himself and others, is
perplexed, still does not understand, and repeatedly pleads with the
Buddha to explain further. The Buddha twice refuses on the grounds

that it would just further confuse things, but finally agrees to teach the full Dharma.

At this point some five thousand monks, nuns, and laypeople in the congregation, so arrogant that they think they have already attained the highest possible wisdom and have no more to learn, get up from their seats, bow to the Buddha and leave. The Buddha does not try to stop them, remarking that the congregation had thus been cleared of little-needed twigs and leaves.

The Buddha then explains again that all the buddhas of the past, all the buddhas of the many worlds of the present, and all of the buddhas of the future use various literary and teaching methods, including a great variety of sutras, as required by the situation, all for the sake of leading people to the One Buddha Way. Such teachings, he insists, are neither empty nor false. In particular, the teaching of nirvana was invented for people not yet ready for the Great Vehicle in order to lead them to enter the Way by which they will become buddhas. Included is a long list of practices, such as bowing to a buddha image or making an offering to or entering a stupa, by which people have entered the way toward becoming a buddha themselves. All of this, he says, is in accord with the Buddha's ancient vow to lead all living beings to full awakening, that is, to lead them to become buddhas themselves.

With this, the Buddha announces that since buddhas very seldom appear in the world he will now teach the One Vehicle, but only to bodhisattvas.

Shariputra, the leading shravaka and not normally regarded as a bodhisattva, feels like dancing for joy because he realizes the truth of the Dharma, the truth that he too is to become a buddha and in that sense is already a bodhisattva. In the third chapter, the Buddha further reassures Shariputra that this is indeed the case and explains that he will become the Buddha Flower Light and describes the era and the buddha land of that Buddha. This, in turn, causes all others in the assembly to rejoice and say that, after the first turning of the wheel of the Dharma at Varanasi, the Buddha has now turned the wheel of the greatest Dharma.

Shariputra, though encouraged by this assurance, on behalf of those devotees who do not yet understand once again begs the Buddha to explain why, if there are not three paths, he has so often preached them in the past. And this time the Buddha does so by means of the famous parable of the burning house.

## THE PARABLE

A rich man's house, now in a terrible state of repair and to which there is only one narrow gate, catches on fire with all of his many children playing inside. Though the father compassionately calls to them, urging them to leave the burning house, they are too absorbed in their play to listen to these warnings. He also considers carrying them out by force, but soon realizes that this too will not work. So he tells the children that, if they go out quickly, outside the gate they will find goat-drawn carriages, deer-drawn carriages, and ox-drawn carriages that he will give them to play with.

Such rare playthings being just what they always wanted, the children rush outside, to the great joy of the father, and soon ask him for the promised carriages. Instead, because he is rich and has many of them, he decides to give each of the children a much larger and fancier carriage drawn by a great white ox. The children, having received something even better than what they had expected, are overjoyed.

The Buddha then interprets this parable for Shariputra, explaining that he, the Buddha, is much like the father in the parable, attempting to save his children from the fires of birth, old age, disease, death, grief, sorrow, suffering, and so on, from which they cannot escape by themselves because they have many attachments. He offers them the three vehicles as a way to get them through the gate, but rewards them in the end with the Great Vehicle—an even better reward than the one promised.

## COMMENTARY

Parables are metaphorical; they are analogies, but never perfect ones. This parable provides an image of four separate vehicles. But if we follow the teaching of the Sutra as a whole, the One Buddha Vehicle is not a separate alternative to other ways; it includes them. Thus, one limitation of this parable is that it suggests that the diverse ways (represented by the three lesser carriages) can be replaced by the One Way (the great carriage). But the overall teaching of the Sutra makes it plain that there are many paths within the Great Path, and the Great Path integrates them all. They are together because they are within the One Vehicle. To understand the many ways as somehow being *replaced by* the One Way would entail rejecting the ideal of the bodhisattva way (the third carriage), which the Sutra clearly never does.

What the parable stresses is the urgency of the human condition, making it necessary for the Buddha to find some way to get people to leave their play and suffering behind in order to enter the Way. The Buddha, we are to understand, has used such means, not to deceive people, but to lead them to awakening. For this, he has used a great variety of ways and means, here represented by the three carriages.

It is extremely important, I believe, to understand that the many skillful means are always within the One Buddha Way, not alternatives to it. The many skillful means are "skillful" only because they skillfully lead to the One Way, and the One Way exists only by being embodied in many skillful means. Understanding the One Way and the many skillful means as separate, alternative ways has been a great mistake, a mistake that has sometimes led to disrespect, intolerance, and disdain for others.

## SMALLER VEHICLES

We should realize that in this story it is the lure of the three "lesser" vehicles that actually saves the children. In running out, the children are pursuing the shravaka, pratyekabuddha, and bodhisattva ways. And here, these three ways, including the bodhisattva way, are essentially equal, as they are equally effective, perhaps with one appealing to some of the children, another to others, and the other to still other children. These "smaller" vehicles, in other words, are sufficient for saving people, that is, for enabling them to enter the One Buddha Vehicle and become bodhisattvas, ones who are on the way to becoming buddhas themselves.

One of the important insights to be gained from the teaching of skillful means is that many things that are not the whole truth are nevertheless important truths. Just as we should seek the potential to be a buddha in ourselves even though we are far from perfect, we should seek the truth, even the hidden truths, in what others say, in their words and in their stories.

"Others" includes of course other religions and their followers. Followers of the Dharma Flower Sutra can be glad when they encounter people of other faiths who have found carriages appropriate for themselves. The Sutra teaches that there are many successful ways, some, no doubt, beyond our imagination.

## CRITERIA FOR SKILLFUL MEANS

The Buddha, like any teacher, has to use appropriate skill in order to lead others to the realization of their own potential. But this does not mean that any trick will do. In general, there appear to be three criteria in the Dharma Flower Sutra for something to be regarded as skillful means: appropriateness, skillfulness, and effectiveness. All of the skillful means recognized in the Dharma Flower Sutra have at least these three characteristics.

First, they are for the sake of helping someone else. Often, in the parables, the person who uses skillful means is rewarded for doing so. In this story the father is full of joy from having rescued his children. But the purpose of the skillful act is to help someone else, in this case the children. The father is rewarded, but he is seeking to save the children, not seeking to be rewarded. There is no possibility of using the term *skillful means* to refer to something that merely shows off one's cleverness or to some expedient that is primarily for one's own benefit. The methods, in other words, are always intended to be appropriate and beneficial for those who hear or receive them.

An action that can be characterized as "skillful means" is selected or created to fit the situation and abilities of the recipients of the method, just as good teachers must consider the situation and abilities of their students. When this notion is extended, however, to practices that need to be developed by followers of the Buddha, then it is helpful to construe such means as needing or having a double appropriateness—appropriateness for the practitioner as well as for the recipient. That is, what makes something appropriate in our own practice is not only the abilities and situation of the person being guided but also the situation, and especially the abilities, of the one doing the guiding. Just as good teachers must consider their own abilities, we have to seriously ask ourselves not only "What needs to be done?" but "What can *I* do?" This is only to say that, insofar as possible, the whole situation, including oneself as part of the situation, needs to be taken into account in order for action to be as appropriate as possible.

In the Dharma Flower Sutra the term *skillful* is used to describe the methods of buddhas or those in parables who represent the Buddha. They are based on intelligence and insight, even wisdom, but such skill does not, especially in the stories, depend on perfect knowledge. In this parable, the father first tries to get the children to leave the burning house by shouting at them to get out. When that does not work, he considers taking them out by force. When he realizes that

that approach will not work either, he comes up with the idea of offering the carriages. It is very important, I think, that the father tells the children that they can have what they most desire. The father, in other words, cannot simply force them out; he appeals to something already in them, and he can do so because he has knowledge and insight into who they are and what they want.

It takes skill to be able to discern what is needed in particular situations. This is one very important lesson of the Dharma Flower Sutra. Rather than offer simple rules that can be followed in all situations, it implores us to analyze the situation and be creative and imaginative, that is, "skillful," in dealing with it.

Sometimes we like to take the shortest, most direct, way to the solution of a problem, just like the father shouting at his children. Often such direct orders do not work, not because the prescription is incorrect, but because it is not presented skillfully, that is, in a way that will be accepted and acted upon. It takes skill to figure out not only what is needed, but what will be effective.

And skillful means must be effective. They work. There are no examples of skillful methods that turn out to be ineffective. In this story, it is very important that the children are actually saved from the burning house. In Buddhism, intentions are very important, but the Dharma Flower Sutra places much more emphasis on results. The Sutra, in other words, while concerned about what goes on in our heads, is even more concerned about what we do with our bodies, that is, with how we behave, with how we live our daily lives.

## MEANS AND ENDS

Even the very fancy carriage that the father gives to the children is, after all, only a carriage, a vehicle. All of our teachings and practices should be understood as devices, as possible ways of helping people. They should never be taken as final truths.

Appropriate means are means, not ends. In this sense they have only instrumental and provisional importance. While it is true that the notion of skillful means is sometimes used to describe something provisional, it is important to recognize that being instrumental and provisional does not mean that such methods are in any sense unimportant. At one point at least, the Dharma Flower Sutra even suggests that it is itself an appropriate means. The context is one in which the Sutra is praising itself and proclaiming its superiority over others ("those who do not hear or believe this sutra suffer a great loss"), but then has those who embrace the Sutra in a future age say:

> When I attain the Buddha way,
> I will teach this Dharma to them
> By skillful means,
> That they may dwell within it. (LS 273)

It is very interesting that what gets the children out of the house is their pursuit of the three kinds of carriages, that is, their pursuit of the shravaka, pratyekabuddha, and bodhisattva ways. At least with respect to getting the children out of the burning house, these so called lesser ways are effective. And they appear to be equally effective. As we will see later, the Sutra champions the bodhisattva way and generally regards it as superior to other ways. But it does not say that these other ways, primarily the shravaka way, cannot be effective. In fact, it says just the opposite—the shravaka way is one of the Buddha's skillful and appropriate ways of saving people.

## ONLY TO BODHISATTVAS?

Why does the Buddha say in this chapter that he will teach the One Vehicle, but only to bodhisattvas? In the first chapter, we saw that the Dharma Flower Sutra celebrates both listening and teaching or preaching. In other words, it takes two to teach—teaching is not teaching unless someone is taught. Thus in the first chapter, heavenly flowers fall on both the Buddha and the audience. That idea is extended here with the idea that the Buddha preaches only to bodhisattvas. The point is that to hear the Dharma is to be already, to that degree, a bodhisattva. This is because to truly hear the Dharma is to take it into one's life, thus to live by it, thus to be a bodhisattva. So it can be said that the buddhas come into the world only to convert people into bodhisattvas.

## LIFETIME BEGINNERS

As a whole, what the Sutra condemns is not lesser vehicles but arrogance, especially the arrogance of thinking one has arrived at some complete truth, at some final goal. Rather, we are called upon by this Sutra to be "lifetime beginners," people who know they have much to learn and always will.[12] The five thousand who walk out of the assembly in the second chapter are said to be like twigs and leaves and not really needed, but apparently in Chapter 8 they too are told that they will become buddhas.

## A LOVING FATHER

In many of the parables in the Dharma Flower Sutra, it is a father figure who represents the Buddha. It is possible that the use of such stories influenced the teachings of the Dharma Flower Sutra, leading it, probably more than any other Buddhist text, to emphasize the father-like nature of the Buddha, personalizing him as it were. Over and over, the Lotus Sutra uses personal language to speak of an ultimately important reality. Far from being "absolute," or even "omniscient," as the Buddhist tradition has sometimes claimed, the Buddha of the Dharma Flower Sutra is someone who is very concerned for his children. This means, in effect, that the happiness of the Buddha, the fulfillment of the Buddha's purpose, depends—again—on us.

It is important to realize that we are similar to the children in this parable of the vehicles. We need guidance, but we will not be forced.

We should think of ourselves as collaborators with the Buddha, helping to do Buddha-work, both within ourselves and in the world.

## OUR BURNING HOUSE

The parable is interpreted as saying that the world is like a burning house. Much more than in my telling of the story above, the verse version of the parable goes to great lengths to describe the terrors inside the burning house, perhaps leading some to think that our goal should be to escape from the burning house that is this world.

But escaping from the world is not at all what the Sutra teaches. Elsewhere it makes clear that we are to work in the world to help or save others. The point here is more that we are like children at play, not paying enough attention to the environment around us. Perhaps it is not the whole world that is in flames but our own playgrounds, the private worlds we create out of our attachments and out of our complacency. Thus leaving the house is not escaping from the world but leaving behind our play-world, our attachments and illusions, or at least some of them, in order to enter the real world.

Awakening is more a road than a destination, more a commencement than a conclusion—a responsibility as much as an achievement. To enter the Buddha Way is not a matter of attaining some great height from which one can boast or look down on others. It is to enter a difficult path, a way. At the end of this parable, the children are very happy, as they have received a gift much greater than they expected, perhaps greater than they could have imagined. But we must not imagine that receiving the gift is the end of the matter.

We can say that their lives and their difficulties—that is, their responsibilities—have now really only just begun.

# SHARIPUTRA

A T THE VERY BEGINNING of the Lotus Sutra's third chapter Shariputra, the leading shravaka—a monk who is not normally regarded as a bodhisattva—tells the Buddha that he is full of ecstasy because he realizes the truth of the Dharma: namely, that he too is destined to become a buddha, and in that sense is, in fact, already a bodhisattva, one who is practicing the bodhisattva way.

Who is this Shariputra? What story does the Darma Flower Sutra tell us about him, and what can we learn from his story?

One of the ten great disciples of Shakyamuni Buddha, Shariputra was usually regarded as first in wisdom, sometimes regarded as first among the disciples, and sometimes even mistaken by Jains as the leader of the Buddhist movement. Shariputra was a brahman, a member of the highest caste in India, who left a wealthy family to follow one of the six great non-Buddhist teachers. This teacher taught skepticism about knowledge of things we cannot see—such things as other worlds, causation, and so forth.

It is said that Shariputra and Maudgalyayana (called "Maha-Maudgalyayana," Great Maudgalyayana, in his only appearance in the Lotus Sutra) were close friends before they became monks. One day when they were in a crowd of people watching dancing girls and enjoying a festival, Shariputra suddenly realized that all of those people now having so much fun, and he himself, would soon be dead. He resolved to seek liberation from a condition in which the conclusion to everything is death. After listening to several other teachers, he decided, with Maudgalyayana, to become a disciple of the skeptic Sanjaya. Later, after meeting a monk who told him only that the Buddha's main teaching was that all things are produced through causation, together with Maudgalyayana and all of the other disciples of Sanjaya, he joined the Buddha's following. This was about a year after Shakyamuni's awakening.

Legend also has it that when he was about to die, Shariputra requested permission from the Buddha to do so before the Buddha himself, as he would not be able to stand the grief of witnessing the Buddha's death. With the Buddha's permission he returned to his home with one disciple. Saying "I have been with all of you for forty years. If I have offended anyone, please forgive me," he lay down on his bed, and quietly passed away.

In the Vimalakirti Sutra, Shariputra is something of a dunce who shows up late to hear a conversation between Manjushri and Vimalakirti, an exceedingly wise Buddhist layman whom Manjushri has gone to visit because he is at home sick. When he enters, Shariputra can't find a seat and asks himself where he should sit. Vimalakirti, reading his thoughts, embarrasses him by asking whether he has come to hear the Dharma or to find a seat.

In other Mahayana sutras as well, Shariputra is often treated as stupid or foolish. To some extent this is true also in Chapter 12 of the Lotus Sutra. There a young girl, a dragon princess, makes him look foolish by suddenly becoming a buddha after Shariputra expresses the conservative view that a woman's body is too filthy to receive the Dharma, much less to embody a buddha.

Shariputra's name occurs often in the Dharma Flower Sutra. Though he does not play much of a role in the first chapter, in the first paragraph of that chapter, Shariputra is introduced as one of twelve thousand great monks who are "well known to everyone"—"arhats without faults, free from afflictions, self-developed, emancipated from all bonds of existence, and mentally free." His name is introduced in a similar way in the first chapter of the Sutra of Innumerable Meanings, where he is called "Great Wisdom Shariputra," but he plays no role at all in that sutra.

In the second and third chapters of the Dharma Flower Sutra, however, it is Shariputra to whom the Buddha explains the practice of skillful means. In these chapters, Shariputra appears in the very important role of spokesman for the whole assembly, pleading with the Buddha to explain himself, and especially to preach the Dharma Flower Sutra for the sake of those who have gathered. Here he does seem to be "first among the disciples."

## THE STORY

Chapter 2 ends with these memorable words:

> There will also be those
> Who are modest
> And purehearted,
> Devoted to seeking the Buddha way.
>
> For all of these
> The One Vehicle way should be praised everywhere.
>
> It should be understood, Shariputra,
> That the Dharma of the buddhas is like this.
> With trillions of skillful means, in accord with what is
>   good
> They teach the Dharma.

Those who have not practiced and studied it
Cannot fully understand this.
But all of you,
Knowing that the buddhas,

The teachers of the worlds,
Use skillful means
According to what is appropriate,
Should have no more doubt.

Your hearts should be filled with great joy,
For you know that you too will become buddhas. (LS 102)

In Chapter 3, we learn that previously Shariputra and other shravakas had understood that bodhisattvas had been told that they would
become buddhas, but not that the shravakas themselves would, and
they had wondered why they had not received this message of universal salvation from the Buddha. Here, Shariputra realizes they had
not really understood skillful means, and that what the Buddha had
taught them was a means to bring them closer to the truth.

Then Shariputra says that, his doubts having been removed, he is
at peace both in body and in mind, and that, having received a share
of Buddha Dharma, he has realized three things: that he is a child of
the Buddha, that he is born from the Buddha's mouth, and that he has
been transformed by the Dharma.

The Buddha tells Shariputra that he had taught him to aspire to
become a buddha in a previous life, but that Shariputra had forgotten
all about that. Thus, the present teaching is only to call Shariputra
back to his own original vow.

The Buddha then goes on to assure Shariputra that in a distant
future life he will become a buddha, the Buddha Flower Light. And he
describes that eon of Flower Light Buddha, called "Adorned with Great

Treasures," and his buddha land, called "Free of Dirt," a kind of paradise with great quantities of gold and jewels and other precious things. But it is called "Adorned with Great Treasures" because in it there will be countless bodhisattvas, and they will be regarded as great treasures.

This assurance of becoming a buddha given to Shariputra by the Buddha was the impetus of a great party and celebration, as everyone in the assembly rejoiced and danced with great joy. At least their hearts danced for joy. Everyone shed their outer garments and offered them to the Buddha. And when the gods or heavenly beings offered their garments to the Buddha, the clothes swirled around in the sky, and the gods made great music and created a wonderful shower of heavenly flowers. Then the gods announced that after the first turning of the wheel of Dharma at Varanasi, the Buddha had now turned the wheel of the greatest Dharma.

## COMMENTARY

Let's look further at each of the three things that Shariputra realized:

*He is a child of the Buddha.* Here, and throughout the Dharma Flower Sutra, the primary meaning of "child of the Buddha" is "bodhisattva." Here, Shariputra realizes that while being a shravaka, he is also a bodhisattva, actually more deeply and profoundly a bodhisattva. But being a child of the Buddha has other implications as well.

What Shariputra originally set out to find was an understanding of the world in which death is not the end of everything—that is, a world in which everything comes to nothing. In other words, he sought meaning in life, he wanted his own life to be meaningful, to amount to something more than death.

Basically, he found two things. First, he found that nothing can separate us from what Christians call the love of God and Buddhists the compassion of the Buddha. The Dharma Flower Sutra teaches repeatedly that the Buddha is all around us, nearer than we think. He is the father of us all, the Compassionate One. The second important meaning of this metaphor is that we owe our lives not only to our biological parents and ancestors, but even more to the process, the Dharma, by which we live and are sustained. Chinese and Japanese Buddhism place enormous stress on the importance of biological ancestors, but in the teaching that we are all children of the Buddha, we should realize that biology is only one of the ways in which we inherit from the past. What we learn from our teachers—usually to be sure in the first instance from our mothers or primary caretakers, but also from a whole company of teachers, including those we encounter in books—has an enormous impact on shaping who and what we are. And those of us who are significantly drawn to the Buddha Dharma will be especially aware of our indebtedness both to the Buddha and to the tradition that has made his Dharma available to us. In an important sense, we ourselves are children of the Buddha.

*He is nourished from the Buddha's mouth.* Just as inheritance is not only biological, nourishment is not only physical, but mental and spiritual as well. Where should we look for mental and spiritual nourishment? We should not, I believe, think that because we are Buddhists or followers of the Dharma Flower Sutra our spiritual nourishment must always come from the Dharma Flower Sutra or from Buddhist sources alone. One of the wonderful things about the Lotus Sutra, as we will see when looking at the simile of the plants, is its recognition that the Buddha Dharma nourishes the whole world, not just Buddhists.

One way of understanding this, then, is to imagine that the Buddha can speak to us and nourish us in innumerable ways. In other words, anything at all, if we penetrate into it deeply enough, can be a revelation to us of Buddha Dharma. No matter how good or bad a person or situation or thing may be, it can be something from which we can learn; if we are open to it, we can find in it something of great value.

*He is transformed by the Dharma.* While the Dharma can be thought of, and is, something that nourishes and sustains us, it can also transform us. Shariputra's life was dramatically changed by the Dharma. Here, hearing the Dharma, he suddenly realizes that the goal he has been pursuing and the kind of life he has been living, while good, is not good enough. He realizes that the way he has taken can be a kind of gateway to more fully following the Buddha. No wonder he is filled with ecstasy! Indeed, almost everywhere you turn in the Dharma Flower Sutra, someone is receiving the Sutra with joy, or is full of joy, or has a heart that is dancing for joy.

The Buddha reminds Shariputra that Shariputra had learned this lesson before but had forgotten his own original vow. This is one of the many ways in which the Dharma Flower Sutra teaches that the potential for being a buddha is fundamental—something given to us originally. His life as a bodhisattva was always his life. Now, quite suddenly, he knows it.

To understand the Buddha Dharma as an ultimate truth about reality is to experience it as liberating. That Shariputra has received only some of the Buddha Dharma means that even though he is enlightened, liberated, and overcome with joy, this is only a new beginning, a rebirth, not a death in which there is nothing more to do. He is set free to live in the Dharma.

## THE SECOND TURNING OF THE WHEEL

Though in the parable of the burning house already discussed Buddhist diversity is symbolized by the three, or four, vehicles, here there are two divisions or kinds of Buddhist teachings, Hinayana and Mahayana. At least two important things are indicated by this two-fold division. One is that here, in Mahayana, which means "great vehicle," something new is being taught, something that goes beyond what was taught at Deer Park. Second is that while the first turning or teaching is superseded, it is not false or to be thrown away. The first turning of the wheel (such teachings as the four noble truths) is superseded by being included within a larger framework of Mahayana teaching.

It is appropriate, I think, that in Rissho Kosei-kai's Dharma Wheel Reception Hall there is a magnificent statue of Kannon Bodhisattva with a thousand arms in the main hall. But in order to get to it one walks through a large reception hall dominated by four great black columns in which are carved the four noble truths. The four truths, in other words, are not to be discarded; they can lead you to the bodhisattva way.

Throughout the Dharma Flower Sutra two things are affirmed: 1) that the Sutra is continuous with what was taught and done in the early years of the Buddha's ministry, and 2) that something new is happening. This is generally true of Mahayana sutras. They both affirm a continuity with older Buddhist traditions and claim that in Mahayana something new has emerged.

Thus, it is significant that Shariputra becomes further enlightened here, "re-born" as he puts it. This can be contrasted with some other Mahayana sutras, in which he is treated as merely stupid, meaning that Hinayana Buddhists are quite stupid and unworthy of the Dharma. In some cases, shravakas were even said to be *icchanti*—hopeless, incorrigible, utterly devoid of buddha-nature.

It is, I believe, unfortunate that the Lotus Sutra includes the Mahayana practice of referring to the twenty or so traditional Buddhist sects of that time with the demeaning term "Hinayana," meaning "inferior," "lesser," or "small." But we should understand that the Sutra teaches that this lesser way is sufficient to save people, as it is the attraction of the lesser vehicles that saves the children from the burning house. Consistent with this, whenever in this Sutra there is a description of a more or less paradise-like, future world, there are plenty of shravakas in it. Rather than reject "Hinayana" teachings and methods, the Dharma Flower Sutra seeks to incorporate them into the One Vehicle.

What's more, teachings about the shravaka way in this Sutra should not be understood as being merely, or even primarily, about monks living many centuries ago. These teachings are for us as well. It is we ourselves, above all, who should not be arrogant or lazy, or feel too comfortable with what we have achieved or too worn-out to do anything more. It is we who need always to remember that we have entered a way that is very difficult and comes to no final end in life.

## SHARIPUTRA'S DOUBT

His doubts having been removed, Shariputra was at peace, mentally and physically. This "doubt" is not a matter of doubting whether something is true or not. It is a matter of not having confidence about one's position or status or importance. In one sense, it is a matter of self-doubt or lack of confidence, but more importantly it is a matter of doubting the benevolence of the Buddha, or the meaningfulness of life, something Christian theologians have sometimes called "existential doubt."

What Shariputra gains from realizing that he is a bodhisattva is not a safe quick trip directly to being a buddha, as on an elevator, but something more like admission to a long stairway. The stairway will be difficult. But the most important point is that there is a stairway, a way to overcome suffering from the unsatisfactoriness of life, and the Buddha's teachings can lead us to such a stairway.

Is life really meaningful? That is what the story of Shariputra is about. And the Sutra's answer is that life is and can be experienced as meaningful, or can be meaningful, because it is meaningful.

The Sutra understands itself to be good news for everyone—in one sense, a kind of wake-up call to enter a new world, or to experience the world in a new way; in another sense, it is a kind of public announcement that everyone is a bodhisattva and therefore that you are already a bodhisattva and are on your way to becoming a buddha. Hearing such an announcement, really hearing such an announcement, we should all be glad and full of joy!

# THE RICH FATHER AND THE POOR SON

A S WE HAVE SEEN, in Chapter 3 of the Lotus Sutra the parable of the three vehicles was used by the Buddha to explain why there is a diversity of Buddhist teachings and why he is now teaching the One Buddha Way. Having heard this explanation, four shravakas—Subhuti, Maha-Katyayana, Maha-Kashyapa, and Maha-Maudgalyayana—all "living a life of wisdom," hearing from the Buddha a teaching they had never heard before, and also hearing the Buddha's assurance of Shariputra's eventual supreme awakening, were astonished and ecstatic with joy. In Chapter 4 of the Sutra they tell the parable of the rich father and the poor son as a way of checking out whether they have understood the Buddha correctly.[13]

## THE STORY

When still a boy, a man ran away from home, only to live a life of desperate poverty, moving from place to place in search of menial work. Meanwhile his father, who had become extremely rich and powerful, searched everywhere for the lost son but could not find him.

One day the son accidentally came to the place where the father lived. He saw his father in the distance surrounded by servants and other signs of great wealth but he did not recognize him and began to flee in fear of such wealth and power. But the father, having secretly longed for his son for many decades and wanting the son to have his inheritance, recognized the man immediately and sent a servant after him. But when the servant caught up with him, the son, fearing that he would be forced to work or even be killed, pleaded that he had done nothing wrong and fell to the ground in a faint. Seeing this, the father told the servant to douse him with cold water to wake him up, tell him he could go wherever he liked, and then leave him alone.

The son went off to another village to look for food and clothing. Later, the father secretly sent two unimposing, poorly dressed servants to go to the son and offer to hire him to work with them at double pay shoveling animal dung. To this the son agreed, and he went to work at his father's house. Later, seeing how poorly the son looked, the father disguised himself as a lowly worker, went to the son, praised his work, and promised him better wages and treatment if he would continue to work for him, explaining that as he was old he wanted to treat the man just like a son. The son was pleased, and continued to shovel dung for another twenty years, gradually becoming more confident and more trusted by the father. But still lacking self-confidence, he nonetheless continued to have a very low regard for himself and live in a hovel outside the gate.[14]

Eventually the rich man became ill. Knowing he would die soon, he asked the son to take charge of his various properties and businesses. As the time of his death grew near, the father called together various officials and all of his relatives and friends and servants and revealed to them that the poor man was in fact his son and would inherit all of his wealth. With such enormous wealth coming to him quite unexpectedly, the son was very amazed.

# COMMENTARY

Imbedded in this story are many of the lessons that are to be found throughout the Dharma Flower Sutra. Let's look at some of them.

## FAITH IN YOURSELF, FAITH IN THE DHARMA

At a meeting some time ago of the International Buddhist Congregation in Tokyo, a young woman described how, dissatisfied with the faith in which she had been raised, she had searched among Christian and Buddhist traditions for an appropriate faith for herself, finally discovering with some joy the importance of having faith in herself. We might think that faith in oneself is not enough. And indeed it isn't. But it is an important beginning. The poor man in this story was not able to become a functioning contributor to his family and society until he gained some respect for and confidence in himself.

The Dharma Flower Sutra stresses that each of us is somebody important—important to himself or herself, important to others, and important to the Buddha. Each of us is a person of great potential. For this reason we are sought after by the Buddha. The Buddha's wealth— supreme awakening or enlightenment—is not something you have to earn or purchase in any way; it already belongs to you; it was yours from before your birth; it is your rightful inheritance.

Self-respect and self-confidence are primarily attitudes, types of emotional and psychological states, but they also entail respecting what has been given to you, including your body. If we eat, or drink, or take drugs to excess, we show disrespect for ourselves and deprive the Buddha of what he is trying to achieve in our lives, through us. The Buddha needs us, needs everyone. The Buddha's compassion is for all the living.

Accordingly, we should not be overly humble or servile—or allow others to be oppressed into such servility. Oppression is the worst kind of evil, because it denies the buddha-nature of all creatures. It is akin to an insult to the Buddha.

Though this story does not directly advocate social responsibility, it makes evident the need for those who seek to follow the Dharma Flower Sutra to be concerned about social as well as individual evil. War, class oppression, racism, and environmental pollution are affronts to the Buddha. They are affronts to the Buddha precisely because they assault and insult the buddha-nature in people and give rise to totally unnecessary suffering.

Apart from the Buddha and blind to the Buddha Dharma, we are like someone wandering around, destitute, impoverished, without purpose, miserable. In a sense, this is the destiny of those who do not, in some way, follow the Buddha Way. This does not mean, however, that one has to be a Buddhist in the ordinary sense. To follow the Buddha is to put one's trust in and devote oneself to the happiness of others and the life of the whole. It is to share in a kind of common human faith that life is meaningful, a faith that finds expression in a variety of religious and other forms.

### THE BUDDHA AND OUR RELATIONSHIPS TO HIM

The focus of this story is the poor son and his attitude toward himself, but it is also, in important ways not always recognized, a story about the Buddha. Here we are told that the Buddha needs his son, yearns for his son, and seeks to find him. Why? Because he wants to give him the great treasure that is his inheritance.

Shakyamuni Buddha was a human being who lived for a time in India, eating and sleeping like other human beings. He left to his descendants, his followers, a great treasure house of profound teachings. He died and his body was cremated, the ashes being distributed and installed in stupas. He is no longer around in the way that he once was. Responsibility for taking care of that great treasure house, for preserving those teachings and developing them by applying them in new situations, and especially for sharing them with others, is given to the Buddha's children. The Buddha's work must be done by us, can only be done by us. It is we who can embody the Buddha in the contemporary world, enabling the Buddha to continue to live.

In the Dharma Flower Sutra, the term "children of the Buddha" is used primarily to refer to bodhisattvas, including those who do not even understand that they are bodhisattvas. A bodhisattva is one who is on the way to being a buddha, one who is becoming a buddha, by doing bodhisattva practices—that is, by teaching and helping others. We are children of the Buddha because our lives have been shaped by the Buddha.

While saying that we are children of the Buddha says something important about us, it also says something important about the Buddha, a "father to the whole world." And this sense of the Buddha as father is reinforced dramatically in several parables, where, as in this one, the Buddha is represented by a father-figure. Far from being some kind of philosophical "absolute," the Buddha of the Dharma Flower Sutra yearns for his lost son, and for all of his children. That is another meaning of being a child of the Buddha.

Furthermore, even when we think we cannot see him, the Buddha can be found right next to us. The Buddha may not even go by the name of a buddha. Sometimes perhaps he goes by the name of Christ, or Krishna, or even Jane. Belonging to a Buddhist temple or organization is not, in itself, the Buddha Way, nor is it the only way to enter or follow the Buddha Way. The "universal gate" is many gates, many more than you or I could possibly know in a lifetime.

Indeed, sometimes we are being led to the Buddha even when we do not know it. Even when we are not looking for the Buddha Way, probably we are being led to it. At the beginning of this story, the son is not looking for his father, at least not consciously. He is satisfied with a very low level of existence, almost bare subsistence. He has no ambition and feels no need to improve himself. It is the father who seeks him out and guides him. But what he guides him to is a gradual recovery of his self-confidence, and hence of his strength and his ability to contribute. The son is given guidance by the father not only because he is weak, but also because he is strong, at least potentially. We can be led by the Buddha precisely because the potential to become awakened, to enter the Way, is already in us.

For followers of the Dharma Flower Sutra, there is no such thing as a "hopeless case." Everyone, without exception, has within himself or herself an inner strength, a great power, to flourish in some way.

And yet, in this story, upon seeing the great power and wealth of the father, the son runs away in fear. Sometimes, when we see how great is the Buddha's treasury—how great the responsibility of compassionate knowing—we too may run away in fear. It is not easy to be a follower of the Dharma Flower Sutra or of the bodhisattva way. It involves taking responsibility, both for one's own life and for the lives of others. And that can be frightening. That is why it is not enough for a religion to teach doctrine; it must provide assurance, over and over again—assurance that life can be meaningful, even wonderful, assurance that can overcome our natural tendency to run away in fear.

But how do we find life meaningful? Sometimes through menial work. Sometimes a very humble task, such as removing dung, is important preparation for something greater. One of the basic lessons of the Lotus Sutra is that one can find in every situation that there is something to be learned. Sometimes an unpleasant situation or task can be understood as being a present given to us by the Buddha, an opportunity for learning and growth, just as the son in this story received from his father the present of shoveling dung. We can learn from just about any situation, even from very unpleasant ones, if we approach it with a right attitude.

Of course, what might be learned in some situations is that the best thing to do is to change the situation or even flee from it. The Dharma Flower Sutra is not a recipe for being passive and accepting every situation no matter how bad. But it *does* urge us not to be mere sufferers or victims, but always, inasmuch as we are able, to learn from and seek the best in any situation.

At the end of this story, the son is happy, as he has acquired great wealth, much greater wealth than he had ever imagined having. But, while it is the end of the story, we must not imagine that it is the end of the matter. We can even say that his difficulties—that is, his responsibilities—have now really only just begun. Awakening is a process—a responsibility as much as an achievement or a gift.

As the shravakas say right after the telling of this parable, we should never become complacent and satisfied with some lesser level of awakening, such as some great experience of nirvana, but always pursue the Buddha Way.

Perhaps above all, this chapter is an exhortation never to be complacent with what one has achieved, an invitation to continue to grow in wisdom, compassion, and service.

That is the bodhisattva way, the bodhisattva way of becoming a buddha.

# ONE GREAT CLOUD AND MANY KINDS OF PLANTS

C HAPTER 5 of the Lotus Sutra is sometimes entitled "The Parable of Medicinal Plants," but in the version translated by Kumarajiva and used in East Asia, and upon which almost all European versions are based, no such parable can be found. While medicinal plants or herbs are mentioned in the central story, which is a simile, they play only a very minor role. In Sanskrit versions of the Lotus Sutra, however, there is a parable about medicinal herbs. As is true with some other parables, in this case too there are both prose and verse versions. Here is a telling of the parable that makes use of both.

## THE PARABLE[15]

Once upon a time there was a man who was born blind. He supposed, therefore, that there was no such thing as a beautiful or an ugly shape and no such thing as living beings who could see beautiful or ugly things—no sun, moon, stars, or planets, and no one to see such things. When people told him there were such things, he did not believe them.

When a certain physician met this blind man, he realized right away that the man's condition was due to something that had happened in a previous life, and he knew that this illness could not be treated effectively with commonly available medicines. He knew also that on the snowy King of Mountains there were four medicinal herbs that would work. One contained all flavors, colors, and tastes; another cured all ailments; another destroyed all poisons; and there was one that brought happiness to all who stood in the right place. Out of compassion for the blind man, and by using some sort of magical device, the physician went to that mountain, climbed it, and searched all over it to find the four herbs. After returning with them, he gave these herbs to the blind man in a variety of ways—chewed, pounded, raw in a mixture with other things, boiled in a mixture with other things, by piercing the man's body, after burning them, and so forth.

The blind man soon was able to see, and he saw such things as the light of the sun and the moon, the stars and planets, and a great variety of shapes. He realized that he had been a fool for not believing those who had told him about such things when he was still blind. And he began to think that since he was no longer blind he could therefore see everything.

There were also in that place some seers, men who were endowed with the five divine powers: the powers to go anywhere and to transform oneself or other things, to see anything at any distance, to hear anything at any distance, to know the thoughts in the minds of others, and to know one's own former lives and those of others. They said to the man who had been blind: "Now you can see, but you still do not know anything. Why are you so arrogant? When you are in your house you cannot see what is outside. You don't know who likes or dislikes you. And you can't hear or understand the voice of someone only five kilometers away, or hear a drum or the sound of a conch off in the distance. You can't go anywhere without lifting your feet and following a path. You can't even remember being in your mother's womb.

How can you say you see everything? What makes you think you are so wise? Do you want to take darkness for light?"

Then the man asked the seers how they had obtained such powers. And they told him, "If you want such powers you should live in a forest, or sit in a mountain cave, and think only of the Dharma. You must get rid of all your faults."

So the man went off into a forest, concentrated on a single thing, got rid of his worldly desires, and obtained the five holy powers. Then he thought to himself, "In the past, no matter what I did, nothing good ever came of it. I was blind and not wise. Now I can go wherever I want."

The text goes on to tell us that a variety of herbs are needed because there is a variety of entrances into the Dharma. The blind man, we are told, just like ordinary people, is blinded by desire, while the man who thinks he can see everything is like the shravakas. Then the man is encouraged to further his awakening.

## A SIMILE

Although there is no parable of medicinal plants in the chapter by that title, what we do have there is a simile that is very important for understanding the Dharma Flower Sutra.[16]

In this simile the Buddha is said to be like a great cloud that covers the entire world and dispenses a universal rain, a rain that falls everywhere. The rain, like the Dharma, is the same everywhere. But the living beings nourished by the rain are like an enormous variety of plants—some large, some small, some red, some blue, some growing on hills, some in valleys, some growing in sand, others in clay or water, and so forth. The rain nourishes all the plants equally, the big, the medium-sized, and the small, penetrating everywhere, from the tops of tall trees to the deepest roots.

The passage itself is so succinct it is worth quoting here: "Kashyapa," says the Buddha, suppose that in the three-thousand great thousandfold world, growing on mountains, along the rivers and streams, in valleys and in different soils, are plants, trees, thickets, forests, and medicinal herbs of various and numerous kinds with different names and colors. A dense cloud spreads over all of them, covering the whole three-thousand great thousandfold world, and pours rain down on all at the same time. The moisture reaches all the plants, trees, thickets, forests, and medicinal herbs, with their little roots, little stems, little branches, little leaves, their medium-sized roots, medium-sized stems, medium-sized branches, medium-sized leaves, their big roots, big stems, big branches, and big leaves. Every tree, large or small, according to whether it is superior, middling, or inferior, receives its share. The rain from the same cloud, goes to each according to nature and kind, causing it to grow, bloom, and bear fruit. Though all grow in the same soil and are moistened by the same rain, these plants and trees are all different.

## COMMENTARY

An interesting aspect of the parable is that, within the same story, the Buddha is likened both to the physician and to the seers. Perhaps this is a way of telling us that the Buddha appears in many guises. An extremely important aspect of Buddhist practice for followers of the Lotus Sutra is the practice of recognizing the buddha-nature in others. This "buddha-nature" is nothing but the Buddha himself as a kind of potential. Thus, we need to develop the ability to see the Buddha in others. And what the Dharma Flower Sutra insists on is that we should learn to see the Buddha not just in special, holy people or leaders, but in all others. Thus, for those of sufficient skill, the Buddha can indeed be found in many guises, as both a physician and a seer.

I am reminded of the many stories in Chinese of how Manjushri Bodhisattva appears in many different disguises—as a beggar or a cripple, for example—in order to lead people to the sacred mountain, Wu-tai, which is the Chinese home of Manjushri. Chapters 24 and 25 of the Lotus Sutra tell us of the many forms in which the bodhisattvas Wonderful Voice and Regarder of the Cries of the World (Kwan-yin/ Kannon) appear to people in need. Such bodhisattvas, of course, embody the Buddha, enabling the Buddha to live in the world by being the Buddha for some. When we encounter someone who might be regarded as a rival or even an enemy, we should pause and consider how this person might be the Buddha in disguise—at least for us.

## UNIVERSALISM, PLURALISM, AND HARMONY

With the simile of the cloud and the rain, the focus of the Sutra has shifted somewhat—from a focus on skillful means in Chapters 2 through 4 to an emphasis on the universality of the Dharma and the equality of living beings.

In the missing half of the chapter, there are two additional similes: a simile of light and one of clay and pottery. According to the first, just as the light of the sun and the moon illuminates the whole world—those living beings who do good and those who do ill, the tall and the short, things that smell good and things that smell foul—so too the light of the Buddha's wisdom shines equally on all the living according to their capacities. Though it is received by each according to what it deserves, the light itself has no deficiency or excess. It is the same everywhere. According to the second simile, the simile of the clay and pottery, just as a potter makes different kinds of pots from the same clay—pots for sugar, for butter, for milk, and even for some filthy things—they are all made of the same clay, just as there is only one Buddha Vehicle.

It is worth noting in passing that in both of these similes there is an obvious inclusion of bad or unpleasant things. This is one of the ways in which the Dharma Flower Sutra expresses universality, the idea that there are no exceptions, no one is left out of the Dharma. Everything is affected by Buddha Dharma. The One Vehicle is for all living beings.

Whereas the parable of the burning house can lead us to believe that the One Vehicle replaces the three vehicles just as the one cart seems to replace the three carts, here we can understand the Sutra's intention to be inclusive of all beings. The many living beings, whether good, bad, both, or neither, are all nourished by the same rain, by the same Buddha Dharma.

It is also important to recognize that the kind of universalism affirmed in the Dharma Flower Sutra does not in any way diminish the reality and importance of particular things. The fact that the pots are made of one clay does not make the pots any less real. Similarly, that many beings of various kinds are illuminated by one light affirms both the oneness of the light and the many-ness of the living beings. Thus the universalism of the Dharma Flower Sutra is at the same time a pluralism, an affirmation of the reality and importance both of unity and of variety.

The central message of the simile of the cloud and rain is that the Buddha's teachings, the Dharma, is equally available to everyone. The Dharma can be found anywhere, ready to nourish each and every one of us. All living beings participate in a process in which they are nourished by the same living energy as everyone else, a living energy that Buddhists call "Buddha Dharma." But we are not all alike. We live in different cultures, have different histories, use different languages, are born in different generations, have different abilities to hear and understand, and so on. That is why the one Dharma has to be embodied in many different teachings and practices.

The variety of teachings is symbolized in Chapter 3 of the Dharma Flower Sutra as three vehicles, but we can see that in these similes, there are not just three ways—there are a great many, just as there are many different kinds of plants.

If plants, at least the vast majority of plants, receive no rain, they soon wither and die. The same is true of us: without the nourishment of the Dharma we would dry up and die. But this Dharma that nourishes all is not something to be found only in the Buddhist religion. It is universal. It is everywhere. The Dharma can be found even in the ordinary food that we eat and the water we drink, making it possible for us to live.

According to the simile of the great cloud and rain, every living being is, in one sense, equally valuable. Each has its own function within the larger whole. Each has its own integrity, its own value for itself, its own goodness, its own purposes, its own beauty. The rain nourishes according to the needs of the various plants. A big tree requires more water than a small shoot of grass. But this does not necessarily mean that the big tree is superior to the small blade of grass; it's just bigger. Different living beings play different roles in the ecology of the planet. Each of us depends on a vast network of living beings, which are dependent on each other. Thus, a certain harmony or peace is required—not necessarily a perfect harmony, but enough of a harmony to enable the system to function and survive through growth and modification.

Today, many believe that the minimal harmony necessary for human survival on earth is being destroyed by earth's dominant group of living beings—human beings. Whole habitats—rainforests, wetlands, uncultivated plains, natural rivers and streams—have been destroyed and are still being destroyed, probably at an increasing rate. Increased economic activity virtually everywhere also means increasing pollution of the air and water and the very soil upon which we depend for much of our food. In addition to such environmental destruction, humankind has developed weapons of enormous destructive power that could hardly have been imagined a century ago.

In this sense, human beings have made themselves more important, that is, more powerful, than other living beings in this ecosystem. They threaten to destroy even the minimal harmony that makes life on earth possible.

This is a situation well beyond what the Indian compilers of the Lotus Sutra could have imagined. It would be foolish to claim that the Sutra provides a recipe for solving the kind of problems that threaten the planet today. But, in principle, the Sutra is hardly silent about such matters. It calls upon us to recognize that—in important respects—all living beings are equal. All are nourished by the same processes, symbolized in the simile as the rain of the Dharma.

The Dharma Flower Sutra calls upon us, not only to transform individuals, but also "to purify buddha-lands." From the point of view of the Sutra, of course, this earth is the buddha land of Shakyamuni Buddha. This world, and especially this world, is Shakyamuni Buddha's world. But the Buddha is not some sort of all-powerful God ruling the universe. The Buddha is embodied, made real, in the Buddha-deeds of ordinary living beings. The Buddha invites us to be partners with him in transforming this world into a pure buddha land, where there is a kind of harmony of beauty enabling living beings to flourish together in many different healthy ways, all equally depending on the Dharma and on one another.

This chapter of the Lotus Sutra encourages us to think of the large picture and to be grateful that we are nourished by the Dharma raining on us. But it is also important to recognize that the Dharma can be rained down by us. In *Zen and Western Thought* the famous Zen scholar Masao Abe wrote that "the greatest debt without doubt is to my three teachers.... Without the Dharma rain they poured upon me, a rain which nourished me for many years, even this humble bunch of flowers could not have been gathered."[17]

In other words, to follow the Buddha Way, the Dharma, is to be nourished by the Dharma, but it is also to nourish others—many kinds of others. In still other words, to follow the Buddha Way of transforming living beings and purifying buddha lands is to become a buddha oneself, at least in small but very important ways.

# DOING THE COMMON GOOD

IN CHAPTER 3 of the Lotus Sutra, the Buddha assures Shariputra that in a future age he would become a buddha—in Chapter 6 he does the same for his disciples Kashyapa, Subhuti, Katyayana, and Maudgalyayana. Thus at least five of the ten "great disciples" of the Buddha have been assured of becoming buddhas in some future age. In Chapters 8 and 9 as well, assurances of becoming a buddha in the future will also be given. But at the very end of Chapter 6, the Buddha says that while he has been talking about the future, he would now like to say something about the past—"mine and yours." "Listen carefully," he says. And then in Chapter 7 he tells a story about the Buddha Excellent in Great Penetrating Wisdom and his sixteen sons who lived in the distant past.

How distant? The Dharma Flower Sutra has many interesting, ingenious ways of depicting huge numbers. Here we find one of the most interesting. "Suppose," the Buddha says, "that someone ground everything in a thousand million worlds into a powder as fine as the powder in ink. Then suppose he went to the East, passing through various worlds until he had passed through a thousand worlds. In that world he deposits one speck of the powder and passes on through another thousand worlds, where he drops another speck of powder.

And he continues doing this until all the specks of powder are gone. This would be a very large number indeed. But now suppose all of the worlds he has passed through, whether a speck of powder was dropped there or not, were themselves all ground into powder as fine as ink powder. The number of eons since Excellent in Great Penetrating Wisdom Buddha passed away is millions of billions of times larger than that!" Like the specks of ink powder, the number of eons is finite, but larger than we can imagine. And that may be the point—stretching our imaginations.

## THE STORY

Such a very long time ago, the Buddha says, there was a prince who earnestly sought supreme awakening by meditating for billions of years but was not successful. To help, some gods from the highest heaven prepared an enormously high seat or throne for him under a bodhi tree, and the kings of the lowest heaven rained flowers over the whole area in which he was sitting. From time to time a fragrant wind would come up and blow away the old flowers so that new ones could fall from the heavens and replace them. The kings of heaven beat their drums, and other gods joined in, to make a kind of concert of heavenly music as an offering to this prince. Still, he sat on that seat, without moving a muscle and without thinking at all, for ten small eons. Finally, the Dharma came to him and he became fully awakened as the buddha named "Excellent in Great Penetrating Wisdom."

Before leaving home, this prince had sixteen sons. When they heard that their father had become a buddha, they gave up their playthings and went to him, followed by their grandfather, the king, hundreds of ministers, and hundreds of thousands of ordinary people. When they arrived before the Buddha, the princes all congratulated, praised, and honored him for doing something from which everyone would benefit, and they begged him to explain the Dharma.

When Excellent in Great Penetrating Wisdom became a buddha, all of the many worlds in each of the ten directions shook in the six different ways in which a world can shake. All of those worlds, even those darkened by shadows, were suddenly filled with light, so that people could see each other well for the first time, and they exclaimed, "Where have all these living beings suddenly come from?"

In the east, Shakyamuni says, continuing the story, the palaces of the kings of heaven were suddenly twice as bright as before, leading the kings of the Brahma heavens to wonder what was going on, and to discuss this strange business among themselves. One of them suggested that perhaps the reason for all the light was that a great god or a buddha had appeared somewhere in the universe. So the Brahma kings in the east all gave up the pleasures of deep meditation and set out toward the world of Excellent in Great Penetrating Wisdom Buddha carrying huge plates full of flowers, and bringing their palaces along behind them.

Soon the kings of the Brahma heavens came to the place where Excellent in Great Penetrating Wisdom Buddha was sitting on his great throne under a great bodhi tree, surrounded by a large variety of people and heavenly beings, and the sixteen princes begging the Buddha to preach. These heavenly kings worshiped the Buddha by walking around him several hundred thousand times, strewing the flowers they had brought and creating a mountain of flowers in the process. They also offered flowers to the bodhi tree. Then they offered their palaces to the Buddha, praising him for doing good for all living beings, and begging him to proclaim the Dharma.

Most honored of human and heavenly beings,
We beg you:

Turn the unexcelled Dharma-wheel,
Beat the drum of the great Dharma,

Blow the conch of the great Dharma,
Rain down everywhere the rain of the great Dharma,
Saving innumerable beings! (LS 190)

Similarly, in a series of short stories, all the kings of the Brahma heavens from all the other ten directions come in turn to the place where the Buddha is sitting, to praise and worship him and offer him flowers and palaces. After each of these groups begged him to teach the Dharma, the Buddha agreed. And when they had all assembled, he taught them the four noble truths and then the teaching of "twelve causes and conditions," teachings that in the Dharma Flower Sutra are associated with shravakas and pratyekabuddhas.

At this point, billions of the people listening to the Buddha's teachings refused to become attached to things, freed themselves from evil passions, gained profound and wonderful meditation, the three kinds of knowledge, the six divine powers, and the eight emancipations, and became shravakas.

The sixteen princes became novice monks, and they begged the Buddha to preach now, not just about awakening, but about supreme awakening, that is, about becoming a buddha. The Buddha agreed, but it was not until another twenty thousand eons had passed that he finally preached the Dharma Flower Sutra. And it took him eighty thousand eons without resting to complete the entire Sutra. The novices and some shravakas received the Sutra fully, while others did not.

Following this, Excellent in Great Penetrating Wisdom Buddha went into a state of deep meditation for eighty-four thousand eons. Seeing this and realizing that someone would need to do the work of the Buddha in his absence, the sixteen novices each taught the Dharma Flower Sutra to monks and nuns and lay men and women for the whole time, thereby helping billions and billions of living beings. When the Buddha emerged from meditation, he praised the novices and asked everyone to make offerings to them. Later, the Buddha says, these sixteen novices also achieved supreme awakening, became buddhas, and are now teaching the Dharma in the worlds of the ten directions, among them, in the east, is Medicine Buddha (Akshobhya) and, in the west, Amida Buddha (Amitabha). And the sixteenth is Shakyamuni Buddha himself, spreading the Dharma in this world.

## COMMENTARY

There is not a lot of humor in Buddhist texts, but here a slight note of humor is introduced into the Dharma Flower Sutra with this story, at the point where the people of the many worlds see each for the first time. Today, Tokyo's Shinjuku Station is probably the busiest train station in the world, always crowded with people coming and going. Imagine being blind and being led through such a busy place every day. You would be aware that there are other people around. But most of them are very quiet, so you would have no idea how many people there were. One day, if quite suddenly you were able to see, you might say in surprise, "Who are all these people?" The buddhas bring light to the dark places of our lives, enabling us to see more than we could see before, surprising us.

Following this almost whimsical note in the story, the Buddha then presents some of the most essential teachings of Buddhism, beginning with the four noble truths.

In brief, these are: the truth that life involves suffering; the truth that the cause or origin of suffering is desire or ignorance; the truth that suffering can be overcome, usually understood to be the state of nirvana; and the truth that the way to overcome suffering is the eightfold path.[18] Closely associated with this teaching in classical Buddhism is the teaching of the "twelve causes and conditions."

In the Dharma Flower Sutra these two teachings are closely

associated with the shravaka and pratyekabuddha ways respectively, and they are mentioned frequently. But only here in this story are they actually described. And here both are associated with the shravaka way. In the Dharma Flower Sutra generally, while the bodhisattva way is presented as more inclusive or more far-reaching, there is no intention to disparage the shravaka way as illustrated by this story.

## KINGS, BODHISATTVAS, AND BUDDHAS

The kings of the Brahma heavens give up the pleasures of meditation to come down to earth and offer their flowers and palaces to the Buddha. This means that even a king of heaven, a god, cannot become a buddha without working in this world of human beings to benefit others. It does not mean that meditation is to be avoided. In this story it is through meditation that the prince became the Buddha Excellent in Great Penetrating Wisdom. But the story does suggest that meditation alone is not sufficient Buddhist practice.

Probably in every religion, people are often attracted to a religious practice because they have a problem and need some help. They pray to be cured of some illness, or to overcome some human relationship problem, to find success in business, to find a suitable husband or wife or to have a good birth. And quite often religious practice does result in some kind of overcoming of such problems, resulting in some kind of comfort.

In the parable of the magic city that is told late within this story and will be discussed in the next chapter, the Dharma Flower Sutra makes quite clear that comfort may be good, or even necessary—but only as a temporary resting place. If someone is comforted by the Buddha's teachings, we should be glad. Shakyamuni Buddha, you will remember, was also born as a prince, initially living in a palace with everything that could possibly make him comfortable and happy. But we should also remember that this is what he abandoned in order to seek awakening in the ordinary, uncomfortable world.

Though it may have such a result, the Dharma should not be practiced merely for the sake of obtaining a peaceful or comfortable life, a kind of palace. We too should give our palaces to the Buddha, which means that we should have deeply felt compassion toward others and a desire to help others. The great teacher Nichiren said that a hundred years of practice in a pure land was not equal to a day of practice in this impure land. We must do the hard work of a bodhisattva.

As a bodhisattva, Excellent in Great Penetrating Wisdom was helped toward becoming a buddha by gods and kings of the Brahma heavens. We can understand that without the help of the gods and kings of heaven, the prince would not have become a buddha at all. This can be understood to mean that Buddhist practice is not primarily a solitary matter, but something done in and for a larger community with the help of others. The sixteen princes praised and honored their father because he was doing the common good, something from which everyone would benefit.

Toward the end of the story, the Buddha Excellent in Great Penetrating Wisdom enters deeply into meditation. Seeing this, the sixteen princes realize that the Buddha is no longer available and that someone else has to do the Buddha's work, especially his work of teaching the Dharma so that all will be helped to become buddhas. And so these princes do the Buddha's work, filling in for him as it were, and enabling countless living beings to enter the bodhisattva path in order to move closer to becoming a buddha. In other words, even a buddha needs help—especially the help of bodhisattvas.

In Buddhism we say that we have faith in or take refuge in the Buddha, the Dharma, and the Sangha or Buddhist community. It expresses the important idea that we need the help from the Buddha, from his Dharma or teachings, and from a supporting community. This sense that we all need the help of others extends, in the Dharma Flower Sutra, even to buddhas and bodhisattvas.

## FOR THE GOOD OF ALL

The sixteen princes thank their father because, by his awakening, "human and heavenly beings as well as ourselves are supremely enriched." And they beg him to "teach for the sake of the world."(LS 183)

At the end of the series of stories of heavenly kings coming to the Buddha, the last group of them says:

> May these blessings
> Extend to all,
> That we with all the living
> Together attain the Buddha way. (LS 193)

This is an important expression for Rissho Kosei-kai and for many other Buddhists as well. It is a kind of summary of the heart of Mahayana Buddhist teaching. The expression "with all the living" is a way of reminding ourselves that we are related to all, and that the highest Buddhist practice is doing something for the good of all.

To speak of doing something for the good of all is a way of talking about serving the Buddha. Nothing is good all by itself. Good is always a blessing *for somebody*. It is relational. Our own personal good is always limited, limited in part by the very limited scope of our experience, our knowledge, and our compassion. The good of our family is larger, less limited, than our individual good, but still very limited. The good of the community is larger than the good of our family. The good of the nation is larger than the good of our community. The good of all people is larger still. But all of these are still limited goods.

The Buddha, who is in all times and places, is not so limited. That is why "serving the Buddha," "doing the Buddha's will," and similar expressions have the meaning of doing something for the good of all, of working for the common good. But doing something for the good of all should not be seen as opposed to doing something for our own good.

The Buddha never asks us to completely give up our own interests, our own good, to be completely selfless, to serve only the good of others. The Buddha does ask us to go beyond our own good, to understand and to feel deeply that we are related to a whole cosmos of living beings, and to know that it is by doing something for the good of all that we ourselves can realize our own highest good—the buddha in us.

# 10

# A FANTASTIC CASTLE-CITY

Mᴏꜱᴛ ᴏꜰ Cʜᴀᴘᴛᴇʀ 7 of the Lotus Sutra tells the story of
the Buddha Excellent in Great Penetrating Wisdom—but
here we'll turn our attention to a parable told by Shakyamuni Buddha late in the story, a parable about a magical, fantastic
castle-city.

## THE PARABLE

Once upon a time there was a very bad road that was many, many
miles long; steep, wild, and difficult; deserted and far from where
anyone lived—a truly frightening place. A group of people wanted
to go along that road to a place where there were rare treasures. This
group was led by a guide who was knowing and wise and who knew
the difficult road well—where it was open and where it was closed, for
example—and who had considerable experience leading groups that
wanted to go across that terrible road.

Along the way, the group became tired and weary and said to the
guide, "We are utterly exhausted, and afraid as well. We can't go any
further. Since the road before us goes on and on, now we want to
turn back."

The guide, a man of many skillful means, thought to himself, "What a shame that these people want to give up on the great and rare treasures and turn back." Having thought about it in this way, he used his skill in appropriate means to conjure up a beautiful and wonderful castle-city that appeared about twelve miles down the difficult road. Then he said to the group, "Don't be afraid! You must not turn back! Look! See that great castle ahead. There you can stop and rest and do whatever you want. When you enter this castle, you will soon be completely at ease. Later, when you are able to go toward the place where the treasures are, you should leave this castle-city."

The hearts of the exhausted group were filled with joy and they exclaimed, "Now we can surely escape from this dreadful road and find some peace and comfort." Then the group went into the fantastic castle and, thinking they had been rescued from their difficulties, soon were calm and comfortable.

Later, seeing that the group was rested and no longer afraid or weary, the guide used his skillful means to cause the fantastic castle-city to disappear. And he said to the group: "We have to go now. The place of the treasures is close. I created this large fantastic castle-city a little while ago just for you to rest in."

## COMMENTARY

While there are several important things one might learn from this story, its central message is quite clear: while we may think that nirvana, a condition of complete rest and quiet, is our final goal, it is not. While we may think that nirvana is salvation, that is only a useful illusion from which we will eventually need to move on. According to the Dharma Flower Sutra, it is always an illusion to think that we have arrived and have no more to do, to think that if we reach some kind of experience of happiness or comfort, we have reached the end of the path.

Similarly, while we may think that the Buddha entered final nirvana, becoming "extinct" and thus no longer active, that too is only a useful illusion, as the Buddha is working still, enabling us to live and work with him to save all the living. In Chapter 16 of the Sutra we can find these words:

> In order to liberate the living,
> As a skillful means I appear to enter nirvana.
> Yet truly I am not extinct.
> I am always here teaching the Dharma. (LS 296)

The Buddha has used teachings, including the teaching of his own final nirvana, to help people along difficult roads.

In part, the message of this story is the same message as that of previous parables—it's about the importance of skillful means used appropriately. But here the focus is not as much on skillful means in general, as it is in the parable of the burning house and the three vehicles or the parable of the poor son and rich father. Here the focus is on one particular teaching—that of nirvana, one of the most important concepts of classical Buddhism—and seeing even that teaching as yet another example of skillful means.

Literally, "nirvana" means "extinction." It was often thought to be the state of awakening achieved by Shakyamuni Buddha, a state in which all illusions and all karma that leads to rebirth are extinguished. While it has been interpreted in various ways by various Buddhist philosophers and schools, nirvana is often said to be the goal of Buddhists or of the Buddhist path. In this story, however, we are to see that nirvana, or at least one understanding of nirvana, is not to be taken as a final goal at all. Quite the opposite—to take the magically created castle-city as the goal would be to remain in a permanent state of delusion, thinking one had arrived at one's destination when one had not.

Yet this does not mean that the teaching of nirvana is unimportant, a "mere" skillful means. To the contrary, here we are to understand that if the guide had not been able to conjure up a castle in which the travelers could rest, they would not have been able to continue toward their goal. The magical castle-city was vitally useful. In other words, it was not merely useful in the sense that it happened to be convenient but not really necessary; it was essential in order for the travelers to be able to move ahead.

The Lotus Sutra is sometimes said to disparage the shravaka way and its emphasis on nirvana. And it is indeed true that some passages in the Sutra can be cited to support this view. For example, in Chapter 2 we can read:

> For those with dull minds
> Who want lesser teachings,
> Who greedily cling to existence,
> Who, after encountering countless buddhas,
>
> Still do not follow
> The profound and wonderful way,
> And are tormented by much suffering—
> For them I teach nirvana. (LS 86–7)

But passages of this kind are rare and, while they are one way of looking at the matter, they do not represent the overall view of the Lotus Sutra, which is basically that shravaka teachings are an important step along the Buddha Way. Already in Chapter 1 we can find:

> By various causal explanations
> And innumerable parables,
> [The buddhas] illuminate the Buddha-dharma
> And open understanding of it to all.

If any are suffering
Or weary from age, disease, or death,
For them they teach nirvana
To bring all suffering to an end.

The shravaka way certainly is not being belittled or disparaged—after all, it brings suffering to an end. For those who sought to be shravakas he taught the Dharma of the four truths for overcoming birth, old age, disease, and death, and attaining nirvana.

Thus we find references to this shravaka nirvana as "incomplete nirvana," or as what shravakas "think is nirvana." Not surprisingly, we find contrasting terms in the text as well, such as "ultimate nirvana." At one point in Chapter 7, the Buddha says, "the nirvana that you have attained is not the real one!" This implies, of course, that there is a greater "nirvana" of some kind. This greater nirvana is often characterized in the Dharma Flower Sutra as "buddha-wisdom." The shravaka nirvana, the Buddha says, is "only close to buddha-wisdom." (LS 199) Sometimes the text goes further, declaring that real nirvana is a matter of being a buddha. Thus, at the end of Chapter 7 we find:

When I know they have reached nirvana
And all have become arhats,
Then I gather everyone together
And teach the real Dharma.

Through their powers of skillful means,
Buddhas make distinctions and teach three vehicles.
But there is really only one Buddha-Vehicle.
It is for a resting place that the other two are taught.

Now I teach the truth for you:
What you have reached is not extinction.

To gain a buddha's comprehensive wisdom,
You have to make a great effort.

When you have gained comprehensive wisdom,
And the ten powers of the Buddha-dharma,
And acquired the thirty-two characteristics,
Then that is real extinction. (LS 206)

Thus, what is taught in the Dharma Flower Sutra, and in the parable of the fantastic castle-city, is that an experience of nirvana that leads you to think you have accomplished all that you need to accomplish is always an illusion. Yet, while it is an illusion, it is not necessarily a *bad* illusion, since, by providing a resting place along the way, it can enable people to pursue the greater goal of acquiring buddha-wisdom, of becoming a buddha. Resting places can be illusions and escapes, but they may be both useful and necessary. Without them many people, including ourselves, might not be able to continue on the way. We should not, then, be too critical of resting places, especially of the resting places of others.

All Buddhist teachings are for the purpose of helping us, but if we cling to them as though they themselves are the goal, they can become more of a hindrance than a help to continuing on the path. We should welcome the Buddha's teachings with joy and make use of them in our lives, but we should not cling to them as though the teachings themselves are the goal.

The Dharma Flower Sutra provides assurance that everyone has buddha-nature, that everyone is endowed from birth with a potential to be a buddha. It teaches that all will follow the bodhisattva way to some degree, however minimal. But it does not say that this way will be easy, or that it will make our lives easy. It promises a happy life, but not a life of comfort and ease. Especially when compared with remaining in a fantastic castle-city, continuing on the long, steep, and arduous road is difficult, and even fraught with danger.

Both patient endurance of hardship and perseverance are required, two of the six transcendental practices of bodhisattvas. In Buddhism this world is known as the "*saha* world," that is, the world in which suffering both has to be and can be endured. Nichiren, the thirteenth-century Japanese Buddhist monk and patriarch of many groups devoted to the Lotus Sutra, understood this all too well. And because the Lotus Sutra taught him to anticipate persecution and suffering, he was able to endure much suffering and cope with the problems that confronted him.

Leaving a resting place or giving up some comfort does not, of course, mean that we should feel miserable all the time. The point is that by resting you gain both strength and joy for pursuing a path that is both arduous and joyful.

11

# GREAT TREASURE IS VERY NEAR

ESPECIALLY IN EARLY CHAPTERS of the Lotus Sutra, one major concern is to understand or explain how the older shravaka way is related to the newer bodhisattva way. What was especially important was to try to explain why the great early disciples of the Buddha, that is, the Buddha's closest disciples, were shravakas and apparently had not taken the path of the bodhisattva. The authors and compilers of Mahayana sutras were trying to create a new tradition, but this new tradition could not be a complete break from the old tradition, symbolized in the Lotus Sutra as the shravaka way. While critical of that older tradition, they wanted to incorporate it into the new.

In Chapter 8 of the Sutra ("Assurance for the Five Hundred Disciples"), the Buddha first explains that the disciple named Purna, son of Maitrayani, has been a most excellent teacher of the Dharma under thousands of buddhas. He has skillfully taught the Dharma in the past, is doing so in the present, and will continue to do so in the future. He is so skillful that innumerable people, supposing him to be a shravaka, have benefited from his teaching. In reality, however, this Purna is a bodhisattva who will eventually become a buddha named Dharma Radiance. By disguising themselves as shravakas in ways like this, bodhisattvas make it possible even for unmotivated people to enter the bodhisattva way, the way of becoming a buddha.

The second section of this chapter in the Sutra can be a little confusing. It begins with twelve hundred arhats wishing that they could be assured of becoming buddhas, just as other shravakas have been assured. The Buddha then says that he will assure these twelve hundred one by one. Assurance of becoming a buddha is then given to another leading monk, Kaundinya, the uncle of Purna, who is to become a buddha named Universal Light. It is said in other texts that Kaundinya was the first to become an ordained disciple of the Buddha at Varanasi and that for some time he was the head of the community of monks. The discussion here of his assurance of becoming a buddha is very short. It is immediately followed by the announcement that five hundred arhats, some of them named, will be assured one by one by their predecessors of becoming buddhas, all with the same name, Universal Light.

Next, the Buddha says that the rest of the shravakas will eventually become buddhas, and he instructs Kashyapa, another of his ten great disciples, to go and tell those shravakas who were not present that they too would eventually become buddhas. The text is not completely clear at this point, but the reference to the rest of the shravakas probably means those in the twelve hundred not among the five hundred who will become buddhas named Universal Light. And the absent shravakas could be the arrogant ones who had left the assembly in a huff in Chapter 2, just as the Buddha was about to preach. If so, this is one of many places where the Sutra shows a spirit of generosity. Even arrogant people who refuse to listen to the Buddha, it says, will eventually become fully awakened buddhas.

At this point, the five hundred arhats, the highest stage of spiritual development pursued by shravakas, ecstatic with joy over receiving their assurance of becoming buddhas, confessed that they had previously been foolishly satisfied with the level of progress that they had already attained. Then to explain their situation to the Buddha they tell the parable of the hidden jewel, or, as I like to call it, "the parable of the gem in the hem."

## THE PARABLE

A poor man visiting the home of a good friend, a rich man, became drunk and fell asleep. The host, having to leave in order to take care of some business, sewed a priceless jewel into the robe of his sleeping friend and went off. After a while the poor man woke up and left. He went to another town, where he had great difficulty earning enough for sufficient food and clothing. Eventually he happened to run into his friend once again, who promptly scolded him, explained that he had given him the jewel so that he would not have to struggle so much, and called him a fool for not making use of his hidden treasure.

The Buddha, we are told, is like that rich friend. He reminds us of good roots planted long ago. An arhat is like the poor man. Being satisfied with what little he has already attained, he does not realize that in reality he is a bodhisattva who will attain supreme awakening.

## COMMENTARY

The central lesson of this parable is, of course, that the greatest treasure is never far off, but intimately close to each of us. Though we may not know it, we already have it. That is, each of us has within us abilities, skills, talents, strengths, potentialities, powers, and so forth with which to do the Buddha's work, abilities that we do not yet know about and have not yet utilized.

The idea that the treasure we seek is very close may seem to conflict with the story of the fantastic castle-city discussed in the previous chapter. In that story, the goal is both very distant and very difficult to reach. But these two stories can be understood to be in harmony: the goal is very distant in one respect and very close in another.

While the term "buddha-nature" is never used in the Dharma Flower Sutra, this is a good example of the use of the basic idea behind the concept that would be developed after the Dharma Flower Sutra was compiled. One way we can understand the term is as a kind of "power" that makes it possible for any one of us to be a bodhisattva for someone else, a strength that makes it possible for us to share in doing the Buddha's work of awakening all the living, a strength that makes it possible for us to go far beyond our normal expectations.

Buddha-nature, the potential to become a buddha, is not something we have to earn; it is something that all of us have received naturally, something that cannot be destroyed or taken away from us. It is, as the parable in Chapter 4 teaches, our inheritance; it is ours by virtue of our very existence. This is why we are taught in this chapter that our treasure is very close.

Our buddha-nature is, in one sense, part of the basis of our very existence. Nothing could be closer. On the other hand, unless we learn to make use of this ability and put it into practice in our daily lives, the goal of realizing it, of becoming a buddha, remains very distant. In light of these two views, gaining the treasure is a matter of more fully understanding and realizing something that was always within us. While our treasure is very close, that full realization and appropriation of it always remains very distant.

In a sense, a hidden treasure has no value until it is disclosed and used in some way. This is the difference in economics between investing and hoarding. If we take our savings and just stuff it in a mattress, the money doesn't "work" for us. It earns no interest or dividends, and accomplishes no ends for anyone. So it is with our abilities and talents. If we hoard them by keeping them hidden and unused, they do no good for ourselves or for others.

In this story, using the treasure clearly means using it to enjoy life. Life is difficult, but we are much freer, more able to appreciate, more able to cope with whatever difficulties life presents us if we have an appropriate attitude toward life and toward ourselves. Having a good attitude toward life, for the Dharma Flower Sutra, means seeing everything that comes to us as a gift, more especially as an opportunity, as what we call a "learning experience." Yes, life can be very difficult, but if we approach the troubles and difficulties that come our way as opportunities for learning, we will enjoy life more fully.

In Mahayana Buddhism, the importance of helping others is often stressed. But we should know that even helping others is never *merely* helping others—it always contributes to our own enjoyment of life as well. The Dharma Flower Sutra encourages us to look for and cultivate the good both in ourselves and in others.

So what does this mean with regard to buddhas and bodhisattvas? Purna, we are told in the first section of this chapter, while seeming to be a shravaka, is actually a bodhisattva in disguise. The Dharma Flower Sutra both retains the classical meaning of bodhisattva as one who is very high in status, on the way to becoming a buddha, and it gives new meaning to the term by proposing that all are, to some degree bodhisattvas. This means that the title "bodhisattva" should be seen, not so much as a mark of status, but rather as a term used to name a kind of activity. Just as a teacher who does not teach is not really a teacher, a bodhisattva who does not do the work of the Buddha is not truly a bodhisattva. On the other hand, anyone who does do the work of the Buddha, regardless of title or status, is—to that degree—a bodhisattva. I sometimes like to say that we should regard the word "bodhisattva" not so much as a noun, but as a verb. Unfortunately, this is much easier to do in Chinese than it is in English!

Here is one version of the surprising revelation that shravakas may indeed be bodhisattvas.

Monks, listen carefully!
Because they have learned skillful means well,
The way followed by children of the Buddha [bodhisattvas]
Is unthinkably wonderful.

Knowing that most delight in lesser teachings
And are overawed by great wisdom,
Bodhisattvas become
Shravakas or pratyekabuddhas.

Using innumerable skillful means,
They transform all kinds of beings
By proclaiming themselves to be shravakas,
Far removed from the Buddha Way.

They save innumerable beings,
Enabling them to succeed.
Though most people are complacent and lazy,
In this way they are finally led to become buddhas.

Keeping their bodhisattva actions
As inward secrets,
Outwardly
They appear as shravakas.

They appear to have little desire
And to be tired of birth and death,
But in truth
They are purifying buddha lands. (LS 210–11)

The point is in part to emphasize the importance of embodying the Dharma in our lives, in our actions and behavior toward others. But equally important is the idea that anyone can be a bodhisattva for us, if we are open to seeing and experiencing the other as a bodhisattva. As is so often the case, this teaching, the idea that a shravaka can be seen to actually be a bodhisattva, is both about how we should regard ourselves and about how we should regard others, an idea that will be developed and emphasized over and over again in subsequent chapters of the Dharma Flower Sutra.

We should notice that the rich friend's initial ploy doesn't really work well. Apparently he expected the poor man to realize that he had the treasure and make use of it. Yet he did not, remaining just as poor as before. Why? In this story it is simply because the poor man is foolish, too dumb to realize that the jewel had been sewn into his garment. This means, of course, that the Buddha depends on others. In this case, making use of the treasure depends on the poor man. A treasure has been given to him, but unless he himself makes use of it, it amounts to nothing.

So it is with us. We should not think that the Buddha is some kind of all-powerful god who can awaken all living beings by himself. The Buddha of the Dharma Flower Sutra, like all beings, lives interdependently with others. He needs his children, his bodhisattvas, to do his work in this world, working both for their own liberation and for the liberation of others.

Shinran, the great founder of the True Pure Land (Jodo Shin-shu) tradition of Japanese Buddhism, thought it important to say that human beings are utterly dependent on the "other-power" of the Buddha and can accomplish nothing good by their "own-power." But in the Dharma Flower Sutra we cannot find this radically dualistic distinction between the power of the Buddha and the power of others. In this Sutra, the power in us, the buddha-nature in us, is always both our own power and the power of the Buddha embodied in us.

Taking interpretation of this parable further, the idea of being given a great treasure is not only an individual matter, but something that can be applied to human beings as a whole. The treasure is the earth, the natural environment and resources that we have inherited. Human beings have been given not only buddha-nature, but all of nature itself. The Buddha (the reality of the world) is basically generous and supportive of human life. We have inherited an incredibly rich earth. With it we are given an enormous opportunity to do good. The question is, will we recognize and appreciate how valuable this treasure is, and, if we do, how will we use this treasure given to us?

Perhaps humanity as a whole is like the poor man in the parable— still stumbling around without realizing that we have such a treasure. Perhaps humanity as a whole needs to wake up to see not only the wonderful treasure that is in us but also the wonderful treasure that is all around us.

## EVEN THE LOTUS SUTRA HAS LIMITATIONS

In this chapter, as in others, when the Buddha describes the future buddha land of Purna after he has become the buddha named Dharma Radiance, he says that his land will be without women, that men will have no sexual desire, and that they will be born without having mothers. Historically, such a misanthropic attitude toward women probably reflects the experience of celibate monks living in India twenty centuries ago. Sexuality and gender has been an ongoing problem for Buddhism. This is in large part because sexual desire in men can be seen as the prime embodiment of desire and greed—everything that Buddhism, especially traditional Indian Buddhism, opposed and sought to abolish. Women were seen as the cause of men's sexual desires, and thus as embodiments of evil.

With respect to attitudes toward women, Buddhism was something of an improvement over Hinduism. Women were, for example, admitted into the community as ordained nuns, as was true in Jainism. But nuns were radically subordinated to monks and it was believed that only through rebirth as a man could a woman have any possibility of awakening fully.

The Dharma Flower Sutra often reflects such attitudes, as appears to be the case in this chapter. But, as we will see later, it sometimes takes a more generous view of women and of their potential to be Dharma teachers and become buddhas in the future. Thus the Sutra is consistent in teaching that every living being has the potential to become a buddha in this world. In doing this, in maintaining the consistent teaching of universal buddha-nature, the Sutra takes an important step toward teaching the equality of men and women.

Yet while the Dharma Flower Sutra does take a step forward with respect to equality, going beyond Hinduism, beyond traditional Buddhism, and even beyond many Mahayana sutras, it only takes a step, and not a very large one at that, falling far short of today's standards. We can, I believe, love the Dharma Flower Sutra and seek to follow its important teachings while still recognizing that, like everything else, it has limitations. We should not forget that the Sutra itself teaches that all Buddhist teachings are skillful means, relative to their time and circumstance, including the details of the Dharma Flower Sutra. In this sense, though ahead of its time in most ways, in some other ways the Lotus Sutra reflects the limitations of the culture and time in which it arose.

# 12

## ANANDA AND RAHULA

Among the stories of the Lotus Sutra, the story in Chapter 9 ("Assurance for Arhats, Trained and in Training") is not at first as interesting as some others in the Sutra. The first time I taught a course on stories in the Lotus Sutra, I almost passed over it completely—but whenever I look carefully in the Dharma Flower Sutra, I find small gems of great wisdom that I hadn't seem before. Chapter 9 is one place I've found them.

## THE STORY

In previous chapters, the Buddha has assured various shravakas that in the future, usually in the very distant future, they will become buddhas. At the beginning of Chapter 9, Ananda and Rahula go up to the Buddha and say that they think that they too are qualified to be assured of becoming buddhas. Then two thousand other disciples also get up from their seats, and go to the Buddha to beg him to assure them of becoming buddhas.

The Buddha assures Ananda that after making offerings to six billion buddhas he would become a buddha known as King of the Wisdom of Mountains and Seas Who Is Unlimited in Power and that he would be responsible for a buddha land called Never Lowered Victory Banner, where he would teach countless bodhisattvas and be praised by an equally large number of buddhas. Of course Ananda is extremely happy. And he suddenly remembers the teachings of billions of past buddhas, and he recalls his own original vow to teach and transform countless beings into bodhisattvas.

Some eight thousand bodhisattvas are sitting in the congregation at that time. They wonder why so many shravakas were being assured of supreme awakening, but not a single bodhisattva. Understanding what was on their minds, the Buddha explained that in a previous life Ananda and he had together aspired to become buddhas. But since Ananda had followed a way of listening while Shakyamuni had vigorously practiced, Shakyamuni had already attained supreme awakening and Ananda had not yet. Since Ananda is now protecting the teachings and will protect the teachings of future buddhas, and will teach and transform many into bodhisattvas, causing them to achieve supreme awakening, he has now been assured of becoming a buddha.

Then the Buddha speaks to Rahula, telling him that in the future he will become the eldest son of as many buddhas as there are specks of dust in the ten worlds, including finally the buddha who is Ananda in a future life. Then he himself will become fully awakened as a buddha named One Who Walks on the Flowers of the Seven Treasures. And then the Buddha explains that while others see Rahula only as the Buddha's son, the Buddha knew Rahula's hidden or quiet practices.

The Buddha then speaks to Ananda about the two thousand other disciples present, and explains that they will make offerings to as many buddhas as there are specks of dust in fifty buddha worlds, honor those buddhas, and protect their teachings. Eventually these disciples will go to the worlds of the ten directions and become buddhas all at the same time, all of them called Jewel Sign. Then the hearts and bodies of these two thousand, "hearing the voice of assurance," are filled with joy.

World-honored One! Bright Lamp of Wisdom!
Hearing this voice of assurance,
We are filled with joy,
As though sprinkled with sweet nectar! (LS 224)

## COMMENTARY

The main characters in this story, Ananda and Rahula, are historical figures, people about whom we know a great deal. This does not, of course, mean that we should accept all of the stories about them as being true. There is a story in the Pali canon, for example, in which Ananda comes to earth from the Tushita heaven and is born on the same day as the Buddha.

The Buddha's early disciples were usually known for being first, or greatest, in something. Ananda was known for being first in listening, particularly in listening to the teachings and sermons of the Buddha. For this reason he probably is the most famous of the disciples, as he is known for having remembered all of the teachings of Shakyamuni that later became the sutras.

Buddhist sutras begin with the words, "This is what I heard." We are to understand that this is Ananda who is speaking and that the sutra that follows is what he heard, and what he recited from memory at the First Buddhist Council shortly after the death of the Buddha. If this is true, or even close to being true, it is a truly remarkable accomplishment, as the Buddha taught for some forty-five years, during which he preached a great many sermons. Apparently there was no writing in India at that time, and it was not until some centuries after the Buddha's death that Buddhist texts could be recorded in written form. Thus it may be that the vast bulk of Buddhist sutras were memorized by Ananda.

A cousin of Shakyamuni and a brother of the infamous Devadatta, Ananda joined the Sangha when he was about twenty, along with six other high-caste young men. At first, the request by Ananda and his brother to be allowed to join the Buddha's following was refused. So they became disciples of another religious teacher. But later, when they approached Shakyamuni a second time, permission was granted for them to join the group and become Buddhist monks. Some twenty years later, Ananda was surprised by his selection to be Shakyamuni's personal attendant—a position he kept for about twenty-five years.

According to legend, Ananda was not able to achieve nirvana, the awakening of an arhat, during the Buddha's lifetime. Right up to the night before the Council at which he would recite the Buddha's teachings, he was unable to reach that highly sought stage. But late that night, before the dawn, as he was in the process of lying down to sleep, he suddenly experienced nirvana, thus becoming eligible to participate in the Council along with all of the other arhats.

Like Shakyamuni, Ananda was a Shakya noble. There are many stories about his kindness, especially toward women, and about his attractiveness to women. It was he, more than any other, who persuaded Shakyamuni to admit women into the Sangha, in particular Shakyamuni's aunt and stepmother Mahaprajapati, thus creating the first Buddhist community for nuns.

There are a great many stories of people going to Ananda for advice or counsel, often on matters of doctrine, not only monks and nuns but also a variety of brahmans and householders. In addition to accounts of Ananda preaching both to monks and to lay men and women, there are also stories of Ananda being appointed to speak for the Buddha, either in place of the Buddha or to complete a sermon the Buddha had started.

Though highly suspect, it is written that Ananda lived to be a hundred and twenty years old. At the beginning of the fifth century, the Chinese monk Fa-hsien traveled to India, reporting extensively on what he saw and heard. At Vaishali, where it is said that the Buddha gave his last sermon, Fa-hsien found two stupas on opposite sides of the river, each containing half of the remains of Ananda. This was said to be a consequence of Ananda's body being cremated on a raft in the middle of the Ganges River. Nuns worshiped at the stupas of Ananda, since it was through his help that the community of nuns had been established.

One Pali text says that Ananda was "a dispeller of gloom in the darkness."[19] This could easily remind us an important verse from the end of Chapter 21 of the Lotus Sutra. About anyone who can teach the truth, it says,

> Just as the light of the sun and the moon
> Can dispel darkness,
> Such a person, working in the world,
> Can dispel the gloom of living beings. (LS 349)

The other main character in this story is Rahula. Rahula was also known as a "first"—first in quietly doing good. It is said that this means that he followed the Vinaya precepts, the rules for monks, very strictly. Like Ananda, he became one of the Buddha's ten principal disciples.

As he was Shakyamuni's only biological son, it was only natural that Shakyamuni Buddha would make an extra effort not to show any favoritism toward him. Thus there are many stories of Rahula being treated by his father just like any other follower.

While the name *Ananda* means "bliss" or "joy," the name *Rahula* means "obstruction," "bond," or "fetter." Born just shortly before the future Buddha left home to pursue enlightenment, it is said that he was named Rahula by his grandfather after the future Buddha announced immediately after the birth of his son that an "obstruction" (*rahula*) had been born. Like many sons of noble Shakya families of the time, the future Buddha apparently had been thinking of leaving home from a fairly young age. It is said that his own father, the king, had arranged for his marriage to Yashodhara when he was nineteen in order to discourage him from leaving home. Ten years later, Rahula was born, and it was said that Shakyamuni called him Rahula because he created "bonds" of affection. This story would later be used to show how a bond of love can be an impediment or hindrance to one who wants to follow the life of a monk.

Though his age at the time is far from certain, Rahula was about seven years old when Shakyamuni returned to his home in Kapilavasthu with many of his followers and stayed in a bamboo grove outside the city. Yashodhara pointed his father out to the boy, but at first Shakyamuni paid no attention to his son. When they were about to leave, Yashodhara told Rahula to ask for his father's blessings. He did so, and Shakyamuni beckoned to him to follow him. When they reached the forest, Shakyamuni told Shariputra to shave the boy's head, put him in monk's robes, and make him the first novice monk. In some accounts, Yashodhara tells Rahula to ask his father for his inheritance and his wealth, and the Buddha instead makes him the inheritor of his spiritual wealth by turning him into a novice monk.

Just as according to Fa-hsien nuns worshiped at the stupas of Ananda, novice monks worshiped at the stupa of Rahula, who apparently died before his father did.

### THE CHALLENGE OF TEACHING THOSE CLOSEST TO US

Why are Ananda and Rahula the last of the disciples to receive assurance of becoming buddhas? Is it because they were closest to the Buddha? Surely being so close to a buddha, or to any other great person, creates both special opportunities and special problems or temptations, especially perhaps the problem of favoritism and the temptation to inflated self-importance. There are signs that favoritism, or the appearance of favoritism, may have been a worry for Shakyamuni Buddha and a problem and danger for both Ananda and Rahula. All three would have wanted to avoid creating jealousy among the monks, and, more positively, to be fair to all of them.

This points as well to the difficulty of leading those closest to us. In many stories in the Dharma Flower Sutra we find that characters who represent the Buddha have problems leading their children. In the early parable of the burning house, for example, the children in the burning house initially refuse to pay any attention to their father. Similarly, the children of the physician in Chapter 16, to be discussed later, also refuse to obey their father's exhortation to take the good medicine he has prepared for them. The poor son in Chapter 4 is a runaway. In addition, we also often find sympathy being expressed for Shakyamuni Buddha because he is responsible for this world of suffering.

Collectively, both of these elements, disobedient children and sympathy from others, and many other things as well, point to the similarity of the Buddha to ordinary human beings. Some might think of the Buddha as being extremely distant and different from ourselves— along the lines of how the famous Christian theologian Karl Barth describes God: "totally other." But in the Dharma Flower Sutra it is the opposite: the Buddha is very close to us, concerned about us, affected by us—thus similar to us. That is why the Buddha's work, so to speak, is difficult. It is only because he cares about this world that his job is difficult.

We will often have the most difficulty leading those who are closest to us, our own children, or parents, or wives, or husbands. Often this can be a sign that things are as they can be. If life is difficult for the Buddha because he is close to the world, we should expect to have difficulties with those who are closest to us. Those difficulties should be taken as a sign that we should strive to improve our relationships with those closest to us, even though we can expect this to be difficult at times.

The Buddha says that only he knows the hidden or quiet practices of Rahula. We cannot be certain about what this means, but it may be an indication of Rahula's modesty. We can imagine that, as the

Buddha's only son, after becoming a monk, he would have been especially careful to try not to draw attention to himself. This would be in order to prevent the Buddha from being accused of favoritism—but it might also have been an effort on the part of Rahula to avoid a false sense of his own self-importance.

The Dharma Flower Sutra does not say that we can become totally selfless, completely pure in our dedication to others. It takes a more realistic approach of assuming that all of our intentions are to some extent self-serving. But it does teach, at least by example, that we should not seek acclaim for our own good deeds. It is better to do good quietly, without drawing attention to ourselves. We can imagine that Rahula was careful not to draw attention to himself, going about doing good quietly, doing good about which only the Buddha would know.

## ANANDA'S ORIGINAL VOW

Like Shariputra in an earlier story, in this story Ananda recollects his original vow to teach and transform countless beings into bodhisattvas. This is basically the vow of buddhas and especially of bodhisattvas to save all living beings. Much earlier, in Chapter 2 of the Sutra, the Buddha said:

> You should know, Shariputra,
> I originally took a vow,
> Wanting to enable all living beings to be equal to me,
> Without any distinctions. (LS 89)

In Mahayana Buddhism there is a distinction between two kinds of vows, special vows (*betsugan* in Japanese) and general vows (*sogan*). Special vows, which might better be termed "resolutions," are relative to time and circumstance, individual ability, and so on. They may change. Here, however, we are talking of the Buddha's original general vow, a vow that is said to be taken by all buddhas and to be good for all. It is sometimes taken to be a four-part vow: to save everyone, to remove all hindrances to awakening, to study all the teachings, and to attain the Buddha Way of supreme awakening. These four are sometimes known as the four great vows of followers of the bodhisattva way.

The idea of making a vow that will last for uncountable eons, a vow that is to be the very basis of one's life, stresses the importance of perseverance, persistence, or diligence. It is a fundamental teaching of the Dharma Flower Sutra that we should set goals for ourselves, such as saving all the living, or world peace, goals that we know very well may never be fully realized. Having set such a goal, we should be devoted to pursuing it. This is why perseverance in the face of difficulties is one of the six transcendental practices or perfections of bodhisattvas. Following this way, we will not easily become discouraged, want to give up, or turn back. Defeats and losses can be expected, but even small victories in the struggle for world peace and human happiness can be a cause for great joy.

## TEACHING AND TRANSFORMING BODHISATTVAS

In the story in this chapter, we are told that Ananda will teach and transform innumerable beings into bodhisattvas. The idea of transforming, or converting, bodhisattvas occurs quite often in the Dharma Flower Sutra. In many variations, it is a central idea of the Sutra, but it is a concept that is a bit complicated, in part because at least two somewhat different things are being taught.

One is the idea that teaching or preaching is not teaching or preaching if no one is affected or changed by the teaching. In the Dharma Flower Sutra, teaching is a relational activity, involving two sides, a teaching side and a learning side. It is not that one side is active and the other passive. Teaching goes on only when both sides are active. That is why the Dharma Flower Sutra often speaks of the importance of receiving the Sutra, and of making it a part of one's life. It is not enough to learn teachings merely as ideas in one's head, or as doctrines that can be recited. Real learning, transformative learning, only takes place when the teaching is integrated into one's very life and every-day actions. That is why in the Chinese version of the Dharma Flower Sutra the words for "teaching" and "transforming" appear together so often, virtually as one word.

The second thing being taught here is the basic idea that human beings should be transformed into bodhisattvas. It is a fundamental tenet of Mahayana Buddhism that we should live a life of helping others—indeed, that our very salvation, our awakening, is a matter of helping others. This is the bodhisattva way of being active in the world. What makes this idea complicated is that, according to the Dharma Flower Sutra, everyone, at least to some degree, already is a bodhisattva. Everyone is already becoming a buddha.

So why is there a need to teach and transform people who are already bodhisattvas into bodhisattvas? Here, I believe, the Sutra holds two teachings that, if reduced to merely intellectual ideas, create a puzzle. It is a truth that has to be grasped imaginatively and exis-tentially rather than purely through the tools of logic. Even though we are already practicing the bodhisattva way to some degree, all of us are also in continual need of being transformed, both by our own prac-tice itself and by following the example of others, whose practice can inspire and teach us. Such transformation, such life-changing teaching and learning, is not something that happens once and then is over and done with; it is needed over and over again.

In this story we find eight thousand bodhisattvas in the great assem-bly grumbling to themselves about the fact that while many shravakas were being reassured by the Buddha of their eventually becoming bud-dhas these bodhisattvas themselves had received no such assurance. They are bodhisattvas—and should know very well that they are to become buddhas. But they are still capable of petty jealousy and need to be reassured.

If bodhisattvas such as these who had learned directly from the Buddha are capable of being jealous and petty, it should not be surprising that ordinary human beings, including ourselves, are also quite capable of such attitudes and behavior.

We too are in constant need of teaching and transformation.

# 13

## DHARMA TEACHERS

E XCEPT FOR A brief interesting parable toward the end, Chapter
10 does not have a dramatic story with characters and activities.
Still, the core message is dramatic in its own way, and elucidates
an important type of skillful means to open our understanding of the
profound meaning of the Lotus Sutra.

## THE STORY

In previous chapters the Buddha has addressed only shravakas. Here in
Chapter 10, for the first time in the Dharma Flower Sutra, the Buddha
addresses a bodhisattva, the Bodhisattva Medicine King. He points to
the great multitude of living beings of many kinds assembled before
them and tells Medicine King that if any of them rejoices for even a
single moment on hearing even a single verse of the Dharma Flower
Sutra, he will assure them of achieving supreme awakening. Further,
he says, if anyone does this after he has passed away, that individual
too will be assured of achieving supreme awakening, of becoming a
buddha.

If anyone, the Buddha says, receives and keeps, reads, recites,
explains, or copies even a single verse of the Sutra, respects it as they

respect the Buddha or makes offerings of any kind to it, or even just puts their hands together respectfully toward it, such a person should be considered to be a great bodhisattva, one who is to become a buddha in a future life. He or she should be respected and given presents and offerings by all. Such a person, having achieved supreme awakening in a former life, has appeared in this world out of great compassion in order to preach the Dharma here.

Any good man or woman who privately explains even a phrase of the Sutra to a single person is a messenger of the Buddha, one who does the Buddha's work. How much more so anyone who explains the whole Sutra to many people. When anyone hears such a person teaching the Sutra, they will attain supreme awakening.

Someone who speaks ill of the Buddha for a whole eon is not as bad as someone who, with only a single word, speaks ill of someone for reading and reciting the Dharma Flower Sutra. Similarly, one who praises the Buddha will receive many blessings, but the good fortune of one who praises someone for upholding the Sutra will be even greater. Though the Dharma Flower Sutra is the most difficult to believe and understand, the Buddha tells Medicine King Bodhisattva, it is the most excellent he has ever taught. It contains the hidden core of all the teachings.

All those who are able to copy, embrace, read, recite, make offering to, and teach the Dharma Flower Sutra for the sake of others after the Buddha's extinction will be covered by the Buddha's robe and protected by buddhas of the other worlds as well; they will have the powers of faith, of aspiration, and of good character. They will live with the Buddha and have their heads patted or caressed by the Buddha.

Medicine King Bodhisattva is then told that stupas should be erected, decorated, praised, and respected wherever the Sutra is taught, read and recited, or copied, or wherever there is a copy of the Sutra. But it is not necessary, the Buddha says, to place any relics in the stupa because it will already contain the Buddha's whole body. Anyone making offerings to such a stupa will thereby approach supreme awakening. Similarly, anyone who sees or hears the Sutra, understands and upholds it, is getting closer to supreme awakening.

This chapter also includes a simile: A bodhisattva who has not heard or practiced this Sutra is like an extremely thirsty man digging for water in the earth. If he sees only dry ground, he is a long way from supreme awakening. But if he keeps digging and eventually sees damp earth and then mud, he knows that he is getting closer to water and will be encouraged to go on until he reaches water.

After the Buddha has passed away, those who would explain this Sutra should "enter the room of the Tathagata," which means having great compassion; should "wear the robe of the Tathagata," which means being gentle and patient; and "sit on the seat of the Tathagata," which means seeing the emptiness of all things.

Though the Buddha will be in another land after passing away, he will conjure up and dispatch various people and other creatures to hear the Dharma Flower Sutra taught, to enable the teacher to see the Buddha from time to time, and to help the teacher if he or she forgets a phrase of the Sutra. Those who follow such a teacher will be able to see many buddhas.

## COMMENTARY

The most important thing about this chapter is its emphasis on the Dharma teacher. Here we can see that the Sutra attempts to break through the limitations of the threefold shravaka-pratyekabuddha-bodhisattva distinction that had been prominent in earlier chapters of this Sutra and elsewhere in Mahayana Buddhism. According to Chapter 10, anyone—bodhisattva, pratyekabuddha, shravaka, or layperson, man or woman—can be a Dharma teacher.

This important point is certainly not unique to this chapter, but it is emphasized here in a special way: it is not only great bodhisattvas, great leaders, or great people who can teach the Dharma and do the Buddha's work, but very ordinary people with even a limited understanding and even of limited faith can join in the Buddha's work, if only by understanding and teaching a little. The point is, of course, that you and I can be Dharma teachers.

Thus the Buddha tells Medicine King Bodhisattva that if anyone wants to know what sort of living beings will become buddhas in the future, he should tell them that the very people before him, that is, all sorts of people, including very ordinary people, will become buddhas.

Up to this point in the Sutra the term *bodhisattva* has been used in at least two distinctly different ways. On the one hand, it is used as a kind of title or rank for great, well-known, and basically mythical bodhisattvas such as Maitreya and Manjushri. Such great bodhisattvas, often called bodhisattva great ones, are very important in Buddhism, as they can symbolize great virtues such as compassion and wisdom, and serve as ideal models of what we can be.

We have seen in earlier chapters that shravakas, beginning with Shariputra, are actually bodhisattvas—they are on the way to becoming buddhas. But we never find such expressions as "Shariputra Bodhisattva." A somewhat different use of "bodhisattva" is being made, one in which the term does not represent a rank and status but a kind of relational activity. Accordingly, anyone can be a bodhisattva *for someone else.* The primary meaning of this is, of course, that we ourselves, the hearers or readers of the Dharma Flower Sutra, can be bodhisattvas and indeed sometimes are.

But with "bodhisattva" being associated in our minds with such great ones as Maitreya and Manjushri, it may be very difficult for us to believe that we are capable of being bodhisattvas. We are too young, we may think, or too old or too stupid or too tired or too lazy or too selfish or too something else to be a bodhisattva! It's impossible, we may feel.

This is where Chapter 10, and the idea of the teacher of the Dharma, comes in. It may be hard for me to believe that I can be a bodhisattva, but not as difficult to believe that I might be a good man or good woman who is able "even in secret, to teach to one person even one phrase of the Dharma Flower Sutra" and, therefore, be an emissary of the Buddha, one who does the Buddha's work. In other words, Chapter 10 gives us what may be perceived to be a more attainable goal.

What's more, the gender gap so often prevalent in Buddhist texts is broken through here. Not only buddhas, but all of the famous, great mythical bodhisattvas are male, almost always dressed as Indian princes. But "any good son or good daughter," the text says, who privately explains even a phrase of the Sutra to a single person is a messenger of the Buddha, one who does the Buddha's work. Later we will learn that the stepmother and the wife of the Buddha are to become buddhas and therefore are to be considered bodhisattvas. Also the dragon princess in Chapter 12 of the Sutra becomes fully awakened and so can be regarded as a bodhisattva. And it is true that the Bodhisattva Regarder of the Cries of the World (known in Japanese as Kannon and in Chinese as Kwan-yin[20]) of Chapter 25 of the Sutra will take on female forms and be regarded as female in China, even as the "Goddess of Mercy." And we are told later in the Dharma Flower Sutra that such great bodhisattvas as Regarder of the Cries of the World and Wonderful Voice are quite capable of taking on any form in order to help someone, including several female forms. Still, not in the Dharma Flower Sutra or elsewhere do we find a woman with the title "Bodhisattva."

I believe it is no accident that Chapter 10 repeatedly uses the expression "good son or good daughter." It wants us to understand and actually embrace the teaching that we, whoever we are, can teach the Dharma. Even if only a little, we can teach the Dharma, and to that degree be a Dharma teacher.

And, if we can realize that we can be a teacher of the Dharma, it is only a short step, perhaps not even a step at all, to realize that anyone else can be a Dharma teacher for us. And when we have reached that double realization, we have truly, I believe, entered into the wonderful flowering of the Dharma known as the Lotus Sutra.

In light of all this, it is sometimes said that the Lotus Sutra offers an easy way to awakening, and that this is why it has been so popular throughout the history of East Asia, and, judging by the large number of fragments that continue to be found, probably it was once popular in India and Central Asia as well. But is the way of the Dharma Flower Sutra so easy?

This matter is a little complicated, because, as is so often the case with this text, two things are asserted that seem incompatible on the surface. On the one hand, it teaches that anyone and everyone can be, and to some degree, no doubt, has already been, a Dharma teacher and bodhisattva for someone else. We can say that all have planted seeds of becoming a buddha, or that they have entered the Way of becoming a buddha. In Chapter 10 we are told that if anyone rejoices even for a single moment from hearing even a single verse of the Sutra, he or she will attain supreme awakening. Please notice, however, that it does not say "has" attained supreme awakening, but "will." What is between the hearing of a single verse and the attainment of awakening is, at least normally, a great deal of effort and work. As we have seen, the treasure we seek is at once both near and very distant—and what the Sutra teaches here is that even a single verse can plant a seed, a starting point for entering the Way. Like any seed, the seed and the bud that springs from it have to be watered and nourished in order to grow, flower, and bear fruit.

## PRACTICES OF THE LOTUS SUTRA

Some traditions maintain that there are five kinds of Lotus Sutra practices taught here: receiving and embracing (or upholding) the

Sutra, reading it, reciting (or chanting) it, explaining it (by teaching or preaching), and copying it.

"Receiving and embracing" involves really hearing and following the Sutra, giving yourself to it, so to speak. It is not merely a matter of hearing with one's ears and mind, but also with one's body. That is, it is a matter of making the Sutra a truly significant part of one's life by embodying its teachings in one's actions in everyday life.

By reading the Sutra, whether alone or with others, aloud or to one-self, and by reciting or chanting the Sutra, the teachings are likely to become more deeply rooted in our minds and hearts. The Sutra does not seem to support, however, the idea that mindlessly reciting the text has any value.

Reciting sutras once meant reciting them from memory. Memorizing sutras was once an extremely important responsibility of monks. For centuries it was the only way they had to store them, as writing had not yet been invented in India. Even after the invention of writing, without printing presses, copies of a sutra written on bark and such, especially copies of a sutra as long as the Lotus Sutra, must have been relatively rare.

Explaining the Sutra to others is good not only for learners, but also for teachers. All good teachers know that, in the process of teaching, they almost always learn at least as much as their students. Even now—after decades of teaching the Dharma Flower Sutra—I still always feel that in a classroom we are all learners and that I am being blessed with the greatest learning of all.

Copying a sutra originally meant, until relatively recently, writing it out by hand. With such a large quantity of sutras, this was a very important practice, the principal way of storing sutras for subsequent use. With written copies there could be much less reliance on memo-rized versions. But while copying Chinese characters by brush can be a pleasant meditative exercise involving concentration, I'm not at all sure that such copying is so important today. What is important is looking at every character or word in the text, not quickly skipping over parts that are boring or difficult. Translating also, I believe, can well serve the purpose of concentrating one's focus on each part of the text. Such practice, too, can be beneficial both to the reader and to the translator.

Actually even in Chapter 10 there are several variations of the formula for five practices and many more throughout the Sutra, usually with five or six different practices being listed. By my count, at least sixteen such practices are cited in the Sutra, though never all in one place. Not all of them are entirely different perhaps, but they are different enough to be represented by different Chinese characters in Kumarajiva's translation and therefore in my English translation.

Here are the sixteen practices with regard to the Sutra: to hear, receive, embrace or uphold, read, recite, study, memorize or learn by heart, remember it correctly, understand its meaning, explain it, teach it for the sake of others, copy it, honor it, make offerings to it, put it into practice, and practice the Sutra as taught or preached. What I want to portray with this list is that the Dharma Flower Sutra is richer and much more complex than standard formulas sometimes suggest. The reduction of the sixteen to a standard five is a useful device for aiding our learning—nothing more. By using a variety of such lists, even in the same chapter, we are being taught, I believe, to be flexible and open-minded when reading or studying the Dharma Flower Sutra.

Whether the list of such practices be five or seven or sixteen, these are practices that can be done by anyone, including you and me, and they can be done just about anywhere. They certainly are not the end of Buddhist practice, but they can be used as skillful means, as useful and important steps in the direction of the life of a true Dharma teacher or bodhisattva.

Though it is not listed as one of the sixteen, erecting stupas wherever the Dharma Flower Sutra is taught as advocated in this chapter is the same sort of thing. As we'll see later, one who erects or even makes offerings to such a stupa is approaching supreme awakening.

Since one of the sixteen practices is making offerings to the Sutra, a kind of worship, it may be useful to discuss the difference between worshiping an idol (or statue) and worshiping *with the help of* an image, or worshiping *through* or *before* an image. Among many Protestant Christians, as in the Bible, idolatry is vigorously condemned. It is understood to be worship of a false god, something that is not God. Virtually all Buddhists, on the other hand, make a great deal of use of physical objects in both personal and public worship. Most prominent among these, of course, are buddha statues and, in Mahayana Buddhism, statues of famous bodhisattvas, especially Kwan-yin/Kannon, Maitreya, Manjushri, and Samantabhadra—all of whom are prominent in the Lotus Sutra—and Kshitigarbha/Ti-tsang/Jizo (who does not appear in the Lotus Sutra). But it is not only such statues and paintings that are used in worship—the Lotus Sutra itself, in physical form, has often been treated as an object of worship in East Asia.

To worship an idol itself is to confuse one's ultimate object of worship or devotion with some physical thing. One morning my wife and I went to the Great Sacred Hall of Rissho Kosei-kai in Tokyo. As Rissho Kosei-kai's main object of worship and devotion, a wonderful statue of the universal or eternal Shakyamuni Buddha dominates the main hall. Inside of this statue is a copy of the Threefold Lotus Sutra in calligraphy inscribed by Founder Niwano. But we did not worship either the statue or its contents. Before, through, and with the help of the statue that was in front of us, we paid our respects to the Buddha who is everywhere. This does not make the statue any less important, indeed it makes it truly more important, for it can lead us to the truth—something that worshiping the statue itself could never do.

## DIGGING FOR WATER

Let's turn our attention to the brief simile found in this chapter: the extremely thirsty man digging in the soil for water. Unlike some parables, this simile is not fully interpreted for us, but it can nonetheless readily be understood in accord with the previous discussion.

The man, a bodhisattva, digs for water on a "high plain." We do not know exactly what this "high plain" means, but presumably it means that he is digging in a place where water is quite deep down but where there is at least a reasonable possibility of water being found. If he dug in a rocky place, for example, he might die of thirst before finding any water at all.

Digging, he comes to damp earth, then mud, and knows that he is getting closer to water. Actually, the dampness itself *is* water. That is, seeing damp earth, while he cannot yet drink, he is seeing a promise of water he'll be able to drink soon, a promise that he knows is good because the dampness and the water he seeks are the same water.

The text interprets this parable in terms of hearing the Dharma:

> Medicine King, you should know
> That this is the way people are.
> Those who do not hear the Dharma Flower Sutra
> Are far from buddha-wisdom.
>
> But if they hear
> This profound sutra...,
>
> And hearing it
> Truly ponder over it,
> You should know that those people
> Are near the wisdom of a buddha. (LS 232)

So too all sixteen simple practices—any of them and many others as well, while not the ultimate goal, can be a kind of taste of the life of a bodhisattva. If we practice one or more of them seriously, we will experience a taste of riches to come and know that we too are nearer to the water after which we thirst: the wisdom of a buddha.

Here as well, we should notice that a kind of relational activity is going on. On the one hand, the man is using his own effort to dig for water. He is motivated, even driven, by something within himself, namely, his thirst. His very life depends on finding water to drink and so he exerts a great effort. On the other hand, the promise of water, the increasingly damp earth, comes to him. As a result of making an effort, he receives a promise. The water is something he finds.

While there is no guarantee that by digging we will find water, at least in this lifetime, we, too, if we make an effort to follow the bodhisattva way, may receive a promise of riches to come. Along the way we too may receive some help from the Buddha. In Chapter 10 we are told that the Buddha will send various people to hear the Dharma taught and to help the teacher when he needs it. We should be prepared to meet such people.

## THE BUDDHA'S ROOM, ROBE, AND SEAT

Toward the end of Chapter 10, we find these words:

If people are to teach this sutra,
Let them enter the Tathagata's room,
Put on the Tathagata's robe,
And sit on the Tathagata's seat.

Facing the multitude without fear,
Let them teach it clearly everywhere,

With great compassion as their room,
Gentleness and patience as their robe,
And the emptiness of all things as their seat.
Doing this, they should teach the Dharma. (LS 232)

In this beautiful poetic expression we have another indication of what it means to follow the bodhisattva way. It means nothing terribly complicated, just the very difficult matter of being compassionate, gentle, and patient and living from an understanding of the emptiness of all things. To enter the room of the Buddha, wear his robe, and sit on his seat is a wonderful metaphor for living the life of a bodhisattva, living the Dharma in a way that goes beyond our sixteen simple practices. This is what it means to be a teacher of the Dharma.

Teachers of the Dharma are called the Buddha's workers—a very important concept. Here again we can see that the Buddha depends on human beings to do his work. It is all too easy to think that everything has already been arranged for us in this life. Here in Chapter 10 we are told that Dharma teachers, having already attained supreme awakening in some former life, have been born into this world out of compassion in order to teach and preach here. But this does not mean that everything has already been decided for us by our actions in former lives. That would make a joke of present life, reducing it to triviality. What we do with our lives, how we live now, is never merely a function of the karma or causation or choices made in previous lives, important as that is. What doing the Buddha's work requires may be an understanding that what we do now makes an important difference, to ourselves, to others, and to the Buddha himself.

By being Dharma teachers doing the Buddha's work, we ourselves can embody the Buddha, enabling the Buddha to live and work in this world, now. To this degree, the very life of the Buddha is determined in part by what we are and do. The Dharma Flower Sutra teaches that we should never accept a lesser teaching, especially any teaching that makes less of us, that makes human beings anything less than Dharma teachers and bodhisattvas.

In Chapter 10 of the Lotus Sutra, it is clear that *what the Buddha taught*—and by extension what bodhisattvas teach—that is, the Dharma, is more`important than the Buddha himself. That is the meaning behind both the sentiment that someone who insults the Buddha is not as bad as someone who insults the Sutra and the idea that stupas need not contain physical remains of the Buddha's body because the Dharma contains his whole body.

The teaching that the Buddha has three or four "bodies," of which the highest is the Dharmakaya, the Dharma-body, is perhaps being alluded to here. But that teaching makes it clear that you cannot have the Dharma-body without the other bodies. To follow, or have faith in, or take refuge in the Buddha is to follow what the Buddha discovered and taught, the Dharma. But equally, to follow the Dharma is to follow what was taught by the Buddha. For a Buddhist, Dharma is always Buddha Dharma.

# 14

## THE GREAT STUPA OF
## ABUNDANT TREASURES BUDDHA

I N CHAPTER 11 of the Lotus Sutra we encounter, as in the first
chapter, a story that is the product of an incredibly fertile imagination. In a sense, this chapter begins a new and long story-within-the-
story that began in Chapter 1—a story that extends through Chapter
22, albeit with interruptions, and that provides a somewhat different
setting from the story thus far. This story, sometimes referred to as the
"ceremony in the air" makes free use of unusual images and events in
order to advance a kind of universalism or unified world view. Here, I
will consider the part of this story found in Chapter 11 of the Dharma
Flower Sutra. Later, we will look at further developments of the longer
story.

### THE STORY

With no introduction or warning of any kind, the chapter begins
with a verbal image of a huge stupa, magnificently adorned with jewels and a great many other ornaments, springing out of the ground
and coming to rest suspended in the air before the Buddha and the

assembly. As offerings to the stupa, the thirty-three gods cause heavenly and rare *mandarava* flowers to rain down from their heaven. Other gods, dragons, satyrs, centaurs, ashuras, griffins, chimeras, pythons, humans, and nonhumans, tens of millions of billions of beings of great variety, make offerings to the stupa with all kinds of flowers, incense, garlands, streamers, canopies, and music, thus revering, honoring, and praising it.

Soon, from within the stupa, comes a loud voice praising Shakyamuni Buddha for teaching the Dharma Flower Sutra. "Well done, well done, World-Honored Shakyamuni! For the sake of the great assembly you are able to teach the Wonderful Dharma Flower Sutra of great impartial wisdom, the Dharma by which bodhisattvas are taught and that buddhas protect and keep in mind. It is just as you say, World-Honored Shakyamuni! All that you say is true." (LS 235)

Astonished at these events, the monks and nuns and laypeople present are all filled with joy and wonder. The bodhisattva known as Great Delight in Preaching, seeing that no one understands what is going on, asks the Buddha why this stupa has emerged from the ground and such a voice has issued from it. In answer, the Buddha explains that in the stupa there is the whole body of a buddha. A very long time ago in a very distant place, he explains, there once lived a buddha named Abundant Treasures. While this buddha was still a bodhisattva, he made a great vow that after he had become a buddha and then extinct, if anyone ever taught the Dharma Flower Sutra he would have his great stupa rise up before such a teacher, both in testimony to the truth of the Sutra and so that he could hear it taught directly and praise the one teaching it. It is, the Buddha says, because he heard the Dharma Flower Sutra being taught that Abundant Treasures Buddha has come to this world in this great stupa.

Great Delight in Preaching responds that the congregation would like to see the buddha inside. The Buddha then explains that Abundant Treasures Buddha had also said that if such an assembly wanted to see him, to see his whole body, the buddha teaching the Sutra would have to invite to that place all of the buddhas embodying him throughout the entire universe. Thus, Shakyamuni Buddha would now need to assemble all of the buddhas embodying or representing him throughout the universe, that is, all the buddhas in the ten directions. Great Delight in Preaching then says to the Buddha that those in the assembly would also like to see the buddhas from all over the universe.

Then Shakyamuni Buddha emits a ray of light from the tuft of hair between his eyebrows, illuminating all of those billions and billions of worlds in every direction, so that the congregation in this world can see the magnificence of those other worlds, each with billions of bodhisattvas and with a buddha in each of them preaching the Dharma.

Then, after this world had been suitably purified and decorated for such a visit, each of those buddhas, accompanied by a bodhisattva, comes to sit before the Buddha on a great lion seat at the foot of an extremely tall tree full of jewels.

But there are not enough of these seats in this world, even for the buddhas and their attendant bodhisattvas from just one direction, let alone ten. So Shakyamuni Buddha must purify billions and billions of worlds neighboring this world and prepare them with lion seats under great, tall, jeweled trees to receive the many buddhas and bodhisattvas. And when that is not enough, he does the same thing with billions and billions of additional worlds neighboring the already greatly expanded world. The whole area is transformed in this way into a single pure buddha land.

After they were all seated, each of the buddhas instructs their attending bodhisattva to go to Shakyamuni Buddha and ask him, "Are your illnesses and troubles few? In spirit and energy are you well? And are your bodhisattvas and shravakas at peace?" After greeting the Buddha and making flower offerings to him, they are to tell him that their buddha would like to see the great stupa opened.

Then, with the whole congregation watching intently, Shakyamuni goes up in the air to the stupa and with his right hand opens its door. From the stupa comes a loud sound, the kind of sound you hear when the bar is removed from a huge gate. Immediately, the whole congregation sees Abundant Treasures Buddha sitting on a seat in the stupa as if in meditation with a still perfect body. Abundant Treasures Buddha then praises Shakyamuni, saying: "Well done, well done, Shakyamuni Buddha! You have preached this Dharma Flower Sutra gladly, which is what I have come to this place to hear."

The congregation then celebrates by strewing a great many beautiful flowers before the two buddhas. Then, invited by Abundant Treasures to come into the stupa, Shakyamuni joins him on the seat in the stupa.

But now, since the two buddhas are high up in the stupa in the air, those in the congregation on the ground can't see them well and want to be raised up into the air also. Sensing this, Shakyamuni Buddha raises everyone up in the air, and expresses his desire to have someone to whom he could entrust the teaching of the Sutra; that is, he wanted to have others promise to teach the Sutra after his extinction.

The buddhas who have come from all directions, the Buddha explains, will use skillful means to ensure that in their own worlds the Dharma will last for a long time.

Now, the Buddha asks, will anyone come forward and vow to receive and embrace, read and recite the Dharma Flower Sutra, so that it will live for a long time in this world?

Among all of my children, the Buddha says, if any is able to embrace the Dharma, they should make a great vow, so that it will continue to live. But, he says, this will be extremely difficult. Compared with teaching all of the other sutras, or with picking up Mount Sumeru and hurling it to innumerable other buddha lands, or using one's toe to pick up an entire world and hurling it far away, or standing on the highest heaven to preach countless sutras, teaching the Dharma Flower Sutra in an evil age following the Buddha's extinction will indeed be difficult. Compared with wandering around with the sky in one's hand, copying or getting someone else to copy this Sutra would be difficult. Similarly, ascending to the Brahma heaven with the earth on one's toenail would be easy compared with reading the Sutra aloud for even a moment. Carrying a load of dry hay into a fire without getting burned would not be difficult compared with teaching the Dharma Flower Sutra even to just one person. Leading many to have holy powers by preaching thousands of sutras for them would not be difficult in comparison with inquiring about the meaning of the Sutra after the death of the Buddha. Compared with leading someone to honor and embrace a sutra such as this one would not be difficult in comparison with teaching the Dharma to billions and billions of living beings, leading them to become arhats with holy powers.

## COMMENTARY

This story presents us with an interesting image of the universe as a place in which Shakyamuni and his world, which is our world, is central, and yet Shakyamuni is far from being the only buddha. First of all, there is the buddha named Abundant Treasures, who comes out of the distant past in a dramatic way in order to praise Shakyamuni Buddha for teaching the Dharma Flower Sutra. The resulting image of two buddhas sitting side by side on a single seat is a unique one. But this image is dependent on another, which reaches not into the distant past, but into distant reaches of contemporary space to reveal the innumerable buddhas in all directions. In other words, it is only after all the worlds have been integrated into a single buddha land that the congregation is able to see Abundant Treasures Buddha and the two buddhas sitting together in the stupa.

Those buddhas present are so numerous that this entire world is not big enough to include even those from just one of the ten directions. We are to understand that the number of buddhas throughout the universe is incredibly large, and that all of them are, in some sense, subordinate to Shakyamuni Buddha. Thus, Shakyamuni Buddha, as well as being the Buddha of this world, in which suffering has to be endured and can be, is also a universal buddha—a buddha who is somehow present everywhere in time and space.

The exact meaning of the Chinese term used for these many buddhas is not very clear. They can be said to be "representatives," or perhaps "duplicates" or "replicas" of Shakyamuni, but I think that they can best be understood as embodiments of Shakyamuni. Certainly, they are not, as some would have it, mere "emanations." The complex point is that they are both independently real apart from Shakyamuni Buddha and in some sense subordinate to him. Put abstractly, we have here one of several images in the Dharma Flower Sutra in which the reality and togetherness of being both one and many is affirmed: here are both the one central reality of Shakyamuni, somehow represented throughout vast reaches of space, and the reality of many buddhas, each with their own lands and their own attendant bodhisattvas. Nowhere in the Sutra is it suggested that these buddhas and their lands are in any way unreal. Other worlds are less important—to us in our daily lives—than is our own world, but that does not mean that they are any less real than our world.

This image of the reality of one and many can also be seen in the image of Shakyamuni Buddha bringing together billions and billions of worlds to create a temporary unification of them into a single buddha land. Their reality as many lands does not disappear when they are brought together to function as one. Later in the Sutra they will return to being, as they were, many. In this way, Shakyamuni Buddha, as well as being the buddha of this world, is at the same time the Universal Buddha—the buddha who, by virtue of his embodiments, is represented or present everywhere throughout the universe.

One reason that this holding together of the reality of both the one and the many is important in the Dharma Flower Sutra is that it provides a general framework for understanding the One Vehicle of many skillful means. It provides, in other words, a way of understanding through images how the many ways of Buddhism can all have an importance and reality within one Buddhism.

Whatever else it is, the great stupa in this story is a literary device providing a reason for assembling all of the buddhas from all directions. This stupa springing out of the earth from the past could be material from a dream, or from a rich imagination. But it can also be said that Abundant Treasures Buddha symbolizes the truth, the Dharma that does not change and is a kind of ground or basis for all teaching of the Dharma. In this way, Shakyamuni Buddha can symbolize the teacher of the Dharma. And the two buddhas sitting together on a single seat would indicate both that the teacher is to be respected as much as the truth itself, and the opposite, namely, that however devoted we may be to Shakyamuni Buddha for teaching, we should remember that our devotion should be based on his teaching the truth. In other words, for followers of the Dharma Flower Sutra, a Dharma that is not alive in the present in this world of suffering is of no use at all, and useful Dharma can live only if it is the truth.

Such an idea leads naturally to the concern expressed toward the end of the story about the survival of the teaching of the Dharma after the Buddha has died. How is the truth to continue to be made available to people? How is the truth to be taught and brought to life after the Buddha has died?

Here it's important to note that the stupa does not come from some distant heaven, but springs up out of the earth. This means that this world and ourselves in it are affirmed, as this is where the truth about the nature of reality is to be found, and to be taught. In other words, this world has a kind of buddha-nature within it, here symbolized by the stupa that comes up out of the earth with Abundant Treasures Buddha in it.

So, too, the fact that all of the buddhas throughout the entire universe come to this world, or at least to a purified version of this world, shows a powerful affirmation of our world. The Pure Land, this story implies, is to be found here. This is the land that Shakyamuni Buddha transforms into a Pure Land, even if only temporarily.

Such affirmations are not just sentiments; they are an indication of where our own energies should go—that is, into purifying this world and realizing the buddha-nature of things in this world, thus enabling us both to see this world as a Pure Land and to transform it into a Pure Land. Thus, three things are here held up together, perhaps inseparably—Shakyamuni Buddha, the buddha of this world, and the teacher of the Dharma Flower Sutra; the Dharma Flower Sutra (the Dharma) that Shakyamuni Buddha teaches in the world; and this world itself, the place where Shakyamuni Buddha lived and taught the Lotus Sutra and where he lives and teaches the Sutra still. Abundant Treasures Buddha, we are told several times, is extinct, having died in the distant past and his body presumably having been cremated. Yet here he is in the present, speaking and acting very much alive. This seems to cast some doubt on the reality of death or the meaning of "extinction." But it expresses an important truth—the past is not merely dead and gone; it is alive, or at least can be, in the present.

This is not to say that the Dharma Flower Sutra denies the pastness of the past or abolishes the reality of time. But it does affirm that in an important sense the past can be alive in the present. This is, of course, an anticipation of what the Sutra affirms about Shakyamuni Buddha. He too died and was cremated long ago, but is alive still.

A related point of secondary interest in this story is the common courtesy in the greetings brought to Shakyamuni. After all the buddhas from all over the universe have assembled and seated themselves on their lion seats in the much expanded and purified world, each of them instructs his attending bodhisattva to go to Shakyamuni Buddha to ask to be included in witnessing the opening of the stupa of Abundant Treasures Buddha. But first, they are told, they should inquire about Shakyamuni Buddha's health, about whether he has any illnesses or worries, and similarly about the health and spirits of the bodhisattvas and shravakas of this world.

These greetings are not just about his physical condition, but about the Buddha's mental or spiritual condition as well. This tells us something not only about common courtesy, but also about the nature of the Buddha in this Sutra. He is not indifferent to what happens in the world, but one who himself suffers, both physically and mentally.

In the Dharma Flower Sutra there are several ways in which the humanity, or what we would now call the "historicity," of Shakyamuni Buddha is affirmed and even insisted upon. He is placed within fantastic stories, such as this one, in which he can be seen as much more than human, but from time to time we are reminded that this same Shakyamuni is a man. We are reminded that he is one who left his father's castle, who became awakened under the bodhi tree, who went to Varanasi to teach, and so on, and, perhaps most importantly, a man who at the end of his life died and his body was cremated.

The human death of Shakyamuni Buddha creates a problem for those who would follow after him—how to keep him alive despite his death, and how to keep his teaching, the Dharma, alive without him to teach it.

Chapter 11 introduces in a special way the idea that the solution to this difficult problem is a matter of embodiment—the Buddha can be kept alive by those who embody him by embracing and following his teachings. And it is precisely because Shakyamuni Buddha was a human being—with a human body and other human limitations— that we human beings can be expected to embody the Dharma, that is, be the Buddha, in our lives, despite our having human bodies and very human limitations. It is through being embodied in very imperfect human beings that the life of the Buddha can become so long that it can even be said to be "eternal."

*Last*, having established through the powerful image of buddhas coming to this world from all directions that the Buddha is somehow represented throughout the universe, the chapter ends with an appeal to those who can take up the difficult task of teaching the Dharma after the Buddha's extinction to make a great vow to do so. The difficulty of teaching the Dharma is expressed in what has come to be known as "the nine easy practices and six difficulties." They dramatically express the difficulty of teaching the Dharma. But this is not done to discourage us. The point, rather, is to have us understand that we too are called, even challenged, *not* to be teachers of a dead Dharma, of dead doctrine from the distant past, but to be teachers of the Dharma by embodying the very life of the Buddha, which is itself the Dharma, in our whole lives.

Through living the Dharma as much as possible ourselves, the Buddha too continues to live in our world.

# 15

# DEVADATTA AND VIOLENCE

I N CHINESE and Japanese versions of the Lotus Sutra and in translations from Chinese, the stories of Devadatta and the dragon princess comprise Chapter 12, while in Indian versions they appear at the end of the previous chapter. This gives a stronger impression of the chapter being an interruption of the longer story that begins in Chapter 11 with the emergence from the ground of the stupa of Abundant Treasures Buddha. Originally these two stories may have circulated independently of the Lotus Sutra as one or two different texts. Putting them in a separate chapter in this way gives more emphasis and importance to them.

Superficially there is not much reason for these two stories to be together. In terms of characters, they have nothing in common. What makes sense—both in terms of their being together in one chapter and of the chapter being inserted at this point in the Sutra—is the teaching of universal awakening found throughout the Lotus Sutra. The chapter reinforces the idea that there can be no exception to the teaching that everyone is to some degree on the bodhisattva path to becoming a buddha—including those regarded as evil, and even women, who too often in India were regarded as inherently evil. The inclusion of the stories of Chapter 12 drives home the point that there are no exceptions to universal awakening. While this is only implicit in the Devadatta story, it is made explicit in the story of the dragon princess. Putting the two together helps us to better understand the function of both, and putting them together in a separate chapter serves to underline one of the main teachings of the Sutra as a whole.

In the next chapter of the present volume, we'll explore the story of the dragon princess, but here let us turn our attention to Devadatta. Though renowned for his evil actions, there is nothing at all in the Lotus Sutra about the evil deeds of Devadatta, not even a hint of the personification of evil he would become in Buddhist legends. Instead, what we find here is a story about a past life and an assurance of becoming a buddha in a future life.

## THE STORY

In the first part of the chapter, the Buddha relates that in an earlier life he himself had been a king who, wanting deeply to become fully awakened, abdicated his throne in order to pursue the Dharma, seeking far and wide for someone who could teach the Lotus Sutra to him. Asita, a kind of seer or wise man, told the king that if he would promise to obey him, he would teach the Sutra to him. So the king became a servant of Asita. Obedient to him for over a thousand years, he learned much from him and eventually received the Dharma from him. This Asita was none other than Devadatta in an earlier life.

Having told this story of the past lives of Devadatta and himself, the Buddha then tells the congregation that the Buddha's awakening and powers are entirely due to Devadatta, his great friend. After a long time, he says, Devadatta (whose name might mean Gift of Heaven) will become a buddha named Devaraja, Heavenly King Buddha, and that he would be the buddha of a world called Heaven's Way.

## BACKGROUND

Some scholars believe that stories of Devadatta's evil deeds were invented later to discredit the leader of a group that was a rival to the main Buddhist organization, a Buddhist saint whose rival organization lasted for several centuries and probably only died with the death of Buddhism in India, long after the time of the Buddha.[21] Nevertheless, it is clear from the function of this story in the Dharma Flower Sutra that the compilers of this chapter supposed that the evil doings of Devadatta are something that everyone already knows and does not need to be told about.

There are many different versions of a wide variety of Devadatta stories in Buddhist texts, some of them quite early. What follows below is a kind of composite of these stories, one in keeping with what is generally accepted and often retold; it undoubtedly includes both some historical and some fabricated material.

According to many stories, Devadatta was the son of King Suppabuddha and his wife Pamita, who was an aunt of the Buddha. His sister, Yasodhara, was the Buddha's wife, making him both a cousin and a brother-in-law of Shakyamuni Buddha. Together with Ananda and others, he became a monk early in the Buddha's ministry. It is said that he was a good monk at first, known for his grace and psychic or magical powers, and that only later did he become greedy for power and start making trouble for the Buddha. As his ill will and jealousy toward the Buddha increased, he is said to have become the greatest enemy of the Buddha.

One day in a large assembly, Devadatta approached the Buddha and asked to be made the leader of the Sangha, the community of monks, a request that was promptly rejected. Devadatta is said to have become very angry, vowing to take revenge on the Buddha. Devadatta had followers, one of whom was Ajatasattu. Together they planned to kill both Ajatasattu's father, King Bimbisara, and Devadatta's enemy, the

Buddha. Ajatasattu succeeded in killing his father, thereby becoming king, but Devadatta failed in several attempts to kill the Buddha.

According to legend, the first attempt to kill the Buddha involved a complicated plot to hire a man to kill the Buddha, who would in turn be killed by two other men, who would in turn be killed by four other men, who would be killed by eight other men. But when the first man came close to the Buddha, he became frightened. Putting down his weapons, he became a follower of the Buddha. Eventually, all the men hired to kill one another became disciples of the Buddha.

Another attempt to kill the Buddha is said to have happened on Holy Eagle Peak, where the Lotus Sutra and many other sutras are supposed to have been preached by the Buddha. From above this Eagle Peak, which is a platform about one-fourth of the way down the mountain, Devadatta pushed a huge stone down at the Buddha. On its way, the stone struck another, from which a smaller piece flew down and hit the Buddha's foot, causing it to bleed—albeit without doing serious damage.

A third attempt to kill the Buddha involved getting a fierce elephant drunk. When the elephant saw the Buddha coming at a distance, it raised its ears, trunk, and tusks and charged at him, but when the elephant came close, the Buddha radiated his compassion toward the elephant, causing it to stop and become quiet. The Buddha then stroked its trunk and spoke to it softly. The elephant took up in its trunk some dust at the Buddha's feet and scattered it over its own head. Then it went away and remained completely tame from that time on.

There are also several stories, which do not agree on details, about Devadatta wanting to split the community of monks into two factions. He asked the Buddha to require all the monks to follow five extremely strict ascetic practices: living always only in forests, living only on alms obtained by begging, wearing only robes made from rags collected from trash piles and cemeteries, sleeping only outdoors at the foot of trees, and not eating fish or meat for the rest of their lives.

Apparently, Devadatta was able in this way to win some five hundred converts to his way of thinking, especially among younger monks, welcoming them within the emerging group of forest monks who made up his followers. By some accounts, all of these followers of Devadatta were subsequently persuaded to go back to the Buddha.

Stories of the end of Devadatta's life vary a great deal from one another. It is said that he was so evil that he fell into a burning purgatory while still alive. In other accounts, though, it is said that toward the end of his life he came to deeply regret what he had done, decided to follow the Buddha again, and set out to join him, but before reaching his destination fell desperately ill and died. Most legends leave Devadatta burning in purgatory, but according to one, in a future age he would become a pratyekabuddha, someone who would be able to become fully awakened through his own efforts.

## COMMENTARY

Basic to the teachings of this Sutra is a kind of promise, an assurance, that each and every living being has the potential to become a buddha. This tells us something about ourselves, of course, but here the light is shining in the other direction, encouraging us to see the buddha in others—regardless of their moral or other qualities.

In an important sense, this story is not so much about Devadatta as it is about Shakyamuni Buddha. It does not teach us that Devadatta was able to become a buddha because his inner intentions were really good, or because he changed his ways and became a good man, or because of anything else he did or did not do. What this story teaches is that the Buddha is one who can see the buddha in others. And that is what we are encouraged by this story to do—to look for and see the buddha in all those we encounter.

This is a story that can also be seen as being about how the Buddha responded to the violence of Devadatta.

How we respond to violence depends heavily on the kind of violence to which we are responding. If we were to approach the theme of violence with Buddhist skillful means, a basic conclusion might very well be that the most important thing to be aware of when thinking about a Buddhist response to violence is, "It all depends." It would be foolish to think that there is one kind of response that one should make to all forms of violence.

Accordingly, without trying to suggest that it is the only Buddhist way to respond to violence or even that it was the best in this situation, I want to share how I did, in fact, respond to the events of "9/11," September 11, 2001.

I was responsible for Dharma talks at a small, English-speaking, Buddhist congregation in Tokyo called the IBC (International Buddhist Congregation) of Rissho Kosei-kai. September 11 was a Tuesday. On September 16, I was expected to give a Dharma talk at the IBC. As the date approached, I felt I had to think and speak about the events of 9/11, in the context of Rissho Kosei-kai and its foundational text, the Lotus Sutra. The title I chose for that talk was "Tuesday's Devadatta." Here I will share much of what I had to say on that September day.

The magnitude of what happened in the United States on 9/11 seemed, at the time at least, to be beyond imagination. Several thousand people were dead or missing, more than ten thousand injured, and hundreds of thousands directly affected. Children returned home to find no parents; parents went to bed knowing their children were probably dead; wives and husbands returned home to no spouse, friends dead, friends missing, friends in grief. The dead were not only Americans but people of more than thirty countries. Almost all of us are related to some of these people in a variety of ways.

The response was predictable and understandable—disbelief, shock, grief, fear, sadness, anger, even hatred. All are forms of suffering.

Most Americans, and many people in other countries as well, felt more vulnerable as a result of that attack, no longer safe, as though their homes and homelands were no longer refuges of safety. Although Pearl Harbor had been attacked by the Japanese in 1941, it was in Hawaii, which most Americans felt to be a long way from their homes on the U.S. mainland, which had not been attacked for nearly two centuries.

Deep in human nature, or at least in Western human nature, there seems to be a need for revenge, retaliation, striking back, and inflicting pain and punishment on those who have offended or wronged us. Usually this is called "justice." In America, the "criminal justice system" is largely for the purpose of *punishing* criminals. In a sense, it is often viewed as a way of "getting even," though this "getting even" is often a matter of "getting back" in such a way as to be more than even. It is likely, I said, that the 9/11 terrorists believed deeply that they were working for justice, giving their own lives for what they believed to be just and right.

In the days following 9/11, and still today, some want to punish Arabs, or even Muslims, everywhere, seeing them as potential "terrorists" or "enemy combatants." Others wanted to bomb the extremely poor country and people of Afghanistan into oblivion. And now we are still in the midst of an invasion of Iraq to rid it of weapons of mass destruction, which apparently never existed, and to bring an end to connections to terrorism, which also apparently never existed. Too often this is the nature of "justice." An eye for an eye, says the Bible— and justice looks back to correct wrongs or to get even by inflicting punishment. These days, people all over the world, perhaps religious people especially, are being encouraged to subscribe to such Western notions of "justice."

This is not, however, the Buddhist way. Buddhists are asked, even in the midst of enormous suffering, to look back and behind events in order to better understand causes and conditions giving rise to suffering. Buddhists have to ask not only who did it, but why? How could someone be led to commit such acts? What are the causes and conditions preceding and surrounding them?

Buddhists are also asked to try to look forward—asking for, seeking for, a way ahead, a better world, a world of peace. We are not asked to look for ways to "right a wrong," but to seek ways to create good; not asked to get back at someone, but how to prevent such things from happening again. It is thus clear that Buddhists have an enormous healing ministry to perform if they are to be part of a movement toward world peace.

Shakyamuni Buddha's response to the violence of Devadatta was to be thankful, and to see in Devadatta the potential to become a buddha. "Thank you," he says in essence, "I learned much from you, and you, too, will become a buddha."

Perhaps it is impossible to be thankful for the devastation of September 11 and its aftermath in Afghanistan and Iraq, and indeed throughout the world. The tragedy and loss is too great and continues still with no end in sight. But even if we cannot quite feel grateful for 9/11, we can learn from it.

We might, for example, learn that violence produces more violence. Retaliation does not cut the chain of violent retribution. Too often, as we can see today, violence leads to more violence in long, perhaps endless, cycles of retaliation.

We might learn that we should look into the causes and conditions creating the attitudes that enable someone to kill thousands of innocent people, along with oneself. The terrorists obviously were not pursuing selfish interests or desires. They apparently thought they were doing justice. If we are to work to create a better future, we need to better understand their motivation and the motivations of people like them.

We might learn that being disrespectful to others, by labeling them as "terrorists" or condemning them as "evil," for example, does not lead to improved relationships or to better understanding or to peace. It leads to resentment and hatred.

We might learn that ignorance of others, especially of the cultural and religious customs of people with whom we are in conflict, does not lead to mutual understanding or trust. It leads to foolish mistakes, abuse of power, tragedy—to much suffering.

But the way to peace is a long and difficult one. By not even mentioning what Devadatta had done or tried to do to the Buddha, does the Dharma Flower Sutra teach that we should ignore evil, that we should, in this case, ignore terrorism? Of course not. We are, rather, urged to do two things: to find the causes or reasons behind current events in order to try to understand them, and to try to see the good in others and to cultivate that to the best of our ability.

And, as we see repeatedly emphasized in the Dharma Flower Sutra, we need to work to spread the Dharma. Too few Buddhist voices are being heard in the West. It is said that Buddhism is becoming more and more popular in the West, but in the weeks following 9/11, I did not hear a single Buddhist voice on American television or radio.

Finally, we might cooperate with those who seek peace. Many Christians, Muslims, and Jews are, in a sense, practicing Buddha Dharma without knowing it by working for peace. Through a variety of international agencies we can try to support and encourage them. The same Bible that demands "an eye for an eye" also says "turn the other cheek." We need to join the peacemakers of every religious tradition, promoting interfaith cooperation and encouraging them to work together to build a more peaceful world.

Once when Rev. Nikkyo Niwano, the founder of Rissho Kosei-kai, found himself under severe and unwarranted attack from a newspaper, he took the very unpopular stance of turning that very unpleasant situation into a learning situation, and began referring to the newspaper as "our bodhisattva." Bodhisattvas, even evil ones, can be our teachers, if we are wise enough to learn from them.

A central teaching of Rissho Kosei-kai's form of Buddhism is that every situation, no matter how difficult or tragic or violent, can be received as an opportunity to learn and benefit in some way. This does not mean, I hasten to add, that every situation is simply to be accepted and lived with in quiescence—far from it! Rissho Kosei-kai is very involved in a variety of what have been called "world-mending" activities and projects. But the teaching does mean that within every situation there is something valuable, something redeemable, something from which we can learn if we follow the example of the Buddha in the story of Devadatta.

"Bodhisattva" means one who seeks to be awakened by working for others, one who is on the way to becoming a buddha. Yet another meaning of "bodhisattva" is one from whom we can learn, just as Shakyamuni learned from Devadatta.

Thus, may 9/11 and all such tragedies be a kind of Devadatta Bodhisattva for all of us.

# 16

## THE DRAGON PRINCESS

T HE DRAGON PRINCESS is one of the most common figures in Chinese Buddhist temples. In a typical Ming-style temple, behind the main buddha and facing in the opposite direction, backing up the Buddha so to speak, one finds a statue of Kwan-yin, the female "South Sea" Kwan-yin. To her left is Sudhana from the Flower Garland Sutra and to her right one always finds the dragon princess from the Lotus Sutra, signifying both the unification of these two scriptures and Chinese Buddhist traditions in Kwan-yin, and the close association of Kwan-yin and the dragon princess.

That this girl is a dragon is interesting in itself. In the Indian text she is a naga, the daughter of the Naga King. Along with the garuda, nagas are very commonly found on South East Asian Theravada Buddhist temples. As was the case for most Indian mythical creatures, there were no corresponding mythical creatures in China. The Chinese had no nagas, but they did have dragons, and, both being associated with the sea, that was close enough to suggest translating "naga" into "dragon." And so it is that in English one sometimes finds this girl referred to as a "Naga Princess."[22]

## THE STORY

In the second part of the Lotus Sutra's Chapter 12, the bodhisattva Accumulated Wisdom—an attendant of Abundant Treasures Buddha, who is still sitting with Shakyamuni Buddha in his great stupa in the air—proposes to Abundant Treasures Buddha that it is time for them to return home. But Shakyamuni stops them, saying that the bodhisattva Manjushri, someone with whom they would enjoy discussing the Dharma, will soon be back, and that they should wait for him.

Soon, Manjushri emerged from the sea, paid his respects to the two buddhas sitting in the stupa, and exchanged greetings with Accumulated Wisdom Bodhisattva. Asked by Accumulated Wisdom how many he had led to the Way, Manjushri asked him to wait a minute to see for himself, and immediately countless bodhisattvas—who had been taught nothing other than the Dharma Flower Sutra by Manjushri—also emerged from the sea.

Then Accumulated Wisdom asked Manjushri if he had ever encountered anyone, anywhere in his vast travels, who had followed the Dharma Flower Sutra so well that they were qualified to become a buddha quickly. Manjushri replied that, yes, "there is the daughter of the dragon-king Sagara. Just eight years old, she is wise and has sharp faculties, and is well acquainted with the abilities and actions of living beings. She has mastered incantations. She has been able to receive and embrace all the profound inner core treasures preached by the buddhas, and has entered deeply into meditation and gained an understanding of all things. Within a moment, she aspired to become awakened and reached the stage of never backsliding. Her eloquence knows no bounds, and she has compassion for all the living as if they were her own children. She is full of blessings, and the thoughts in her mind and the explanations from her mouth are both subtle and great. Compassionate and respectful of others, kind and gentle, she is able to attain awakening." (LS 251)

Accumulated Wisdom, recalling that Shakyamuni had devoted enormous time and effort to achieving awakening, expressed doubt that this girl could do so in a moment. "It's unbelievable," he said.

Even before he had finished saying this, however, the girl herself appeared and went over to Shakyamuni and bowed deeply before him, expressing the thought that only he could know whether or not she is qualified to attain awakening because he alone knows that she has truly heard the Dharma and will preach the way of the Great Vehicle in order to save all beings from suffering.

Shariputra then spoke to the girl, expressing conventional belief: "You think that in no time at all you will attain the unexcelled way. This is hard to believe. Why? Because the body of a woman is filthy and impure, not a vessel for the Dharma. How could you attain unexcelled awakening? The Buddha Way is long and extensive. Only after innumerable eons of enduring hardship, accumulating good works, and thoroughly carrying out all the practices can it be reached." Adding that she could never become a Brahma-king, an Indra, a Mara-king, a holy wheel-rolling king, or a buddha, since they all have male bodies, he asked how she could possibly expect "in a woman's body, [to] so quickly become a buddha."(LS 252–3)

The girl offered a valuable jewel she had with her to the Buddha, who accepted it immediately. Then she asked Shariputra and Accumulated Wisdom whether the Buddha had accepted the gem quickly or not. The two of them responded, "Most quickly." And she said, "Use your holy powers to watch me become a buddha even more quickly than that!" (LS 253)

Then the whole congregation saw her suddenly change into a man, carry out all the bodhisattva practices, and go to the pure world in the South, where she sat upon a jeweled lotus flower, attained supreme awakening, acquired the thirty-two major and eighty minor marks of a buddha, and began to teach the Dharma all over the universe.

Shariputra, Accumulated Wisdom, and everyone else in the congregation—the bodhisattvas and shravakas, the monks and nuns, and the human and nonhuman beings—accepted her teaching amid great rejoicing.

## COMMENTARY

Taken in context, the main purpose of this story is very clear: women are as capable of becoming fully awakened buddhas as any of the monks who would have been the early hearers of the story. Later, this story would be used appropriately to say the same thing to women. As indicated in the previous chapter, Chapter 12 of the Lotus Sutra contains a message of universal salvation, a powerful reinforcement of the idea found throughout the Sutra that all living beings have within them the potential to become fully awakened buddhas.

Some have made much of the fact that the body of the girl in this story is transformed into that of a male before she becomes a buddha.[23] There are many stories in the sutras of such gender transformations. All can be seen to be reflections of a belief that a buddha must have a male body, as the thirty-two marks of a buddha always include reference to the male sex organ.

This belief that buddhas always have male bodies was seldom if ever challenged in India. It remained basically unchallenged in East Asia as well, with the remarkable exception that in Chinese culture the Indian bodhisattva Avalokiteshvara, who was always taken to be male, was transformed into Kwan-shih-yin (Kanzeon in Japanese),[24] the bodhisattva Regarder of the Cries of the World, who is both male and female and widely recognized in East Asia not only as a bodhisattva but also as a buddha. While this remarkable bodhisattva will be discussed later in this book, we would do well to recognize here that the textual basis for this understanding of Kwan-yin is Chapter 25 of the Lotus Sutra, in which it is said that Kwan-yin can take on any form in order to help others. Thirty-three such forms are listed, the first of which is the form of a buddha.

The compilers of the Lotus Sutra no doubt assumed that Avalokiteshvara would have to be male. While today we can regret the fact that early Buddhists failed to challenge the assumption that a buddha must always have a male body, it is not surprising that this was simply assumed in this story of the dragon princess.

It is an incorrect representation of the story, however, to claim that the Sutra "insists" on such a transformation. What is insisted on is the claim that "even" a girl can become a buddha. Since by definition buddhas are male, the story simply says in one brief phrase that her body was transformed into that of a male during the process of her becoming a buddha. There is no insistence. It is simply assumed to be a necessary step in becoming a buddha.

Many generations took this story to be a proclamation that women are as capable of becoming buddhas as men. When Japan's Emperor Shomu (701–756) established a kind of national temple system throughout the country, in each district one temple was established for ten monks and another, a nunnery, for ten nuns. While the whole system was related primarily to Mahavairocana Buddha and the Flower Garland Sutra[25] rather than to Shakyamuni and the Dharma Flower Sutra, in the nunneries it was the Dharma Flower Sutra that was installed and recited for the protection of women, most likely because it contained the story of the dragon princess.

Today much, if not all, of the world is gradually undergoing something of a transformation with respect to what people think about gender. Women insist on equality with men, resulting in some quite remarkable changes in social structures and cultural habits in much of the world. The story of the dragon princess can be used to support the ideal of equality between men and women, as that was its obvious purpose, at least with respect to the ability to become fully awakened.

That the story retains what we see as an incorrect assumption that buddhas are always male can be used as an occasion for us to challenge our own assumptions about gender and gender roles. It is easy for us to recognize that the assumption in the Sutra that buddhas must be male is both unnecessary and undesirable, but it is not as easy to see our own unchallenged assumptions about the nature and appropriate roles of men and women. We might even think that the assumption found in this Lotus Sutra story comes to us a gift from the Buddha—is an opportunity for us to become more awakened, especially with respect to gender issues.

In the context of the Dharma Flower Sutra, it is not surprising to find that a dragon or young person can become a buddha, but that someone can do so suddenly is quite surprising—because it goes against the Sutra's often repeated assertion that the way to becoming a buddha is long and arduous. Indeed, this is the point of the tale of the weary travelers and the fantastic castle-city in Chapter 7. This story about the dragon princess is the only place in the Dharma Flower Sutra where it is said that one can become a buddha suddenly.

At least in Japan and China, and quite likely in India as well, there was controversy over whether or not sudden awakening is possible. What we find in the Dharma Flower Sutra can be taken as another example of its tolerance of diverse views. Taken as a whole, it seems to say that becoming a buddha is normally, perhaps almost always, a long and difficult path, but that there can be exceptions. Rather than articulating this exception as a kind of doctrine, however, the Sutra simply makes it part of a story, illustrating the exception without entering into debate on the subject.

True awakening is difficult and rare; sudden awakening is much rarer still. If profound awakening happens at all, and certainly if it happens suddenly—in ourselves or in others, like those at the end of this story—we too should be amazed and grateful. But let us not suppose that there is some shortcut to true awakening through the use of drugs or some other esoteric practices. True awakening takes much time and effort.

We might also note that the sudden awakening in this story is highly qualified by Manjushri's observations about what the dragon princess had already attained. From his description, we know that she had already become a bodhisattva who aspired to become a buddha. She had already made considerable progress on the Way and demonstrated great compassion before becoming a buddha suddenly. Thus, she was especially ready to become a buddha suddenly.

There are other elements of this story that might be held up for our own benefit. For example, like Shakyamuni Buddha, the girl is the child of a king. She leaves a palace—which in the Dharma Flower Sutra is always a symbol of luxury and comfort—in order to come into the world to help others by becoming a buddha. Princes and princesses are supposed to stay in their palaces, where all is clean and comfortable, and settle down with another prince or princess to produce royal heirs. Not many of us live in palaces today.

Or do we? The palace can be understood as the comfort and security of tradition and conventional wisdom. Like Shakyamuni himself, the dragon princess, this buddha-in-the-making, is a convention-breaker who does the unexpected. Imagine how shocked the venerable Shariputra and Accumulated Wisdom, both presumably monks well up in years, must have been when this young girl turned to them, demanded to know whether or not her jewel had been accepted by the Buddha quickly, and instructed them to watch her. This is not the way young girls are supposed to behave toward their elders. It was not the way things were done then; it is not the way they are done now.

Like many great religious leaders, this girl is highly unconventional. Jesus, Saicho, Dogen, Nichiren, Gandhi, and even Nikkyo Niwano were not conventional either. We have heard the story about Shakyamuni Buddha leaving his father's palace and his own wife and child so often that we forget that that story too is about shockingly unconventional behavior. For that matter, virtually the whole story of early Buddhism is about unconventional behavior and lifestyles—a group of young men leaving comfortable homes to become wandering beggars who encourage other young men to leave their homes and families to take up a life of begging!

The dragon princess resorts to unconventional behavior not to be unconventional but to make a point. She needed to get the attention of these men in order to teach them something. In other words, she was unconventional, but unconventional for the purpose of helping others not for the sake unconventionality. Maybe the world needs more people who are willing and able to be unconventional for the sake of helping others.

We are told at the end of the story that, as a buddha, the dragon princess began teaching the Dharma all over the universe. But it is also relevant that in her very being and in her actions in the process of becoming a buddha, she teaches the Dharma to Shariputra and Accumulated Wisdom Bodhisattva. And this is witnessed by the whole congregation, which in turn is then taught by the girl who has become a buddha. And we hearers or readers of the story are also offered an opportunity to witness this whole scenario. In this way the dragon princess is our teacher, one who leads us to buddha-wisdom. It is important to see that she can be a teacher of the Dharma and a buddha for us even during the process of becoming a buddha. In challenging Shariputra and Accumulated Wisdom Bodhisattva, though still in the body of a girl, she was already a buddha—even though they cannot yet see that.

The idea of seeing a buddha is almost a constant theme in the Dharma Flower Sutra. At times, *seeing* a buddha can be equated with *being* a buddha. As we saw in the story of the Buddha and Devadatta, at least one of the things that make the Buddha a buddha is his ability to see the buddha in others. So it is not insignificant that toward the end of this story the dragon princess tells Shariputra and Accumulated Wisdom that they should watch with their supernatural ability to see. Such holy powers are nothing less than the fantastic powers of the human imagination. Shariputra and Accumulated Wisdom learned to see what others could not see—a mere girl becoming a buddha—because they were enabled to transcend their normal vision and their normal, conventional ways of thinking. They were transformed by the dragon princess into men who could see like a buddha, men who could see the buddha in the girl.

That is what we are asked to do by the Dharma Flower Sutra—to use our imagination to see further and deeper than we have ever seen before: to see the buddha in others, to see the positive potential in others—both their inherent good and their good for us. It is seldom if ever easy to do this, but we already have such holy powers, and they can be awakened through the story of the dragon princess—a girl who becomes a buddha and who is a buddha in the process of becoming a buddha.

# 17

## TWO NUNS

THE NUN MAHAPRAJAPATI, accompanied by six thousand followers, and the nun Yashodhara, mother of Rahula, with her own followers, are mentioned together in Chapter 1 of the Dharma Flower Sutra as among those present in the great assembly that had gathered to hear the Buddha. Curiously, they are mentioned after a list of shravakas, monk-arhats who are part of a group of twelve thousand, and before a contingent of eighty thousand bodhisattvas. A number of both shravakas and bodhisattvas are named individually. Here the two nuns do not seem to fit into either category, shravaka or bodhisattva.

Chapter 13 is where these two nuns make their main appearance in the Dharma Flower Sutra. This brief chapter, entitled "Encouragement to Uphold the Sutra," is about a succession of bodhisattvas, arhats, and other people, including the two nuns, who vow before the Buddha that after his death they will continue to teach and spread the Sutra far and wide. Because of the earlier close family relationships, the underlying psychology may be complex, but on the surface the story of Mahaprajapati and Yashodhara found here is quite simple.

## THE STORY

Mahaprajapati, described as the sister of the Buddha's mother, along with six thousand nuns all get up from their seats, put their palms together in veneration, and look intently at the face of the Buddha. Then the Buddha, speaking to her with a term of familiar address, "Gautami," asks her why she was looking so perplexed. "Deep down," he asks, "are you wondering why I have not mentioned your name to assure you of supreme awakening?"

Then he proceeds to assure her that in ages to come, still accompanied by the six thousand nuns, she will become a bodhisattva who is a great Dharma teacher, gradually fulfilling the bodhisattva way and eventually becoming the buddha named Seen with Joy by All the Living. As that buddha, she would in turn assure six thousand bodhisattvas, presumably her six thousand nun followers, of supreme awakening.

Yashodhara, here described as the mother of Rahula and a nun, thinks to herself, "Among the Buddha's assurances of supreme awakening, I'm the only one here who hasn't been mentioned!" Then the Buddha assures her that she too will become a great Dharma teacher by doing bodhisattva practice under hundreds of thousands of billions of buddhas in ages to come, gradually fulfilling the bodhisattva way and eventually becoming the buddha called Having Ten Million Shining Characteristics.

The two nuns, full of joy, then praise the Buddha for giving them peace of mind and promise to go everywhere to proclaim the Dharma Flower Sutra, even to other lands in other regions.

### BACKGROUND

According to legends not found in the Lotus Sutra, the mother of Shakyamuni, Maya (or Maha-Maya), died shortly after giving birth to the future Buddha, Gautama. Maya's younger sister, called Gautami, was responsible for raising Gautama, subsequently married his father, King Shuddhodana, and thus became Gautama's stepmother.

Some years later, one source says it was five years after the beginning of the community of Buddhist monks, and following the death of her husband, Gautami, along with others, requested permission from the Buddha to become a nun. At first the Buddha was very reluctant to admit women to the growing society of monks, but following Ananda's insistence that she be admitted, with the Buddha's consent she became the first Buddhist nun, possibly the first nun of any kind,[26] and was given the name Mahaprajapati.

Most stories about Mahaprajapati are not so much about her as they are about her efforts to keep the future Buddha from fleeing the palace where he was raised, by surrounding him with innumerable beautiful young women, seeing that his every desire was met, and so on. In the Dharma Flower Sutra, however, the very brief story is about Mahaprajapati herself being reassured of becoming a fully awakened buddha.

Yashodhara was one of possibly several wives of Shakyamuni, and the mother of their son Rahula. In Buddhist sutras and other texts a great many stories can be found about Yashodhara, often mentioning her good looks and her haughty personality.

She was a cousin of Shakyamuni, famous for her beauty, as was Shakyamuni himself. Their first meeting is said to have occurred in this way: Wanting to find a proper bride for his son, Shakyamuni's father had a collection of jewelry made for Shakyamuni to distribute at a party to which all of the lovely young women of the land were to be invited. The king's aides were told to watch carefully to see which woman was most attractive to him. But when the women actually came to the party, Shakyamuni showed no interest in any of them.

Just as the party was about to end, a young woman came in late, with a huge entourage. This was Yashodhara. She approached the handsome prince without hesitation or embarrassment to ask for her gift. "I'm sorry," said Shakyamuni, "the jewelry is all gone. You should have come earlier." "Well," she replied, "why didn't you save something for me?" Then Shakyamuni offered her his own ring and necklace. But she declined these presents, turning away from Shakyamuni. In another version of this story, she accepted his necklace and then asked, "Is this all I'm worth?" In either case, she had gained his attention!

The king, Shakyamuni's father, soon sent a messenger to Yashodhara's father to ask for his daughter's hand in an arranged marriage. But he refused, indicating that he would give his daughter only to a young man who could prove that he was superior to all others. Thus, a kind of Indian Olympics was held, with contests in such things as mathematics, writing, swordsmanship, horseback riding, boxing, and so on. Naturally, Shakyamuni won all the contests and he and Yashodhara were soon married at a great, splendid wedding ceremony.

Yashodhara became famous for her independence. For example, she refused to wear the traditional veil. When criticized for this, she replied that a noble woman who controls her mind and senses will be properly veiled even when she is naked, for one's sins cannot be covered even by a whole pile of robes and veils.

When Shakyamuni returned home for the first time after becoming a monk, his father the king was overjoyed, but Yashodhara was still overcome with sadness and grief because her husband had left her. On this occasion, she alone did not leave her room to come to meet him. So Shakyamuni went to her room along with two disciples and was able to help her overcome her grief, in part by explaining that he had found a very great treasure.

Several days later, when Yashodhara arranged for their son, Rahula, to see his father for the first time, she told him to ask his father to give him a great treasure. The boy did this and then followed the Buddha into the forest, later becoming a monk himself.

Yashodhara then turned into a kind of recluse, keeping to herself inside the palace. But several years later, after King Shuddhodana had died and Mahaprajapati had become a nun and established a community of nuns, Yashodhara walked to where the nuns were staying and became a nun herself. Subsequently she studied with Shakyamuni frequently, saw her son, Rahula, often as well, and became a great nun.

## COMMENTARY

The reason for the chapter title, "Encouragement to Uphold the Sutra," may be obscure, as it is not so much that the bodhisattvas or nuns are encouraged as that they themselves promise or make a vow to endure and persist in teaching the Sutra despite rejection and persecution.

This concern and promise follow from the request of the Buddha at the end of Chapter 11, where Shakyamuni Buddha asks that anyone who can embrace, read, and recite the Sutra come before him now and make such a vow.

Now, here in Chapter 13, bodhisattvas respond: "We will cherish neither our bodies nor our lives, but care only for the unexcelled way. In ages to come, we will protect and uphold what the Buddha has entrusted to us." And they promise that they will go to preach the Dharma to anyone who seeks it. "We are emissaries of the World-Honored One," they declare, and say that they will teach the Dharma well, facing multitudes without fear. (LS 259–60)

Words such as these were very important to Nichiren and to many of his followers over the centuries who suffered abuse and persecution as a consequence of being ardent, sometimes fanatical, devotees of the Lotus Sutra.

Who then is being encouraged to uphold the Sutra in Chapter 13? It is we the hearers or readers who should be encouraged, just as Nichiren was. If so many arhats and bodhisattvas and nuns can uphold the Sutra in dark times despite abuse and persecution, surely we can. The encouragement of the title should be taken as our encouragement.

Though it may not seem obvious to us now, a central point of the story of Mahaprajapati and Yashodhara is related to the main doctrinal theme of the whole Sutra—universal salvation or the potential of all living beings to become a buddha. If, as many scholars believe, Chapter 12 with its story of the dragon princess was added to the Dharma Flower Sutra relatively late, this chapter would have been needed to make it quite clear that becoming a bodhisattva and eventually achieving full awakening is not something limited to men.

Not only Mahaprajapati and Yashodhara but Mahaprajapati's six thousand nun followers as well, who are to become great Dharma teachers, gradually fulfilling the bodhisattva way, are assured of reaching supreme awakening as buddhas. In contrast with the story of the dragon princess, there is no mention of these nuns having to become male. Clearly, as Dharma teachers and bodhisattvas at least, they are female.

This teaching of universal salvation, of the potential in all living beings to become buddhas, is always also about us, the hearers and readers of the Dharma Flower Sutra. The focus of the chapter is the question of how the Dharma will survive in a hostile world without Shakyamuni Buddha to teach it. The answer is that it is a responsibility of bodhisattvas to teach and proclaim the Dharma everywhere. Among such bodhisattvas are women. This means that anyone can grow spiritually through encountering women and that one can meet the Buddha in a woman. This was very important in the development of Buddhism in China, and subsequently in the rest of East Asia, as it fostered the growth in devotion to Kwan-yin, in which the Buddha is encountered in female form.

That the women in this story are both nuns should not, of course, be taken to mean that nuns are the only women in whom we can meet the Buddha. Mahaprajapati is a nun, but she is also Shakyamuni's aunt, and Yashodhara is a nun, but she is also Shakyamuni's wife and the mother of their son, Rahula. The fact that they have had non-monastic roles is important. It means that while we can see the potential to be a buddha in nuns, this potential and power can also be seen in aunts and mothers, and, of course, in any woman.

We might wonder why these two women come last in a succession of assurances of becoming a buddha. Perhaps it was to give them a special place, but more likely it has to do with the enormous importance in the Sutra of Chapter 10, "Teachers of the Dharma."

In earlier chapters of the Sutra various shravakas, beginning with Shariputra, are assured of becoming buddhas in the future. This is brought to a kind of conclusion in Chapter 9, in which Ananda and Rahula and two thousand shravakas are given assurance of becoming buddhas.

Then Chapter 10 opens with the Buddha expressing as fully as possible the central theme of the Dharma Flower Sutra. "Do you see in this assembly," he says to Medicine King Bodhisattva, "the innumerable gods, dragon kings, satyrs, centaurs, ashuras, griffins, chimeras, pythons, humans and nonhumans, as well as monks, nuns, laymen and laywomen, those who seek to become shravakas, those who seek to become pratyekabuddhas, and those who seek the Buddha way? I assure all such beings…that if they hear a single verse or a single phrase of the Wonderful Dharma Flower Sutra and respond in joy even for a single moment, they will attain supreme awakening." (LS 225)

Then he goes on to say that after his extinction "if there is anyone who hears even a single verse or a single phrase of the Wonderful Dharma Flower Sutra, and responds in joy for even a single moment, I assure that one also of supreme awakening." Further, he says, if anyone receives and embraces, reads, recites, explains, or copies even a single verse of the Wonderful Dharma Flower Sutra, or looks upon it with reverence as if it were the Buddha himself, or makes any kind of offering to it, or even shows reverence toward it by putting their palms together, they have already worked to fulfill their great vow under many millions of buddhas. And he says to Medicine King Bodhisattva that if anyone asks him what sort of living beings will become buddhas in the future, he should show them that such good sons and daughters will become buddhas. Anyone who shows devotion to the Lotus Sutra should be honored by the whole world. Offerings should be given to them as they are to buddhas, as they are great bodhisattvas.

If anyone after the Buddha's extinction, the Buddha says to Medicine King, "is able, even in secret, to teach to one person even one phrase of the Dharma Flower Sutra, then you should understand that they are emissaries of the Tathagata, sent by the Tathagata to do the work of the Tathagata. How much more true this is of those who teach this Sutra everywhere for others before great crowds of people!" (LS 225–26)

It would be difficult to be any clearer than this: anyone is capable of receiving and embracing the Sutra and of teaching it to others. With this clearly established as the teaching of the Dharma Flower Sutra, the reader should be prepared for Chapter 13 and its emphasis on nuns and women as bodhisattvas. In Chapter 13, it is said that the two nuns are to become "Dharma teachers." In no previous occurrence of the Buddha giving assurance to someone of their becoming a buddha was this done.

We might wonder also about the initial reluctance of the Buddha to admit women into the monastic community. Undoubtedly there was some tension in the early Buddhist community of monks between two matters: on the one hand is the teaching that all are equal in that all are bodhisattvas with the potential of becoming buddhas, and on the other hand is the reality of sexual desire in monks who had renounced their sexuality. The reality of the monks' desire and consequent disrespect for women did not go away, but by admitting women into the Sangha as nuns, the teaching won out.

## UPHOLDING THE SUTRA

The Dharma Flower Sutra makes frequent reference to "upholding" the Sutra. What does it mean to "uphold" the Sutra? The Chinese character used here can mean such things as "keep," "hold," "uphold," or "take care of." Usually, when translating it in the Dharma Flower Sutra, I have used the term "embrace." It occurs in several combinations that are important in the Sutra, especially (in Japanese pronunciation) as *juji*, "receive and embrace"; *buji*, "honor and embrace"; *goji*, "protect and embrace"; and *jisetsu*, "embrace and explain"; and there are many others. I like to use "embrace" because, for the Dharma Flower Sutra, what is involved is not a matter either of storage or of defending, but of following or adhering to the teachings of the Sutra by embodying them in one's life.

But in Chapter 13, what is of most direct concern is *propagating* the Sutra in the face of great difficulties, spreading its teachings to others despite many obstacles, leading others to embrace it. So here, in the title of Chapter 13, it seems fitting to think of being encouraged to "uphold" the Sutra.

Then an enormously large group of bodhisattvas spoke to the Buddha, telling him not to worry as after his extinction, "in a frightful and evil age," even if cursed and abused or attacked with swords and sticks they would teach the Sutra everywhere. In such an evil age, "full of dreadful things, evil spirits will take possession of others to curse, abuse, and insult us." In order to teach this Sutra they will wear "an armor of patient endurance" and "endure all such difficult things." "We will cherish neither our bodies nor our lives," they say, "but care only for the unexcelled way," protecting and upholding in ages to come "what the Buddha has entrusted to us." Repeatedly driven out from stupas and monasteries, they will endure such troubles, going wherever there are those who seek it to teach the Dharma entrusted to them by the Buddha. We are, they say, "emissaries" of the Buddha, "facing multitudes without fear," in order to spread the Dharma. (LS 257–60)

We do not know what circumstances in India led to this kind of anticipation of abuse and persecution of followers of the Dharma

Flower Sutra, but, especially for Nichiren and his followers, these words could be seen as anticipating their own experience. They were a powerful encouragement to endure suffering and persist in teaching the Sutra to others no matter how great the difficulties.

Today, few of us have to face such extreme persecution for teaching the Lotus Sutra. But most followers of the Sutra certainly do face difficulties, especially from those who are antagonistic toward the Sutra and toward those who seek to teach it. And in most, if not all, of the world such antagonism may be directed more intensely toward women. We know that Mahaprajapati and Yashodhara had to overcome great difficulties and even hostility toward women in order to become nuns and teachers of the Dharma.

There are other kinds of difficulties as well, difficulties in understanding the Sutra, difficulties in translation and interpretation, difficulties adequately embodying the teachings in our everyday lives, difficulties in teaching or preaching it, difficulties in sharing our enthusiasm for it. Indeed, for those who want to uphold the Dharma Flower Sutra, there is no shortage of difficulties. It is all too easy to become disheartened and discouraged and want to give up.

Chapter 13, especially perhaps in the final verses, "We will cherish neither our bodies nor our lives, but care only for the unexcelled way," can be a wonderful encouragement to continue despite such difficulties. If others have faced terrible abuse and persecution, surely we too can face difficulties and survive.

# 18

# THE JEWEL IN THE TOPKNOT

T HE PARABLE of the jewel in the topknot is found in Chapter
14 of the Lotus Sutra. In Japanese this chapter is called *Anraku
Gyo*. It is one of the more troublesome Lotus Sutra chapter
titles to translate into English. The Chinese character for *gyo* is used
in many different ways, but in this Buddhist context it means "to
conduct oneself, practice, or behave in some way." Though "conduct"
would also work fine, I translate it as "practice." The problem comes
with *anraku*, which basically means comfort. So you can find this
chapter title translated as "Comfortable Conduct," or "Ease in Practice," or "Peaceful Practices." The trouble is that while "comfortable
conduct" is a perfectly good translation for the title by itself, none of
these translations even approaches the meaning of the content of the
chapter. This chapter is not about being comfortable.

I have sometimes used "Carefree Practices" to translate this title,
but the chapter is also not really about being carefree. It's mainly about
practices that will keep bodhisattvas out of trouble. Perhaps they
could be called "safe" practices. They are practices that make it possible to be free from worry. For now, I have translated the chapter title
as "Safe and Easy Practices" but perhaps it should be called "Practice
That Will Keep You Out of Trouble," or more simply "Staying Out of

Trouble." Still, we should understand that what is involved is not just a matter of *avoiding* trouble; it is, as we can learn from the parable of the jewel in the topknot, much more a matter of seeking the good or positive by facing unavoidable difficulty. A Japanese proverb says, if you avoid troubles, they will chase after you; if you face them, they will run away.

At the beginning of the chapter, Manjushri refers to the bodhisattvas in the previous chapter who have promised that no matter how difficult it may turn out to be, no matter how much hostility they have to face, they will teach the Dharma in the evil ages following the death of the Buddha. Now Manjushri asks the Buddha how these bodhisattvas should go about it. It is important to recognize that an evil age, a terribly difficult age, is the setting for this chapter.

The Buddha responds to Manjushri by outlining four kinds of practice and association with others that such bodhisattvas should follow. One has to do primarily with outward behavior, one with speech, one with mental attitudes, and one with intentions. The description of the first is far longer than those of the other three.

First, a bodhisattva should behave well, avoid temptations, and preach the Dharma. Behaving well includes being patient, mild, and unattached to anything, including nonattachment. Avoidance of temptations includes not getting too close to or receiving special gifts from kings, princes, government officials and the like, participants in dangerous sports, heretics, entertainers, people who raise animals or fish, those who seek to become shravakas, and so on. Also male bodhisattvas should have no desire for women, being especially careful around them, and should never desire children or young disciples. They should, of course, teach the Dharma to all—including those with whom they should not be closely associated.

Such a bodhisattva should first seek a quiet place for meditation. One should also disregard differences, such as, for example, those between what is viewed as superior and inferior Buddhist ways, or between what is real and what is unreal, or between men and women. And, finally, a bodhisattva should recognize the truth of the central Buddhist philosophical idea of the insubstantiality and impermanence of all things—the truth of the interdependent origination or becoming of all things.

Second, when teaching or preaching, bodhisattvas should make "safe and easy practices part of their lives," never showing contempt toward other teachers of the Dharma, never finding fault with them by pointing out their weak points, and never in any way showing hostility toward them. Rather, bodhisattvas should feel compassion toward them and enjoy inner peace of mind in order to bring peace of mind to others. They should not seek expensive gifts from those they teach, but rather seek only two things: their own awakening and the awakening of others. Free from such things as jealousy, anger, and illusions, bodhisattvas need not have any sorrows or fears. They will never be threatened or driven out of monasteries. They will be free of worry, at least of this kind of worry.

Third, true bodhisattvas should not despise or speak ill of those who follow other ways and should avoid fruitless quarrels with them. They should never tease or make fun of those who seek to follow any of the three ways. They should look upon all the buddhas as their loving fathers and upon all bodhisattvas as their teachers. With great compassion, patience, and gentleness, they should teach the Dharma impartially to all, never causing others to have doubts or worries. As a result they will have many good friends, and many followers who come to receive the Dharma from them.

Fourth, true bodhisattvas should feel great compassion and kindness toward monks and laypeople who have not taken the bodhisattva way, and vow to lead them to embody the Buddha in their own lives. Such a teacher of the Dharma will have many listeners among all kinds of human beings and even heavenly beings will come to hear and protect such a teacher.

At this point in the chapter, ostensibly to praise the Dharma Flower Sutra, the Buddha tells the parable of the jewel in the topknot.

## THE PARABLE

A powerful, holy wheel–rolling king sought the surrender of many lesser kings, and when they did not yield he went to war, winning many battles. In combat, many of his soldiers distinguished themselves, and so he presented them with all sorts of rewards—houses, fields, cities, gold, jewels, garments, elephants, servants—all sorts of good and valuable things. But there was one thing he held back—an extraordinarily precious and unique jewel that he kept in the topknot of his hair. Yet this great king, when finally he saw a soldier of especially great merit, gave that soldier the precious jewel from his own topknot.

The Buddha is like that king, he tells Manjushri. He became king of this world and had to go to war with Mara,[27] the evil one, and his followers with his own army of followers led by sages and saints. To them he has given many gifts—many different sutras, various kinds of meditation practice, teachings such as nirvana, and so on. But he did not, until now, give the Sutra of the Lotus Flower of the Wonderful Dharma. Now, like the king, the Buddha gives the Dharma Flower Sutra for the benefit of all living beings for their flowering. He does this because he sees that there are many people of great merit. Thus the Sutra is the most excellent and profound of teachings, given last as the core of all the buddhas' teachings.

## COMMENTARY

In this story, we are told, the jewel kept in the king's topknot represents the Dharma Flower Sutra. Here the symbolic meaning of "jewel" is quite different from that in the story in Chapter 8 of the "hidden jewel," where the jewel symbolizes the potential that lies dormant within all living beings to become awakened. The main point here, once more, is to describe symbolically the relationship between earlier forms of Buddhism and the Mahayana, or Great Vehicle, and to explain why the Dharma Flower Sutra was not taught earlier. Here, the Dharma Flower Sutra is seen as the crowning achievement of the Buddha and Buddhism. The Buddha has given many gifts and treasures, many sutras, many practices, and so on, but there is one that stands above all the others—the Wonderful Dharma Flower Sutra.

It is important, however, to see here that the earlier or "lesser" rewards really are, first and foremost, rewards. There is no suggestion that the earlier teachings of the shravaka way are wrong or bad or even misleading. Just as in the very first parable in the Lotus Sutra, the parable of the burning house, it is by pursuing the three small vehicles that the children are led to the great vehicle; here too there is no hint of going from bad to good, or from wrong to right, or from false to true. It is the case that the Dharma Flower Sutra proclaims itself to be better in some sense than other sutras, but this is a relative difference. The holy wheel-rolling king rewarded his soldiers with all sorts of good and valuable things before deciding that one was worthy of the jewel in his topknot.

The final verse portion of the chapter says that the Buddha has taught many sutras as skillful means, and when he knows that people have gained sufficient strength from them, he at last and for their sake teaches the Dharma Flower Sutra. In other words, it is because other sutras have been taught and people have gained strength from them that the Buddha is at last able to teach the Dharma Flower Sutra. Other sutras and teachings prepare and open the way for the teachings of the Dharma Flower Sutra.

This means, of course, that while followers of the Dharma Flower Sutra may think it is the greatest of sutras, they should not disparage other sutras or other teachings, just as is taught in the four trouble-free practices in the early part of the chapter.

Yet in what way is the Lotus Sutra superior to or better than other sutras? In this story, this is not explicit, but if we look below the surface, we may find an answer to this question.

The jewel in the topknot is very valuable, but we are not told in what way it is more valuable than other valuable things. The text says that the Dharma Flower Sutra is "supreme," the "greatest," the "most profound," the "highest." But there are only a couple of hints or suggestions as to how it is supreme among sutras. One hint is that the Sutra, like the jewel in the topknot, is withheld to the last. But, surely, merely being last is not necessarily a great virtue and would not automatically make this Sutra any better than any other. The second thing we are told is that the Dharma Flower Sutra "can lead all the living to comprehensive wisdom." Thus, we may think, the reason that being last is important in this case is because being last makes it possible for the Dharma Flower Sutra to take account of what has come before and be more inclusive than earlier sutras. While much use is made here of what are basically spatial metaphors, such as highest, or most profound, what is suggested here is that the real superiority of this Sutra lies in its *comprehensiveness*. And this is not so much a matter of repeating doctrine and ideas found in earlier sutras as it is a matter of having a positive regard both for the earlier sutras and for those who teach or follow them, and thus being more comprehensive.

This is why three of the four practices urged on bodhisattvas at the beginning of the chapter involve having a generous, respectful, positive, helpful attitude toward others. Rather than reject other teachings and sutras, the Dharma Flower Sutra teaches that all sutras should be regarded as potentially leading to the larger, more comprehensive, more inclusive wisdom of the Lotus Sutra itself.

It is quite interesting, I think, that here the reason for teaching the Dharma Flower Sutra last is not because other sutras have not worked well, but that because of them there are many people of great merit now present to hear the Lotus Sutra. The Sutra teaches that there have been many kinds of Buddhist teachings and sutras in the past. Now the supreme Dharma Flower Sutra is to be preached. Why now?

Indeed, this same question has to be faced by any religion that claims to have a special revelation, even just a special beginning. Usually, the answer is some kind of great evil, terrible pollution, or awful sin, something extremely negative that makes some kind of special intervention necessary. But not in the Dharma Flower Sutra. Here it is because of the *goodness*, that is, because of the merit, of many of his followers that the king at last gives the great jewel to one of them.

The king understands his responsibility to be one of rewarding people for, and according to, the merit of the good they have done. That is, he is looking for the good in people and for the good things they have done. What the Dharma Flower Sutra teaches is that we too should be about the business of seeking out the good in other people and rewarding it where possible. It is very easy to be critical of others, to find fault with them, especially perhaps when it comes to those to whom we are the closest, such as those in our families and those with whom we work every day. For those who would be followers of the Dharma Flower Sutra, while it is important to understand the teaching of buddha-nature, understanding or accepting the idea of universal buddha-nature is nowhere near as important as actually embodying that idea in everyday life by seeing and respecting the buddha-nature in those around us.

Such a practice is likely to lead to a happier and more rewarding life for all involved. Thus, it is not accidental that this parable, which might at first seem unrelated to the first part of the chapter, is actually quite closely related to the whole idea of practice that leads to a rewarding life. The theme of the parable is not just the withholding of the jewel, but rewarding others with all kinds of treasures, including, and especially, the greatest treasure one has to give. This is a practice that leads to a trouble-free life, that is, to a life that is relatively free of worries, in part because one has many friends and few if any enemies.

In the prose section of this chapter, it is said that the radiance of the wisdom of those who follow the Dharma Flower Sutra will shine like the sun. The point is that one can see nothing in darkness. All there is, is a lack of light. If we provide light, even a very little light, darkness will disappear. That is why the radiance of the wisdom of one who follows the Sutra is like the radiance of the sun—it lights up the world, bringing happiness both to others and to oneself.

## THE WHEEL-ROLLING KING

While this story is about a king and his army, compared with many other religious texts, the Lotus Sutra is remarkably free of military imagery. Apart from this story, the only armies mentioned in the sutra are the armies of Mara, a sort of Indian version of the devil or Satan. Terms such as "soldier," "general" (except for the "generals of heaven"), "war," "military," "battle," and so on simply are not used in the Dharma Flower Sutra.

Even here, it is relevant to note that the powerful, holy, wheel-rolling king who is at the center of the parable is not primarily a warrior. He is a holy *chakravartin-raja*, an ideal ruler or king in Indian mythology, a king who rules not by force but by righteousness and doing good. *Chakra* is the Indian word for wheel and a *chakravartin* is a wheel-turner, a title that could be given to any powerful ruler, the idea being that, as the wheels of his chariot roll along, all obstacles in the ruler's path are destroyed. In Buddhism, however, the wheel becomes the Dharma wheel, and the *wheel-rolling king* can become a symbol of one whose teachings are so powerful that they overcome all obstacles.

Today, when so many seem to think that the only way to safety and happiness for humanity is through war, and through constantly looking for evil in order to punish it, it is good to know that the Dharma

Flower Sutra teaches that the way to peace is through seeking out and rewarding the good in others. For many, it is precisely this positive thrust of the Dharma Flower Sutra—its affirmation of the opportunities offered to us within this life, where suffering is pervasive—that makes it the supreme sutra. In this story, this parable of the jewel in the topknot, we can see both the idea that the Dharma Flower Sutra is supreme and the idea that it is supreme precisely because it directs us to seek out and reward the good that we can find everywhere.

After all, it is not only holy wheel-rolling kings who have jewels to give. Anyone, by seeking to reward others, can find their own life greatly enriched. Even if such a practice does not always lead to comfort, and you can be sure that there will be times when it will not, it can lead to a kind of equanimity that might be called "trouble-free."

The chapter closes with the idea that those who read the Sutra will be rewarded in many ways and will have marvelous dreams assuring them of ultimately becoming buddhas. That is, receiving the Sutra not only changes our lives by making us more positive and happy, it even helps make our dreams more pleasant.

# 19

## BODHISATTVAS OF THE EARTH

C HAPTER 14 of the Lotus Sutra ends speaking about dreams, saying that those who behave well will not only enjoy happy lives while awake, but have wonderful dreams as well. The story of bodhisattvas springing up from below the earth in Chapter 15 is a bit like such a wonderful dream.

We should remember that in Chapter 11, millions and millions of buddhas came from all over the universe to this world to see Abundant Treasures Buddha in his magnificent stupa, and that each of those buddhas was accompanied by a great many bodhisattvas. Now, in Chapter 15, the time is approaching for those buddhas and bodhisattvas to return home to their own distant worlds.

## THE STORY

The chapter begins with some of those bodhisattvas from other worlds asking Shakyamuni Buddha to allow them to help him by staying in this world to preach the Dharma Flower Sutra after Shakyamuni's death. But the Buddha promptly declines their offer on the grounds that he does not need their help because there are many bodhisattvas already in this world who can protect and embrace, read and recite, and teach the Dharma Flower Sutra after his death. "There is no need," he says, "for you to protect and embrace this sutra. Why? Because in my world itself there are as many bodhisattva great ones as there are sands in sixty thousand Ganges. And each one of these bodhisattvas has as many followers as there are sands in sixty thousand Ganges." (LS 279)

At this point the ground quakes and splits open and a fantastically enormous number of bodhisattvas and their attendants spring up from the earth, where they have been living in empty space below the earth. They go before the two buddhas in the stupa in the air, Abundant Treasures and Shakyamuni, pay respects to them, then go to all the other buddhas seated on lion seats to pay respects to them, and then return to the two buddhas sitting in the stupa.

These bodhisattvas are led by four great bodhisattvas—Superior Practice, Unlimited Practice, Pure Practice, and Firm Practice[28]— who inquire about the health of Shakyamuni Buddha. "Is the World-honored One at ease," they ask,

> With few ailments and troubles?
> In teaching all the living,
> Are you free from weariness?
> And are all the living
> Readily accepting your teaching?
> Don't they make
> The World-Honored One tired? (LS 281)

Then Maitreya Bodhisattva, who in stories in the Dharma Flower Sutra is often surprised and confused, in effect asks the Buddha, "Who are all these bodhisattvas that I have never seen before, and where have they come from, and who taught them the Dharma? In all of this multitude there is not one that I know." And the bodhisattvas who had accompanied the buddhas from all of the other worlds ask their buddhas the same question and are told by them to be quiet and listen to Shakyamuni Buddha's response to Maitreya.

Shakyamuni then explains that he himself has been teaching and leading these bodhisattvas ever since sitting under the bodhi tree in Gaya, when he attained supreme awakening. "But," protests Maitreya, "it has only been a little over forty years since you became an awakened buddha. How could you have taught these innumerable bodhisattvas in such a short period of time? It is as impossible to believe as a twenty-five-year-old man claiming to have a hundred-year-old son! Or it is as if a hundred-year-old pointed to someone very young and claimed that the young man was his own father. No one can believe this. The whole world will find it hard to believe such a thing as this!" (LS 287–90)

## COMMENTARY

The bodhisattvas are said to spring up from the sky or empty space that is below the earth. Exactly what is meant by the empty space below the earth is unclear. Probably this was simply the most convenient way to have this huge number of bodhisattvas be hidden from view, yet not be in less-than-human regions, nor be among the heavenly beings, yet still be in this world. The dramatic effect of the story is dependent on the existence of these bodhisattvas being unknown to all but Shakyamuni, so they have to be hidden somewhere. But it is also important for the thrust of the story that they not be from some other world, or even from one of the heavens or purgatories associated with this world. In other words, both for the sake of the story and for the sake of the central message of the Dharma Flower Sutra, it is important that these bodhisattvas be both hidden and somehow of this world. Thus the Buddha says, "They are my children, living in this world...." (LS 286)

Indian people at the time of the Buddha had a complex cosmology in which there are heavens above the earth and purgatories below, but the earth itself, though dominated by a mountain in the middle, is relatively flat; that is, it is not a globe. There could be a sky below the earth, just as there is above it. Apparently it is from such a sky, a sky that cannot be seen, that this great multitude of bodhisattvas emerge.

Some interpreters of the Lotus Sutra may prefer to think that this space below the earth is a symbolic reference to the popular Mahayana Buddhist idea of emptiness. These bodhisattvas, they claim, emerge from emptiness. This could be right. But the Lotus Sutra is not much concerned with the concept of "emptiness," using it in a positive sense only very few times. So it seems to me to be unlikely that it is what is behind this story. What this story wants to affirm, I believe, is not the reality of emptiness, but the reality and importance of this world, this world of suffering, a world that is, after all, Shakyamuni Buddha's world and our world.

How long have these bodhisattvas been living in this space below the earth? In the text the Buddha says two things: that he has been teaching these bodhisattvas ever since he became awakened under the bodhi tree and began to turn the Dharma-wheel, which "was not long ago," and for a much longer time—"for innumerable eons" and "from the long distant past." Thus here in Chapter 15 is a vision of time that will have to be discussed in greater detail in the next chapter.

That the bodhisattvas are from the earth has traditionally been taken to be an affirmation of this world, usually called the "*saha* world" in the Sanskrit *Saddharma-pundarika Sutra*. That it is the *saha* world means that this world is the world in which suffering both must be and can be endured. There is a pattern in the Dharma Flower Sutra in which some great cosmic and supernatural event demonstrates or testifies to the cosmic importance of Shakyamuni Buddha, and, since Shakyamuni is uniquely associated with this world, its reality and importance is also affirmed in this way; and, since what Shakyamuni primarily gives to this world according to the Sutra is the Dharma

Flower Sutra itself, it too is very special and important; and, since the Dharma Flower Sutra is not the Dharma Flower Sutra unless it is read and embraced by someone, the importance of the life of the hearer or reader of the Sutra is also affirmed; and, since the most appropriate way of life for a follower of the Dharma Flower Sutra is the bodhi-sattva way, it too is elevated and affirmed. These five—Shakyamuni Buddha, this world, the Dharma Flower Sutra, the hearer or reader of the Sutra, and the bodhisattva way—do not have to appear in this particular order. Any one of them leads to an affirmation of the others. But there is a pattern in the Dharma Flower Sutra, wherein there is a radical affirmation of this world, this world of suffering, but an affirmation that is necessarily linked to the importance of Shakya-muni Buddha and the Dharma Flower Sutra on the one hand and to the lives and bodhisattva practices of those who embrace the Sutra on the other.

Thus, we can say that to truly love and follow the Buddha is also to love and care for the world, which is also to love and care for other liv-ing beings. And the reverse is equally true: to really care for others is at the same time devotion to the Buddha. To be devoted to the Dharma Flower Sutra and to Shakyamuni Buddha is to be vitally concerned about the welfare of others, the common good, and therefore about the welfare of our home, the earth.

None of these five items radically affirmed by the Dharma Flower Sutra—Shakyamuni Buddha, this world, the Dharma Flower Sutra itself, those who embrace and follow the Sutra, and the bodhisattva way—should be understood as being static or unchanging. All are alive and dynamic or they are nothing. All are in processes of learning and growth and change, often through enduring trials and suffering. This can be seen as an extension of the very basic Buddhist idea that all things are related and interdependent, always coming to be by being dependent on others.

It may seem strange to say that the Dharma Flower Sutra is alive, but what we mean by that is that unless the Sutra is somehow embodied and brought to life in the actual lives of someone, unless it makes a real difference in the actual lives of people, it amounts to nothing at all, or at least to no more than a dead book on some shelves. The Sutra does not spread itself. Its spread depends on Dharma teachers, human beings—on all of us.

It is quite revealing that the Buddha declines the offer of bodhisattvas from other worlds to help in this world. It indicates that we who live in this world have to be responsible for our own world. We can rely neither on gods nor extraterrestrial beings of any kind to fulfill our responsibilities. In recent years we have experienced extremely severe "natural calamities" all over the world. No doubt some of these were unavoidable, but almost certainly some were related to the warming trend of the earth's climate, which results directly from human activity, from releasing greater and greater quantities of carbon dioxide into the earth's atmosphere. Some potential disasters can be avoided if we realize that this is the only home we or our descendants will ever have and begin to take better care of it.

Of course, the authors and compilers of the Dharma Flower Sutra had no idea of modern environmental issues such as global warming. Still, they did have a very keen sense of the importance of this world as the home both of Shakyamuni and of themselves. They too thought that what we human beings do with our lives, how we live on this earth, is of the utmost importance.

Thus, this story is not only about affirmation of the earth. As is always the case when a text is read religiously, it is also about ourselves, in this case, the hearers or readers of the Dharma Flower Sutra. It tells us who we are—namely, people with responsibilities for this world and what it will become, people who are encouraged to follow the bodhisattva way toward being a buddha, people for whom, like Shakyamuni Buddha, this world of suffering is our world, our field of bodhisattva practice.

In this story there is also an affirmation of human life, reflecting a humanistic, positive regard for human life in this world. In greeting the Buddha, the bodhisattvas from below ask the Buddha whether he is in good health and peaceful, whether the living beings here are ready to receive the Dharma, and whether they are exhausting him. His reply is that he is in good health, that the living beings of this world are ready to receive the Dharma, and that they do not wear him out because they have already learned some important things in previous lives, where they have planted roots of goodness. Thus, a positive regard for human beings is affirmed: just as in the story of the gem in the hair, the treasure, the Dharma Flower Sutra, is given because there are many of great merit; here too there is a positive regard for human beings in general.

Nikkyo Niwano, founder of Rissho Kosei-kai, connects this story and its message of world-affirmation with the idea that Shakyamuni Buddha became awakened not as someone sent to earth by a god or as one who received a divine revelation from a transcendent realm, but through his own efforts as a human being. In this respect, Buddhism, he said, is quite different from most, perhaps all, other religions.[29]

It is appropriate, therefore, that Master Hsing Yun, founder of Fo Guang Shan—a great monastery in Taiwan, with branches all over the world, which is strongly oriented to serving people in this world and in this time—calls his teaching "Humanistic Buddhism."[30]

## THE BODHISATTVA WAY

The bodhisattva way is affirmed throughout the Dharma Flower Sutra. The Sutra does not reject other ways, neither the shravaka way nor the pratyekabuddha way, but it does make them subordinate to the way of bodhisattvas, which, revealingly, is also called "the Buddha Way." This is because the bodhisattva way is understood to be a path leading one to becoming a buddha, that is, to embodying the Buddha in one's life. Lesser goals may be useful and effective in leading one to the bodhisattva way, but they should be regarded as entrances to the way, or resting places along the way.

Thus it is that the four great bodhisattvas—Superior Practice, Unlimited Practice, Pure Practice, and Firm Practice—who lead the great horde of bodhisattvas who emerge from the earth are said to display, or correspond to, the four great bodhisattva vows:

> *Firm Practice:* However innumerable living beings are, I vow to save them all;
> *Pure Practice:* However innumerable hindrances are, I vow to overcome them all;
> *Unlimited Practice:* However innumerable the Buddha's teachings are, I vow to master them all;
> *Superior Practice:* However supreme the Buddha Way is, I vow to reach it.

These four vows make clear what the way of the bodhisattva is: It is devotion to the goal of helping everyone to attain the potential they have within themselves to be a buddha.

It is important to recognize that the bodhisattvas who spring up from the earth are not merely historical beings of the past. They include ourselves. Shakyamuni Buddha was a historical person. He was born, lived, and died on earth. So too were the leading shravakas who appear in the Dharma Flower Sutra—Shariputra, Ananda, Subhuti, Katyayana, Kashyapa, Maudgalyayana, and others. These are the names of historical people. But the famous, and not so famous, bodhisattvas are not historical, at least not in the same sense. Manjushri, Maitreya, Universal Sage (Pǔxián/Fugen/Samantabhadra), Earth Store (Dìzàng/Jizo/Kshitigharba), and Kwan-yin (Kannon/Avalokiteshvara) are the five most prominent bodhisattvas in East Asian religion and art. Though all, especially Manjushri, Maitreya, and Kwan-yin, are believed to have been embodied in a variety of historical figures, none is an actual historical figure. The same is true of other bodhisattvas who have important roles in the Dharma Flower Sutra, bodhisattvas such as Never Disrespectful, Medicine King, and Wonderful Voice, and the four leading bodhisattvas who emerge from the earth in Chapter 15. Though some are believed to have been embodied in one or more historical figures, none is historical in the sense that Shakyamuni, Shariputra, and you and I are historical. Rather, they are models for us, setting examples of bodhisattva practices that we can follow.

But the enormous horde of bodhisattvas who well up from the earth with the four leaders are perhaps a little different. They appear, not in historical time, but in a powerful story. The text says that the four groups, the monks and nuns, laymen and laywomen, could see these bodhisattvas "by the divine powers of the Buddha." This is another way of referring to the human imagination, to the power that we all have to transcend everyday life, the power to see the buddha in others. The bodhisattvas are nameless, and, except for greeting and showing respect to all the buddhas, in this story and in subsequent chapters of the Sutra they do nothing. We can understand this to mean that in a sense they are not yet. The emergence of bodhisattvas from the earth is not a one-time event in ordinary time, but an ongoing process— bodhisattvas are emerging from the earth still. And not only, of course, in India, but virtually everywhere there are human beings. If we use our own powers of imagination, we can see bodhisattvas emerging from the earth all around us! We ourselves can be among them.

Much of the time the bodhisattva in us is hidden, but from time to time it emerges out of the ground of everyday life of both suffering and joy. One way to understand the Lotus Sutra, the Dharma Flower Sutra, is to see it encouraging the emergence of bodhisattvas from the earth, like lotus flowers.

These children of the Buddha,

...

Have learned the bodhisattva way well,
And are untainted by worldly things,
Just as the lotus flower in the water
Emerges from the earth. (LS 289)

They are of the earth. They have their roots in the mud, but they also rise above the mud to blossom, bringing beauty to the world. The Dharma Flower Sutra teaches us to believe that each and every one of us can be such a bodhisattva, a gift of beauty to the world.

## THE UNIVERSAL BUDDHA

Taken together, Chapters 11, 15, and 16 of the Lotus Sutra teach the important idea of the Universal Buddha—the Buddha of every place (Chapter 11) and every time (Chapters 15 and 16). You will remember that in Chapter 11 buddhas from all over the universe are brought together by Shakyamuni Buddha in a purified and expanded version of this world to see Abundant Treasures Buddha in his stupa. These many buddhas from all over the universe are said to embody Shakyamuni Buddha. They are, thus, a powerful expression of the idea that Shakyamuni Buddha is represented everywhere and in that sense is everywhere, in all places. In Chapters 15 and 16, we learn that Shakyamuni Buddha is also in infinitely extended time, or at least something approaching infinite time, stretching back through countless ages and forward into equally countless ages.

The universality of the Buddha will receive further attention when Chapter 16 is discussed, but here I want to point out that this Chapter 15 is an important part of one of the central teachings of the Dharma Flower Sutra—that Shakyamuni Buddha is both a historical person and the one Universal Buddha, the Buddha of all times and places, one who is infinite both spatially and temporally, from the infinite past into the infinite future and in all parts of an infinite universe.

Perhaps the main purpose of the story in Chapter 15 is to set up, or provide a reason in the story for, the "revelation" of the everlasting life of the Buddha that is found primarily in Chapter 16, and to be discussed in the next chapter of this book.

# THE GOOD PHYSICIAN

C HAPTER 16 of the Lotus Sutra, titled "The Lifetime of the Tathagata," is traditionally regarded as the heart of the second half of the Sutra, just as Chapter 2 is regarded as the heart of the first half. Certainly, the central teaching of Chapter 16—that the Buddha is alive even now—is pivotal for understanding the Sutra as a whole.

In an important respect, this chapter of the Sutra is a continuation and culmination of a story found in Chapters 11 and 15, and it needs to be understood in relation to them. In Chapter 11 Shakyamuni is portrayed as the Buddha of all worlds. In order that the whole body of Abundant Treasures Buddha may be seen, Shakyamuni assembles buddhas from all over the universe. As we have seen, these other buddhas are in some sense representatives of Shakyamuni Buddha. They can be called embodiments of Shakyamuni Buddha. Thus it is clear that Shakyamuni Buddha is represented or present in the vast expanse of space.

In Chapter 15 Shakyamuni is portrayed as having been a buddha for countless eons: Shakyamuni says that the many, many bodhisattvas who emerge from below the earth have been taught by him over countless eons. Here the Buddha is present in a vast expanse of time. "Thus, since I became Buddha a very long time has passed, a lifetime of innumerable countless eons of constantly living here and never entering extinction." (LS 293)

That chapter ends with Maitreya Bodhisattva and others wondering how someone who has been living and teaching for only a few decades can be the teacher of countless bodhisattvas who lived ages and ages ago.

In Chapter 16, all of this is brought together in the teaching that Shakyamuni Buddha is the one Universal Buddha, the Buddha of all times and places, one whose life is extended indefinitely both spatially and temporally, from the extremely distant past into the distant future and in all the directions of the vast universe. This teaching has naturally given rise to calling the Buddha "Eternal Buddha" or "Eternal Shakyamuni Buddha"—though it should be noted that there is no use of such terms in the Dharma Flower Sutra itself. In the Sutra itself, the lifetime of the Buddha is said to be extremely long, but not *outside of time*—which is the most common use of "eternal" in Western philosophy and theology.

The Buddha explains that in different times and different worlds he has assumed different names, taught different sutras, used different teaching devices, and so on as appropriate to the situation, all for the one purpose of leading all living beings to buddha-wisdom.

To illustrate this, the Buddha relates the parable of the good physician.

## THE PARABLE

Once upon a time there was a wise and good doctor with many sons. One day, after the father had left home on business, the sons unknowingly drank some poison that they had found in the house. Returning home, the father found the children writhing on the floor, sick from the poison. By that time, some of them had completely lost their minds, while others were not yet so seriously affected.

Seeing that the father had come back, the sons were very happy and begged him to cure them of the poison. The father consulted his books, prepared an appropriate medicine, and urged the sons to take it to free themselves from their illness, suffering, and agony. The sons who had been least affected by the poison saw right away that the medicine was good for them, took it, and were immediately cured. Others, however, were further gone and could not see that the medicine would help them, and so refused to take it.

The father, realizing this, decided to devise a way to reach them and get them to take the medicine. He told them that he was getting old and would soon die, but was leaving a good medicine for them, with the recommendation that they take it. Then he went away again, and sent back a messenger with news that he had died.

The sons, hearing that the father had died, felt lonely, deserted, and helpless. "If our father were alive he would have been kind to us, and would have saved us. But now he has abandoned us and died in a distant land. We think of ourselves as orphans, with no one to rely on." (LS 295) But this grief caused them to come to their senses, whereupon they realized that the medicine would indeed be good for them, took it, and were completely cured. Learning that his sons had recovered, the father returned home.

## COMMENTARY

The physician-father, of course, represents the Buddha, and his supposed death is like the Buddha's entry into final nirvana, his human death. In reality, though, the Universal Buddha, the loving father of the world who is working even now to save all from suffering, did not die. The Buddha's death and entry into final nirvana, like the physician-father's report of his own death, is a story told in order to get people's attention, to get them to wake up and take greater responsibility for their own lives.

One other lesson we might see is that the same medicine is not always good or equally effective for all. Some of the children are immediately cured by the father's medicine; others are not because they don't take it. This medicine is like the rain of the Dharma in Chapter 5, the same rain that goes everywhere to nourish all kinds of plants, but is received differently because people are different in their abilities, in what they like and dislike, and in their backgrounds. In other words, Buddha-medicine needs to be different for different people. What is important is to discern what medicine will actually work for someone. The medicine prepared for and given to the children is not really medicine at all for them until they actually take it. A medicine that is not taken, no matter how well prepared and no matter how good the intentions of the physician, is not effective, not skillful, not yet really medicine.

The same is true of the Buddha Dharma. It has to be taken or embraced by somebody, has to become real spiritual nourishment for someone, in order to be effective. Again, this is why in the Dharma Flower Sutra teaching is always a two-way relationship. The Dharma is not the Dharma until it is received and embraced by someone. And, of course, people are different—so the Dharma has to be taught in a great variety of ways, using different stories, different teachings, poetry as well as prose, and so on.

The same is true of religious practices. For some Buddhists, meditation is effective; for others, recitation; for others, careful observance of precepts; for still others, sutra study; and so on. It is through an ample variety of teachings and practices that the Dharma has been effective and can be effective still. If we insist that there is only one proper way to practice Buddhism, it would be as if the physician in this story decided to let the children die because they did not immediately take the medicine he had offered.

A closely related idea is that even the most heavily poisoned can be saved—though saving them may require more wisdom, more effort, and more creativity. The father in this parable does not give up just because at first he does not succeed. Though the idea of universal salvation—the idea that all are capable of becoming a buddha—is certainly not unique to the Dharma Flower Sutra, it is central to the teachings of the Sutra, and is taught and suggested there in a great many ways. No doubt one of the reasons for the near extinction of the doctrine that there are beings with absolutely no possibility of awakening in them, who are, therefore, beyond hope of any kind of salvation—the so-called *icchantika*[31]—has been the enormous popularity of the Dharma Flower Sutra in East Asia. Under the influence of this Sutra and other teachings, the universality of buddha-nature won out over the idea that some people are beyond any possibility of awakening.

Though he does not appear in the Lotus Sutra, Medicine (or Healing) Buddha (Yakushi Nyorai in Japanese, Yao-shi Ju-lai [Yàoshī Rúlái] in Chinese, Bhaiṣajya-guru in Sanskrit) is very popular in East Asia as one who is prayed to for long life, and who cures people of illness—including disease and ignorance. He is often portrayed as one of a trio of buddhas along with Shakyamuni Buddha and Amida Buddha. Many sutras are dedicated to him, including an entire sutra dedicated to his vows. Yet in this story it is not Medicine Buddha but Shakyamuni Buddha who is portrayed as a medicine buddha, as one who has profound knowledge of medicine and seeks to cure those who have become deranged by the poisons of the world. This is one reason why these three buddhas—Shakyamuni Buddha, Medicine Buddha, and Amida Buddha—are often conflated, or integrated, in the minds and hearts of ordinary Buddhists in East Asia. Shakyamuni himself is a medicine buddha, a healing buddha.

We should notice that, as in the parable of the burning house of Chapter 3 of the Sutra, the dangers—the fire and many other terrible things in Chapter 3 and the poison in Chapter 16—are found in the fathers' houses. Some have raised questions as to why the Buddha would be so careless as to have such a fire-hazard of a house or why he would leave poison lying around in a house full of children. This kind of question probably presupposes that the Buddha is somehow all-powerful and creates and controls the world. But that is not a Buddhist premise. In the Dharma Flower Sutra the point of having the danger occur in the Buddha's home is to indicate a very close relationship between the Buddha and this world. The world that is dangerous for children is the world in which the Buddha—like all of us—also lives.

While Medicine Buddha is the Buddha of the East, just as Amida Buddha is the Buddha of the West, Shakyamuni Buddha is the Buddha of this world in which suffering both has to be endured and can be. He is, in other words, our Buddha in a special way. Because he is not all-powerful, and even suffers himself, he can understand the sufferings of others, be compassionate toward them, and offer wise and compassionate help, just like a wise and good physician. Thus Shakyamuni is our Medicine Buddha, the Medicine Buddha of this world.

The parables in the Dharma Flower Sutra do not say that the fathers created the burning house or the poison found in the home of the physician. Shakyamuni Buddha has inherited this world, or perhaps even chose to live in this world, in order to help the living. The dangers in this world are simply part of the reality of this world. Indeed, it is because of them that good medicine and good physicians are needed here.

In both of these stories of a father and his children, and in the parable of the rich father and poor son (as well as in other stories in the Dharma Flower Sutra), it is important to recognize that the father *helps* the children, *facilitates* the liberation of the children—he does not, and indeed cannot, somehow rescue them by force. Nor does he save them by demanding their obedience; he does not set up laws and punish offenders. Rather, he skillfully creates a situation in which his children are encouraged to save themselves. The important lesson here is, of course, that we too need to recognize and lead others to recognize that while we have all been offered good medicine by the Buddha, while always and everywhere we are being helped by the Buddha, still, we too have to save ourselves. Neither Shakyamuni Buddha nor Medicine Buddha nor any other buddha will do it for us; no one will carry us out of the burning house or force us to take our medicine. We too have to be finally responsible for our own actions, for our own way of life, for our own health and salvation.

The Buddha has come into the world of suffering and suffers with the living beings of this world. Like others, he participates in the creation of the world at every moment. He does so by being a teacher and medicine giver, not by being a kind of external, unilateral power. Above all, the Buddha is a teacher. And it is precisely in reference to his being a teacher that bodhisattvas are so frequently referred to in the Dharma Flower Sutra as children of the Buddha. Those whose lives are shaped by the teachings of the Buddha, by the Buddha Dharma, have been created as much by the Buddha's words as by their biological parents. But, like normal parents, the Buddha does not have absolute power over his children. Like the father in the parable of the rich father and poor son in Chapter 4, the Buddha longs for his children to be ready to receive their inheritance from him, his great wealth of the Dharma.

The Buddha can be called the loving father of all, not because he has complete power over others, but precisely because he does not. Far from demanding that human beings be obedient to him, the Buddha challenges us to enter into and take up the way of the bodhisattva, a way to which we can be led but cannot be forced to enter. Like the poor son in Chapter 4, we may need encouragement in order to learn gradually to accept responsibility for the responsibilities we have inherited, for the buddhas' business, or, like the weary travelers in Chapter 7, we may need a resting place, even an illusory one, in order to pursue the valuable treasure in our own lives, but finally it is we ourselves who have to be responsible.

Various reasons are given in the Sutra as to why the Buddha has announced his entry into final nirvana when actually he is still alive in this world. For example: "If the Buddha lives for a long time in this world, people of little virtue will not plant roots of goodness, and those who are poor and of humble origins will become attached to the five desires and be caught in a net of assumptions and false views. If they see that the Tathagata is always alive and never extinct, they will become arrogant and selfish or discouraged and neglectful. Unable to realize how difficult it is to meet him, they will not have a respectful attitude toward him." (LS 293)

It is useful to understand these terms through the vehicle of the parables. The children in the parable of the burning house are too absorbed in their play to notice what is going on around them, including their father's attempts to warn them of the dangers. The son in the parable of the rich father and poor son is simply lacking in self-confidence and self-respect. The children in this parable are stricken by poison. All are in need of help and guidance, but what they need guidance for is to accept greater responsibility for the direction and quality of their own lives. In this way, they can, perhaps only very gradually, become bodhisattvas, and take responsibility for doing the Buddha's work in this world.

And yet, even though stories have been told about the death of the Buddha, even now the Buddha is not really dead. He is still with us, alive in this world, living the bodhisattva way, doing the bodhisattva work of transforming people into bodhisattvas and purifying buddha lands. "From the beginning," he says, "I have practiced the bodhisattva way, and that life is not yet finished...." (LS 293)

When the Dharma Flower Sutra says that the Buddha is somehow embodied or represented in all directions throughout time and space, it is not claiming that the Buddha is somehow beyond time and history—in fact, it is saying something that is nearly the opposite: namely, that no matter where we go, whether on foot or by spaceship, and no matter when in our lives, whether celebrating our eighteenth birthday or lying on our deathbed, there is no place and no time in which the Buddha is not available to us.

The father returns home after the children have been shocked into taking the medicine and have recovered. The children are able to see him once again. By taking good medicine, the Dharma, people are able to see the Buddha, even though he died some twenty-five hundred years ago. To incorporate the Dharma into one's life is to be able to see the Buddha. The Buddha can be found in anybody and anything at all. This is what it means for the Buddha to be universal: he is to be found whenever and wherever we look for him.

Chapter 16 ends with an interesting and important verse, spoken by the Buddha:

> I am always thinking:
> "How can I lead all the living
> To enter the unexcelled way
> And quickly perfect their Buddha-bodies?" (LS 299)

The Buddha's purpose is to lead the living to enter the unsurpassed way and quickly take on the body of a buddha, embody the Buddha. The Chinese verb that I have here translated as "perfect" might more literally be rendered as "fulfill" or "realize." The point is that it is something we *do* or *can do*. It is an activity, not a dead end. It is an opportunity more than an achievement. The purpose of the Dharma, in other words, is to lead people to act like buddhas, that is, to be *doers* of the bodhisattva way, and, in this sense, the wider purpose is to enable each of us to be the Buddha in the world for anyone to see. When we do that, when we make it possible for others to see the Buddha, we ourselves will be able to see countless buddhas, not only when we are dreaming, but even when we are most awake.

By embodying the Buddha in our own lives through living the bodhisattva way, we give life to the Buddha in the present. In a sense, we are creating the Buddha, contributing to the shaping of the life that is the ongoing life of the Buddha.

# 21

# NEVER DISRESPECTFUL BODHISATTVA

I N A STORY told by Manjushri Bodhisattva in the first chapter of the Lotus Sutra, we find a bodhisattva named Fame Seeker. This bodhisattva, we are told, "was greedily attached to lucrative offerings, and, though he read and memorized many sutras, he gained little from it and forgot almost all of them.... But because he had planted roots of goodness, this man too was able to meet innumerable hundreds of thousands of billions of buddhas, make offerings to them, revere, honor, and praise them."(LS 67) In a subsequent life Fame Seeker became Maitreya Bodhisattva, the future Buddha of this world.

In the story told by Shakyamuni Buddha in Chapter 20, we find a somewhat similar bodhisattva, one named Never Disrespectful.

## THE STORY

The Buddha tells the bodhisattva Great Strength about another buddha named Majestic Voice King who lived long, long ago and taught what was appropriate to those who were seeking to become shravakas or pratyekabuddhas as well as to bodhisattvas seeking supreme awakening. His exceedingly long lifetime was followed by that of another buddha of the same name, who was succeeded one by one by two tril-lion other buddhas, all with the same name.

Following the first of these buddhas, during an age of superficial, merely formal Dharma when there were many arrogant monks, there was a bodhisattva monk known as Never Disrespectful. He was called this because whenever he encountered any individual or any group of people, be they monks or nuns or laypeople, he would announce that he would never dare to disrespect them or make light of them because they were all actually bodhisattvas on the way to becoming buddhas.

He did not devote himself to reading or chanting sutras, but simply went around bowing to people and telling them why he would never disrespect them, never put them down or make little of them. And yet people resented his constant assurances that they would become bud-dhas in the future, and they often cursed and abused him, sometimes throwing things at him and forcing him to run away and hide in the distance. Yet he continued for many years the same practice of always respecting others, constantly refusing to make little of anyone, and assuring everyone that they were on the way to becoming buddhas.

When he was about to die, from the sky Never Disrespectful Bodhi-sattva heard the entire Dharma Flower Sutra that had been preached by Majestic Voice King Buddha. By embracing this Sutra, his eyes, ears, nose, tongue, body, and mind were purified, enabling him to prolong his life for countless ages and to preach the Dharma Flower Sutra to a great many people.

Seeing his fantastic powers, many people, including those who had abused him, came to respect and follow him and receive the Dharma from him. And after the end of his extremely long life, he was able to meet millions and millions of buddhas and could preach the Dharma Flower Sutra to them and to their followers. As a consequence of this, he was able to meet still more millions and millions of buddhas and preach in their presence.

This bodhisattva, the Buddha says, was Shakyamuni Buddha himself in a previous life. It was Shakyamuni's preaching of the Dharma Flower Sutra in former lives that enabled him to attain supreme awakening. And the monks and nuns and laypeople who abused Never Disrespectful Bodhisattva, after suffering for an enormously long time from not seeing a buddha or hearing the Dharma or being in the community, are now, says the Buddha, present in the congregation as the five hundred bodhisattvas, five hundred nuns, and five hundred laypeople who do not falter in their pursuit of supreme awakening.

## COMMENTARY

In some translations of the Lotus Sutra this bodhisattva is called "Never Disparaging" or "Never Despise." This is a curious matter. In the existing Sanskrit versions he is called Sadāparibhūta, which means "always held in contempt" or perhaps "always despised." But the Chinese translation, Ch'ang Pu-ch'ing (Cháng Bùqīng; Jōfugyō or Jōfukyō in Japanese pronunciation), means "never treating lightly," though this name by itself can easily be understood to mean "never despise." Thus in Chinese translation his name has been reversed from "always despised" to "never despising"—though there is no contradiction in these terms.

In the Dharma Flower Sutra, bodhisattvas, especially those appearing in the last eight chapters, including this bodhisattva, are intended to be models for us, at least to some degree. I do not mean that we are supposed to behave exactly like any of these bodhisattvas, especially not like Medicine King Bodhisattva in Chapter 23 who burns himself. But these bodhisattva stories are clearly intended as examples having to do with the conduct of our own lives.

So what is being taught in this story? Most people, I believe, never, or at least nearly never, *despise* other people. We might occasionally meet someone we do not like, but we do not usually go around *despising* others. But all of us, all too often I believe, do in fact speak and act in ways that are disrespectful of others. Usually, I suppose, this is not deliberate or intentional, but arises from being careless or busy or self-absorbed or just ignorant of what may create feelings of being belittled in others. So never being disrespectful is a serious challenge for each of us. And that, I believe, is what this chapter intends to teach us—that we should always and everywhere respect other people, all other people. This means finding the good in others, even if, as in the case of Never Disrespectful Bodhisattva, they are throwing sticks and stones (or worse!) at us.

Never Disrespectful Bodhisattva, we are told, lived in an era of merely formal Dharma. In Buddhism it is often taught that there are three or four phases of the Dharma, what we might think of as phases in the life of the Dharma. The first can be called the phase of true Dharma; the second, merely formal Dharma; and the third, the end of the Dharma. One common interpretation has it that in the first phase, the phase of true, real, correct, or right Dharma, following the life of a buddha in the world, the Buddha's teachings are taught and practiced and awakening is sometimes achieved. We can think of this as a time of living Dharma, a time when the Dharma has a deep impact on people's lives. In the second phase, the teachings are practiced but awakening is generally not possible because the teachings are only superficially held and practiced. In the third phase the teachings exist but they are not practiced at all, not embodied in the lives of people. Sometimes a fourth phase is added, a period in which the teachings themselves are no longer even present. Eventually, another Buddha emerges and the cycle begins again.

While this pattern of phases is quite common in Buddhism, we do not find it in the Dharma Flower Sutra. There we find the end of the Dharma mentioned directly only twice, and perhaps indirectly twice, but never in connection with the phases of true Dharma and merely formal Dharma. These first two phases, on the other hand, are often mentioned together, suggesting that there is a two-phase cycle in which a new phase of true Dharma follows a phase of merely formal Dharma. In Chapter 20, this two-phase cycle is clearly endorsed. Setting the scene for the appearance of Never Disrespectful Bodhisattva, we are told that "after the true Dharma and merely formal Dharma had entirely disappeared, another buddha appeared in that land." (LS 338) And this event of a period of true Dharma not only preceding but also following a period of merely formal Dharma is said to have happened two trillion times in succession!

The term that I have translated as "merely formal Dharma" is sometimes called "semblance," "imitation," or "counterfeit" Dharma. The Chinese character used for the name of this phase basically means "image," as a statue or picture of a buddha is an image of a buddha. In such a period, Buddhism is characterized by formality and lack of depth. Buddhist monks become proud of learning the teachings, sutras, and ceremonies, but there is little real application of the teachings in the world. Institutions and other teaching devices, formalities of various kinds, tend to be elevated to ultimate importance. People fail to see the buddha-nature in themselves or in others.

We can only speculate as to why this three-phase cosmology is not in the Dharma Flower Sutra. My sense of it is that in the context of the Dharma Flower Sutra it is not appropriate to believe that the end of the Dharma, the third phase, is inevitable. Virtually the whole thrust of the Sutra is to encourage keeping the Dharma alive by embodying it in everyday life. It simply would not make good sense to repeatedly urge people to keep the Dharma alive by receiving, embracing, reading, reciting, and copying it, and teaching and practicing it if a decline of the Dharma were inevitable. The Dharma Flower Sutra teaches that the bodhisattva path is difficult, even extremely difficult, but it cannot be impossible. Even the many assurances of becoming a buddha that we find in the first half of the Sutra should, I think, be taken as a kind of promise that supreme awakening is always possible.

We can, of course, understand the three phases not as an inevitable sequence of periods of time, but as existential phases of our own lives. There will be times when the Dharma can be said to be truly alive in us, times when our practice is more like putting on a show and has little depth, and times when the life of the Dharma in us is in serious decline. But there is no inevitable sequence here. There is no reason, for example, why a period of true Dharma cannot follow a period of merely formal Dharma. And there is no reason to assume that a period has to be completed once it has been entered. We might lapse into a period of decline, but with the proper influences and circumstances we could emerge from it into a more vital phase of true Dharma. A coming evil age is mentioned several times in the Dharma Flower Sutra, but while living in an evil age, or an evil period of our own lives, makes teaching the Dharma difficult, even extremely difficult, nowhere does the Dharma Flower Sutra suggest that it is impossible to teach or practice true Dharma.

In the West we like to see things neatly divided into two. If something is not true, it is false. If it is not real, it is fake. If it is not good, it is evil. If it is not alive, it is dead. Such an attitude, I believe, is deeply rooted in Western religious ideas of there being a final determination of all souls as worthy either of everlasting bliss or everlasting punishment.

If we approach the idea of three phases of the Dharma with such a dualistic assumption, from a perspective of true Dharma, it is nearly inevitable that we will think of the second phase, the Merely Formal phase, as simply not-true, lumping the phases of merely formal Dharma and of end of the Dharma together and failing to appreciate the very important notion here that there are three phases of the Dharma, not merely two. If, on the other hand, we were to look at the first and second phases from a perspective of the third, we could say that they, both the first and the second, are not the decline or end of the Dharma. Both perspectives are partly correct: the second phase, the phase of merely formal Dharma, is neither true Dharma nor the end of the Dharma.

It is a fact that Shakyamuni Buddha, who was once alive and who taught the Dharma, died. He became a "historical figure," someone really dead in an important sense. In his place as objects of devotion were such things as relics, stupas, pictures, and statues. Compared with a living human being, such things are dead. And then these dead things are put into museums and become even less alive. Or temples housing them become museums, tourist attractions, or funeral parlors, where the Dharma can be said to be dead. Teachings may be followed, but not in a very profound or sincere way.

But while an "image" of the Buddha is not the real thing, neither is it without value. It can be a way of keeping the Buddha alive in the world and in ourselves, though not in the way he was alive as a historical human being. I will always be grateful to "the Buddha" in the basement of Boston's Museum of Fine Arts with whom I sat quite regularly when experiencing difficult times as a student. I did not receive the whole Dharma, the living Dharma, from that Buddha, but I did receive something very valuable. So, too, if a temple comes to function mainly as a tourist attraction, or as only a place for funerals and memorial services for the dead, it may serve as a skillful means to lead some to deeper interest in the Buddha Dharma. And teachings that are not followed in a very profound way can nonetheless be gateways to more sincere practice. This is, I believe, one reason that in the Dharma Flower Sutra, periods of merely formal Dharma are not followed by periods of the decline of the Dharma but rather by new periods of true Dharma.

## BODHISATTVA PRACTICE BEGINS WITH RESPECTING OTHERS

Teachers of the Lotus Sutra often say that it teaches the bodhisattva way of helping others. Unfortunately, this is sometimes understood to mean intruding where one is not wanted, interfering with the lives of others, in order to "do good." But the story of Never Disrespectful Bodhisattva may lead us to see that doing good for others begins with respecting them, seeing the buddha in them. If we sincerely look for the potential in someone else to be a buddha, rather than criticizing or complaining about negative factors, we will be encouraged by the positive things that we surely will find. And furthermore, by looking for the good in others, we can come to have a more positive attitude ourselves and thus move along our own bodhisattva path.

In earlier chapters of the Lotus Sutra, it is the Buddha who is able to see the potential to become a buddha in others. But here it becomes very clear that seeing the buddha or the buddha-potential in others is something we all should practice, both for the good of others and for our own good.

Respecting others, recognizing their buddha-potential, though it may *involve* being kind, is not the same as kindness. Nor does it mean always praising others. Sometimes criticism is what is most needed. In my own experience as an employer, I have sometimes found it necessary to take the harsh measure of firing people from a job, forcing them to do something about a serious problem, such as alcoholism. In the Lotus Sutra as well, in Chapter 4 we find the father speaking to his workers, including his son, in a "rough" manner, saying such things as "Get to work! Don't be so lazy!" (LS 144) Knowing when to be critical and how to be critical without being hurtful is itself an art, for which there are few rules.

Over and over again in the Dharma Flower Sutra we are encouraged to "receive, embrace, read, recite, copy, teach, and practice" the Dharma Flower Sutra. Thus, the fact that Never Disrespectful Bodhisattva did not read or recite sutras is quite interesting. I think it is an expression of the general idea in the Dharma Flower Sutra that, while various practices are very important, what is even more important is how one lives one's life in relation to others. The references to bodhisattvas who do not follow normal monastic practices, including reading and recitation of sutras, but still become fully awakened buddhas indicates that putting the Dharma into one's daily life by respecting others, and in this way embodying the Dharma, is more important than formal practices such as reading and recitation.

Yet showing respect for others needs to be as sincere as possible. If we take being respectful to be only a matter of mere formality, only a matter of being polite, then we will likely miss the significance of what is being taught in the story of Never Disrespectful Bodhisattva. Bowing to others is one of the ways in which he shows respect for those he meets; the bowing is not his respect itself. Respect for others is something in one's heart that can be expressed, more or less well, with words and gestures such as bowing, but that should not be confused with its expressions.

The relation between sincere respect and its expressions in gestures and words is something like the relation between true Dharma and merely formal Dharma. And yet expressions of respect even when respect is not sincerely felt can still be good. What we can think of as ritual politeness—saying "Thank you" when receiving something, even if we do not feel grateful; asking "How are you?" when greeting someone and not even waiting for a response; saying "I'm sorry" when we do not really feel sorry—can all contribute to smoother social relations. Just as true Dharma is greater than merely formal Dharma, being truly grateful is greater than expressing gratitude in a merely formal way, and heartfelt sincerity is greater than merely conventional politeness, but even social conventions and polite expressions can be an important ingredient in relations between people and can contribute to mutual harmony and respect.

When we bow in respect before a buddha image, is it an expression of deep respect or merely a habit? When the object of our sutra recitation is to get to the end as quickly as possible or to demonstrate skill in reading rapidly, is our recitation anything more than a formality?

When we take a moment to pray with others for world peace, are we expressing a profound aspiration for world peace, an aspiration that is bound to lead to appropriate actions, or are we simply conforming to social expectations? Probably in most cases, the truth lies somewhere in the middle, where our gestures and expressions are neither deeply felt nor completely superficial and empty. It is possible, after all, to be a little sincere or a little grateful. We should, of course, try to become more and more genuinely grateful and sincere, but we should not disparage those important social conventions, often different in different cultures, found in one way or another in virtually all cultures.

In Chapter 2 of the Lotus Sutra we find such expressions as this:

If anyone, even while distracted,
With even a single flower,
Makes an offering to a painted image,
They will progressively see countless buddhas. (LS 94)

If making an offering with just a single flower while being distracted can be a sign of taking the Buddha Way, surely such things as expressions of gratitude or apology, even superficial ones, can be signs of respect for others. Just as "merely formal" Dharma is better than no Dharma at all, small signs of respect are much better than no respect at all.

Never Disrespectful Bodhisattva tells everyone he meets, even extremely arrogant monks, even those who are angry, disrespectful, and mean-spirited, that they have taken the bodhisattva way. If what he says is true, surely whenever we make even superficial expressions of gratitude or apology, we are to some degree showing respect, a sign that, like Never Disrespectful Bodhisattva, we too have—to some slight but very important degree—taken the bodhisattva way that will lead to our awakening.

It is significant that Never Disrespectful Bodhisattva tells everyone he meets, including those who are arrogant, angry, disrespectful, and mean-spirited, that they are bodhisattvas. Often in Buddhism, bodhisattvas are thought to be extremely high in rank, second only to buddhas. In typical Buddhist art this is expressed by showing bodhisattvas dressed in the fine clothes and wearing the jewelry of princes. But here we are to understand that everyone, including very ordinary people, is a bodhisattva. Though his appearance is not described, it is easy to imagine Never Disrespectful Bodhisattva himself as an ordinary monk. Of course we should respect great bodhisattvas and great people, but part of the message of this story is that there is a bodhisattva to be respected in everyone we meet.

# 22

## DIVINE POWERS OF A BUDDHA

FROM THE TIME of its early interpretations in China, the Lotus Sutra has been taken to have two halves. The early fifth-century Chinese commentator Tao-sheng (Daosheng), for example, made a division of the book between the present Chapters 14 and 15, regarding Chapters 1 through 14 as the first half of the Sutra, revealing that the cause of the three vehicles is the one vehicle, and regarding Chapters 15 through 22 as the second half, revealing that the effect of the three vehicles is the same as that of the one vehicle. And he saw the remaining chapters, now numbered 23 through 28, as a kind of appendix.[32]

In the sixth century, T'ian-t'ai Chih-i (Tiantai Zhiyi),[33] the most influential interpreter of the Lotus Sutra, basically followed this same division, understanding the two "halves" to be like gateways or entrances to the Dharma. Subsequently the first half was often associated with the teaching of one vehicle, which is found especially in Chapter 2, sometimes with the historical Shakyamuni Buddha. The second half was associated with the Original, or Eternal, Shakyamuni Buddha.

Thus the Lotus Sutra proper was understood to come to a kind of end and logical conclusion with the "Entrustment" of Chapter 22.

The brief Chapter 21, "Divine Powers of the Tathagata," particularly the symbolism of its story, has traditionally been taken to signify the unity of the Sutra. Despite the seeming duality of the two halves, the symbolism of the story is taken to express the unity in principle of the two. Analyzing the Sutra into two halves, in a sense, divides it. In this chapter we are encouraged to remember that the two halves are two halves of a whole, of a unity.

## THE STORY

All of the billions of bodhisattvas who had sprung up from below the earth in the story in Chapter 15 promise the Buddha that they will continue to preach the Dharma Flower Sutra everywhere, both in the worlds where the Buddha is embodied in other buddhas and in this world in which the Buddha has died. "Why?" they ask rhetorically, "Because we too want to gain this true and pure, great Dharma, to embrace, read and recite, explain, copy, and make offerings to it." (LS 345)

The Buddha then displays his divine powers by extending his long and broad tongue up to the Brahma heaven and emitting from the pores of his body a magnificent, many-colored light that illuminates all the worlds in all directions. Similarly, the other assembled buddhas seated on lion seats under jewel trees stretch out their tongues and emit rays of light from their own bodies.

After hundreds of thousand years, all these buddhas draw back their tongues, cough simultaneously, and snap their fingers in unison. These two sounds travel throughout the universe, causing the earth in each of the lands to shake in the six ways.

Through this display of divine powers, all of the living beings in all the other worlds are able to see all of the buddhas and bodhisattvas and others assembled in this world, making them full of great joy as a consequence of obtaining something they had never had before, the ability to see this world. Then heavenly beings, gods, and others, singing in loud voices, proclaim that Shakyamuni Buddha is now preaching the Lotus Sutra in this world and that all should rejoice and make suitable offerings to him.

All the living beings then praise the Buddha, saying "Praise to Shakyamuni Buddha! Praise to Shakyamuni Buddha!" They take flowers, incense, necklaces, banners, ornaments, jewels, all sorts of decorations, and toss them in the direction of this world, where they come together like clouds and form a canopy over the place where the buddhas are assembled. Then the way between all the worlds opens up, as though there were a single world.

The Buddha then tells Superior Practice and the other bodhisattvas that all of the Buddha's teachings, divine powers, secrets, and profound matters are revealed and taught in this Sutra. For this reason, bodhisattvas should embrace, read and recite, explain and copy, and cultivate and practice it as they had been taught. Wherever this is done a stupa should be erected, as such a place is a place of turning the wheel of the Dharma and of supreme awakening.

In the verses that conclude the chapter, the Buddha promises again that anyone who keeps the Sutra and teaches according to its true meaning will illuminate the gloom of living beings. Causing others to enter the Mahayana way, they will be able to attain the awakening of a buddha.

> Just as the light of the sun and the moon
> Can dispel darkness,
> Such a person, working in the world,
> Can dispel the gloom of living beings,
> Leading innumerable bodhisattvas
> Finally to dwell in the one vehicle. (LS 349)

## COMMENTARY

The Chinese/Japanese term which is translated here as "divine powers" is *jin-riki* in Japanese pronunciation, literally god-power, where both "god" and "power" can be understood as either singular or plural. Often the term is translated as "supernatural powers." But in Asian Buddhism there is not as sharp a distinction as there is in the West between what is natural and what is supernatural. In the midst of everyday life, marvelous things happen. They are extraordinary, even supernatural in some sense, but they are not necessarily a consequence of external powers or of divine intervention in the workings of nature.

The divine powers displayed in this story are said to be ten in all, five having to do with the past and five with the future. The second five can be understood as consequences of the first five being widely implemented. While these ten are known as "divine powers," they are actually events—events that display special, magical powers, some by buddhas, some by others. Let's look at each briefly in turn and explore its significance.

*The Buddha's long and broad tongue.* The long and broad tongue reaching to the Brahma heaven testifies to the truth of what had been taught. It is a way of affirming that what the Buddha teaches is true, especially true in the sense of being effective in relieving suffering. This tongue symbolizes the length and breadth the Dharma: it is both broad or inclusive and long in that it can reach everywhere. Though it takes many forms, the Dharma goes everywhere and is one; that is, it is neither divided nor fragmented.

Thus this image of the long and broad tongue reaching to the heavens is called a symbol of *nimon-shin'itsu*, "two gateways, one in faith." That is, in faith the two halves of the Sutra are one, and Shakyamuni Buddha and the Original Buddha are one. This is why in Rissho Kosei-kai, for instance, the central object of religious devotion is called "Eternal Shakyamuni Buddha."

This unity of Shakyamuni Buddha and the Original Buddha is related to the Dharma Flower Sutra's repeated affirmation of the reality and importance of this concrete, actual world. The original, universal Buddha is always an embodied Buddha—for us, principally Shakyamuni Buddha, who is uniquely the Buddha of this world, the one declared in the Lotus Sutra to be the "father of this world." The abstract universal and original Buddha has to be embodied in order to make a difference in this world. Without Shakyamuni Buddha, for us at least, there might be no buddha at all. Even the three Pure Land Sutras, which are the textual basis for devotion to Amida Buddha, like the Dharma Flower Sutra are said to have been preached on Eagle Peak by Shakyamuni Buddha. Regardless of what buddha is the main object of art or devotion, the whole Buddhist tradition has its historical origin in Shakyamuni Buddha.

*Emitting light of innumerable colors from every pore.* The light of truth dispels the darkness both of delusion and of despair. This points to the truth that it is better to illuminate the darkness than to complain about it, that is, to the importance of being positive. With its emphasis on the potential of all living beings to become buddhas, its affirmation of the reality and importance of actual life, its insistence on making the best of every situation, the Dharma Flower Sutra is an affirmative book, affirming not only life and the world, but especially the life and world of the hearer or reader of the Sutra.

Light is something positive; darkness, merely the absence of light. Similarly, ignorance can be understood as an absence of truth, and delusion as an absence of reality. The Dharma Flower Sutra encourages us to focus not on the negativities of darkness, ignorance, and delusion, but on ways to limit and overcome them by spreading light and truth and compassion.

That all of the other buddhas also stretch out their tongues and emit light from their pores should be taken to mean that all buddhas have realized and teach the same truth. It is a symbol of *nimon-ri'itsu*, "two gateways, one in principle." Even though there are two apparently different gateways to the path of awakening, in principle they are united as one.

That the light from the Buddha is of innumerable colors means that even though the Buddha's teachings are united into a coherent unity, they are also rich in variety. The Dharma Flower Sutra itself seldom, if ever, teaches anything in only one way, but puts things in a variety of ways.

*The buddhas cough simultaneously.* This strange event, not easily interpreted, may signify the oral preaching of the Dharma, as one often has to clear one's throat with a slight cough before speaking before an audience. That this coughing is done simultaneously has been taken to signify that all buddhas teach the same thing. This event is also taken as signifying that the teachings are united as one. This is a symbol of *nimon-kyo'itsu,* "two gates, one in teaching," affirming that in principle the way of the shravakas and the way of the bodhisattvas are united as one teaching.

*The buddhas snap their fingers in unison.* This equally strange event is said to represent giving assurance to someone, or making a pledge or a promise. It is called *nimon-nin'itsu,* "two gateways, one in humanity." It is taken to symbolize the important activity of identifying with others, an essential and vital part of bodhisattva practice. One might even say that fundamental to the practice of the bodhisattva way is sympathy for others, a sense of being united with someone else in a profound way. And, as Rissho Kosei-kai's Founder Niwano wrote, "the entire teaching of the Lotus Sutra is ultimately resolved into the spirit of union between oneself and others."[34]

With the dramatic acts of coughing and finger-snapping, the text invites us not only to see something marvelous with the eyes of imagination but also to imagine hearing the marvelous sounds of countless buddhas coughing simultaneously and snapping their fingers in unison. That these sounds are extremely powerful is signified by their being heard in all of the worlds throughout the universe.

*These sounds cause all the buddha lands to tremble and shake.* The trembling and shaking in the six ways[35] of all the lands in all the worlds expresses the idea that the entire universe and everything in it is moved by the fantastic powers of the Buddha. Here divine powers are displayed not by the buddhas directly but by the buddha lands. An influence of Buddha Dharma over nature is affirmed here. The Dharma Flower Sutra proclaims over and over that the Dharma is not only a human thing but a cosmic reality. Also recognized here is the sense that when we hear the Sutra preached we should be moved, even shaken, from our normal pursuits, to the point of actually following the teachings in daily life.

The Japanese expression for this is *nimon-gyo'itsu,* "two gateways, one practice." This does not mean that the same practice is suitable for everyone, but that there is a profound unity among authentic practices. As is said clearly in Chapter 2 of the Dharma Flower Sutra, skillful means are many, but they serve one common purpose.

*All of the living beings of all the worlds are able to see those in this world.* In the first chapter of the Lotus Sutra, the Buddha emits a light by which people in this world can see everything in all the other worlds, but in this case it is the opposite. By emitting light from this world, all of the living beings in other worlds can see Shakyamuni Buddha and Abundant Treasures Buddha and all of the buddhas, bodhisattvas, monks and nuns, and laypeople in this world. That all kinds of living beings can see by the buddhas' light means that all can live by the wisdom of the Dharma—that all living beings, human and nonhuman, even those in other worlds, can live by the Buddha's light.

This is called *mirai-ki'itsu,* "in the future, unity of opportunity." This means that there is no essential difference in the capacity to receive the Dharma among living beings—all can become awakened in the future.

*Heavenly beings in the sky sing in loud voices that Shakyamuni Buddha is teaching the Lotus Sutra.* What is expressed here is the importance of the Buddha Dharma not only for beings in this world, but also for gods and other heavenly beings, another expression of its cosmic reality and importance. But the hearing of heavenly beings singing in loud voices in the sky also suggests that living beings can be inspired by what they hear from the sky.

This is a dramatic way of affirming the human imagination as a source of inspiration. With the imagination, human beings can soar above the ordinary world, gaining inspiration to return to it with renewed dedication to transforming it into the ideal pure land.

This is called *mirai-kyo'itsu*, "in the future, unity in teaching." It means that while in reality there are now conflicts among teachings, often with various ones claiming that only their teachings are correct, in the future this will no longer be so. As people realize and practice "two gates, one in teaching," they will come to realize that apparently conflicting teachings can be brought into a unity by the power of the Dharma Flower Sutra.

*All the living beings in other worlds put their hands together, face this world, and praise the Buddha.* This has been understood as a prediction that all living beings will eventually take refuge in the Buddha—*mirai-nin'itsu*, "in the future, a unity of humanity." Now there are terrible conflicts among people—frequent wars, competition for scarce resources, ethnic feuds, high levels of crime, family quarrels, and so on. But if, the Dharma Flower Sutra teaches, people learn to practice *nimon-nin'itsu*, that is, if they learn to respect other people, listen to them, and have sympathy for them, the world will become a more peaceful place.

*The living beings in the other worlds toss all sorts of decorations in the direction of this world, where they come together like clouds, forming a canopy over the assembled buddhas.* The coming together of a variety of offerings to form a single canopy represents the variety of practices coming together to form one harmonious practice. It is called *mirai-*

*gyo'itsu*, "in the future, unity in practice." This does not mean that everyone will practice in the same way, but that the variety of practices can be made into a coherent unity.

*The passage between all the worlds opens up as though there were a single world.* By following the Buddha Way—basically recognizing the potential in others to become a buddha, their ability to be a buddha for someone, and by practicing appropriately, that is, helpfully—all sorts of differences can be overcome—ethnic, national, religious, gender, language, educational, economic, and so on. All sorts of people— who are equal in the Buddha's light—become united in purpose. This is termed *mirai-ri'itsu*, "in the future, unity in principle." Here, unity in principle does not mean in theory (in contrast with actuality), but more like unity in truth. It points to the potential to transform this world into a pure land of beauty, harmony, and peace.

## UNITY AND DIVERSITY

Though not the heart of the story or message of this chapter, we should make note of the fact that these great bodhisattvas, said in Chapter 15 to have golden-colored bodies and the thirty-two features of a buddha, want to teach the Dharma because they want to continue to improve themselves in embodying it by embracing, reading and reciting, explaining, copying, and making offerings to the Sutra. In other words, even great bodhisattvas need to continue to hear and embrace the Dharma.

Then, we are told, the Buddha reveals his great divine powers. It would be easy to assume that nothing important is being taught here, because in this story we are being challenged to go beyond doctrine. But here dramatic imagery is used primarily to have us feel the importance of the teachings and want to follow them ourselves. From the perspective of the Dharma Flower Sutra, knowledge and theoretical understanding of the Dharma is not enough. For it to become part of our deeply lived experience, a powerful emotion has to arise, a desire not only to learn from the teachings but also to follow them by taking them into our lives.

This is what makes someone a bodhisattva, this ability to incorporate the Dharma in one's life. It is a great mistake, I think, to understand the Buddhist tradition that we inherit as being nothing but a history of great thinkers and leaders. Saints such as Tao-sheng and Chih-i, Saicho, and Nichiren are extremely important for what they have contributed to the tradition, but we should never forget that the Buddhism we inherit with gratitude is a product as well of countless less well-known and now unknown people who have emerged from everyday life on this earth to become bodhisattvas by doing good, by contributing to the welfare of others. Unlike well-known monks and their royal supporters, the vast majority of such bodhisattvas have been ordinary laypeople.

If we can understand this, with our hearts as well as with our minds, we will realize that we too can be among the bodhisattvas who emerge from the earth, that is, from engagement in the actual world.

It is important to recognize that here again, as in earlier stories, the Dharma Flower Sutra reveals a consistent affirmation of unity and diversity. The unity found and affirmed is not a oneness in which difference disappears. Here, unity requires diversity, that is, something to unify. Diversity of faith, teachings, practices, humanity, and the like are not going to disappear; nor would it be good if they did. Precisely because different beings have different backgrounds and experiences, and different levels of ability in various undertakings, variety is needed. Without depth of diversity, the Dharma would never flourish. But such diversity requires coherence, some unity, if it is to be effective. Unity and diversity require each other.

As pointed out earlier, Chapter 21 is taken to express the unity of the Sutra—but it goes beyond that. The unity is taken to be a bringing together of all the Buddha's teachings, divine powers, secrets, and profound matters. "In brief," it says toward the end of the prose section, "all the teachings of the Tathagata, all the unhindered, divine powers of the Tathagata, the hidden core of the whole storehouse of the Tathagata, and all the profound matters of the Tathagata are proclaimed, demonstrated, revealed, and preached in this sutra." (LS 347)

The Dharma Flower Sutra, therefore, should never be used as a way of disrespecting or rejecting other sutras. Rather, its aim is to integrate them into a unity of opportunity, teaching, humanity, practice, and truth.

At the end of the story in the Sutra is a very interesting passage, a part of which is often used in Buddhist liturgical services. Let's look at the entire paragraph:

> After the extinction of the Tathagata, you should all wholeheartedly embrace, read and recite, explain and copy, and practice [this sutra] as you have been taught. In any land, wherever anyone accepts and embraces, reads and recites, explains and copies, and practices it as taught, or wherever a volume of the sutra is kept, whether in a garden, or a woods, or under a tree, or in a monk's cell, or a layman's house, or in a palace, or in a mountain valley or an open field, in all these places you should put up a stupa and make offerings. Why? You should understand that all such places are places of the Way. They are where the buddhas attain supreme awakening; they are where the buddhas turn the Dharma wheel; they are where the buddhas reach complete nirvana. (LS 347)

Here, putting up a stupa is a dramatic way of indicating that all places where the Dharma is embodied in actual life are sacred places, as holy as any stupa. In a sense, it is a rejection of the idea that only temples and stupas and such are holy places. For the Lotus Sutra, any place at all can be a holy place, a place of awakening, a place of the Way, simply by being a place in which the Dharma is embodied by being put into practice. And it is precisely in such places, wherever you are, that "the buddhas attain supreme awakening, . . . the buddhas turn the Dharma-wheel, . . . the buddhas reach complete nirvana." This is a fantastically powerful affirmation of the reality and importance of the holy ground on which we all stand. In a sense, wherever Buddha Dharma is successfully shared or taught a stupa has already emerged.

If you take refuge in the Buddha, the Buddha has refuge in you— your practice is what enables the Buddha to be alive in this world. Not yours alone, of course, but your practice of the bodhisattva way, along with the practice of others, is what can dispel the darkness and the gloom of living beings.

The final verses of Chapter 21 have sometimes been taken to be the final teaching of the Sutra and therefore to be especially important. They express, quite simply, the power and possibility that each of us has to make a positive difference wherever we are.

> After the extinction of the Tathagata,
> Anyone who knows the sutras preached by the Buddha,
> Their causes and conditions and proper order,
> Will teach them truthfully in accord with their true meaning.
> Just as the light of the sun and the moon
> Can dispel darkness,
> Such a person, working in the world,
> Can dispel the gloom of living beings,
> Leading innumerable bodhisattvas
> Finally to dwell in the One Vehicle.

# ENTRUSTING THE DHARMA TO US

CHAPTER 22 of the Lotus Sutra brings the main body of the Sutra to a close. The long story—which begins in Chapter 1 and teaches the integration of many skillful means into the One Buddha Vehicle, the sudden appearance of the stupa of Abundant Treasures Buddha and the assembling of buddhas from all over the universe in Chapter 11, and the emergence of the great host of bodhisattvas from the earth in Chapter 15—comes to an end with Chapter 22. Chapters 23–28, along with Chapter 12, which is a kind of interruption of that story, are regarded as a distinct group of chapters, as a kind of appendix, in terms of the order of composition of the Lotus Sutra.

This does not mean, however, that the later chapters are necessarily later in composition than those appearing earlier in the Sutra. These chapters may have existed for centuries in oral versions only, passed along from generation to generation by word of mouth. Since they can be understood to illustrate the bodhisattva tradition, the addition to the Lotus Sutra of these chapters is completely natural. No doubt some, and perhaps all, of them existed and circulated independently until incorporated into the Lotus Sutra.

The story in Chapter 22 is very brief.

## THE STORY

Shakyamuni Buddha places his right hand on the heads of all the many assembled bodhisattvas three times and entrusts the teaching of the Dharma Flower Sutra to them, urging them to spread it with all their hearts and make it known far and wide. He tells them that they should receive and embrace, read and recite, and proclaim the Sutra, so that all living beings everywhere may hear and understand it. This is because the Buddha, the "great gift-giver" for all living beings, has great compassion, is not stingy or begrudging, has no fear, and gives to living beings buddha-wisdom, tathagata-wisdom, natural wisdom. The bodhisattvas respond by promising three times to do what they have been asked, and by pleading with the Buddha not to worry about that. Then the Buddha tells all of the assembled buddhas, including Abundant Treasures Buddha in his stupa, to return in peace to where they had come from.

With this, everyone in the assembly is filled with joy.

## COMMENTARY

In ancient India placing one's hand on the head of another apparently was a sign of trust. Clearly something like that is intended here—but perhaps something more is involved. Though not in this chapter, in various places in the Dharma Flower Sutra, Shakyamuni Buddha has said that he is the father of this world. Further, bodhisattvas are regarded as children of the Buddha. There is, in other words, a kind of familial relation, a relation of affection between the Buddha and bodhisattvas. Here, the placing of his hand on the heads of bodhisattvas indicates that the relationship is not only one of trust in a formal sense, but displays a religious faith which goes beyond calculations of ability and such. Just as in early chapters of the Sutra he has assured shravakas of becoming buddhas, here the Buddha assures bodhisattvas that they can do the job that needs to be done.

The bodhisattvas, in turn, assure the Buddha that they will indeed carry on his ministry of spreading the Dharma. In other words, the relationship of trust between the Buddha and the bodhisattvas is a mutual one, based on personal assurance. The Buddha assures the bodhisattvas that they can do what needs to be done and they assure him that they will do it.

And what is the job that needs to be done? The more general answer is that the Dharma needs to be widely shared—so, especially with the Buddha no longer able to do so directly, bodhisattvas are responsible for teaching, and thus perpetuating, Buddha Dharma. The Sutra is concerned not only with teaching the Dharma in the ordinary sense; it is concerned with having the Dharma be embodied, having it be a central part of the lives of people. Early in this chapter, Shakyamuni Buddha says, "For incalculable hundreds of thousands of billions of eons, I have studied and practiced this rare Dharma of supreme awakening." (LS 351) Notice that he says both "studied" and "practiced." Practicing the Dharma goes beyond studying it to embody it in one's life. Thus bodhisattvas have a responsibility not only of teaching the Dharma by words, but also by demonstrating and exemplifying it in their actions.

It is because of this role as exemplars of the Dharma that bodhisattvas, both mythical and human, can be models for us. Because they are said to have many marvelous powers, people may pray to a bodhisattva for relief from some kind of danger or suffering, but that is not the most useful way to understand our relationship to such bodhisattvas. They have been entrusted by the Buddha to be exemplars of the Dharma who in their very being can inspire us to follow our own bodhisattva ways. If various bodhisattvas have found skills and powers with which to help others, we too can develop skill in ways of helping others.

As the Dharma Flower Sutra often praises itself and asserts its own excellence or superiority, it is very important to notice that in this chapter, which entrusts the teaching to bodhisattvas, the Buddha says that if in the future there are people who cannot have faith in or accept the Dharma Flower Sutra, other profound teachings of the Buddha should be used in order to teach the Dharma Flower Sutra. In other words, the teachings of the Lotus Sutra are not only in the text called the Sutra of the Lotus Flower of the Wonderful Dharma, they are also to be found in all of the profound teachings of the Buddha found in numerous sutras. By clinging too strongly to the text and words that we call the Dharma Flower Sutra, we may limit our ability to spread the teachings of the Sutra, the teachings that comprise the "real" Dharma Flower Sutra.

One of the things this means is that the Buddha Dharma is at once both cultural and transcultural. That is, it can be found in many languages and cultures and in that sense is "beyond" culture. Though we may not know exactly what he and his assistants translated from, Kumarajiva's translation is a translation into Chinese in which the Dharma Flower Sutra is embodied, for the most part, in Chinese terms and ways of thinking. Similarly, Japanized versions take on, to some degree, characteristics of Japanese language and culture. I have translated the Chinese version into English. In doing this, I know very well that a great deal is lost, but I also believe that it is possible that something is gained, for by being rendered in additional languages and cultural contexts, the transcultural Dharma Flower Sutra once again, to some extent, finds embodiment and life.

By entrusting the Dharma to bodhisattvas, who themselves are largely mythical and therefore a-cultural, the Buddha is indicating that Buddha Dharma is good medicine for all people and should be made available to all. This does not mean that everyone should become a Buddhist. But the mission to spread the Dharma to all does imply that everyone should have an opportunity to hear Buddha Dharma and decide for themselves whether it is suitable for them. This means that translations, even good translations, are not enough. For it to be effectively taught, the Dharma has to be embodied in the lives of contemporary people, in bodhisattvas of today—bodhisattvas who may or may not be Buddhist. Indeed, it is entirely possible for one to embody the Lotus Sutra in one's life without ever having heard of Buddhism or the Lotus Sutra. This is well illustrated in an excellent book by Taigen Dan Leighton, called *Faces of Compassion: Classic Bodhisattva Archetypes and Their Modern Expression.*[36]

Though not the only way, reading, reciting, and writing the Dharma Flower Sutra are sound practices for truly embracing the Buddha Dharma and integrating it into one's life. Thus, this chapter, which entrusts the care and propagation of the Dharma to all bodhisattvas, commissions all of us to spread the Lotus Sutra and its teachings.

This means, in effect, that anyone who has been enriched by and loves the Dharma Flower Sutra is obligated to share it with others. Just how this should be done will depend heavily on the abilities and locations, both social and geographical, of each person. But the point I want to stress here is that spreading the Dharma beyond oneself, and beyond one's communities and country, is not just a kind of something extra to be added to one's religious practice, something nice to do if one has time; it is an essential part of the practice of the Lotus Sutra. It is what those who have been enriched by the Dharma Flower Sutra have been entrusted by the Buddha to do.

## GENEROSITY IN TEACHING

The text says, "The [Buddha] is the great gift-giver for all living beings. You too should follow the teachings of the [Buddha] and not be stingy or begrudging." (LS 351)

It is common for people who are enthusiastic about something to want to protect it by preserving it just as it is and by taking pleasure in making it difficult for it to be understood or appreciated by the uninitiated. Being inflexible about how a text is to be translated and expressed, insisting, for example, on using unfamiliar Sanskrit terms or quaint English expressions, may make it very difficult for others to enter a particular circle of understanding and appropriation. In such ways we may be establishing an in-group/out-group situation in which we are on the inside, in some way perhaps protected from what is outside. Traditionally, secret religious doctrines or ceremonies often functioned in this way.

Perhaps this kind of group bonding through special, esoteric language is necessary to some degree. Certainly it is very common among religious groups. But when it means that the Dharma Flower Sutra, which entrusts us to spread it everywhere, is not taught generously to others, we fail to fulfill the commission of the Buddha.

I believe that teaching generously should mean that we share the Sutra in whatever ways are most appropriate to the intended audience, always, of course, within the real limits of our abilities. While it might be nice if everyone learned enough Chinese to be able to read Kumarajiva's Chinese version of the Lotus Sutra, this is neither necessary nor necessarily desirable. It is good, I believe, that we have versions of the Dharma Flower Sutra that make it more intelligible to Japanese people, and it is good that there are English versions that make it more available to English-speaking people. This is not merely a matter of translation into other languages; it is important that the Sutra be rendered in ways that make it as understandable as possible.

This kind of generosity, a generosity in which one tries to understand and appreciate the linguistic and cultural situation of others, a generosity in which we do not insist that our own way of expressing something in the Sutra is the only good way, this kind of generosity is what the Sutra expects of those who are its genuine followers.

If we do not approach teaching the Sutra with such a generous attitude we will, I fear, fall into one more version of "merely formal Dharma." In other words, we will be going through the motions of teaching and practicing, but very few will be deeply moved by such teaching. This kind of failure to be generous is largely unconscious, making it difficult, but not impossible, to detect and overcome. But another problem often stands in the way of our being generous in teaching: Often we are all too conscious of it, making it difficult to overcome. This is manifest in reticence or shyness in speaking and teaching.

Throughout the Dharma Flower Sutra there are references to the eloquence of bodhisattvas. Already at the beginning of Chapter 1 we are told that the eighty thousand bodhisattvas present had all "taught with delight and eloquence." (LS 53) Later, in Chapter 17, the Buddha says, "When I taught that the length of the [Buddha's] life is very long…bodhisattva great-ones as numerous as the specks of dust in an entire world delighted in being eloquent and unhindered in speech." (LS 301) Even the bodhisattva called "Never Disrespectful," because he always went around bowing to people and telling them that he would never disrespect them, is said to have "powers of joyful and eloquent speech." (LS 339) And of the dragon princess, a young girl, it is said that her "eloquence knows no bounds." (LS 251)

Such an emphasis on eloquence is simply another indication of the importance of the teaching role of bodhisattvas. Of course, not everyone who follows the Dharma Flower Sutra will become truly eloquent, and certainly not automatically. But there is a strong suggestion that those who seek to spread the Dharma must strive to overcome reticence and shyness in order to be able to speak freely without being hindered by worries about embarrassing oneself. In many cases, this may require training and much practice, but it is an integral part of the bodhisattva path. Being shy should not be an excuse for leaving the teaching of the Dharma to others.

## BUDDHA-WISDOM

The Buddha, the text says, gives to living beings "buddha-wisdom, tathagata-wisdom, natural wisdom." This phrase has sometimes been taken to refer to three different kinds of wisdom, but I think the three terms are intended to be equivalent, three different ways of saying "buddha-wisdom." The fact that *Tathagata*, often translated as "Thus Come One," is simply another of the ten epithets of the Buddha, would indicate that there is no difference between buddha-wisdom and tathagata-wisdom, and the logic of the phrase would suggest that if there is no difference between these two, there is no difference among the three; they are just three ways of talking about the same thing.

If this is correct, it means that buddha-wisdom, or at least the buddha-wisdom given to human beings, is a kind of natural wisdom. Natural wisdom is a kind of inherent wisdom, a wisdom that is not given from outside but arises naturally. Thus, we are being told here that in teaching Buddha Dharma we can rely on our own inherent wisdom. This is, of course, entirely consistent with the idea that we all have a buddha-nature, a capacity to be a buddha for others.

Such wisdom should not be understood, as terms such as "inherent" might suggest, as something independent of others. In the first place, it is not something we ourselves individually create. It is a gift to us, something we have all received. Second, just as having buddha-nature does not mean that we are already fully buddhas, having natural wisdom does not mean that our wisdom cannot or should not be developed and enhanced by knowledge. What it does mean is that we have a natural capacity to do this, a capacity to become better informed, more knowledgeable, wiser in dealing with others.

Our buddha-wisdom is like the inheritance of the poor son in the parable in Chapter 4 of the Dharma Flower Sutra and discussed here in Chapter 7. Our inheritance is ours—it cannot be taken away from us. But it can be severely restricted in use, or it can be expanded greatly through experience and education.

And thus we come to the closing lines of this story. It is very interesting, especially from the perspective of one raised in the West with notions of divine omnipotence, to see Shakyamuni Buddha here being urged by bodhisattvas not to worry and in turn telling the assembled buddhas that they should now go in peace.

Then Shakyamuni Buddha had all the buddhas embodying him, who had come from all directions, return to their own lands, saying: "Buddhas, go in peace." (LS 352)

The Buddha, in other words, like any teacher, is concerned about whether his teaching has really been effective. Here he is reassured that the teaching that he has been doing will be continued by bodhisattvas. Just as the Buddha has assured many that they will become buddhas, here the Buddha is assured that the bodhisattvas will fulfill the commission given to them by the Buddha.

In turn, the Buddha can then tell the assembled buddhas to go in peace, that is, without worry as to whether what is needed will be done. There would be no point in telling the buddhas to go in peace unless there was some possibility that they would be anxious. But the earthly bodhisattvas have just promised to preach the Buddha Dharma. For that reason, all the buddhas can be put at ease.

This means, as we have said many times, buddhas depend on bodhisattvas to carry out their mission. Shakyamuni Buddha is not independently powerful. His power is embodied in the actions and lives of bodhisattvas. Shakyamuni Buddha could tell the other buddhas to go in peace because the Dharma had been entrusted to us!

# 24

# SEEN WITH JOY BY ALL THE LIVING

CHAPTER 23 of the Lotus Sutra tells a story about previous lives of Medicine King Bodhisattva, when he was a bodhisattva called Seen with Joy by All the Living, a bodhisattva who burned his whole body as a sacrifice to a buddha and later burned just his arms as a sacrifice to a buddha. It then praises the Dharma Flower Sutra and those who follow it.

Like the Sutra as a whole, this chapter has had enormous impact on East Asian Buddhism. Many will remember the sight of Vietnamese monks burning themselves to death in the 1960s during the Vietnam War, beginning with the monk Thich Quang Duc in 1963. It has been said that these monks and nuns used their bodies as torches to illuminate the suffering of the Vietnamese people so that the world might see what was happening in Vietnam. Theirs was an extremely powerful message. And it is a fact that the story and pictures of Thich Quang Duc burning himself were soon seen all over the world. And within a few months the regime of President Diem was overthrown and his anti-Buddhist policies ended.

A great many Chinese monks right down to the middle of the twentieth century followed the practice of burning off one or more of their fingers as a sign of dedication and devotion. Until very recently, virtually all Chinese monks and nuns, and I believe those in Vietnam as well, when receiving final ordination, used moxa, a kind of herb used in traditional Chinese medicine, to burn small places on their scalps, where the scars usually remained for life. This ritual burning was taken to be a sign of complete devotion to the three treasures—the Buddha, the Dharma, and the Sangha.

While deeply sympathetic with those who show such great devotion by sacrificing their bodies by fire, it is not a practice I can recommend to anyone. It is much better, I believe, to sacrifice our bodies through dedicated work, in a sense burning our bodies much more slowly. Since Chapter 23 is naturally read as advocating self-immolation, it has been my least favorite chapter in the Lotus Sutra, one that I sometimes wish had not been included. And yet the last part of the chapter contains some of the most beautiful aphoristic poetry in the Dharma Flower Sutra.

## THE STORY

In response to a question by Constellation-King Flower Bodhisattva as to why Medicine King Bodhisattva is traveling around in this world of suffering, doing many difficult and painful things, the Buddha explains that many ages ago there was a buddha named Pure and Bright Excellence of Sun and Moon whose world was a special kind of paradise, a world without difficulties of any kind. This buddha preached the Lotus Sutra to one and all, including a bodhisattva named Seen with Joy by All the Living.

After doing various austerities and strenuously seeking to become a buddha for thousands of years, this bodhisattva gained the ability to transform himself by taking on any form. But instead of doing so, he made many offerings of flowers and incense to the Buddha. Then, thinking his own body would be an even better offering to the Buddha, he drank fragrant oil, put perfume and oil on his body, dressed himself in perfumed robes, and set fire to himself. The light from that fire lasted for twelve thousand years, illuminating countless worlds, where the buddhas praised him for making such an offering out of pure devotion.

After being consumed by the fire, Seen with Joy by All the Living was born once again in the same world under the same Buddha, this time as the son of a king. There, after explaining the need to do so to his father, he rode a platform of seven precious materials into the sky to pay tribute to the Buddha of that land. The Buddha, announcing to Seen with Joy by All the Living Bodhisattva that he would soon enter final nirvana, entrusted all of his teachings to the bodhisattva, including the Dharma of supreme awakening, and all of his disciples, lands, and physical remains, instructing him to distribute the remains widely and to build stupas for them.

After that Buddha died, Seen with Joy by All the Living Bodhisattva, saddened and in grief, burned the Buddha's body on a sandalwood pyre. He collected the remains, made eighty-four thousand urns for them, and erected a stupa for each of the urns. But, still not satisfied with himself, he announced that he would make an offering to the remains of the Buddha. Then he burned his arms before the stupas and offered the light from the fire to the remains of the Buddha for seventy-two thousand years, causing many to aspire to supreme awakening.

Seeing their teacher without arms, many bodhisattvas, gods, and others became troubled and sad. But Seen with Joy by All the Living Bodhisattva explained that having sacrificed his arms he surely would eventually obtain the golden body of a buddha and that his arms would soon be restored. And they were, to the great joy of all.

Then the Buddha explains to Constellation-King Flower Bodhisattva that Seen with Joy by All the Living Bodhisattva was actually Medicine King Bodhisattva in previous lives. He does not mind doing austerities in this life, the Buddha explains, because he has offered his body to buddhas countless times in previous lives. Everyone who aspires to supreme awakening, the Buddha says, should offer a light to a stupa by burning a finger or toe, as the reward for this will be much greater than the reward for giving even the greatest of material offerings. Yet greater still will be the reward of one who keeps even a single verse of the Dharma Flower Sutra, the king of all sutras, because it saves all living beings. Those who hear this chapter of the Sutra especially will be highly rewarded. For example, a woman who hears and keeps this chapter will be reborn in the paradise of Amitabha Buddha as a man, as a great bodhisattva, who sees and is praised by billions and billions of buddhas and is surpassed only by buddhas.

## COMMENTARY

Despite the fact that this chapter is taken by some as praising the actual sacrifice of one's body or body parts by burning, I believe that the Lotus Sutra does not teach that we should burn ourselves or parts of our bodies. The idea that keeping even a single verse of the Lotus Sutra is *more rewarding* than burning one's finger or toe suggests this. And further, suicide would go against the teachings of the Sutra as a whole as well as the Buddha's precept against killing. The language here, as in so much of the Lotus Sutra, is symbolic, carrying a deeper meaning than what appears on the surface.

There is no evidence to suggest that such practices as burning body parts or one's whole body was taken literally in India. It was in China and Vietnam especially, with finger burning and self-immolations occurring even as late as 1948, that such language was taken literally. This is one danger of literalism. It can lead to extreme acts that benefit no one. Devotion is good; devotion to the Buddha is good; devotion to the Dharma Flower Sutra is good. But acts of devotion have to be examined with additional criteria to determine whether they are in accord with the Dharma as a whole, whether they promote or retard one's progress along the way, and whether they are likely to lead to a reduction in suffering. There could be very exceptional circumstances, perhaps once in ten million eons, when such a sacrifice is called for. It may be that Vietnam in the 1960s was one such time. But the monk Thich Quang Duc, who burned himself in 1963, did not do so merely to express his devotion. His act of devotion was also a political act aimed at improving the lives of millions of people.

Religious devotion not tempered by intelligence and wisdom can be dangerous, both to others and to oneself. Sound practice, skillful practice of the Buddha Way, requires that we develop to the fullest all of our capacities for doing good.

Certainly we should devote our whole selves to the Dharma, to the Truth. This is the most important meaning of "burning our bodies." Does it mean abandoning the bodhisattva practice of service to others in order to serve the Dharma? Of course not. It is by serving the Dharma that we serve both others and ourselves. Serving the Dharma and serving others cannot be separated, just as serving others cannot be completely separated from serving ourselves. This integration of interests—in contrast with Western individualism and with certain Christian ideas of completely selfless devotion and sacrifice—is one of the great insights of Buddhism.

Let your practice be a light for others, helping them to dispel the darkness. This is a second symbolic meaning of "burning" our bodies or arms. It is similar to a very famous passage in the Christian New Testament:

> You are the light of the world. A city set on a hill cannot be hid. Nor do men light a lamp and put it under a basket, but on a stand, and it gives light to all in the house. Let your light so shine before people, that they may see your good works and give glory to your Father who is in heaven. (Matthew 5:14–16)

It is not enough to receive, preserve, or believe Buddhist teachings in one's head. One must put them into practice in daily life. This cannot be done in isolation, for the very meaning of bodhisattva practice is serving others. This is the most important meaning of offering a light to the Buddha.

Returning to the story, before Seen with Joy by All the Living Bodhisattva sacrificed his body in the fire, he drank perfumed oil, and put various perfumes both on his body and on his clothes. I think we should understand this to be a kind of purification in preparation for what he was about to do, offering himself to the Buddha Pure and Bright Excellence of Sun and Moon.

While we normally think of purification as a cleansing or washing, usually with water, in human history many different things have been taken to be agents of purification—especially water, fire, smoke, salt, and blood. This is one reason that even today a typical Chinese temple is usually full of smoke and incense. But long before the invention of the bathroom shower, the washing machine, and dry cleaning, many people used perfume and incense as a way of "removing" unwanted aromas and, in a sense, purifying themselves, their clothing, and their special spaces. Though we do not think of it as purification, perfume and perfumed things of various kinds are still used to mask odors felt to be undesirable.

Purification of ourselves in preparation for sacrificing ourselves to the Buddha can still be an important part of Buddhist practice. For followers of the Dharma Flower Sutra, the highest act of devotion to the Buddha is not meditation or chanting or burning incense, though they may be helpful. The most important display of devotion is bodhisattva practice, the practice of helping others. And for this, preparation is often needed. One kind of preparation is the development of appropriate skills, perhaps especially skill in listening. But more foundational than the development of skills is the matter of purifying ourselves of things that get in the way of our being actually helpful.

As part of the Threefold Lotus Sutra, the Dharma Flower Sutra itself is often followed by a "closing sutra," the Sutra of Meditation on the Dharma Practice of Universal Sage Bodhisattva. This sutra is often called the Repentance Sutra and has been used in purification rituals because it is about purifying ourselves, especially our senses.

Another way to approach purification is through the idea of the three poisons. The three poisons are mentioned several times in the Lotus Sutra, but are never discussed. In this chapter, in accord with tradition, they are said to be greed, anger, and folly. Actually, while "greed" and "anger" are very common designations of the first two poisons, the third has sometimes been taken to be delusion, foolishness, or stupidity. Here we might best think of it as confusion. If we are going to be helpful to others, we need to purify ourselves of these three poisons. Our actions should not arise from greedy, selfish motives. Our actions should not be based on anger. And we should not be confused about what we are doing.

With the sense of purification we find in Chapter 23, however, purifying ourselves would not necessarily mean getting rid of our greed, anger, and confusion. Human beings are selfish. To think that one is completely free of selfishness and self-centeredness is probably always a kind of self-deception. It's unlikely that human beings are ever completely free of greed, of wanting more than they need. Human beings get angry. It is a natural, though not inevitable, response to the anger of others, for example. As I suspect we all know, simply saying we are not angry does not make it so. It's unlikely that human beings are ever completely free of anger. And while we want to be as free from confusion as possible, it probably is good that some confusion, some lack of clarity, some caution remains, at least usually.

What we see in the case of Medicine King Bodhisattva is a kind of purification that is a masking. This might mean, for example, that rather than trying to pretend to ourselves that we are purely selfless, we need to recognize that we are actually interested in what we are doing and even expect to gain from it in some way. If we can recognize our own interest in everything we do, we might be able to avoid the kind of purely self-serving activity, selfishness, and self-centeredness that gets in the way of actually being helpful to others. Similarly, if we can recognize our own anger and the reasons for it, we need not express it in ways that lead others to become angry. We can wear the perfume of a smile!

Such purification is, of course, itself both for our benefit and for the benefit of the Buddha. By being aware of our desires and anger and confusions, and, at the same time, purifying ourselves of them with perfume, we can improve both our own lives and the lives of others.

In this chapter we find the curious idea that from the mouth of those who joyfully receive this chapter will come the fragrance of blue lotus flowers and from their pores will come the fragrance of sandalwood. In other words, if we purify ourselves, both our words and actions will smell good! This means that those who truly hear the Sutra will not only be changed themselves, they will also influence others in beneficial ways.

Seen with Joy by All the Living Bodhisattva lived for many lifetimes in the land of the Buddha Pure and Bright Excellence of Sun and Moon. The text describes it in this way:

> In his land there were no women, no one living in purgatories, no hungry spirits, no animals, no ashuras, and no difficulties of any kind. The land was as level as the palm of one's hand and made of lapis lazuli. It was adorned with jeweled trees, covered with jeweled curtains, and hung with banners of treasured flowers. Jeweled vases and incense burners were everywhere. There were platforms made of the seven precious materials, with trees for each platform.... Under all these jeweled trees, bodhisattvas and shravakas were seated. And above each of the platforms tens

of billions of gods were making heavenly music and singing praises to the Buddha as an offering. (LS 353–54)

Like Purna's buddha land, the land of this buddha is very unlike the world in which we live, the world of Shakyamuni Buddha. I suppose it should not be surprising that celibate monks sometimes thought that a paradise would be without women. No doubt sexual desire was a major problem for men who wanted to be rid of desire. This is why, a bit later in the story, Seen with Joy by All the Living Bodhisattva was reborn in that same land without having a mother, through a metamorphosis like that of an insect.

Perhaps such monks actually yearned for the kind of paradise described here and elsewhere in the Dharma Flower Sutra, but I wonder if even they would really want to live in such a place, a place with no difficulties of any kind. I wonder also, at least for more contemporary readers of the Dharma Flower Sutra, whether such a paradise might not be seen as extremely boring and uninteresting. I know I would not welcome going there, at least not for more than a few days!

Is it possible that such a description of a supposedly ideal state in some way enhances our appreciation of the fact that this world is not flat, is not without difficulties, is not without sexuality and sexual desire, is not without its purgatories, and so on? Is it possible that the difficulties and challenges we face in life contribute not only to our sorrows but also to our joys? Perhaps the greatest joy comes not from life in a pure land with no difficulties of any kind, but from the very struggle with, and occasional overcoming of, difficulties that life in this world presents to us. In other words, Medicine King Bodhisattva comes to this world and travels around in it just because it is a land in which suffering has to be endured and can be, which is the only kind of land in which a bodhisattva can really be a bodhisattva.

Toward the end of this chapter we read that if there is a woman who hears this Sutra and acts in accord with its teachings, she will become a bodhisattva, one who is becoming a fully awakened buddha, in the pure land of Amitabha Buddha. Because she has been able to "embrace, read and recite, and ponder over this sutra and teach it for others," she will obtain boundless merit, be praised by countless buddhas throughout the universe, be protected by hundreds of thousands of buddhas, and become equal to the Buddha; in other words, she will become a buddha. (LS 359–60) Here, in a sense, we have an alternative vision to that of a paradise in which there are no women—one in which a woman becomes a buddha through embracing the Sutra, by living the Sutra in this world.

A great Taiwanese monk, Master Yin Shun, passed away at the age of 100 in June of 2005. Normally, in Taiwan, the name of Amitabha, the buddha who presides over the Western Paradise, the land of happiness and bliss, is chanted for the benefit of someone who has died. But shortly before he died, Master Yin Shun requested that the name of Shakyamuni Buddha be chanted after his death because Shakyamuni Buddha is the Buddha of the world in which we live now. Master Yin Shun wanted to be reborn into this world of suffering and hardship rather than in a world of eternal happiness and bliss, so that he could continue promoting Buddha Dharma where it is most needed.

## TWELVE SIMILES

Toward the end of the chapter we find what I believe to be one of the more beautiful passages in the Lotus Sutra. It is a set of twelve similes that can be understood to be prayers not unlike these famous "beatitudes" of the New Testament:

Blessed are the poor in spirit, for theirs is the kingdom
  of heaven.
Blessed are those who mourn, for they shall be comforted.
Blessed are the meek, for they shall inherit the earth.
Blessed are those who hunger and thirst after righteousness,
  for they shall be satisfied.

. Blessed are the merciful, for they shall obtain mercy.

Blessed are the pure in heart, for they shall see God.

Blessed are the peacemakers, for they shall be called sons
of God.

Blessed are those who are persecuted for righteousness' sake,
for theirs is the kingdom of heaven.

Blessed are you when men revile you and persecute you and
utter all kinds of evil against you falsely on my account.
(Matthew 5:3–11)

These beatitudes can be a kind of prayer because they express, not a prediction of what is to happen in some future, but a hope about what will be. They have served down through the ages to give encouragement to people in conditions of need.

In Chapter 23 of the Lotus Sutra we find these twelve similes:

This sutra can bring great and abundant benefit to all the living and fulfill their hopes.

Just like a clear, cool pool, it can satisfy all who are thirsty. Like fire to someone who is cold, like clothing to someone naked, like a leader found by a group of merchants, like a mother found by her children, like a ferry found by passengers, like a doctor found by the sick, like a lamp found by people in the dark, like riches found by the poor, like a ruler found by the people, like a sea lane found by traders, and like a torch dispelling the darkness this Dharma Flower Sutra can enable all the living to liberate themselves from all suffering, disease, and pain, loosening all the bonds of mortal life. (LS 359)

This passage can readily be understood to be not only describing the wonderful powers of the Dharma Flower Sutra but also expressing hope for all those in need:

May those who are thirsty find cool, clear water.
May those who are cold find a warm fire.
May those who are naked find clothing.
May those who are without leadership find a leader.
May children who are lost find their mothers.
May those who need to cross over water find a ferry.
May those who are sick find a doctor.
May those who are in the dark find a lamp.
May those who are poor find riches.
May those in need of one find a ruler.
May those who trade find a sea lane.
May those in darkness find a light.

In other words, the twelve similes are not merely claims about what the Lotus Sutra can do, though they are that; they are also a poetic expression of the many kinds of human needs and of the hope that they be met.

Thus the meaning of "this sutra can save all living beings" is that if it is heard and applied—by us—people will be saved. Those who are thirsty will find cool water and those in the dark will find light.

The text says:

> Even if someone were to give a three-thousand great thou-
> sandfold world full of the seven precious materials as an
> offering to the Buddha, great bodhisattvas, pratyekabud-
> dhas, and arhats, the blessings such a person would gain
> would not equal those of someone who receives and
> embraces even a single four-line verse of this Dharma
> Flower Sutra. Happiness greater than this will not be found.
> (LS 357–58)

We should, I believe, understand this to mean that the greatest happiness comes from putting the Lotus Sutra into practice by following the bodhisattva way of traveling around in this world helping others, thus enabling the Dharma to live in the world.

Why does Medicine King Bodhisattva travel around in this world of suffering? This is the question with which the chapter begins. He does so because he wants to help all those in need, and over many lifetimes has prepared himself to do so. We too, the story of Seen with Joy by All the Living suggests, can bring comfort and satisfaction to those in need by embodying the Dharma Flower Sutra in our own lives, that is, by being Dharma flowers.

# 25

## WONDERFUL VOICE BODHISATTVA

THAT THE TITLE FIGURE of this chapter's story is named "Wonderful Voice," or perhaps "Wonderful Sound," is another curiosity of the Lotus Sutra: absolutely nothing is said about his voice or sounds. "Wonderful Body" would be more appropriate, as his wonderful body is described in some detail: some forty-two thousand leagues tall, radiant and brilliant, powerful, pure gold in color, with eyes the size of lotus leaves, and a face as beautiful as millions of moons together. But there is not a word about his voice!

## THE STORY

Emitting beams of light both from the protuberence on the top of his head and from the tuft of hair between his eyebrows, Shakyamuni Buddha illuminated countless worlds to the East. Beyond all these worlds to the East was still another world, called Adorned with Pure Light, where there lived the buddha Wisdom King of the Pure Flower Constellation and the bodhisattva Wonderful Voice, along with countless other bodhisattvas.

This Wonderful Voice Bodhisattva had already succeeded in many things, including the planting of many good roots, serving many different buddhas in different ages, acquiring great wisdom, and attaining millions of different kinds of concentration. When the light from Shakyamuni Buddha fills his world and shines on him, Wonderful Voice tells the Buddha of his land that he wants to go to Shakyamuni's world, the world in which suffering has to be endured and can be, to pay tribute to Shakyamuni Buddha and visit various bodhisattvas. The Buddha of his world warns him that even though this world is not flat or clean and its buddha and bodhisattvas are small and short, he should not make little of this world or think that its buddha and bodhisattvas are inferior. "Just because our own bodies are fantastically tall and yours is perfect in every way," he said, "do not make light of the buddha, bodhisattvas, or the land of Shakyamuni Buddha." (LS 364)

Then, through the power of entering one of his concentrations, Wonderful Voice makes eighty-four thousand bunches of gold and silver lotus flowers and other valuables appear not far from where Shakyamuni Buddha was sitting on Holy Eagle Peak. Seeing them, Manjushri Bodhisattva asks Shakyamuni Buddha what they signify. And when the Buddha explained that the flowers mean that Wonderful Voice Bodhisattva is coming to visit, Manjushri wants to know what that bodhisattva had done to gain such great powers and says he wants to see him. The Buddha replies that Abundant Treasures Buddha will summon him.

Summoned by Abundant Treasures to come to see Manjushri, this extremely tall and handsome Wonderful Voice Bodhisattva, accompanied by eighty-four thousand other bodhisattvas, flies to this world on a platform made of the seven precious materials, passing through all the worlds to the East, where they quake in the six ways, flowers made of the seven precious materials rain down, and musical instruments sound in the heavens.

Arriving at Holy Eagle Peak, Wonderful Voice, with his big beautiful eyes, gorgeous face, and powerful golden body adorned with signs of countless blessings, descends from the platform, approaches Shakyamuni Buddha, prostrates himself at at his feet, presents him with a magnificent and extremely valuable necklace, delivers various greetings from the Buddha Wisdom King of the Pure Flower Constellation, and expresses the desire to see Abundant Treasures Buddha. Abundant Treasures, in turn, praises him for coming. Then Bodhisattva Excellent Flower wants to know what Wonderful Voice has done to merit such great powers.

Shakyamuni Buddha explains that once upon a time there was a buddha named King of the Sound of Thunder in whose realm Wonderful Voice Bodhisattva lived. Because he offered many kinds of beautiful music and jeweled bowls to King of the Sound of Thunder Buddha, he was reborn in the land of Wisdom King of the Pure Flower Constellation Buddha and was able to obtain great, supernatural powers. This bodhisattva is none other than the present Wonderful Voice. In previous lives he had taken many different forms—including those of women and girls, animals, gods and other heavenly beings, buddhas, and so on—in order to preach the Dharma Flower Sutra. He protects all living beings by taking whatever form is appropriate for liberating them by teaching them the Dharma.

When the Buddha teaches this, the eighty-four thousand bodhisattvas who had come with Wonderful Voice, together with numerous other bodhisattvas of this world, win the ability to transform themselves into the forms of other living beings. Then Wonderful Voice makes offerings to Shakyamuni Buddha and to the stupa of Abundant Treasures Buddha, and, as before with lands shaking, flowers raining down, and music resounding in the heavens, returns home to the land of Wisdom King of the Pure Flower Constellation Buddha and reports his adventure to him.

## COMMENTARY

This story begins with an event not unlike that in the very first chapter of the Dharma Flower Sutra, in which the Buddha emits light of such power that it illumines very distant worlds. Since light is virtually always a symbol of wisdom, we can assume that here too we have a visual image indicating that the influence of Shakyamuni's wisdom is not limited to his world, our world, but also goes to the far reaches of the universe. He is, in other words, the light of all the worlds. Though he is the Buddha of this world, he is also, in some way not clearly spelled out, the Buddha of all worlds. This has been indicated many times in the Dharma Flower Sutra, most dramatically perhaps in Chapter 11, where Shakyamuni Buddha assembles the buddhas and bodhisattvas from all over the universe.

Here, however, it might be relevant to remember that this display of light by Shakyamuni Buddha has happened in Chapter 1. There we learn that it has happened many times in the past, always signifying that the Buddha was about to preach the Dharma Flower Sutra. Should we assume that this meaning has simply been forgotten here? Or might it be the case that in the story of Wonderful Voice Bodhisattva the Dharma Flower Sutra is being preached in some way? But here its teaching is seen not so much as something oral or written, but as a kind of action. That is, Wonderful Voice Bodhisattva can be understood to be preaching or teaching the Dharma Flower Sutra not so much by words as by embodying it by taking on whatever forms are needed to help others. The voice of Wonderful Voice then, is wonderful not by being loud or beautiful but by being absent! His voice, in a sense, is his body, which takes on whatever form is needed by others.

The Dharma Flower Sutra, as we have seen, is action-oriented. At the end of Chapter 16 we are invited to perfect our buddha bodies. The Sutra, in other words, is as much concerned, perhaps even more concerned, about what we do with our hands and feet as it is with what happens in our minds. This is not to say that what happens in our minds is unimportant. It is exceedingly difficult to imagine a peaceful world without there being peaceful minds. But I think it would be a great mistake to assume that, at least for the Dharma Flower Sutra, the end or goal of Buddhism is some kind of experience of being enlightened or awakened. For the Lotus Sutra, the goal is the way itself, the way of awakened action—the practice and the way of the bodhisattva, one who is becoming a buddha through taking on whatever forms are needed to help others.

Though hardly unique to this chapter of the Lotus Sutra, one very clear message here is the one given by his buddha to Wonderful Voice Bodhisattva: Don't make light of Shakyamuni's world! Even though its ground is not made of gold or other precious materials but of dirt, even though it is not smooth but includes many high and low places and even rocks and mountains, even though its buddha and bodhisattvas are extremely short and unattractive compared with ours, one should never think that world is inferior.

We can only guess what is behind the concern contained in this statement. Obviously, the writers believed that someone was not taking this world seriously enough. Does it indicate a time and place where people thought some distant land, some faraway paradise, was to be preferred to this world? Does it indicate a reaction to a worldview that rejected the reality and importance of this world in favor of some ideal world? We cannot be sure. But it is very clear that both here and in many other places the Dharma Flower Sutra emphasizes the value and importance of life in this world, the home of Shakyamuni Buddha, in which the path of the bodhisattva can be taken, the land that is our only home and place of practice.

Though life here may be very difficult, with suffering of many kinds all around, with many difficulties to face, we should consider ourselves fortunate to have so many opportunities to be of service, to practice the bodhisattva way of helping others, and, which is part of the same thing, being helped by others. This is a world in which interdependence, the mutual dependence of living beings upon one another, is abundantly realized. We depend upon our ancestors and our descendants depend upon us; we depend upon our neighbors and our neighbors depend upon us; we depend upon the Buddha and the Buddha depends upon us. This world is through and through a world of interdependent relationships.

In a way, the interdependent character of this world is also shown in the greetings that Wonderful Voice Bodhisattva brings to Shakyamuni Buddha: "World-honored one," he says:

> Are your ailments and troubles few? Is your daily life and practice going smoothly? Are the four elements in you in harmony? Are the affairs of the world tolerable? Are living beings easy to save? Are they not excessively greedy, angry, foolish, jealous, and arrogant? Are they not lacking in proper regard for their parents? Are they not disrespectful to novice monks? Do they not have wrong views and inadequate goodness? Are their five emotions not out of control? (LS 366)

Here we can clearly see that the same Buddha who can illuminate the entire universe, the same Buddha whose land this is, the same Buddha who provides us with infinite opportunities to experience joy in service to the Dharma, this same Buddha is far from all-powerful or utterly independent in the fashion of both Indian and Western gods. This is a buddha who is supremely interdependent, one who both serves all others and at the same time is dependent on all others. This Buddha needs bodhisattvas, and needs ordinary human beings to be bodhisattvas in order to accomplish the Buddha's work of saving all the living.

That is why Wonderful Voice Bodhisattva can take on the form of a buddha. He can become the Buddha for anyone who needs saving grace to come to them in the form of a buddha.

In the previous chapter of the Sutra, about the previous lives of Medicine King Bodhisattva, it is said that Seen with Joy by All the Living Bodhisattva attained a concentration that enabled him to take on any form. It was gaining the ability to take on any form that led this bodhisattva to sacrifice his body to the Buddha of his world. But in Chapter 23 we are not told what the name of this concentration means. Here, in Chapter 24, we can see more clearly what this ability to take on any form is about. It is an extraordinary ability to serve others.

Then the Buddha tells Flower Virtue that while he can see only one body of Wonderful Voice Bodhisattva, this bodhisattva appears in many different bodies, everywhere teaching this Sutra for the sake of the living. He appears as the king Brahma, as Indra, Ishvara or Maha-Ishvara, or as a great general of heaven. Sometimes he appears as Vaishravana, or as a holy wheel-rolling king, or as a lesser king; or he appears as an elder, an ordinary citizen, a high official, a brahman, or a monk, nun, layman, or laywoman; or he appears as the wife of an elder or householder, the wife of a high official, or the wife of a brahman, or as a boy or girl; or he appears as a god, a dragon, satyr, centaur, ashura, griffin, chimera, python, human or nonhuman being, and so on. He can help those who are in a purgatory, or are hungry spirits or animals, and all who are in difficult circumstances. And for the sake of those in the king's harem he transforms himself into a woman and teaches this Sutra.

For those who need the form of a shravaka, a pratyekabuddha, or a bodhisattva to be liberated, he appears in the form of a shravaka, pratyekabuddha, or bodhisattva and teaches the Dharma. For those who need the form of a buddha to be liberated, he appears in the form of a buddha and teaches the Dharma. According to what is needed for liberation, he appears in various forms. Even if it is appropriate to enter extinction for the sake of liberation, he shows himself as one who enters extinction. (LS 367–68)

This variety of forms is remarkably inclusive. While clearly advocating and emphasizing the importance of the bodhisattva way, the Dharma Flower Sutra wants its hearers and readers to understand that appearing in the form of a bodhisattva is only one way among many, any of which can be effective. This variety of forms can be seen as an expression of the emphasis found in the first few chapters of the Sutra on the variety of skillful means. But here, in a sense, the message is even more direct. If, it says, you are "the wife of a brahman," or "a boy or girl," or anyone else, you too can be a bodhisattva, you can be Wonderful Voice Bodhisattva!

This ability to serve others by taking on different forms was made most evident in East Asian Buddhism by Kwan-yin Bodhisattva, the Regarder of the Cries of the World known as Kannon in Japanese. The textual basis for this is, of course, Chapter 25 of the Lotus Sutra, where some thirty-three forms of Kwan-yin are listed. These thirty-three "bodies" are very often depicted in Chinese Buddhist art, especially outside of temples. But in China the ability to take on different forms or bodies in order to help others is by no means restricted to Kwan-yin. Numerous stories are told, for example, of Manjushri Bodhisattva taking on various forms, such as that of an old lady or sick dog, in order to lead someone to Mount Wutai.

Perhaps the most famous case of a bodhisattva taking on a special form is the incarnation of Maitreya Bodhisattva in the form of a historical tenth-century saintly, heterodox, and enormously overweight monk who was especially kind to children. In Japan he is known as Hotei, and is one of the Seven Gods of Good Luck, and, sold in souvenir shops all over the world, he is often called "the laughing Buddha." But in virtually every Chinese Buddhist temple he is known as Mile-fo—Maitreya Buddha. But this form is not the only embodiment of Maitreya in an actual, historical person. Many Chinese historical figures, some political, others religious, either claimed to be or were widely taken to be incarnations of Maitreya. For example, the sixth-century Buddhist teacher, reformer, and champion of peasants known simply as Fu was widely thought to be Maitreya descended from his Tushita heaven to take on the form of Fu.

While Kwan-yin, Manjushri, and Maitreya are famous, especially in China and throughout East Asia, for taking on whatever body is needed in order to be helpful to others, Wonderful Voice Bodhisattva is hardly known outside of the Dharma Flower Sutra, or even outside of Chapter 24 of the Dharma Flower Sutra. He seems, for example, to have been completely neglected by artists. I do not know why this is so. It certainly cannot be because this story is any less encouraging to women than the Kwan-yin chapter. Here, by indicating numerous ways in which Wonderful Voice takes on female bodies, the text goes to some lengths to assure women that they too can become bodhisattvas, that they themselves can become Wonderful Voice Bodhisattva. Perhaps one reason that this bodhisattva failed to attract artists is that it is difficult to portray a face as beautiful as millions of moons together!

Nor do we know whether the story of Wonderful Voice Bodhisattva is older or younger than the story in the Dharma Flower Sutra of Kwan-yin Bodhisattva. But I think it is no accident that in the Dharma Flower Sutra this story is placed just before the Kwan-yin chapter. Kwan-yin is enormously famous for being able to take on any form in order to save others. One could easily think that this special power to take on different forms belongs to Kwan-yin alone. But in the Dharma Flower Sutra we are clearly shown that almost exactly the same power and list of forms is also attributed to Wonderful Voice. The point, I believe, is not that there are two bodhisattvas with such power, but that *every* bodhisattva has such power. We are not talking about magical tricks here. The ability to take on different forms according to what is needed means just that, an ability to adapt to different situations, particularly to the different needs of people. Taking on different forms is no more and no less than the ability to serve others usefully, practically, and effectively. This is a power given not only to the bodhisattvas Kwan-yin and Wonderful Voice, but to each and every one of us.

Thus, one obvious meaning of this story for us is that we too can become bodhisattvas who take on different forms and roles in order to help others. And there is another side to this, even its opposite—anyone can be a bodhisattva for us. If Wonderful Voice Bodhisattva can take on any form, anyone we meet might be Wonderful Voice Bodhisattva in a form designed to help us! But very often at least, someone can be a bodhisattva for us only if we let them, only if we open ourselves in such a way as to enable someone to be a bodhisattva for us.

As we see in Chapter 12 of the Dharma Flower Sutra, there are two stories, both of which suggest the importance of enabling by seeing. The first is ostensibly a story about Devadatta, someone whom everyone, at least in the Buddhist world, knows is the epitome of evil. But in Chapter 12 we find none of this, which everyone knows already. Instead we find the Buddha telling a story about a previous life in which Devadatta was his teacher. We may think this story is mainly about Devadatta, but, more importantly, it is a story about the Buddha, especially about the Buddha's ability to see the bodhisattva in Devadatta. The Buddha enables Devadatta by assuring him that he too is to become a buddha.

The second story in Chapter 12 is about the dragon princess who becomes a buddha in an instant. Present are two men, Shariputra, who thinks that it is impossible for a woman to become a buddha, and Accumulated Wisdom Bodhisattva, who thinks it is crazy to think that a little girl could become awakened suddenly. What the dragon princess says to them is very interesting. "Just watch," she says, "use your holy powers to watch me become a buddha even more quickly than it took for Shakyamuni Buddha to take a jewel from my hand."

(LS 253) In a sense, a little girl becomes a buddha for them, but she can do this only if they used their "holy powers," their vision, to allow her to be a buddha for them, to open themselves to her being a buddha for them.

Normally we think of Buddha Dharma as coming from the Buddha. This is correct, of course. But it is also essential to see that the Dharma, and therefore the Buddha, can come to us from many sources—if we open ourselves to it.

The title of the English version of the autobiography of the founder of Rissho Kosei-kai, Nikkyo Niwano, is *Lifetime Beginner*. The term "beginner" has connotations of being inexperienced or green. The implication of this is, of course, that one always needs to be learning, always needs to be open to new experience, new stories, new ideas. It is easy to think of this remarkable man as being self-taught, which in a sense he was. But he was self-taught only by learning from others, a great variety of others. He learned, for example, about Buddhist teachings from Buddhist scholars, including some very famous Buddhist scholars, but he also learned about Buddhism, and received the Buddha Dharma from ordinary members of Rissho Kosei-kai. He was a lifetime learner. The importance of being open to others, of learning from them, even of seeing the Buddha in them, is something we might learn from the story of Wonderful Voice Bodhisattva.

In the Christian New Testament, the Gospel According to John speaks of "the Word." The Word was with God and was God; the Word "became flesh and dwelt among us." Wonderful Voice Bodhisattva is such a living word, the awakening that can come to us, not just as words spoken and written, but embodied in living beings, and not just in the body of one bodhisattva, but in many different bodies—bodies that are female as well as male, bodies that belong to the lowly as well as to the high, bodies that are nonhuman as well as human. Anyone we meet can be our extremely tall and handsome Wonderful Voice Bodhisattva. Truly, this is wonderful!

# 26

# KWAN-YIN

O NE COULD EASILY devote an entire chapter of this size to a discussion of the names of the bodhisattva Kwan-yin, without doubt the most popular and most often portrayed of Buddhist figures of any kind. Though there are variations, in Sanskrit this bodhisattva is known primarily as Avalokiteshvara. This name was translated into Chinese characters written in Wade-Giles transliteration as Kuan-shih-yin, which is often shortened to Kuan-yin. The Pinyin forms of these names are Guanshiyin and Guanyin.[37] These same Chinese characters are pronounced in slightly different ways in other Chinese dialects, such as Cantonese, where Kwan-yin becomes Kwun Yum, and in other languages such as Korean, where it is Gwaneum, or Japanese, where it becomes Kannon. In addition, the name Kuan-shih-tzu-tsai (Kanzejizai in Japanese pronunciation) or, in the shorter version, Kuan-tzu-tsai (Kanjizai) can often be seen. In the West, Kwan-yin is also known as the Goddess of Mercy, but this is not a translation.

While there is no universal agreement on how best to translate any of these names, the three characters involved in Kwan-shih-yin (Kanzeon in Japanese pronunciation) mean approximately this: *Kwan* has to do with seeing, sensing, observing, or perceiving; *shih* means "world"; and *yin* basically means "sound." So a very literal rendering of this name might be "perceiver of the world's sounds." But the kind of perception involved here is not an indifferent observing, not mere perception; it involves compassion. And the sounds involved are not just any noises but the cries of the suffering of the world. So I translate this name as "Regarder of the Cries of the World." While useful as a translation, that is too long to be convenient for some purposes, so, as Kwan-yin is one of the most commonly used names in English, as in Chinese, that is what I will primarily use here.

In similar fashion, Kuan-shih-tzu-tsai can mean "Regarder of the World's Freedom." From Sanskrit there are also other names, such as "Light of the World's Cries," and so on. And this same bodhisattva also has a great variety of names derived from numerous portrayals in Chinese and Japanese Buddhist art, images that for the most part are derived from stories about the bodhisattva's many different manifestations, both male and female. The most common of these include "Thousand-armed" or "Thousand-handed" or "Thousand-armed and thousand-eyed" Kwan-yin, so named because the image has a great many arms, typically with forty-two being used to represent a thousand. Often each of those hands has an eye in it. More often they hold a symbol of some kind, quite often some kind of implement or tool, such as a willow branch to drive away illness, a conch to summon friendly spirits, a vase or bottle for dispensing water or nectar, a monk's staff, a sutra, a bowl, and so on. Other popular forms include the "Sacred" or "Holy" Kwan-yin, the Water and Moon Kwan-yin, the White-robed Kwan-yin, the Kwan-yin of Eleven Faces, the Fish-basket Kwan-yin, the South Sea Kwan-yin, and the Wish-fulfilling Kwan-yin. It is often said that there are six forms of Kwan-yin, corresponding to the six kinds of living beings who are subject to rebirth, but there are at least two very different sets of six, and many popular forms of Kwan-yin are not included in either set of six. There are also lists of the thirty-three embodiments of Kwan-yin found in Chapter 25 of the

Lotus Sutra. Other East Asian sets show Kwan-yin in fifty-three forms, combining images from various Chinese sources.

In India, as Avalokiteshvara, Kwan-yin was associated with the god Shiva. Both are called Maheshvara (Great Lord) and descriptions of the two are often the same. Potalaka, Avalokiteshvara's mountain home, is also very similar to Shiva's. In China, this Potalaka would be identified with an island in Hangzhou Bay called "Puto-shan" (Universal Buddha Mountain, despite the fact that it really is not a mountain), a major site for tourists and Kwan-yin devotion.

In addition to Chapter 25 of the Dharma Flower Sutra, probably the most influential appearance of Avalokiteshvara in Buddhist sutras of Indian origin is in the Pure Land sutras, especially the Sutra on Contemplation of the Buddha of Infinite Life. There Avalokiteshvara appears, along with Mahasthamaprapta Bodhisattva,[38] as an attendant of Amitabha Buddha. The two bodhisattvas, whose features are described in great detail, serve primarily for guiding the spirits of the dead to Amitabha Buddha's Pure Land in the West. In artistic images, these two bodhisattvas often appear as a triad, with Amitabha in the middle, Mahasthamaprapta on his right, and Avalokiteshvara on his left. Both Mahasthamaprapta and Avalokiteshvara are dressed as Indian princes, with ample robes and jewelry of various kinds, and can be distinguished from each other mainly by the fact that Avalokiteshvara has an image of Amitabha Buddha in his headdress. Most images of Avalokiteshvara adopt this convention of having Amitabha Buddha's image in the headdress.

The close association of Kwan-yin with Amitabha continues to the present day, especially among followers of Pure Land Buddhism, a very large percentage of Chinese, Japanese, and American Buddhists. Kwan-yin's rise to preeminence among Buddhist figures in East Asia can be attributed in large part to the rise in popularity of Pure Land Buddhism among ordinary people, both in China and in Japan.

The primary discussion of Kwan-yin found in Buddhist sutras is the twenty-fifth chapter of the Dharma Flower Sutra, titled "The Universal

Gateway of Kwan-shih-yin Bodhisattva." In East Asia this chapter has frequently been circulated and used as an independent sutra, typically known as the Kwan-yin Sutra. But it is important to recognize that there are a great many other Chinese texts, some also known as sutras, some of which are Buddhist, some Taoist, some simply Chinese, that are devoted to Kwan-yin or in which Kwan-yin plays a major role. And there are other scriptures from India, especially the Avatamsaka Sutra, in which Kwan-yin plays an important role.

Though elements of it subsequently became very important in East Asian Buddhism, the story found in the Dharma Flower Sutra is not particularly dramatic or memorable.

## THE STORY

A bodhisattva named Inexhaustible Mind asks the Buddha why the bodhisattva Kwan-yin is called "Regarder of the Cries of the World." The Buddha explains that if those who are suffering sincerely call Kwan-yin's name with all their heart, they will immediately be heard and will be able to free themselves from suffering. A wide variety of possible misfortunes from which one can be saved and a large variety of benefits that can accrue from worshiping the Bodhisattva are mentioned. If a huge ship with thousands and thousands of fortune-seekers is caught in a storm at sea and blown ashore on an island of terrible beasts, if just one person calls to Kwan-yin, all of them will be saved. One has only to call out the name of the Bodhisattva in order to be saved from various calamities and dangers. One can be saved not only from external dangers but also from the three inner poisons—from lust or greed, from anger or rage, and from folly or foolishness. Praying to Kwan-yin can also result in having a baby of the desired gender, one who will be blessed with great merit, virtue, and wisdom if a boy and one who will be marked with great beauty and by long ago having planted roots of virtue and being loved and respected by all if a girl.

The Buddha says to Inexhaustible Mind Bodhisattva: "If there were countless hundreds of thousands of billions of living beings experiencing suffering and agony who heard of Bodhisattva Regarder of the Cries of the World and wholeheartedly called his name, Regarder of the Cries of the World Bodhisattva would immediately hear their cries, and all of them would be freed." (LS 371)

The Bodhisattva sometimes takes the form of a buddha, a pratyeka-buddha, a shravaka, a king, a prime minister, a wife, boy, or girl, or any of thirty-three bodies in order to help those who can be helped in such a way.

Inexhaustible Mind Bodhisattva then takes an extremely valuable necklace from around his neck and offers it to Kwan-yin. But the Bodhisattva does not accept it, until the Buddha pleads with Kwan-yin to do so out of compassion both for Inexhaustible Mind Bodhisattva and for all other living beings. Then Kwan-yin accepts the necklace and divides it into two parts, offering one to Shakyamuni Buddha and the other to the stupa of Abundant Treasures Buddha.

## COMMENTARY

The two elements that have been lifted out of this story and widely used for various purposes are the idea that calling the name of the Bodhisattva will be sufficient to save one from any kind of difficulty and the idea that Kwan-yin takes on a great variety of forms or bodies.

Nikkyo Niwano of Rissho Kosei-kai said that Chapter 25 is the most misunderstood chapter of the Lotus Sutra.[39] What he meant by this is that, properly understood, bodhisattvas are not gods from whom we should expect to receive special treatment, even in times of great trouble; bodhisattvas should be models for how we ourselves can be bodhisattvas, at least some of the time. In the Horin-kaku Guest Hall at the Tokyo headquarters of Rissho Kosei-kai there is a very large and magnificent statue of the Thousand-armed Kannon. In each of the hands we can see an implement of some kind, tools that represent skills that can be used to help others. When Founder Niwano first showed that statue to me, he emphasized that it should not be understood to mean that we should pray to Kannon to save us from our problems; rather, we should understand that the meaning of Kannon's thousand skills is that each one of us should develop a thousand skills for helping others.

In fact, however, Kwan-yin has more often been understood by devotees to be one who can do things for those who are devoted to her. This is based, at least to a degree, on the part of the story in the Lotus Sutra in which we are told that one has only to call out the name of the bodhisattva in order to be saved from a long list of calamities and dangers.

The list of misfortunes from which one can be saved by calling upon Kwan-yin is interesting but not terribly important, as the meaning is quite clear—Kwan-yin can save anyone from any misfortune. The list simply provides concrete examples. This power to save is why early Jesuit missionaries to China invented the term *Goddess of Mercy* to refer to Kwan-yin and relate her to Mary, the mother of Jesus. Kwan-yin, in fact, has been and still is a goddess of mercy for a great many, answering their prayers and bringing them comfort.

Of course, those who would follow the bodhisattva way should see great bodhisattvas as models for us and not be looking to gods or goddesses for special favors.

A Chinese poem of unknown origins says:

> The Dharma-body of Kwan-yin
> Is neither male nor female.
> If even the body is not the body,
> What attributes can there be? . . .
> Let it be known to all Buddhists:

Do not cling to form.
The bodhisattva is *you:*
Not the picture or the image.

Still, respecting the hidden wisdom of ordinary people, we might see Kwan-yin devotion as a skillful means used by the Buddha to bring the Dharma to ordinary people in the midst of their suffering. By offering them, through countless indigenous images, texts, poems, and devotional practices, a kind of access to Kwan-yin's compassion, a great many people have gained strength to embody compassion in their own lives.

Buddhism, perhaps especially Indian Buddhism, was closely associated with the goal of "supreme awakening," and therefore with a kind of wisdom, especially a kind of wisdom in which doctrines and teachings are most important. Even the term for *Buddhism* in Chinese and Japanese means "Buddhist teaching."

With the development of Kwan-yin devotion, while wisdom remained important, compassion came to play a larger role in the relative status of Buddhist virtues, especially among illiterate common people. Thus, there was a slight shift in the meaning of the "bodhisattva way." From being primarily a way toward an enlightened mind, it became primarily the way of compassionate action to save others.

The Dharma Flower Sutra itself, I believe, can be used to support the primacy of either wisdom or compassion. When it is teaching in a straightforward way, the emphasis is on teaching the Dharma as the most effective way of helping or saving others. But, taken collectively, the parables of the Dharma Flower Sutra suggest a different emphasis. The father of the children in the burning house does not teach the children how to cope with fire; he gets them out of the house. The father of the long-lost, poor son does not so much teach him in ordinary ways as he does by example and, especially, by giving him encouragement. The guide who conjures up a fantastic city for weary travelers does not teach by giving them doctrines for coping with a difficult situation; instead, he gives them a place in which to rest, enabling them to go on. The doctor with the children who have taken poison tries to teach them to take some good medicine but fails and resorts instead to shocking them by announcing his own death. All of these actions require, of course, considerable intelligence or wisdom. But what is emphasized is that they are done by people moved by compassion to benefit others.

Compassion is a useful virtue, in that it can be effectively used by anyone. One of the most impressive things one can experience, as I have on many occasions, is the compassion that dying people often have for those around them. On many occasions I have seen dying people attempt to calm and cheer friends and relatives at their bedside. Of course, everyone can be wise to some degree as well, but there surely is a sense in which the way of compassionate action is more open to everyone than a way that emphasizes the acquisition of wisdom.

Compassion is best embodied in skill, in compassionate action. The tools in the hands of the Thousand-armed Kwan-yin symbolize the many means by which Kwan-yin can help living beings in need. This imagery is, I believe, revealing of the kind of wisdom embodied in Kwan-yin—not some kind of esoteric knowledge of the mind alone, but the practical wisdom found not only in minds but also in hands.

But skill is, after all, a kind of wisdom. So compassion should not be seen in contrast to wisdom but only in contrast to *disembodied* wisdom. To be compassionate is to embody compassion, not just to feel it or think about it or contemplate it. It is to actualize compassion in the world, wherever we are, and thus in our relationships with relatives, neighbors, friends, and even strangers. It is to be compassionate. This is to embody the Buddha, that is, to give life to the Buddha in the present world.

Being embodied can be contrasted with being "on high," as Avalokiteshvara is described in some Indian Buddhist texts. To be embodied is to be a physical presence in this world. This means that we can see Kwan-yin not only in many splendid images in temples and museums but also in our mothers or sons or neighbors. Kwan-yin is not only a symbol of compassion, she *is* compassion, so that wherever compassion can be seen, Kwan-yin can be seen. Kwan-yin is not some god looking down at the world from a distance but the Buddha's compassion embodied in the actual world of quite ordinary men and women.

Tradition also says that we should understand that we ourselves should embody Kwan-yin, that if, for example, we concentrate on Kwan-yin or recite the Kwan-yin chapter, we can open ourselves to compassion, not to some abstract compassion from a distance, but to actually embodying compassion by being compassionate in our own lives and behavior.

The title of the twenty-fifth chapter of the Lotus Sutra is "The Universal Gateway of Kwan-shih-yin Bodhisattva." This implies that while the way of monks and nuns, the way of wisdom, the road to supreme awakening, may be extremely difficult, the way of Kwan-yin is open to all. This may be seen as dependent on the idea of universal buddhanature, the idea that every living being has the capacity and power to become a buddha. But the universal gateway of Kwan-yin is not necessarily dependent on the idea of buddha-nature. It is dependent, rather, on the idea that everyone can be compassionate, a far more accessible goal than that of becoming a buddha.

In the Dharma Flower Sutra this idea is suggested by a kind of list of the embodiments of Kwan-yin. Though these are often counted as thirty-three, and are sometimes even associated with other groups of thirty-three, such as the Heaven of the Thirty-three Gods, the Sutra does not mention the number thirty-three but only provides a list that can easily be counted as thirty, thirty-two, thirty-three, or even thirty-five. At temples in China, it is not uncommon to see a set of thirty-two or thirty-three panels depicting the various ways in which Kwan-yin can be embodied.

For each of the embodiments, the text says that for those who need someone in such and such a body, Kwan-yin appears in that body and teaches the Dharma to them. This means that the way in which Kwan-yin appears to someone is dependent on what the perceiver needs. In other words, Kwan-yin appears to people in many forms not as a way of showing off some sort of magical power but as a way of responding to the needs of people; this is precisely what is called "skillful means" earlier in the Dharma Flower Sutra. This is why, with the exception of a few named gods, the list is a list of generic titles. For example, it says that Kwan-yin appears in the form of a king but does not say that he appears in the form of "King So-and-So." This means that Kwan-yin can appear to us as any king, or as any housewife, in the form of anyone we meet. It means that anyone at all can be Kwan-yin for us.

The list includes shravakas, pratyekabuddhas, and gods but begins with the embodiment of Kwan-yin as a buddha. Any Buddhist scholar, indeed any educated monk, can tell you that Kwan-yin is a bodhisattva, not a buddha. But countless laypeople, and not a few nuns as well, can tell you that Kwan-yin is a fully awakened buddha who has chosen to be in this world to help relieve the suffering of all living beings, an idea that can also be found in much Chinese Buddhist literature. The assertion in the Lotus Sutra that Kwan-yin appears in the body of a buddha to teach the Dharma to those who need someone in the body of a buddha in order to be saved suggests that it is quite reasonable for Kwan-yin to be the Buddha for someone. This tendency of ordinary people in East Asia to regard Kwan-yin as the Buddha can be seen as a certain kind of wisdom, an understanding that the Buddha can come to us in many different forms, including those of Kwan-yin. While often seen by scholars as a departure from scriptures, popular devotion to Kwan-yin can be seen as a fulfillment of the claim in the Dharma Flower Sutra that Kwan-yin can take on the body of a buddha.

The story related above is found in Chapter 25, but, much more than with any other story in the Dharma Flower Sutra, the story of Kwan-yin develops more profoundly and significantly outside the Sutra, in Chinese religion and culture, beginning around the end of the tenth century. Centering on Kwan-yin devotion rather than doctrine, Chinese Buddhism gradually evolved from a religion of aristocrats and monks into a popular religion of common people. In images, Kwan-yin was portrayed less and less as an Indian prince and more often in a relaxed pose, sitting on a rock for example. Kwan-yin is portrayed, in other words, as accessible to common people. And like virtually all Chinese gods but unlike Indian bodhisattvas, Kwan-yin was increasingly seen as a human being, even one who has a birthday.

While both the concept of appealing for help by calling the name of the bodhisattva and the idea that Kwan-yin takes on many forms remained important elements in Kwan-yin devotion and religious practices, a great many other stories, extra-canonical stories, especially stories of embodiments of Kwan-yin, attracted popular attention in China. The most common of these stories to come down to the present day is the story of Princess Miao-shan.[40] Taught to them by their mothers and grandmothers, it has had much influence on how Kwan-yin is perceived and understood by Chinese Buddhists.

Miao-shan (meaning "wonderfully good") was the third daughter of King Miao-chuang. She was naturally attracted to Buddhism, keeping a vegetarian diet from a young age, reading Buddhist scriptures during the day, and meditating at night. Having no sons, the King hoped to choose an heir from among his sons-in-law. When Miao-shan became old enough to marry, unlike her two older sisters who had married men chosen by their father, she refused to be married to anyone. This angered her father so much that he found a variety of ways in which to punish her. For a while, for example, she was made to do hard work in the garden. When those tasks were completed, she was allowed to go to the White Sparrow nunnery, where she underwent further trials designed to discourage her from becoming a nun. But she persevered. So the King burned down the temple, killing the five hundred nuns who lived there, and he had Miao-shan executed for disobedience.

While her body was being protected by a mountain spirit, Miao-shan's spirit traveled to a purgatory, where she was able to save many beings by preaching the Dharma to them. Returning to earth, she went to Fragrant Mountain, meditated for nine years, and became fully awakened.

By this time her father the King had become very ill with a mysterious incurable disease. Disguised as a wandering monk, Miao-shan went to her father and told him that there was only one thing that could save him—a medicine that was made from the eyes and hands of someone who had never felt anger. And she even told him where such a person could be found. There she secretly offered her own eyes and hands to be turned into medicine, which was taken by the King, curing him of his disease.

The King then went to Fragrant Mountain to give thanks to the one who had saved him. There he immediately recognized the ascetic without eyes or hands as his own daughter. Overwhelmed with remorse, the King and his entire family converted to Buddhism. And Miao-shan was transformed into her real form—Kwan-yin with a thousand arms and eyes. Soon after this, Miao-shan died and her remains were placed in a pagoda.[41]

In the process of becoming popular in China, for reasons that are both obscure and complicated, and including identification with Princess Miao-shan, Kwan-yin began to be perceived and portrayed not only as a male figure but also as female, and quite often as androgynously male and female. Female Kwan-yin figures are often dressed in a white robe, perhaps signifying that Kwan-yin is not a monastic but a layperson. As far as I know, there is no precedent for such female, white-robed Kwan-yin images outside China. She is a Chinese development. While it is sometimes said that in China the male Avalokiteshvara was transformed into a female, I think it is important to recognize that the tradition of both male and female forms has continued in East Asia down to the present. Thus Kwan-yin should not be regarded as a male transformed into a female but as one who is both male and female and is recognized as such in East Asian Buddhist art by being given both male and female forms.

Several of the forms listed in the Lotus Sutra are explicitly female. Included are a nun, a female lay believer, four kinds of housewives, and a girl. Some others could be male or female, such as that of "an ordinary citizen." Thus we can see that the transformation in China of Avalokiteshvara from male to both male and female is entirely in accord with what is written in the Lotus Sutra.

Another Chinese development in which Kwan-yin plays a unifying role is the common portrayal of her as being accompanied by, or served by, Sudhana and the dragon princess, a boy and a girl—one from the Avatamsaka Sutra, the other from the Lotus Sutra, two sutras which are closely associated with two different and rival schools of Buddhism.

All human beings, I believe, have both male and female qualities, but strict adherence to the ideas that all buddhas are male, and that nuns should always be subservient to monks, restricts access in both women and men to their female selves. By being a buddha who is both male and female, Kwan-yin provides a kind of balance to the over-whelmingly male-oriented weight of Buddhist tradition, enabling women to appreciate their value and men to appreciate the woman often hidden in themselves.

Kwan-yin, I have said on many occasions, represents a kind of "lowland Buddhism." By this I mean that in contrast to those who would see religions as a matter of climbing to a mountaintop to enjoy some kind of "peak experience," the Dharma Flower Sutra, especially as it is embodied in Kwan-yin, is a way that emphasizes the importance of being earthly, of being this-worldly, of being involved in relieving suffering.

The longer, Sanskrit Heart Sutra has Avalokiteshvara looking down from on high, but the shorter, Chinese Heart Sutra knows nothing of that. In East Asia, Kwan-yin is a bodhisattva of the earth, one who sits on rocks, one who wears a simple white robe, one who takes on a great variety of human forms, including female forms, one who appears in a great variety of indigenous stories and scriptures as one who embodies compassion in this world.

I believe that we should also be lowland Buddhists like Kwan-yin, seeking the low places, the valleys, even the earthy and dirty places, where people are suffering and in need. That is how we will meet the bodhisattva Kwan-shih-yin, at least if we are lucky or perceptive. That is where we will find those who hear and respond with compassion to the cries and sorrows of this world. They too are bodhisattvas of compassion, Kwan-shih-yin embodied.

# 27

# THE FAMILY OF
# KING WONDERFULLY ADORNED

F OR THE FIRST fifteen centuries or so of its life, Buddhism was almost exclusively a religion of monastics, usually supported by laypeople. Initially it was exclusively a society of male monks, who separated themselves from ordinary life and responsibilities by leaving home to follow the Buddha.[42] The Buddha himself abandoned his home and family in order to pursue an ascetic life. For the most part, monks do not have a lot of interest in family life; it is after all what they have abandoned.

In the Dharma Flower Sutra we have three parables that have to do with fathers and sons. In all of them no mother and no women appear at all. So it is very interesting that we find in Chapter 27, nearly at the end of the Lotus Sutra, a family drama, the story of a king named Wonderfully Adorned, his wife, and their two sons.

## THE STORY

The Buddha tells the assembly that long ago there was a buddha with the very long name of Wisdom Blessed by the King of Constellations

Called the Sound of Thunder in the Clouds. (Here, I'll call him "Wisdom Blessed" for short.) Like Shakyamuni, Wisdom Blessed Buddha taught and preached the Dharma Flower Sutra. And it was during the age of his Dharma that there lived a king by the name of Wonderfully Adorned, with his wife, Queen Pure Virtue, and their two sons, Pure Treasury and Pure Eyes.

The two sons had acquired great magical powers as a result of doing everything a bodhisattva should do, including perfecting seven bodhisattva practices, having good attitudes toward others, practicing thirty-seven ways to awakening, and achieving seven types of contemplation. But their father was a follower of a non-Buddhist way. So the sons went to their mother and pleaded with her to go with them to hear the Buddha preach the Lotus Sutra. The mother agreed, but told them to first get their father's permission, and, with sympathy for him, to use their magical powers to persuade him.

The sons then went up into the air before their father and performed a variety of magical wonders—standing, walking, sitting, and lying down in the air, emitting water and fire from their bodies, suddenly becoming giants or dwarfs, diving into the earth as though it were water, walking on water as though it were earth, and so on. In this way they were able to open their father's mind, enabling him to understand and have faith in the Dharma.

Naturally, the King was filled with joy, and wanted to know who their teacher was. To this they replied that it was Wisdom Blessed Buddha, who teaches the Dharma Flower Sutra everywhere. Of course the father wanted to go with them to see the Buddha.

Then the sons went back to their mother and begged her to allow them to leave home so that they could practice the Way under Wisdom Blessed Buddha. As it is extremely difficult to see a buddha, she said, the mother agreed. Then the sons asked both parents to go with them to see the Buddha. Thus, all four went to meet the Buddha, accompanied by tens of thousands of various ministers and servants.

The Buddha taught the King, showing him the Way and making him very happy. The King and Queen removed the extremely valuable necklaces they were wearing and tossed them over the Buddha, whereupon the necklaces flew up into the sky and were transformed into a jeweled platform on which there was a jeweled couch and billions of heavenly garments. And the Buddha, sitting cross-legged on the couch, emitted great rays of light and announced to everyone that, after much study and practice as a monk, King Wonderfully Adorned would become a buddha.

Following this, the King abdicated his throne, gave up his home, and with his wife and two sons, practiced the Buddha Way according to the Dharma Flower Sutra for eighty-four thousand years under Wisdom Blessed Buddha. Following contemplation, the former king went to Wisdom Blessed Buddha up in the air to praise his sons for doing the Buddha's work, enabling him to see the Buddha and inspiring the roots of goodness which were already in him. "These two sons," he said, "are my good friends." (LS 391)

And the Buddha agreed, praising such friends and explaining that anyone who plants roots of goodness will subsequently have good friends. "A good friend," he said, "is the great cause and condition by which one is transformed, led to see the Buddha, and aroused to seek supreme awakening." (LS 391) After praising the Buddha at length, the former king promised never again to follow his own whims, allow himself a wrong view, or experience pride, arrogance, anger, or other evil states.

Shakyamuni Buddha then explained to the assembly that King Wonderfully Adorned was a previous life of the present Padmashri Bodhisattva, Queen Pure Virtue was a previous life of Marks of Shining Adornment, who appeared in that other world out of compassion for the King, and the sons were the present bodhisattvas Medicine King and Superior Medicine, who had gained such powers by planting roots of goodness under countless buddhas.

## COMMENTARY

This story is primarily about the relationship of the father, King Wonderfully Adorned, with his sons. But we may find the role of the mother, Queen Pure Virtue, also of interest. In India at that time, women were very subordinate to men and therefore wives were to their husbands. Of course, this queen does not challenge her husband directly. In fact, she insists that their sons respect their father, even though he is of a different religion. As is often the case with modern mothers, however, this mother seems to be the glue holding the family together, a kind of mediator between the father and the sons. More than anyone else in the story, she displays great skill, in effect teaching the sons how to persuade and convert their father to the Buddhist path.

It is also interesting that we find the Dharma Flower Sutra here being sensitive to the possibility of families having members with different religious perspectives. Sometimes the term "heretical" has been used to translate the Chinese/Japanese term *gedo* which literally means "off the path," where the path is the Way of the Buddha. It simply means non-Buddhist. Actually, one could say that Buddhism itself is a Hindu heresy. "Heresy" means departure from something already established, some "orthodoxy," and is always more or less within some tradition. Thus "Christian heresy" is possible and so is "Buddhist heresy" but that is not what is meant by *gedo*, especially here, where the King is a follower of brahman views, that is, of orthodox views.

So the King's beliefs are different, perhaps even more "orthodox" than those of the sons, who have decided to follow the Buddha of that time. What should the sons do in such a case? Here they are urged by their mother to continue to respect and honor their father.

Buddhism does not reject family life as such. And yet, by setting up an alternative, celibate, monastic institution, traditional Buddhism did have and continues to have a problematic relation to families. But the Lotus Sutra says little about monastic rules and life as such, emphasizing the importance of life in the world being dedicated to the work, especially to the teaching work, of the Buddha. Thus, we can understand this story as saying that it is good if a whole family can devote itself to the Buddha Way.

The Buddha in this story says that anyone who plants roots of goodness will have good friends. This idea of "roots of goodness" or "wholesome roots" can be compared to buddha-nature, but is not exactly the same. Buddha-nature is understood to be given by nature and unavoidable. In Buddhist literature, "roots of goodness," on the other hand, are typically "planted" in former lives, and are thus not inherent.

The main point in the use of "roots of goodness" here is that acts have consequences. Each of us has resources to draw upon. We don't start from nothing. Those who have preceded us, even those who have preceded us by many centuries, have laid foundations for our own lives. But, in the same way, we too can plant roots of goodness, making the world, even into the distant future, a more wholesome place for those who will come after us.

In this story, leaving home is the primary indication of personal transformation. The Dharma Flower Sutra frequently uses a phrase that means "teach and transform." Usually it involves a transformation from ordinary monastic life to the life of a bodhisattva, that is, undergoing a change from being focused on one's own salvation to being focused on helping others. Here, however, leaving home is used to indicate the transformation from being a householder to being a full-time follower of the Buddha. We are not told whether King Wonderfully Adorned and his family shaved their heads and became monks and nuns, as what is important here is not so much their status as it is their behavior. "The practice of [the Buddha's] teachings and precepts," says the King, "will bring peace and comfort and good feelings. From this day forward, I will no longer follow my own whims, nor will I allow myself wrong views, pride or arrogance, anger, or any other evil states." (LS 392)

What is involved, then, is essentially the forsaking of more purely selfish interests for the good of the whole—that is, doing the work of the Buddha. This is a radical change in life, a kind of conversion. Thus, though not the same, it can be related to and compared with the central theme of Christianity, expressed there both as conversion and as resurrection—that is, the ever-present possibility of a radically new, transformed life.

In Rissho Kosei-kai, for instance, Founder Niwano thought that such conversion is symbolized in this story by the "magic" of the two sons. By performing fantastic stunts, they showed their father that the Buddha Dharma had changed their lives—their bodies and their behavior—and not just their words.[43] Especially with those who are closest to us, teaching by example may be more important than attempting to teach by words alone. Of course, some things can probably only be taught by words, but when it comes to teaching religious faith, how one lives or embodies one's faith may be more persuasive than what one says about it.

The Lotus Sutra teaches that we should reflect the Dharma in our own lives, especially in relation to those who are close to us, such as other members of our family. Just thinking we are Buddhist, or saying we are Buddhist, or belonging to a Buddhist organization, or even regularly performing Buddhist practices such as meditation or recitation, is not enough. It doesn't mean much unless it affects how we behave in everyday life.

And when this happens, all kinds of transformations are possible. When the King and Queen give their extremely valuable necklaces to the Buddha, the necklaces are transformed into a jeweled platform with a seat for the Buddha from which he emits light. The point of this, I think, is that when we devote ourselves to the Buddha, not only can our lives be transformed, but ordinary things as well. The necklaces can symbolize any gift to the Buddha. Here the necklaces are exceptionally valuable because they are from a king and queen. But every gift to the Buddha is valuable in its own way. In Rissho Kosei-kai, there is a program called the Donate-a-Meal Campaign, a simple program through which members and others forgo meals in order to contribute to a fund for peace. Such donations are a kind of gift to the Buddha. Such gifts, though individually small, by being combined with those of others may be transformed into something very great.

It is no accident that the first of the six transcendental bodhisattva practices is generosity, often understood as giving, or making donations.

## FRIENDS, FAMILY, AND TEACHERS

King Wonderfully Adorned praises his sons, calling them his friends or teachers, and Wisdom Blessed Buddha responds that good friends or teachers do the work of the Buddha, showing people the Way, causing them to enter it, and bringing them joy.

The term used here, *zenchishiki* in Japanese, is not easy to translate. Some use "good friends," some "good teachers." Perhaps good "acquaintances" or "associates" would be a good translation, for there is a sense in which our good friends are always also our teachers. The point is that the help or guidance of others can be enormously useful. Entering the Way, becoming more mindful or awakened, is not something best done in isolation. We all need good friends and teachers.

In the Lotus Sutra, the term *pratyekabuddha* is used to refer to monks who go off into forests by themselves to pursue their own awakening in solitude. But while the term is used frequently in the early chapters and pratyekabuddhas are made prominent by being named as one of the four holy states of buddhas, bodhisattvas, pratyekabuddhas, and shravakas, we never learn anything at all about any particular pratyekabuddha. While we hear the names of a great many buddhas, bodhisattvas, and shravakas in the Lotus Sutra, we never encounter the name of even a single pratyekabuddha. This leads me to think that, at least for the Lotus Sutra, pratyekabuddhas are not very important.

Though there probably was a historic forest-monk tradition in India, in the Lotus Sutra the pratyekabuddha seems to fill a kind of logical role. That is, there are those who strive for awakening primarily in monastic communities, the shravakas, and there are those who strive for awakening in ordinary communities, the bodhisattvas. There needs to be room for those who strive for awakening apart from all communities—the pratyekabuddhas. But from the bodhisattva perspective of the Dharma Flower Sutra, pratyekabuddhas are in a sense irrelevant. Since they do not even teach others, they indeed do no harm, but neither do they contribute to the Buddha's work of transforming the world into a buddha land.

For the Dharma Flower Sutra, the ideal is the life of the bodhi-sattva, which is also the life of the Buddha. And that life cannot be led in isolation. It necessarily involves both being informed by and teaching others. Some of those we teach or learn from may be our teachers or students or close friends in a more or less formal sense, but many only become our friends in relation to the Dharma—they become our friends in an important sense because of the Dharma relationship we have with them. Such others, while not our teachers or friends in a formal sense, can nevertheless be true teachers and friends.

Though the amount of time I enjoyed in direct conversation with the founder of Rissho Kosei-kai was not very great, and we were never close friends in the ordinary sense, I always think of him as being among my most important teachers and closest of friends. He was and is my Dharma teacher. In this story, the formal relationship is father and sons, even king and princes, but the Dharma relationship is one of teacher and student or true friends.

In Japan during Bon festival season many people visit a temple associated with their families to invite and guide their ancestors' spirits to return home for a brief visit. And they light small fires with which to welcome them back home. In other words, Bon is a special time for remembering what our ancestors have contributed to our own lives. But it would be inaccurate, I think, to restrict our respect for our ancestors only to those with whom we have a blood relationship. Those who have had an important influence on our lives include not only such ancestors in a narrow sense, but all of those who have taught us, including some we've never known personally. That is why it is appropriate that in the ritual "transfer of blessings" we recognize a great host of spirits, both related and unrelated to us in a biological sense.

Another way of putting the point of this story is that we should care about the social environment in which we live. It's a well-known fact that if people who are "rehabilitated" in prison return to the same social environment, they will soon revert to the kind of behavior that led to their being in prison. Many years ago, I had the privilege of working with disturbed adolescent children at a residential treatment center for such children. There, too, we knew that after months and sometimes years of working to restore highly disturbed young men and women to normal lives, if they were returned to the same social environment there was a very great likelihood that they would revert to the kind of depression and ugly behavior that resulted in their being sent to the treatment center. Finding an alternative social environment for those who were ready to leave was often not easy, but those who worked with such young people knew that the kind of social environment in which they were placed would make an enormous difference in what became of them.

And, coming from the other side, it comes as no surprise to parents that the young can teach and lead their elders. Every parent knows this. But there is more than that involved in the story at hand. Buddhism sometimes breaks radically with social conventions—and the most important symbol and reality of that is the exhortation to children to break with their parents and leave home. In this story, the break with convention is that the sons become teachers of the father, rather than the expected opposite.

In parables in early chapters of the Dharma Flower Sutra, a father teaches his children, but here, toward the end of the Sutra, we are reminded that it is not always so, that the opposite can also be the case, and that children can be teachers of their parents. Part of the significance of this is that we should expect the Dharma to come to us from surprising places, including our children. Earlier we have seen that it can come even from our enemies, or from a young girl.

This is related to the idea of the Universal Buddha—the Dharma is everywhere for those who have the eyes to see it and the ears with which to hear it. If we are open to the buddha-nature in others, we will see potential buddhas everywhere.

Just as Buddhism breaks with conventional traditions, the Dharma Flower Sutra sometimes breaks from Buddhist traditions. Almost everywhere they are mentioned, including in other parts of the Lotus Sutra, there are six special bodhisattva practices, often called "perfections" from the Sanskrit term *paramita*, because they are practices through which bodhisattvas should try to perfect or improve themselves.

Though they have been translated in other ways, the usual six are: generosity in giving; morality, sometimes understood as following commandments or precepts; patiently enduring hardship; perseverance or devotion to one's goals; meditation or meditative concentration; and wisdom. To these six a seventh is added in this chapter—the practice of skillful means.

On the one hand, it is appropriate that the practice of skillful means is added to the normal bodhisattva practices. Among other things, it makes clear that the use of skillful means is not, as some have said, something that can be done only by a buddha—but indeed by any Dharma teacher. Here it is made abundantly clear that use of skillful means is a practice of all who follow the bodhisattva path.

As you teach or share Buddha Dharma, you may want to devise your own list of bodhisattva practices. I once gave a talk about the eleven practices of the Lotus Sutra. If I were doing that talk again today, I would have to make it a list of twelve. The point is that the Lotus Sutra encourages us to adapt the Dharma and our ways of teaching it creatively, in accord with what is most likely to be useful in our own place and time.

## FOLLOWING THE TRUTH

The King follows the truth when it is shown to him, even though it is his own sons who lead him to the truth. This probably is the main point intended in the story. The Dharma Flower Sutra wants us to realize that we too must follow the truth, regardless of the source.

Following the truth means not only recognizing it, but also acting in accord with it. The King sees truth in the deeds of his sons and he follows them to see the Buddha.

In this sense, Buddhism can be seen as radically anti-authoritarian. We should follow the truth regardless of convention, regardless of from where or from whom it comes. But, at the same time, this final authority of the individual has to be kept in check by having good associations, good friends, and teachers.

Thus, Buddhism is here again a kind of middle way—saying follow the truth as you yourself see it, but be sure that you are looking in the right places, that you are looking critically, and that your perceptions are shared by good friends. Doing so makes you a "child of the Buddha."

Especially in early chapters of the Lotus Sutra, the expression "child of the Buddha" is frequently used as equivalent to "bodhisattva." For some this might signify leaving home in order to become a monastic, as in this story King Wonderfully Adorned and his entire family leave home to follow Wisdom Blessed Buddha. "Leaving home" in Chinese and Japanese means becoming a monk or nun, and thus becoming what was often thought of as a true Buddhist.

One of the truly liberating teachings of the Dharma Flower

Sutra and Mahayana Buddhism generally is that one does not have to become a monk or nun in order to follow the bodhisattva way of being, just like the Buddha himself, a Dharma teacher. As we see most explicitly in Chapter 10 of the Dharma Flower Sutra, anyone can be a Dharma teacher for others. Such Dharma teachers are all children of the Buddha. But here being a child of the Buddha is not so much an alternative, as it is when one leaves home to follow a buddha, as it is an addition, a kind of fulfillment of being a child of one's biological parents. This is what is symbolized in this story by the fact that the whole family—father, mother, children, and servants—gives up domestic life in order to follow a buddha together.

Thus, the meaning of this story for us is that we can be children of our parents and parents of our children, or have no children at all, and still be children, true followers, of the Buddha. This potential to be a true child of the Buddha, according to the Dharma Flower Sutra, is not initially something we have to earn or learn, it is given to us, just as both our parents and our children are given to us. Relationships created by birth can be grossly distorted or even forgotten, but cannot be completely destroyed or abolished. So, from the moment of our birth, our relationship with the Buddha, a relationship that has close affinities to the relationship of a parent with a child, is always being given to us and can never be completely rejected or abolished.

In a way, this is the lesson of the story of Devadatta in Chapter 12 of the Dharma Flower Sutra. No matter how hard he tried to harm the Buddha, he could not prevent the Buddha from seeing the potential in him for becoming a buddha himself. So too with us. No matter how much we may fail to follow the bodhisattva path, no matter how much we may fail to deal adequately with the poisons of greed, anger, and foolishness in us, no matter how weak or sick or tired we may become, nothing on heaven or earth, not even a buddha, can remove or destroy our ability to do good by being a bodhisattva for others.

# 28

## UNIVERSAL SAGE BODHISATTVA

THE TITLE OF Chapter 28 of the Lotus Sutra can reasonably be translated as "Encouragement of Universal Sage Bodhisattva." There is widespread agreement among translators about the term "encouragement" in this title, but not about the name of the bodhisattva, in Sanskrit known as Samantabhadra.

In Chinese he is consistently known as P'u-hsien (Puxian) and in Japanese, pronouncing the same Chinese characters, he is known as Fugen. The first of the two Chinese characters in the name means "universal" or "universally." It is the same character as that found in the title of Chapter 25 of the Dharma Flower Sutra, the chapter on the Universal Gateway of Kwan-shih-yin Bodhisattva. In both cases, this universality has not so much to do with being everywhere as with being open or available to everyone.

The meaning of the second character in the name of this bodhisattva is more problematic. It clearly can mean "virtue" or "virtuous," and most often does. Thus, the name has been rendered as "Universal Virtue" or "Universal Good." And since to be virtuous is to be worthy, one translator has used "Universally Worthy." The character in question can also mean "wise" or "wisdom." And so the name has also been translated as "Universally Wise." In an attempt to combine virtue and wisdom in a single term, like one other translator of the Lotus Sutra, I think "Universal Sage" is the most appropriate name in English, as a sage is normally both virtuous and wise. The excellent translation of the Lotus Sutra into modern French also uses "Sage."[44]

Here we are concerned with Chapter 28 of the Dharma Flower Sutra, but we should understand that this Sutra is not the primary textual source for accounts of Universal Sage Bodhisattva. Long associated in East Asia with the Dharma Flower Sutra as its "closing" sutra is the Sutra of Meditation on the Dharma Practice of Universal Sage Bodhisattva. Though short, this sutra is a kind of visualization meditation in which there is a great deal of interesting symbolic imagery. But even that sutra is not the most important source for Universal Sage Bodhisattva. For that we have to turn to the much larger and dramatic Avatamsaka Sutra, known in Chinese as the Huayan, in Japanese as the Kegon, and often in English as the "Flower Garland Sutra" or just the "Garland Sutra."

Here is how Universal Sage appears in Chapter 28 of the Dharma Flower Sutra.

## THE STORY

Universal Sage Bodhisattva comes from the East accompanied by numerous other bodhisattvas and surrounded by a great assembly of uncountable numbers of various gods, dragons, satyrs, centaurs, ashuras, griffins, chimeras, pythons, people, nonhuman beings, and others, all displaying dignity, virtue, and divine powers. As usual in such stories, in all the lands through which he passes the land shakes, lotus flowers rain down from the heavens, and marvelous music can be heard in the sky.

Arriving at Holy Eagle Peak, the bodhisattva pays respect to the Buddha by prostrating himself before him and circling around him. He then explains to the Buddha that in a distant world he had heard

Shakyamuni Buddha preaching the Dharma Flower Sutra and had come to hear and receive it directly. Now, he says, he wants to learn how people would be able to obtain this Sutra after the Buddha's death.

The Buddha says that one would need to meet four conditions: to be protected and kept in mind by buddhas, to plant roots of virtue, to join those who are determined to be awakened, and to be determined to save all living beings.

Universal Sage then promises the Buddha that he will protect anyone who receives and embraces the Sutra in the last five hundred years of the evil age. Accompanied by other great bodhisattvas, he will go to such people mounted on a great white elephant with six tusks in order to protect them, "free them from weakness and disease, give them peace and comfort, and make sure no one takes advantage of them." (LS 394) And he will help them to learn the Dharma Flower Sutra, reading and reciting it with them, and enabling them to remember parts they had forgotten.

Having seen him, people who seek, accept, embrace, read, recite, or copy this Dharma Flower Sutra, people who want to study it and put it into practice, should completely devote themselves to it for twenty-one days. Then Universal Sage Bodhisattva will come to them on his elephant, filling them with joy and enabling them by seeing him to remember and understand the Sutra and acquire various concentrations and incantations.

Universal Sage then recites some incantations before the Buddha, and tells the Buddha of the various wonderful rewards that will come to those who read, copy, recite, or keep the Sutra of the Lotus Flower of the Wonderful Dharma.

People who do no more than copy the Sutra will be reborn in the heaven of the thirty-three gods, where eighty-four thousand goddesses, performing all kinds of music, will welcome and entertain them. And if there are people who receive and embrace the Sutra, read and recite it, remember it correctly, and understand its meaning, the hands of a thousand buddhas will be extended to them when their lives come to an end, freeing them from fear and preventing them from falling into evil ways. They will go straight to the Tushita heaven where Maitreya Bodhisattva is surrounded by other great bodhisattvas and hundreds of thousands of billions of goddesses.

Then Universal Sage Bodhisattva promises that after the death of the Buddha, he will protect the Sutra, making it possible for it to spread throughout the land and never come to an end. The Buddha, in turn, praises Universal Sage, especially for vowing to protect the Sutra, and he promises to protect those who receive and embrace the name of Universal Sage.

Anyone, the Buddha says, who receives and embraces, reads and recites, remembers correctly, practices, and copies this Sutra should be regarded as having seen the Buddha, heard the Sutra from the Buddha, made offering to the Buddha, been praised by the Buddha for doing good, been patted on the head by the Buddha, and covered by the Buddha's robe. They "will never again be greedy for or attached to worldly pleasures." They will have no liking for scriptures of non-Buddhists or "other jottings," nor ever again take pleasure in associating with such people or with other evil people. They will be virtuous in every way, completely untroubled by the three poisons or by such things as envy, pride, and arrogance. Their few desires will be easily satisfied, enabling them to do the work of Universal Sage Bodhisattva. Unattached to things, they will be happy in this life. They will soon become supremely awakened buddhas. Those who abuse such a person will suffer horribly, while those who praise and make offerings to such people will be richly rewarded.

## COMMENTARY

In East Asian Buddhist temples and art one can find portrayals of many different bodhisattvas, but only five are found over and over again, in nearly all temples and museums. Their Indian names are Avalokitesh-vara, Maitreya, Manjushri, Kshitigarbha, and Samantabhadra. In English they commonly called Kwan-yin (from Chinese), Maitreya, Manjushri (both from Sanskrit), Jizo (from Japanese), and Universal Sage. All except Jizo are prominent in the Lotus Sutra, though in different ways. While both Kwan-yin and Universal Sage have entire chapters devoted to them, except for a mention of Kwan-yin as present in the great assembly of Chapter 1, they do not otherwise appear in the rest of the text, while Manjushri and Maitreya appear often throughout the Sutra. In typical Chinese Buddhist temples, where the central figure is a buddha or buddhas, to the right one can see a statue of Manjushri mounted on a lion, and to the left Universal Sage riding on an elephant, usually a white elephant with six tusks.

While both Kwan-yin and Maitreya are said to symbolize compassion and Manjushri usually symbolizes wisdom, Universal Sage is often used to symbolize awakened action, embodying wisdom and compassion in everyday life. Above the main entrance to Rissho Kosei-kai's Great Sacred Hall, for instance, there is a wonderful set of paintings depicting Manjushri and wisdom on the right, Maitreya and compassion on the left, and in the middle, the embodiment of these in life—Universal Sage Bodhisattva.

Here, in Chapter 28 of the Dharma Flower Sutra, Universal Sage becomes the vehicle for specifying the four conditions necessary for acquiring the Dharma Flower Sutra. Three of these are matters of action, things we do or can do. At least to some extent we can choose to plant roots of virtue, choose to join those who are determined to be awakened, and choose to be determined to save all the living. The first of the four, on the other hand, is quite different. Being protected and kept in mind by buddhas is not something we can choose; rather, it is more like a gift. Faith, at least in one of its dimensions, is the trust and confidence that we are always under the care of buddhas.

Being under the protection and care of buddhas does not mean that no harm can come to us. We should know that even with the protection of buddhas, the world is a dangerous place. Shakyamuni Buddha, we should remember, was harmed more than once during his teaching career and probably died from food poisoning. We can never entirely escape from a whole host of dangers, including disease, aging, crime, and war. What the Lotus Sutra teaches is not that we can be completely free from danger, but that no matter what dangers we have to face, there are resources, both in ourselves and in our communities, that make it possible for us to cope with such dangers. By having faith in the Buddha, doing good by helping others, genuinely aspiring to become more and more fully awakened through wise and compassionate practice, and by extending our compassion not only to our family and our friends but to all living beings, the dangers we face will recede into the background. They will not go away, but we will not be dominated by them.

To have faith in the Buddha is to take refuge in the Buddha. It means that embodying the Buddha in our everyday lives is our highest good. This is to live in faith, to trust life itself. Such faith is not a license to stupidly do dangerous things, but it does make it possible to live an abundant life, without undue fear or caution, even perhaps in the eyes of the world to be a little foolish. This is part of what it means to be in the care of the buddhas.

Next on the list is "planting roots of virtue," which is a kind of metaphor for the general Buddhist interest in causality. It is based on the idea that, in general, good deeds produce good effects. In the Chinese and Japanese versions of the Dharma Flower Sutra, there are three different terms, all of which I think mean practically the same thing. Here, and in other places in the Sutra, we have "roots of virtue." A little later in the chapter, and in other places in the Sutra, we find "roots of goodness." And in still other places in the Sutra we can see a different term that means "good roots." Like roots of goodness, roots of virtue are typically planted in former lives. But the main point is that acts have consequences. Just as good roots are likely to produce good fruit, good acts are likely to produce good consequences. The metaphor is apt. Just as there is no guarantee that good apple tree roots will result in good apples, as many things can intervene, such as drought, insects, disease, or frost, so too there is no guarantee that good deeds will produce good results, as bad habits, greed, anger, stupidity, and so on can easily intervene. In this sense, life is always precarious. What we think is doing good can always turn out to have been the wrong choice. But if we plant roots of virtue, if we do what we believe is really good, the likelihood that good will result from our actions is vastly increased.

From the day we are born, each of us has resources to draw upon, resources provided by nature, by our mothers and fathers, by our communities, and by our teachers and ancestors. We do not start from nothing. Those who have preceded us as our biological ancestors, and those who are our religious ancestors and teachers as well, have laid foundations for our own lives for which we can be grateful. In the same way, we too can plant roots of goodness, seeking to make the world a more wholesome place for our descendants, for all those who will come after us in the future. The future is forever, but it is also tomorrow. What we do now is important for what will be tomorrow as well as for the more distant future.

Next, joining those who are determined to be awakened, is the third of the conditions for fulfilling the Dharma Flower Sutra. Here two things are involved: being determined to become awakened and joining similarly minded people.

Most simply, being determined to become awakened, the aspiration to awakening, called *bodhichitta* in Sanskrit, is a condition, because awakening does not happen by accident. The Dharma Flower Sutra, and Buddhism in general, does not say that faith is enough. It teaches, as in the parable of the fantastic castle-city of Chapter 7 for example, that the way is arduous and difficult and that we have to work to make our way toward awakening. Some traditions may hold that firm faith in an external power or powers is all that is needed. Others may hold the opposite—that one can only save oneself. But the Dharma Flower Sutra teaches that both are needed—self-determination and the help of others. The need for self-determination is strongly indicated by such teachings as the six bodhisattva practices—generosity, morality, patient endurance of hardship, perseverance, meditation, and wisdom. All require initiative and effort, which must come finally from within, from a powerful aspiration to become awakened.

This is why for the Dharma Flower Sutra one of the worst failings of human beings is an arrogance that leads to supposing that one has arrived at the truth and has no more to do. Anyone who truly wants to fulfill the Lotus Sutra and become a bodhisattva or buddha for others always has more to do. Followers of the Sutra refer to Shakyamuni Buddha as "Eternal Buddha Shakyamuni." Some might misunderstand this appellation as meaning that the Buddha has arrived at his goal, is finished or perfect, and has no more to do. But in Chapter 16, which is entitled "The Lifetime of the Tathagata" and is about the extremely long life of the Buddha, the Buddha says that he has been practicing the bodhisattva way, that is, helping others, for a fantastically long time—and that he is not yet finished. In other words, the long life of the Buddha, rather than being an indication that he has arrived at some static nirvana, indicates nearly the opposite—that he still has a lot of work to do. It follows, of course, that if the Buddha still has a lot of work to do, so do we. And, for that, we have to remain determined to be awakened.

But the third condition not only calls for being determined to seek one's awakening; it says that we should join others who are similarly determined to pursue awakening. Here, as elsewhere in the Dharma Flower Sutra, what is stressed is the social context in which one pursues the Buddhist path, the "associations" of Chapter 14. It is an expression of the obvious truth that it is much easier to live a wholesome life among others who live wholesome lives than it would be to live such a life amid a gang of thieves. But this third condition is more than that—it is an expression of a basic Mahayana idea that our salvation, our liberation from attachments and bad habits, depends on others.

The Buddha invited his closest followers to become a group of monastics, the *Sangha*, reflecting the importance for him of a community of people of similar aspiration. As Buddhism spread, that community took on some different features in different cultural contexts, but remained remarkably similar throughout Asia. Later, particularly in East Asia, a different kind of Buddhist community would evolve to meet changed conditions—lay Buddhist movements such as the "White Lotus Teachings."[45] In both monastic and independent lay-Buddhist organizations, there is a recognition of the importance of having a community of like-minded people to encourage the aspiration and work of individuals. Even the practice of meditation, which is basically a highly individual practice, is often done sitting together with others.

In Rissho Kosei-kai, *hoza*, literally "Dharma sitting," which means sitting together to help one another apply Buddhist teachings to problems of everyday life, is practiced as an important way in which people can be helped by others to fulfill the Lotus Sutra. Participation in hoza is voluntary of course. No one can force another to participate actively in such a group, where one can listen to and learn from others.

The fourth condition is to be determined to save all beings. And what a fantastically simple, yet fantastically difficult, condition that is! Often known as "the bodhisattva vow," in the Lotus Sutra it is at once the Buddha's original vow, the vow of a bodhisattva, and the vow that each of us should make. It is a good example of how the Sutra teaches that the bodhisattva way is for all, including the Buddha himself.

Determination to save all is reflected in the idea of the universal gateway found in the title of Chapter 25, "The Universal Gateway of the Regarder of the Cries of the World." The Sutra teaches that the

Sutra itself is just such a universal gateway—a gateway that is open to all. It both announces the universal availability of the gateway and invites the reader or hearer through the gateway. But on the other side of this gate we will find not the end of the way but the beginning, the bodhisattva way of life, a way of life in which one is determined to save the whole world. Entering the Buddha Way is more like getting on a launching pad than entering a resting place. It is more of an opening than a closure. It's a destination that is a path, a new beginning.

If entering the bodhisattva way is a beginning, we should not expect to be finished any time soon. But we can expect that the way itself will be very rewarding, that it will enable us to experience the joy of seeing countless buddhas along the way.

## THE WORK OF BUDDHA DHARMA

When viewing Buddhist art one of the ways often used to identify a particular bodhisattva is by the animal on which the bodhisattva rides. In the paintings in the entrance to Rissho Kosei-kai's Great Sacred Hall mentioned earlier, Manjushri is riding a lion, Maitreya rides what I like to think is a cow (though others may say it is a bull), and Universal Sage is on a white elephant with six tusks.

In the Chapter 28 story, Universal Sage Bodhisattva promises that if anyone accepts and upholds the Dharma Flower Sutra he will come to that person mounted on a white elephant with six tusks. This can be understood to mean that taking the Sutra seriously gives one extraordinary strength or power. The elephant itself is often a symbol of strength or power, the whiteness of the elephant has been taken to symbolize purity, and the six tusks have been taken to represent both the six paramitas or transcendental bodhisattva practices and purification of the six senses. But if the elephant is taken to be a symbol of power, we should understand that this is not a power to do just anything. It is a power to practice the Dharma, strength to do the Buddha's work in the world, power to be a universal sage.

Though the image does not come from this story but from the much more involved visualization of the Sutra of Meditation on the Dharma Practice of Universal Sage Bodhisattva, the elephant on which Universal Sage Bodhisattva rides is very often depicted as either walking on blossoming lotus flowers or wearing them like shoes. If the elephant is not standing, a lotus flower will be under the foot of Universal Sage. Such lotus blossoming should be understood, I believe, as an attempt to depict in a motionless picture or statue something that is actually very dynamic—the flowering of the Dharma.

Another interesting aspect of these elephants in Chinese Buddhist art is that they are often grinning or perhaps even laughing. We should understand, I think, that the elephant, one of the largest of all creatures and one of the most intelligent, is very happy to be carrying Universal Sage Bodhisattva, very happy to be contributing to giving strength to others, such that these elephants multiply as they do in the Sutra of Meditation on the Dharma Practice of Universal Sage Bodhisattva.

It is significant that Universal Sage and his elephant come not to offer us a ride to some paradise above the masses of ordinary people but to bring the strength of an elephant for doing the Buddha's work in the world, so that the Dharma can blossom in us, empowering us to be bodhisattvas for others, enabling us to see the Buddha in others and to experience the joy of seeing buddhas everywhere.

In doing the work of the Buddha, we should recognize that there are many kinds of Dharma—teachings, truths, and correct ways of doing things. In the Buddha's time there were Hindu dharmas and Jain dharmas, dharmas stemming from one's birth or caste, and dharmas appropriate to one's stage of life. In many respects, the Buddha's teachings provided an alternative to conventional Indian dharmas. Thus, in Buddhism, Dharma is always Buddha Dharma. In other words, Buddha Dharma is such that without the Buddha there is no Buddha Dharma and, since the Buddha is first and foremost a teacher, the Buddha is not the Buddha without Buddha Dharma. The Buddha and his Dharma, the Dharma and its teacher, cannot be separated into independent realities.

There is a very interesting passage in Chapter 28: "If there are any who receive and embrace, read and recite, remember correctly, practice, and copy this Dharma Flower Sutra, it should be known that they have seen Shakyamuni Buddha. It is as though they heard this sutra from the Buddha's mouth. It should be known that they have made offerings to Shakyamuni Buddha. It should be known that the Buddha has praised them for doing good. It should be known that Shakyamuni Buddha has touched the heads of such people with his hand. It should be known that such people are covered by the robes of Shakyamuni Buddha." (LS 397)

The Sutra itself, in other words, is not just an embodiment of Buddha Dharma but of Shakyamuni Buddha himself, and thus is one of the ways in which the Buddha appears to and for us.

### REWARDS AND PUNISHMENTS

Universal Sage promises that anyone who receives and embraces, reads, recites, remembers correctly, and understands the meaning of the Dharma Flower Sutra and puts it into practice as taught is doing the work of Universal Sage Bodhisattva and will receive many wonderful rewards, such as being touched on the head by a buddha. Even someone who merely copies the Lotus Sutra will go to the heaven of the thirty-three gods right after death and be received by eighty-four thousand music-making goddesses. And to anyone who receives and embraces, reads and recites, remembers correctly and understands the meaning of the Dharma Flower Sutra, the hands of a thousand buddhas will be extended, preventing them from falling into evil realms, and they will be reborn in the Tushita heaven, where Maitreya Bodhisattva, the next Buddha of this world already bearing the thirty-two features of a buddha, is accompanied by an enormous number of goddesses. The Buddha also promises rewards, including "never again being greedy for or attached to worldly pleasures," becoming free from pride, conceit, or arrogance, enjoying happiness, and gaining "visible rewards in the present world."

That there are goddesses in the two heavens is interesting in light of the fact that in the paradise-like buddha lands described earlier in the Dharma Flower Sutra often there are no women. I can only speculate that while early chapters of the Sutra were addressed primarily to monks, for whom female figures could easily be a problem, this chapter is addressed primarily to lay followers of Universal Sage Bodhisattva.

Going to the Tushita heaven as a reward can be taken to mean that the Dharma Flower Sutra has transformative power—that by following it one can become truly compassionate like Maitreya.

It is written that terrible things—leprosy, missing or bad teeth, ugly lips, a flat nose, squinty eyes, deformed hands and feet, body odor, severe illness, and so on, often for many generations—will come to those who expose the faults of followers of the Sutra. (LS 397–98) This passage is often used by the Sutra's detractors to show that the Lotus Sutra is extremely intolerant. But we should be careful about this. At least a couple of things need to be said.

One is that the context makes it clear that what is being talked about primarily is not evil-doers but followers of the Lotus Sutra. The passage concludes with "Therefore, Universal Sage, if anyone sees someone who receives and embraces this sutra, they should get up and greet them from afar, as if they were paying reverence to the Buddha." (LS 398) The purpose of the passage is not, in other words, an attempt to describe consequences of evil actions; rather, it is to urge that special respect be given to those who embrace the Sutra.

Second, the passage does not point to supernatural intervention or action to punish evil-doers. It is not about literal punishment at all. At most, it should be taken to mean, again, that actions have consequences. Thus, just as planting good seeds is likely to produce good results, planting rotten seeds by doing bad things is likely to have bad results.

Having said this, perhaps we should also take a quick look at an earlier passage, one in which it is said that those who follow the Dharma Flower Sutra not only will no longer be attached to worldly pleasures, they will have no liking for scriptures of non-Buddhists or other jottings, nor ever again take pleasure in associating with such people or with other evil people, be they butchers or those who raise pigs, sheep, chickens, and dogs, or hunters, or pimps. The common thread here, of course, has to do with profiting from the sale of flesh, animal or human. It shows that some Buddhists have taken very seriously the prohibition against killing or profiting from killing and, in this case, prostitution.

The Dharma Flower Sutra, in my experience, is a wonderful flowering of Buddha Dharma. Whenever I pay close attention to some passage in it, something I had never seen before is revealed to me and I learn from it. But it is also a book that arose in a particular historical context and was composed and translated within particular social settings. It is not entirely free from error, or at least not free from perspectives that we now regard as deficient or even morally wrong. In saying that followers of the Lotus Sutra should not associate with butchers or those who sell meat, with those who raise animals for their meat, or with those who hunt, the Sutra is reflecting values embodied in the Indian caste system, in which such people were despised.

Rather than taking such a view literally, we can understand it to be an exhortation to think carefully about whom we associate closely with. And this consideration brings us back to the third of the four conditions discussed earlier—the idea that we should be most closely associated with a group of people who are determined to follow the bodhisattva way as best as they are able. Having gained the strength that comes from meeting the four conditions and encountering Universal Sage Bodhisattva on his white elephant with six tusks, we need to have no fear of associating with butchers, ranchers, or hunters, or even with pimps. For it is the compassion of the Buddha, modeled for us in the Dharma Flower Sutra by Kwan-yin, the Regarder of the Cries of the World, that will encourage us to be rooted in the suffering and misery of this world, shunning no one. And for some followers of the Dharma Flower Sutra at least, this might mean, not only not avoiding those who are despised by the society in which we live, whether they be a racial minority, or a minority identified by disease or mental illness, or some other despised group, but actively being with and supporting such people.

That this Chapter comes last and therefore can be seen as a kind of conclusion to the Sutra means that the Dharma is not complete without being put into practice—that is, without being put into action in everyday, concrete life. It is not enough to study and gain wisdom, not enough to feel compassion. One must also embrace the Sutra by embodying it in one's life. Faith is not faith if it is only believed, or only felt; it must be lived. One must strive to become a buddha by being a bodhisattva for others, which means nothing more and nothing less than embodying Buddha Dharma by helping others in whatever ways are appropriate and in whatever ways one can. Among those ways is giving encouragement and strength to others, being Universal Sage Bodhisattva for them.

# ACKNOWLEDGMENTS

A GREAT MANY PEOPLE have contributed to the development of these essays. Yoshiro Tamura and Nikkyo Niwano were my first teachers of the Dharma Flower Sutra. It is not possible for me to express how great a debt of gratitude I owe to them for leading one who was initially very skeptical about the virtues of the Sutra to one who has devoted much of his life to sharing its profound meanings. From long conversations with Tamura, some in Japan but most in Chicago, I gained both knowledge about the Dharma Flower Sutra and a kind of fascination with it. His death, only a few months after I moved to Japan in part to work with him, was an enormous loss to me personally and to all those with interest in Tendai Buddhism and the Dharma Flower Sutra. I learned from Nikkyo Niwano mostly from writings, actually translated writings, especially from the book *Buddhism for Today*. Niwano did not speak English, and when I started down this path I knew very little Japanese. We conversed on numerous occasions only through skillful translators. Still, he had a profound impact on me through his books, articles in *Dharma World*, translated Dharma talks, and, very importantly, through others who had learned from him. One cannot be around Rissho Kosei-kai very much without learning much from "Founder Niwano." Even today he is an inspiration for me and for millions of others.

One of the skillful oral translators of Niwano was Masuo Nezu. Like others, I will never know how much of what I took to be Niwano actually came from Nezu! But whether his translation was literal or creative, I am confident that he was always faithful to Niwano's intentions. Like many others, I am very indebted to Nezu for being a vehicle for conveying Nikkyo Niwano's understanding of Buddhism to me, and to many others.

My first reading of the Dharma Flower Sutra in Chinese was guided by Rikkyo University's Akio Tsukimoto, a Christian and Old Testament scholar. He spent many hours with me going through Chinese and Japanese versions of the Sutra, patiently guiding my understanding of Chinese characters. During this same period, Yoshiko Izumida, daughter of Niwano, patiently tried to improve and deepen my understanding of her father's teachings.

Parts of these essays have been used in a variety of class situations, initially at the University of Tsukuba, and later both at Meadville Lombard Theological School at the University of Chicago and at the University of Peking. I have also enjoyed teaching a great many classes at Rissho Kosei-kai in which I not only shared what I had learned, but learned much from students. Some of those students have been especially faithful over many years. Though it is unfair to recognize only a few students among the many who could be recognized, Yasuyo Suzuki and Kunisaku Yasuda do stand out, for they never fail to attend carefully to my talks and offer helpful suggestions, and both of them reviewed early drafts of my translation of the Lotus Sutra and made positive suggestions.

Two others who have devoted a great deal of helpful attention to my work are Michio Shinozaki and Yukimasa Hagiwara. Shinozaki has been a wonderful companion for me in Japan and a collaborator in many projects related to the Lotus Sutra. It is in part by editing essays or talks by him that I have learned from Founder Niwano. On many occasions, Hagiwara has been able to provide logistical support for my work, beginning with helping me move into Tokyo from a suburb during my first months in Japan. But logistical support is far from the whole story. Hagiwara has also devoted much time, both his own and in recent years time of his staff, to attending to my talks and writings and bringing a critical eye to them, something that is all too rare in Japan.

As I imagine every teacher knows, one learns as much, often more, from being a teacher as from being a student. So I am grateful as well to all of those who have provided me with opportunities to think carefully about the Dharma Flower Sutra in order to teach it to others.

For about fifteen years Michio Shinozaki and I have been responsible for organizing nearly annual seminars on the Lotus Sutra, held sometimes in Japan, sometimes in China, and most recently in Hawaii. At all of those seminars I have been a learner as well as an organizer, and from some participants I have been able to learn much, even when disagreements were serious. One of the joys of academic work is learning from colleagues, being enriched through conversations. Out of the dozens of scholars, Buddhist and Christian, who have participated in those seminars it may be unfair to single anyone out, but I would like to express special gratitude to Hiroshi Kanno and Brook Ziporyn. Though not as well known in the West as he deserves to be, Kanno has a vast knowledge of Chinese Buddhism. He has helped me to improve my own understanding on numerous occasions. Ziporyn's ability to understand Buddhism and especially the Lotus traditions playfully has helped me to understand Buddhism more deeply and even more philosophically.

Among my important collegial associations has been the Tokyo Buddhist Discussion Group, meeting monthly in my home. I am grateful to all who have participated over the years in that group, but perhaps especially to Charles Muller and Ken Tanaka, in addition to Hiroshi Kanno, who have been at the core of that group from its beginning quite a few years ago. And for a long time David Loy regularly contributed significantly both to that group and to my growth in understanding Buddhism. At times, this group has patiently improved my thinking and writing.

I was trained in philosophy, not Buddhist studies, to which I came quite late in life. Perhaps even more than most Buddhist scholars, I have also benefitted from academic associations with Buddhist scholars, especially from participation in sessions of the Buddhism Section of the American Academy of Religion, from meetings of the International Association for Buddhist Studies, and from a great many conferences organized in Taiwan, Japan, the United States, and elsewhere. Many of the same colleagues who participate in such meetings and conferences, and some who do not, have contributed to my development through writing, no doubt the main way in which scholars learn from one another.

Earlier versions of most of these essays appeared previously in the magazine *Dharma World*. Throughout the ten or so years in which they were published, the chief editor of that magazine was Kazumasa Osaka. Undoubtedly I owe more than I will ever know both to his editing ability and to his diplomacy and support of my endeavors.

I have also benefited from editors and readers at Wisdom Publications, most of whom are completely unknown to me. But in one case, what was initially an anonymous association through Wisdom has become a good friendship, one that is beneficial intellectually as well as personally and religiously: Taigen Dan Leighton has been both critical and supportive. One could not ask for more than that. David Kittelstrom first brought me into Wisdom and encouraged me to publish with them, and for that I will always be grateful, and senior editor Josh Bartok has not only encouraged me and sometimes come up with creative and constructive suggestions, he has provided excellent assistance with copyeditors, proofreaders, and book designers. I am very indebted to the staff of Wisdom Publications for their work both on this book and on my translation of the Lotus Sutra.

It is quite normal to express gratitude to those who have already contributed in some way to the creation of a book. But I want to stress that this is a reading, only one reading, of this important text. There are other readings and other ways of reading this text, both actual and possible. Among the possible readings are your own. If this book does what I hope it will, you will be stimulated to really read the Dharma Flower Sutra, read it in ways that lead to your own reading of it. Thus, perhaps strangely, I want to express a special sense of gratitude to you who read this book.

# NOTES

1 *The Lotus Sutra: A Contemporary Translation of a Buddhist Classic* (Boston: Wisdom Publications, 2008). In this text this translation will be referenced simply as "LS" followed by a page number. Mentions of a numbered chapter, e.g. "Chapter 28," refer to a chapter in that translation.

2 In Chinese this Sutra is commonly called the *Fahua-jing* and in Japanese as *Hoke-kyō*, pronunciations of 法華経, which the Chinese text most often uses to refer to itself. This term can most directly be translated into English as "Dharma Flower Sutra." The common substitute for this in English is "Lotus Sutra," for which there is no corresponding term in Chinese or Japanese. The "lotus" does appear both in the title of the extant Sanskrit version, *Saddharmapuṇḍarīka-sūtra*, and in the full title of Kumarajiva's Chinese version, which is *Miao-fa-lian-hua jing* (*Myō-hō-renge kyō* in Japanese pronunciation). Word for word, this is "Wonderful Dharma Lotus Flower Sutra." This full title may be the reason that the first translation into a Western language was called *Le lotus de la bonne loi*, translated into French by Eugene Burnouf in 1852. Interestingly, in the earliest Chinese version, by Dharmaraksha in the third century, the term "lotus" does not appear even in the full title—*Zheng-fa-hua jing* (True Dharma Flower Sutra).

The symbolism of the lotus flower, rooted in mud and blooming in the air, is important for Mahayana Buddhism in general and for this Sutra. But, at least it seems to me, as important is the symbolism of flowering, of blossom-ing and blooming. This has to do, at least in part, with the Mahayana sense of the Buddhist tradition as dynamic, rooted in the past to be sure, particularly in the life and teachings of the historical Buddha, but concerned also with the ongoing development or blossoming of that tradition. Except for the fact that this book is already known everywhere in English as the Lotus Sutra, it might be better to use Dharma Flower Sutra for its short title. In this book I will use both.

3 "Symbol and Yūgen: Shunzei's Use of Tendai Buddhism," in William R. LaFleur, *The Karma of Words: Buddhism and the Literary Arts in Medieval Japan* (Berkeley: University of California Press, 1983), pp. 80–106.

4 LaFleur, p. 97.

5 LaFleur, p. 106.

6 *Ginga Tetsudo no Yoru* (Tokyo: Kadokawa Shoten Publishing Co., 1985), pp. 201–2.

7 *The Lotus Sutra: The Sutra of the Lotus Flower of the Wonderful Dharma*, translated by Senchū Murano, 2nd ed. (Tokyo: Nichiren Shu Shimbun, 1991).

8 While these six ways in which the earth can shake are often referred to in the Lotus Sutra, they are never listed or described there. In the Flower Garland (Avatamsaka) Sutra, however, they are listed as: moving, rocking, springing out or gushing, shocking, quivering, and roaring.

9 The term *śrāvaka* (聲聞 Chinese *shēngwén*, Japanese *shōmon*) literally means "voice-hearer," and probably referred originally to those who heard the voice of the Buddha directly. It is used in the Lotus Sutra, especially in the early chapters of the Sutra, to indicate those who follow an older tradition in which the highest goal is to become an awakened *arhat*, one truly worthy of receiving offerings. In one sense, it simply means an ordinary monk, living primarily in a monastery. The shravaka way is contrasted with the bodhisattva way, in which the goal is to become a buddha. It is also one of the three ways indicated by the three vehicles—the shravaka, the pratyekabuddha, and the bodhisattva.

10 A *pratyekabuddha* (緣覺 Chinese *yuánjué*, Japanese *engaku*) is one of the four kinds of holy ones in Buddhism, along with shravakas, bodhisattvas, and buddhas. The meaning is obscure, but they are often regarded as solitary practitioners.

11 方便 (Chinese *fāngbiàn*, Japanese *hōben*, Sanskrit *upāya*).

12 The title of the English version of Nikkyo Niwano's autobiography is *Lifetime Beginner* (Tokyo: Kosei Publishing Co., 1978).

13 The Chinese/Japanese title of this chapter 信解 (*xìn jiě* in Chinese pronunciation and *shinge* in Japanese) can be reasonably translated as "Faith and Understanding," "Faithful Understanding," or something similar. But the meaning of the chapter title in Sanskrit, *adhimukti*, is quite different. It means something more like a disposition or attitude. It is a reference to the son's attitude toward his own life. So it seems that Kumarajiva, rather than translating, may have devised a new chapter title. Though the term is used in a scattering of places throughout the Sutra, it does not appear at all in Chapter 4 itself.

14  It is worth noting that when the shravakas who have told this story explain it, they say that "nirvana" is "like a mere day's pay"—it gets you somewhere, but not far. Very often in the Lotus Sutra, nirvana, which is often taken elsewhere to be the goal of Buddhist practice, is understood to be a lesser goal, something that facilitates one's going on to bodhisattva practice and to the goal of becoming a buddha.

15  This version of the parable is based on the translation from Sanskrit by Leon Hurvitz, in *Scripture of the Lotus Blossom of the Fine Dharma* (The Lotus Sūtra) (New York: Columbia University Press, 1976), pp. 110–19. Because my translation is from Chinese, this half of the chapter including this parable is not in it.

16  Parables and similes are forms of metaphorical language. In a parable, of which there are several in the Lotus Sutra, characters in a story represent someone else. Thus, for example, in the two parables we have already discussed in this book there is a father figure who represents the Buddha. In a simile, on the other hand, one kind of thing is said to be like another. Strictly speaking, there is no story in a simile, just a likeness or similarity.

17  Abe, *Zen and Western Thought* (Honolulu: University of Hawaii Press, 1985), p. xxiv.

18  Never actually mentioned in the Lotus Sutra, the eightfold holy path normally includes: 1) right views or understanding, 2) right thinking, 3) right speech, 4) right action, 5) right way of life, 6) right effort, 7) right remembering, and 8) right concentration.

19  *Theragatha*, verses 1047–49 (Pali Text Society, 1913).

20  For a brief explanation of the names of this bodhisattva, see the first paragraph of Chapter 26 of this volume.

21  For a very full account of this matter, see Reginald A. Ray, *Buddhist Saints in India* (New York & Oxford: Oxford University Press, 1994), pp. 162–78.

22  Nagas are a kind of sea serpent, often depicted as large king cobras. In Southeast Asia, however, they are thought of as mythical sea serpents and are often depicted a such in Southeast Asian Buddhist temples, usually resembling large snakes more than dragons. But Chinese translators of Buddhist texts did not have nagas in their imaginations. They were, however, quite familiar with dragons, an old symbol of good fortune in China. Thus, typically, *naga* was translated into *lóng*, the Chinese word for "dragon." That is why dragons are so prominent in East Asian Buddhist temples and absent from those in Southeast Asia.

Though repeatedly referred to as a dragon princess, in this story it is as if the girl were human, and, apart from her introduction, that is the way she is treated in the story, and in subsequent Buddhist art. Almost always she is not imagined or depicted as a dragon but as a girl.

23  See, for example, Lucinda Joy Peach, "Social Responsibility, Sex Change, and Salvation: Gender Justice in the Lotus Sutra," in *A Buddhist Kaleidoscope: Essays on the Lotus Sutra*, Gene Reeves, ed. (Tokyo: Kosei Publishing Co., 2002), pp. 437–67.

24  "Kwan-shih-yin/Guanshiyin" is the Chinese pronunciation of the most common translation of Avalokiteshvara into Chinese. It is often shortened to Kwan-yin. In modern Pinyin and English publications, these names are often seen as Guanshiyin and Guanyin. In Japanese, they are pronounced "Kanzeon" and "Kannon."

25  The Avatamsaka Sutra, in Japanese "Kegon," in Chinese "Huayan." The name of this sutra is often translated as "Flower Ornament" or "Flower Garland."

26  The Jains also admitted nuns at about the same time. Whether Jains or Buddhists were first is probably unknowable.

27  Mara, variously called the evil one, the god of death, and the god of temptation, is an individual in early Buddhist texts, which contain many stories of his attempts to frustrate the Buddha both before and after his awakening. In stories of the Buddha's encounter with Mara just before his awakening, Mara comes to him on an elephant and disguised as a great wheel-rolling king, a *chakravartin-raja*. Later, this Mara became many devils, and the idea that there are four Mara kings emerged.

28  Viśiṣṭa-cāritra (Jōgyō in Japanese), Ananta-cāritra (Muhengyō), Viśuddha-cāritra (Jōgyō), and Supratiṣṭhitacāritra (Anryūgyō).

29  See *Buddhism for Today* (Kosei Publishing Co., 1976), pp. 177–78.

30  Master Hsing Yun wrote about "Oneness and Coexistence" emphasizing the importance of equality in Buddhism for *Dharma World* (May/June 2000, pp. 25–27). For a book-length account of Master Hsin Yun and Foguang Shan, see Stuart Chandler, *Establishing a Pure Land on Earth* (Honolulu: University of Hawaii Press, 2004.) The idea of "Humanistic Buddhism" comes from an earlier great Chinese Buddhist reformer monk, Taixu. See Don A. Pittman, *Toward a Modern Chinese Buddhism: Taixu's Reforms* (Honolulu: University of Hawaii Press, 2001).

31  The origins of the term *icchantika* are not well understood. Generally it was used for a class of people who are incapable of attaining the Buddhist goal of awakening. The concept is probably best-known as a component in the five-nature taxonomy of people articulated by the Yogâcāra school and defended in Japan especially by the Hosso school. According to this concept, inherently there are five kinds of human beings: shravakas, those who will become arhats; pratyekabuddhas, those who will become pratyekabuddhas; bodhisattvas, those who will become buddhas; an indeterminate group, those who can reach any of the first three goals; and the *icchantika*, those who are incapable

of attaining any of these goals. The existence of such a class of beings was denied by followers of the Lotus Sutra, who strongly advocated the possibility of becoming a buddha for all sentient beings. This matter is discussed at length in the *Buddha-nature Treatise.*

32  See Young-Ho Kim, *Tao-sheng's Commentary on the Lotus Sūtra: A Study and Translation* (Albany: State University of New York Press, 1990). Tao-sheng (355–434) was considered to be the founder of the Nirvana school of Chinese Buddhism. He was especially famous for maintaining that all living beings have buddha-nature and at one time was expelled from his monastery for holding that all beings are capable of attaining liberation, even so-called *icchantika.* See also Walter Liebenthal, "A Biography of Chu Tao-sheng," *Monumenta Nipponica* 11, no. 3 (1955).

33  Chih-i (Zhiyi) (538–597) technically listed as its fourth patriarch, was the actual founder of T'ian-t'ai (Tiantai) Buddhism, the first indigenous Chinese school of Buddhism. He gave special importance to the Lotus Sutra. His interpretation of it is especially influential to this day.

34  Niwano, *Buddhism for Today,* p. 331.

35  See note 8.

36  Rev. ed., Boston: Wisdom Publications, 2003.

37  With diacritics these names are Avalokitêśvara, Guānshìyīn, and Guānyīn.

38  Known as Shìzhì/Seishi or Dàshìzhì/Daiseishi Bodhisattva in Chinese and Japanese, the literal meaning of the name is "one who has attained great energy or power."

39  *Buddhism for Today,* p. 377.

40  For this and much of this article, I am indebted to Chün-fang Yü's wonderful book *Kuan-yin: The Chinese Transformation of Avalokitesvara* (New York: Columbia University Press, 2001). Anyone with even a passing interest in Kwan-yin or East Asian Buddhism should read this book, remarkable not only for insights gained from familiarity with Kwan-yin devotion but also for extensive use of popular materials often ignored by scholars.

41  This account of Miao-shan follows quite closely the account given by Chün-fang Yü in *Kuan-yin,* pp. 293–94.

42  One common Japanese term for becoming a Buddhist priest literally means "leaving home."

43  *Buddhism for Today,* pp. 400–401.

44  *Le Sûtra du Lotus,* translated by Jean-Noël Robert (Paris: Fayard, 1997).

45  See B. J. Ter Haar, *The White Lotus Teachings in Chinese Religious History* (Honolulu: University of Hawaii Press, 1999).

# BIBLIOGRAPHY OF WORKS IN ENGLISH
# RELATED TO THE LOTUS SUTRA

THIS BIBLIOGRAPHY is not inclusive, though it leans in that direction. One reason for not including everything relevant is that there are works which I simply do not know about and would include if I did. Another reason for being less than fully inclusive is the large volume of literature in English produced and elicited by Soka Gakkai. Soka Gakkai is clearly within the Nichiren tradition. Some of this literature is included here as it is clearly related either to the Lotus Sutra or to the Nichiren tradition, but much is not included, simply because, while it is from within that tradition, it is not about that tradition. On the other hand, I have not tried to separate "scholarly" from non-scholarly works in any systematic way. It's a distinction that does not work very well in this case. Some non-scholars produce quite scholarly works, while some scholars produce decidedly non-scholarly works. In constructing this bibliography I've leaned toward being inclusive. When in doubt about an item, I have included it.

The bibliography is divided into five sections. The first is the Lotus Sutra itself in English translation and transliteration. The second section includes books written primarily about the Lotus Sutra. It is followed by a list of books and articles that are at least in part about the Lotus Sutra. The last two sections are lists of works about the T'ian-t'ai/Tendai and Nichiren traditions respectively. Naturally, some works could easily be included in two or more of these lists. One cannot write much about Nichiren, for example, without also writing about the Lotus Sutra. I've made choices, sometimes arbitrary I suppose, to have works appear in only one of these lists, including them in the list that seemed most appropriate.

Like all such bibliographies, this one is dependent on prior bibliographies, but the final, Nichiren, section of this bibliography is especially indebted to the Nichiren tradition bibliography which appeared in Fall 1999 "Revisiting Nichiren" issue of the *Japanese Journal of Religious Studies* edited by Ruben Habito and Jacqueline Stone.

## THE LOTUS SUTRA IN ENGLISH TRANSLATION AND TRANSLITERATION

The Buddhist Text Translation Society, trans. *The Wonderful Dharma Lotus Flower Sutra*. With commentary by Tripitaka Master Hua. 10 vols. San Francisco: Sino-American Buddhist Association, 1976–1982.

Hurvitz, Leon, trans. *Scripture of the Lotus Blossom of the Fine Dharma (The Lotus Sutra)*. Rev. ed., with a new foreword by Stephen F. Teiser. New York: Columbia University Press, 2009. Originally published 1976.

Katō Bunnō et al., trans. *The Threefold Lotus Sutra: Innumerable Meanings, The Lotus Flower of the Wonderful Law, and Meditation on the Bodhisattva Universal Virtue*. Tokyo: Kosei Publishing Co., 1971, 1975.

Kern, H., trans. *Saddharma-puṇḍarīka* or *The Lotus of the True Law*. New York: Dover Publications, 1963. Originally published as Volume XXI of *The Sacred Books of the East*, London: Clarendon Press, 1884.

Kern, Hendrik, and B. Nanjio, eds. *Saddharmapuṇḍarīka*. Bibliotheca Buddhica 10. Tokyo: Meicho fukyūkai, 1977.

Kubo Tsugunari and Akira Yuyama, trans. *The Lotus Sutra: The White Lotus of the Marvelous Law*. 2nd ed. Tokyo and Berkeley: Bukkyō Dendō Kyōkai and Numata Center for Buddhist Translation and Research, 2007. Originally published 1993.

Murano Senchū, trans. *The Lotus Sutra: The Sutra of the Lotus Flower of the Wonderful Dharma*. 2nd ed. Tokyo: Nichiren Shu Shimbun, 1991.

Ogiwara (Wogihara) Unrai, and C. Tsuchida, eds. *Saddharmapuṇḍarīka-sūtram: Romanized and Revised Text of the Bibliothecs Publication by Consulting a Skt. Ms. and Tibetan and Chinese Translations*. Tokyo: Sankibo Buddhist Book Store, 1994. Originally published 1935.

Reeves, Gene, trans. *The Lotus Sutra: A Contemporary Translation of a Buddhist Classic*. Boston: Wisdom Publications, 2008.

Soothill, W.E., trans. *The Lotus of the Wonderful Law or The Lotus Gospel: Saddharma Puṇḍarīka Sūtra, Miao-fa Lien Hua Ching*. Atlantic Highlands, NJ: Humanities Press, 1987. Originally published Oxford: Clarendon Press, 1930.

Toda Hirofumi, ed. *Saddharmapuṇḍarīkasūtra: Central Asian Manuscripts, Romanized Text*. Tokushima, Japan: Kyoiku Shuppan Center, 1983.

Watson, Burton, trans. *The Lotus Sutra*. New York: Columbia University Press, 1993.

———. *The Lotus Sutra and Its Opening and Closing Sutras*. Tokyo: Soka Gakkai, 2009.

## BOOKS PRIMARILY ON THE LOTUS SUTRA

Davidson, J. Leroy. *The Lotus Sutra in Chinese Art*. New Haven: Yale University Press, 1954.

Dykstra, Yoshiko K. *Miraculous Tales of the Lotus Sutra from Ancient Japan: The "Dainihonkoku Hokekyōkenki" of Priest Chingen*. Honolulu: University of Hawaii Press, 1983.

Fuss, Michael. *Buddhavacana & Dei Verbum: A Phenomenological & Theological Comparison of Scriptural Inspiration in the Saddharmapuṇḍarīka Sūtra & in the Christian Tradition*. Leiden: E.J. Brill, 1991.

Ikeda Daisaku. *The Flower of Chinese Buddhism*. New York: Weatherhill, 1986.

Ikeda Daisaku et al. *The Wisdom of the Lotus Sutra*. 6 vols. Tokyo: World Tribune Press, 2000–2003.

Kim, Young-Ho. *Tao-sheng's Commentary on the Lotus Sūtra: A Study and Translation*. Albany: State University of New York Press, 1990.

Karashima Seishi. *A Glossary of Dharmarakṣa's Translation of the Lotus Sutra*. Bibliotheca Philologica et Philosophica Buddhica I. Tokyo: The International Research Institute for Advanced Buddhology, Soka University, 1998.

———. *A Glossary of Kumārajīva's Translation of the Lotus Sutra*. Bibliotheca Philologica et Philosophica Buddhica IV. Tokyo: The International Research Institute for Advanced Buddhology, Soka University, 2001.

Kubo Tsugunari. 道 *(tao) in Kumārajīva's Translation of the Lotus Sūtra: A Study Concerning the Acceptance and Reconstruction of a Philosophy in its Assimilation into a Different Culture*. Studia Philologica Buddhica, Occasional Paper Series XVIII. Tokyo: The International Institute of Buddhist Studies, 1994.

Leighton, Taigen Dan. *Visions of Awakening Space and Time: Dogen and the Lotus Sutra*. Boston: Wisdom Publications, 2008.

Montgomery, Daniel B. *Fire in the Lotus: The Dynamic Buddhism of Nichiren*. London: Mandala, 1991.

Nhat Hanh, Thich. *Opening the Heart of the Cosmos: Insights on the Lotus Sutra*. Berkeley: Parallax Press, 2003.

Niwano Nikkyō. *Buddhism for Today: A Modern Interpretation of the Threefold Lotus Sutra*. Tokyo: Kosei Publishing Co., 1976.

———. *A Guide to the Threefold Lotus Sutra*. Tokyo: Kosei Publishing Co., 1981.

Pye, Michael. *Skilful Means: A Concept in Mahayana Buddhism*. London: Routledge, 2003. Originally published London: Duckworth, 1978.

Reeves, Gene, ed. *A Buddhist Kaleidoscope: Essays on the Lotus Sutra*. Tokyo: Kosei Publishing Co., 2002.

Sangharakshita. *The Dream of Cosmic Enlightenment: Parables, Myths, and Symbols of the White Lotus Sutra*. Glasgow: Windhorse Publications, 1993.

Shen Haiyan. *The Profound Meaning of the Lotus Sutra: T'ien-t'ai Philosophy of Buddhism*. 2 vols. Delhi: Originals, 2005.

Stevenson, Daniel B., and Hiroshi Kanno. *The Meaning of the Lotus Sūtra's Course of Ease and Bliss: An Annotated Translation and Study of Nanyue Huisi's (515–577) "Fahua jin anlexing yi."* Bibliotheca Philologica et Philosophica Buddhica 9. Tokyo: The International Research Institute for Advanced Buddhology, Soka University, 2006.

Suguro Shinjo. *Introduction to the Lotus Sutra*. Freemont, CA: Jain Publishing Co., 1998.

Tamura Yoshirō and Bunsaku Kurata, eds. *Art of the Lotus Sutra*. Tokyo: Kosei Publishing Co., 1987.

Tanabe Jr., George J., and Willa Jane Tanabe. *The Lotus Sutra in Japanese Culture*. Honolulu: University of Hawaii Press, 1989.

Tanabe, Willa Jane. *Paintings of the Lotus Sutra*. Tokyo: Weatherhill, 1988.

Teiser, Stephen F., and Jacqueline I. Stone, eds. *Readings of the Lotus Sutra*. New York: Columbia University Press, 2009.

———. *Buddhist Positiveness: Studies on the Lotus Sūtra*. Delhi: Motilal Banarsidass, 2009.

Yuyama Akira. *A Bibliography of the Sanskrit Texts of the Saddharmapuṇḍarīkasūtra*. Canberra: Australian National University Press, 1970.

———. *Eugène Burnouf: The Background to His Research into the Lotus Sutra*. Bibliotheca Philologica et Philosophica Buddhica III. Tokyo: The International Research Institute for Advanced Buddhology, Soka University, 2000.

Wang, Eugene Y. *Shaping the Lotus Sutra: Buddhist Visual Culture in Medieval China*. Seattle: University of Washington Press, 2005.

## ARTICLES AND ESSAYS ON THE LOTUS SUTRA

Benn, James A. "The *Lotus Sūtra* and Self-Immolation." In *Readings of the Lotus Sutra*, edited by Stephen F. Teiser and Jacqueline I. Stone, 107–31. New York: Columbia University Press, 2009.

Berthrong, John. "Considering the Lotus Sutra." *Dharma World* 23 (July–August 1996): 37–42; also in *A Buddhist Kaleidoscope: Essays on the Lotus Sutra*, edited by Gene Reeves, 95–106. Tokyo: Kosei Publishing Co., 2002.

Bielefeldt, Carl. "The One Vehicle and the Three Jewels: On Japanese Sectarianism and Some Ecumenical Alternatives." *Buddhist-Christian Studies* 10 (1990): 5–16.

———. "Expedient Devices, the One Vehicle, and the Life Span of the Buddha." In *Readings of the Lotus Sutra*, edited by Stephen F. Teiser and Jacqueline I. Stone, 62–82. New York: Columbia University Press, 2009.

Bloom, Alfred. "The Humanism of the Lotus Sutra." *Dharma World* 3, no. 10 (October 1976): 18–20.

Boucher, Daniel, "Gāndhārī and the Early Chinese Buddhist Translations Reconsidered: The Case of the *Saddharmapuṇḍarīkasūtra*." *Journal of the American Oriental Society* 118, no. 4 (1998): 471–506.

Campany, Robert F. "The Earliest Tales of the Bodhisattva Guanshiyin." In *Religions of China in Practice*, edited by Donald S. Lopez Jr., 82–96. Princeton, NJ: Princeton University Press, 1996.

Chandra, Lokesh. "The Lotus Sutra and the Present Age: The Philosophy of SGI President Daisaku Ikeda." *The Journal of Oriental Studies* 6 (1996): 20–27.

Chappell, David W. "Organic Truth: Personal Reflections on the Lotus Sutra." *Dharma World* 23 (March–April 1996): 9–13; (May–June 1996): 19–22; also in *A Buddhist Kaleidoscope: Essays on the Lotus Sutra*, edited by Gene Reeves, 55–70. Tokyo: Kosei Publishing Co., 2002.

———. "Global Significance of the Lotus Sutra." *The Journal of Oriental Studies* 6 (1996): 1–10.

Ch'en, Kenneth K.S. *Buddhism in China: A Historical Survey*, 378–82. Princeton, NJ: Princeton University Press, 1964.

Deal, William E. "The Lotus Sutra and the Rhetoric of Legitimation in Eleventh-Century Japanese Buddhism." *Japanese Journal of Religious Studies* 20, no. 4 (December 1993): 261–95.

Dolce, Lucia. "Between Duration and Eternity: Hermeneutics of the 'Ancient Buddha' of the Lotus Sutra in Chih-i and Nichiren." In *A Buddhist Kaleidoscope: Essays on the Lotus Sutra*, edited by Gene Reeves, 223–39. Tokyo: Kosei Publishing Co., 2002.

Dykstra, Yoshiko K. "Tales of the Compassionate Kannon: The Hasedera Kannon Genki." *Monumenta Nipponica* 31, no. 2 (1976): 21–50.

Eckel, Malcolm David. "By the Power of the Buddha." *Dharma World* 22 (September–October 1995): 9–15; (November–December 1995): 14–18; also in *A Buddhist Kaleidoscope: Essays on the Lotus Sutra*, edited by Gene Reeves, 127–48. Tokyo: Kosei Publishing Co., 2002.

Education Section of Rissho Kosei-kai. "A Guide to the Lotus Sutra." *Dharma World* (January 1986): 20–26; (February 1986): 36–43; (March 1986): 36–43; (April 1986): 24–31; (May 1986): 22–29; (June 1986): 32–36; (July

1986): 30–36; (August 1986): 20–25; (September–October 1986): 29–31; (November–December 1986): 22–24; (January–February 1987): 36–39; (March–April 1987): 29–33; (May–June 1987): 40–42; (July–August 1987): 40–42; (September–October 1987): 34–37; (November–December 1987): 40–42; (January–February 1988): 40–43.

Endo Takanori. "The Lotus Sutra and the Philosophy of Soka Gakkai." *The Journal of Oriental Studies* 6 (1996): 41–57.

Federman, Asaf. "Literal Means and Hidden Meanings: A New Analysis of 'Skilful Means'." *Kokoro: Journal of The Essential Lay Buddhism Study Center* 4, no. 1 (February 2009): 43–50.

Florida, Robert E. "The Lotus Sutra and Health Care Ethics." In *A Buddhist Kaleidoscope: Essays on the Lotus Sutra*, edited by Gene Reeves, 421–35. Tokyo: Kosei Publishing Co., 2002.

Fujita Kōtatsu. "One Vehicle or Three?" Translated by Leon Hurvitz. *Journal of Indian Philosophy* 3 (1975): 79–166.

Fuss, Michael A. "*Upāya* and *Missio Dei*: Toward a Common Missiology." *Dharma World* 23 (September–October 1996): 36–41; also in *A Buddhist Kaleidoscope: Essays on the Lotus Sutra*, edited by Gene Reeves, 115–25. Tokyo: Kosei Publishing Co., 2002.

Grapard, Allan G. "Lotus in the Mountain, Mountain in the Lotus." *Monumenta Nipponica* 41, no. 1 (1986): 21–50.

———. "The Textualized Mountain—Enmountained Text: The *Lotus Sutra* in Kunisaki." In *The Lotus Sutra in Japanese Culture*, edited by George J. Tanabe Jr. and Willa Jane Tanabe, 159–89. Honolulu: University of Hawaii Press, 1989.

Griffiths, Paul J. "The Lotus Sūtra as Good News: A Christian Reading." *Buddhist-Christian Studies* 19 (1999): 3–17.

Habito, Ruben L.F. "Buddha-body Theory and the Lotus Sutra: Implications for Praxis." *Dharma World* 23 (November–December 1996): 47–53; also in *A Buddhist Kaleidoscope: Essays on the Lotus Sutra*, edited by Gene Reeves, 305–17. Tokyo: Kosei Publishing Co., 2002.

———. "The Experience of Lotus Buddhism." In *Experiencing Buddhism: Ways of Wisdom and Compassion*, 172–87. New York: Orbis Books, 2005.

———. "Bodily Reading of the *Lotus Sūtra*." In *Readings of the Lotus Sutra*, edited by Stephen F. Teiser and Jacqueline I. Stone, 186–208. New York: Columbia University Press, 2009.

Hardacre, Helen. "The *Lotus Sutra* in Modern Japan." In *The Lotus Sutra in Japanese Culture*, edited by George J. Tanabe Jr. and Willa Jane Tanabe, 209–24. Honolulu: University of Hawaii Press, 1989.

Hirakawa Akira. "The Lotus Sutra." In *A History of Indian Buddhism From Sakya-*

*muni to Early Mahayana*, translated by Paul Groner, 282–86. Honolulu: University of Hawaii Press, 1990.

Hubbard, Jamie. "Buddhist-Buddhist Dialogue? The Lotus Sutra and the Polemic of Accommodation." *Buddhist-Christian Studies* 15 (1995): 119–36.

———. "A Tale of Two Times: Preaching in the Latter Age of the Dharma." In *A Buddhist Kaleidoscope: Essays on the Lotus Sutra*, edited by Gene Reeves, 201–21. Tokyo: Kosei Publishing Co., 2002.

Hunter, Doris. "The Nature of the True Self: A Comparison of Parables." *Dharma World* 15 (May–June 1988): 30–33.

Hurvitz, Leon. "The Lotus Sutra in East Asia: A Review of *Hokke Shisō.*" *Monumenta Serica* 29 (1970–71): 697–792.

Ignatovich, Alexander. "The Lotus Sutra into Russian" (an interview). *Dharma World* 23 (September–October 1996): 30–32.

———. "Echoes of the Lotus Sutra in Tolstoy's Philosophy." In *A Buddhist Kaleidoscope: Essays on the Lotus Sutra*, edited by Gene Reeves, 297–301. Tokyo: Kosei Publishing Co., 2002.

Jiang Zhongxin. "The Lotus Sutra and the Twenty-first Century." *The Journal of Oriental Studies* 8 (1998): 106–118.

de Jong, J.W. Review of *The Threefold Lotus Sutra*, translated by Bunnō Katō, and *The Sutra of the Lotus Flower of the Wonderful Law*, translated by Senchū Murano. *Eastern Buddhist* 8, no. 2 (October 1975): 113–43.

———. Review of *Scripture of the Lotus Blosssom of the Fine Dharma (The Lotus Sūtra)*, translated by Leon Hurvitz. *Eastern Buddhist* 10, no. 2 (1977): 169–74.

———. Review of *The Lotus Sutra*, translated by Burton Watson. *Eastern Buddhist* 28, no. 2 (1995): 303–4.

Kajiyama Yuichi. "Buddhist Eschatology, Supernatural Events and the *Lotus Sūtra.*" *The Journal of Oriental Studies* 8 (1998): 15–37.

———. "The Saddharmapuṇḍarīka and Śūnyatā Thought." *The Journal of Oriental Studies* 10 (2000): 72–96.

Kalupahana, David J. "The *Saddharmapuṇḍarīka-sūtra* and Conceptual Absolutism." In *A History of Buddhist Philosophy*, 170–75. Honolulu: University of Hawaii Press, 1992.

Kanno Hiroshi. "An Overview of Research on Chinese Commentaries on the Lotus Sūtra." *Acta Asiatica, Bulletin of the Institute of Eastern Culture* 66 (1994): 87–103.

———. "A Comparison of Zhiyi's and Jizang's Views of the *Lotus Sūtra:* Did Zhiyi, after all, Advocate a 'Lotus Absolutism'?" In *Annual Report of the International Research Institute for Advanced Buddhology at Soka University for the Academic Year 1999*, 125–47. Tokyo: The International Research Institute for Advanced Buddhology, Soka University, 2000.

———. "The Reception of Lotus Sūtra in Japan." Translated by Sessen International. *The Journal of Oriental Studies* 10 (2000): 31–46.

———. "The Reception of Lotus Sūtra Thought in China." *The Journal of Oriental Studies* 11 (December 2001): 106–22.

———. "The Practice of Bodhisattva Never Disparaging in the Lotus Sūtra and Its Reception in China and Japan." *The Journal of Oriental Studies* 12 (December 2002): 104–22.

———. "The Three Dharma Wheels of Jizang." In *Buddhist and Indian Studies in Honour of Professor Dr. Sodo Mori*, edited by the Publication Committee, 399–412. Hamamatsu, Japan: International Buddhist Association, 2002.

———. "Huisi's Perspective on the *Lotus Sūtra* as Seen Through the *Meaning of the Course of Ease and Bliss in the Lotus Sūtra*." *The Journal of Oriental Studies* 14 (October 2004): 146–66.

———. "A General Survey of Research Concerning Chinese Commentaries on the Lotus Sutra." In *Annual Report of the International Research Institute for Advanced Buddhology at Soka University for the Academic Year 2006*, 417–44. Tokyo: The International Research Institute for Advanced Buddhology, Soka University, 2007.

———. "The Bodhisattva Way and Valuing the Real World in the *Lotus Sūtra*." *The Journal of Oriental Studies* 17 (October 2007): 180–97.

Karashima Seishi. *The Textual Study of the Chinese Versions of the Saddharmapuṇḍarīkasūtra in the Light of the Sanskrit and Tibetan Versions*. Bibliotheca Indologica et Buddhologica 3. Tokyo: Sankibō Press, 1992.

———. "Who Composed the Lotus Sutra? Antagonisms between wilderness and village monks." In *Annual Report of the International Research Institute for Advanced Buddhology at Soka University for the Academic Year 2000*, 417–44. Tokyo: The International Research Institute for Advanced Buddhology, Soka University, 2001.

———. "Some Features of the Language of the *Saddharma-puṇḍarīkasūtra*." *Indo-Iranian Journal* 44 (2001): 207–30.

———. "A Trilingual Edition of the Lotus Sutra—New editions of Sanskrit, Tibetan and Chinese versions." In *Annual Report of the International Research Institute for Advanced Buddhology at Soka University for the Academic Year 2002*, 85–182. Tokyo: The International Research Institute for Advanced Buddhology, Soka University, 2003.

Kasimow, Harold. "A Buddhist Path to Mending the World." In *A Buddhist Kaleidoscope: Essays on the Lotus Sutra*, edited by Gene Reeves, 337–47. Tokyo: Kosei Publishing Co., 2002.

Kawada Yoichi. "The Lotus Sutra as a Doctrine of Inner Reformation." *The Journal of Oriental Studies* 6 (1996): 28–40.

———. "Redemption in Mahâyâna-Buddhism with Special Consideration of the Lotus Sutra." *Annals of the European Academy of Sciences and Arts* 31, no. 11 (2001): 43–53.

Keown, Damien. "Paternalism in the Lotus Sūtra." In *A Buddhist Kaleidoscope: Essays on the Lotus Sutra*, edited by Gene Reeves, 367–78. Tokyo: Kosei Publishing Co., 2002.

Kubo Tsugunari. "The Fundamental Philosophy of the Lotus Sutra with Respect to the Practices of the Bodhisattva." In *Hokkekyo bosatsu shisō kiso*. Tokyo: Shunjūsha, 1987.

———. "Characteristics of the Lotus Sūtra with Regard to the Human Spirit." *Kokoro: Journal of The Essential Lay Buddhism Study Center* 2 (April 2007): 25–29.

———. "*Bodhi* and *Anuttarā Samyak-Saṃbodhi* in the Lotus Sutra." *Kokoro: Journal of The Essential Lay Buddhism Study Center* 4, no. 1 (February 2009): 1–8.

Kuno Takeshi. "The Precious Stupa of the Lotus Sutra." *Dharma World* 22 (May– June 1995): 25–27.

LaFleur, William R. "Symbol and Yūgen: Shunzei's Use of Tendai Buddhism." In *The Karma of Words: Buddhism and the Literary Arts in Medieval Japan*, 80–106. Berkeley: University of California Press, 1983.

Lai, Whalen. "The Predocetic 'Finite Buddhakaya' in the *Lotus Sutra*: In Search of the Illusive Dharmakaya Therein." *Journal of the American Academy of Religion* 49 (Spring 1981): 447–69.

———. "The Humanity of the Buddha: Is Mahayāna Docetic?" *Ching Feng* 14, no. 2 (June 1981): 97–107.

———. "Seno'o Girō and the Dilemma of Modern Buddhism: Leftist Prophet of the Lotus Sutra." *Japanese Journal of Religious Studies* 11 (March 1984): 7–42.

———. "Why the Lotus Sutra?—On the Historic Significance of Tendai." *Japanese Journal of Religious Studies* 14, nos. 2–3 (June–September 1987): 83–100.

———. "Tao-sheng's Theory of Sudden Enlightenment Re-examined." In *Sudden and Gradual Enlightenment: Approaches to Enlightenment in Chinese Thought*, edited by Peter N. Gregory, 169–200. Honolulu: University of Hawaii Press, 1989.

Levering, Miriam L. "The Dragon Girl and the Abbess of Mo-Shan: Gender and Status in the Ch'an Tradition." *Journal of the International Association of Buddhist Studies* 5, no. 1 (1982): 19–35.

———. "Is the Lotus Sutra 'Good News' for Women?" In *A Buddhist Kaleidoscope: Essays on the Lotus Sutra*, edited by Gene Reeves, 469–91. Tokyo: Kosei Publishing Co., 2002.

Lopez Jr., Donald S. "Introduction." In *Buddhism in Practice*, edited by Donald S. Lopez Jr., esp. 28–31. Princeton, NJ: Princeton University Press, 1995.

Matsumoto Shiro. "The *Lotus Sutra* and Japanese Culture." In *Pruning the Bodhi Tree: The Storm Over Critical Buddhism*, edited by Jamie Hubbard and Paul L. Swanson, 388–403. Honolulu: University of Hawaii Press, 1997.

Mattis, Susan. "Chih-i and the Subtle Dharma of the Lotus Sutra: Emptiness or Buddha-nature?" *Dharma World* 27 (March–April 2000): 28–32, 241–59.

Mayer, John R.A. "Reflections on the Threefold Lotus Sutra." In *A Buddhist Kaleidoscope: Essays on the Lotus Sutra*, edited by Gene Reeves, 151–59. Tokyo: Kosei Publishing Co., 2002.

Miya Tsugio. "Pictorial Art of the *Lotus Sutra* in Japan." In *The Lotus Sutra in Japanese Culture*, edited by George J. Tanabe Jr. and Willa Jane Tanabe, 75–94. Honolulu: University of Hawaii Press, 1989.

Mochizuki Kaishaku and Nikkyō Niwano. "The Lotus Sutra and Modern Society." *Dharma World* 11 (May 1984): 10–14.

Morgan, Peggy. "Ethics and the Lotus Sutra." In *A Buddhist Kaleidoscope: Essays on the Lotus Sutra*, edited by Gene Reeves, 351–66. Tokyo: Kosei Publishing Co., 2002.

Murase Miyeko. "Kuan Yin as Savior of Men: Illustrations of the Twenty-fifth Chapter of the *Lotus Sutra*." *Artibus Asiae* 33, nos. 1–2 (1971): 39–74.

Nakamura Hajime. "The Lotus Sutra and Others." In *Indian Buddhism: A Survey with Bibliographical Notes*, 183–93. Delhi: Motilal Banarsidass, 1987.

Nattier, Jan. "The Lotus Sutra through American Eyes." *Dharma World* 25 (September–October 1998): 23–26.

———. "Gender and Hierarchy in the *Lotus Sūtra*." In *Readings of the Lotus Sutra*, edited by Stephen F. Teiser and Jacqueline I. Stone, 83–106. New York: Columbia University Press, 2009.

Niwano Nichiko. "I Am Always Abiding Here, Teaching the Dharma." *Dharma World* 37 (January–March 2010): 22–25.

Niwano Nikkyō. "Can the Lotus Sutra Rescue a World in Crisis?" *Dharma World* 2, no. 3 (March 1975): 2–7.

———. "How to Read the Lotus Sutra." *Dharma World* 4, no. 12 (December 1977): 2–6.

———. "How Do We Read the Lotus Sutra?" *Dharma World* 7 (December 1980): 2–6.

———. "The Perfection of the Lotus Sutra: Action." *Dharma World* 8 (June 1981): 2–6.

———. "The Seven Parables of the Lotus Sutra: Many Teachings, but One Meaning." *Dharma World*, Special Issue 1991, 56–63.

———. "The Three-fold Lotus Sutra: An Introduction." In *A Buddhist Kaleido-

*scope: Essays on the Lotus Sutra*, edited by Gene Reeves, 27–49. Tokyo: Kosei Publishing Co., 2002.

———. "The Threefold Lotus Sutra: A Modern Commentary." *Dharma World* 18 (March–April 1991). Ongoing translation of the ten-volume *Shinshaku Hokke Sambukyo.*

Ochō Enichi. "From the *Lotus Sutra* to the Sutra of Eternal Life: Reflections on the Process of Deliverance in Shinran." *The Eastern Buddhist* 11, no. 1 (May 1978).

Odin, Steve. "The Lotus Sutra in the Writings of Kenji Miyazawa." *Dharma World* 26 (November–December 1999): 13–19; also in *A Buddhist Kaleidoscope: Essays on the Lotus Sutra*, edited by Gene Reeves, 283–96. Tokyo: Kosei Publishing Co., 2002.

Ogden, Schubert M. "The Lotus Sutra and Interreligious Dialogue." *Dharma World* 22 (July–August 1995): 14–18; also in *A Buddhist Kaleidoscope: Essays on the Lotus Sutra*, edited by Gene Reeves, 107–14. Tokyo: Kosei Publishing Co., 2002.

Ohnuma, Reiko. "Teaching the Lotus Sutra." *Dharma World* 25 (November–December 1998): 33–39.

Peach, Lucinda Joy. "Social Responsibility, Sex Change, and Salvation: Gender Justice in The Lotus Sutra." In *A Buddhist Kaleidoscope: Essays on the Lotus Sutra*, edited by Gene Reeves, 437–67. Tokyo: Kosei Publishing Co., 2002.

Pye, Michael. "Hoben & Shinjitsu." *Dharma World* 1, no. 4 (August 1974): 10–12.

———. "The Lotus Sutra and the Essence of Mahāyāna." In *Buddhist Spirituality*, edited by Takeuchi Yoshinori, 171–87. New York: Crossroad, 1997.

———. "The Length of Life of the Tathagata." In *A Buddhist Kaleidoscope: Essays on the Lotus Sutra*, edited by Gene Reeves, 165–75. Tokyo: Kosei Publishing Co., 2002.

Reeves, Gene. "A Buddhist Practice for the Modern World: Rissho Kosei-Kai and the Lotus Sutra." In *1990 Anthology of Fo Kwang Shan International Buddhist Conference.* Taiwan: Fo Kwang Shan, 1990.

———. "The Lotus Sutra and Process Thought." *Process Studies* 23 (Summer 1994): 98–118.

———. "Appropriate Means as the Ethics of the Lotus Sutra." In *A Buddhist Kaleidoscope: Essays on the Lotus Sutra*, edited by Gene Reeves, 379–92. Tokyo: Kosei Publishing Co., 2002.

———. "The Lotus Sutra as Radically World-affirming." In *A Buddhist Kaleidoscope: Essays on the Lotus Sutra*, edited by Gene Reeves, 177–99. Tokyo: Kosei Publishing Co., 2002.

———. "The Compassion and Wisdom of Kuan-yin." *Dharma World* 35 (April–June 2008): 4–8.

————. "Togetherness of Past, Present and Future in the Dharma Flower Sutra." *Kokoro: Journal of The Essential Lay Buddhism Study Center* 4, no. 1 (February 2009): 9–14.

————. "Think Big!" *Dharma World* 37 (January–March 2010): 29–31.

Saito Eizaburo. "The Lotus Sutra in My Political Life." *Dharma World* 14 (May–June 1987): 34–36.

Sekido, Gyoukai. "The Influence of the Lotus Sutra's Dramatic Aspects on Japanese Culture." *Kokoro: Journal of The Essential Lay Buddhism Study Center* 4, no. 1 (February 2009): 51–60.

Shimazono Susumu. "Bodhisattva Practice and Lotus Sutra-Based New Religions of Japan: The Concept of Integration." *Dharma World* 36 (July–September 2009): 32–40.

Shimoda Masahiro. "How Has the Lotus Sutra Created Social Movements? The Relationship of the Lotus Sutra to the Mahāparinirvāṇa-sūtra." In *A Buddhist Kaleidoscope: Essays on the Lotus Sutra*, edited by Gene Reeves, 319–31. Tokyo: Kosei Publishing Co., 2002.

Shioiri Ryōdō. "The Meaning of the Formation and Structure of the *Lotus Sutra*." In *The Lotus Sutra in Japanese Culture*, edited by George J. Tanabe Jr. and Willa Jane Tanabe, 15–36. Honolulu: University of Hawaii Press, 1989.

Silk, Jonathan A. "The Place of the Lotus Sutra in Indian Buddhism." *The Journal of Oriental Studies* 11 (2001).

Steuber, Jason. "Shakyamuni and Prabutaratna in 5th and 6th Century Chinese Buddhist Art at the Nelson-Atkins Museum of Art." *Arts of Asia* 36, no. 2 (March–April 2006): 85–103.

Stevenson, Daniel B. "Tales of the Lotus Sutra." In *Buddhism in Practice*, edited by Donald S. Lopez Jr., 427–51. Princeton, NJ: Princeton University Press, 1995.

————. "Buddhist Practice and the *Lotus Sūtra* in China." In *Readings of the Lotus Sutra*, edited by Stephen F. Teiser and Jacqueline I. Stone, 132–50. New York: Columbia University Press, 2009.

Stone, Jacqueline. "Chanting the August Title of the *Lotus Sūtra*: Daimoku Practices in Classical and Medieval Japan." In *Re-Visioning "Kamakura" Buddhism*, edited by Richard K. Payne, 116–66. Honolulu: University of Hawaii Press, 1998.

————. "Inclusive and Exclusive Perspectives on the One Vehicle." *Dharma World* 26 (September–October 1999): 20–25.

————. "Lotus Sutra millennialism in Japan: From militant nationalism to postwar peace movements." In *Millennialism, Persecution and Violence: Historical Cases*, edited by Catherine Wessinger, 536–72. Syracuse, NY: Syracuse University Press, 2000.

————. "When Disobedience Is Filial and Resistance Is Loyal: The Lotus Sutra and Social Obligations in the Medieval Nichiren Tradition." In *A Buddhist Kaleidoscope: Essays on the Lotus Sutra*, edited by Gene Reeves, 261–81. Tokyo: Kosei Publishing Co., 2002.

————. "Not Mere Written Words: Perspectives on the Language of the Lotus Sūtra in Medieval Japan." *Discourse and Ideology in Medieval Japanese Buddhism*, edited by Richard K. Payne and Taigen Dan Leighton, 160–94. London: Routledge, 2006.

————. "Realizing This World as the Buddha Land." In *Readings of the Lotus Sutra*, edited by Stephen F. Teiser and Jacqueline I. Stone, 209–36. New York: Columbia University Press, 2009.

Sueki Fumihiko. "The *Lotus Sūtra* and Japanese Buddhism." In *Buddhist and Indian Studies in Honour of Professor Sodo Mori*, 425–35. Tokyo: Kokusai Bukkyoto Kyokai, 2002.

Sugitani Gijun. "The Lotus Sutra and Religious Cooperation." *Dharma World* 33 (April–June 2006): 12–13.

Swanson, Paul L. "The Innumerable Meanings of the Lotus Sutra." *Dharma World* 19 (May–June 1992): 42–43; also in *A Buddhist Kaleidoscope: Essays on the Lotus Sutra*, edited by Gene Reeves, 51–53. Tokyo: Kosei Publishing Co., 2002.

Tamura Yoshirō. "The Lotus Sutra." In *Art of the Lotus Sutra*, edited by Tamura and Bunsaku Kurata. Tokyo: Kosei Publishing Co., 1987.

————. "The Ideas of the Lotus Sutra." In *The Lotus Sutra in Japanese Culture*, edited by George J. Tanabe Jr. and Willa Jane Tanabe, 37–51. Honolulu: University of Hawaii Press, 1989.

Tanabe, Willa Jane. "The Lotus Lectures: *Hokke Hakkō* in the Heian Period." *Monumenta Nipponica* 39, no. 4 (Winter 1984): 393–407.

————. "Visual Piety and the Lotus Sutra in Japan." In *A Buddhist Kaleidoscope: Essays on the Lotus Sutra*, edited by Gene Reeves, 81–92. Tokyo: Kosei Publishing Co., 2002.

————. "Art of the *Lotus Sūtra*." In *Readings of the Lotus Sutra*, edited by Stephen F. Teiser and Jacqueline I. Stone, 151–85. New York: Columbia University Press, 2009.

Tatz, Mark, trans. *The Skill in Means (Upāyakauśalya) Sūtra*. Delhi: Motilal Banarsidass, 1994.

Teiser, Stephen F., and Jacqueline I. Stone. "Interpreting the *Lotus Sūtra*." In *Readings of the Lotus Sutra*, edited by Stephen F. Teiser and Jacqueline I. Stone, 2–61. New York: Columbia University Press, 2009.

Tola, Fernando, and Carmen Dragonetti. "Apologetics and Harmony in the Lotus Sūtra and Bhavya." *Kokoro: Journal of The Essential Lay Buddhism Study Center* 2 (April 2007): 1–24.

————. "The *Universalism* and *Generosity* of the *Lotus Sūtra*: An Emblematic Reaction for a New World." *Kokoro: Journal of The Essential Lay Buddhism Study Center* 4, no. 1 (February 2009): 29–42.

Tsuda Shin'ichi. "Significance of the Fulfillment of Shakyamuni Buddha's Vow as the Foundation of the Soteriology of the *Lotus Sutra*." *Kokoro: Journal of The Essential Lay Buddhism Study Center* 4, no. 1 (February 2009): 15–28.

Unno, Taitetsu. "The Somatic in Religious Life." *Dharma World* 23 (January–February 1996): 13–17.

————. "Somatic Realization of the Lotus Sutra." In *A Buddhist Kaleidoscope: Essays on the Lotus Sutra*, edited by Gene Reeves, 71–80. Tokyo: Kosei Publishing Co., 2002.

Venturini, Riccardo. "The Lotus Sutra and Human Needs." *Dharma World* 19 (May–June 1992): 43–64.

————. "A Buddha Teaches Only Bodhisattvas." In *A Buddhist Kaleidoscope: Essays on the Lotus Sutra*, edited by Gene Reeves, 333–36. Tokyo: Kosei Publishing Co., 2002.

Watson, Burton. "The Lotus Sutra and the Twenty-first Century." *The Journal of Oriental Studies* 6 (1996): 11–19.

Wiseman, James. "Buddhist-Christian Dialogue on the Lotus Sutra." *Dharma World* 22 (May–June 1995): 46–47.

Williams, Paul. "The *Saddharmapuṇḍarīka (Lotus) Sūtra* and its influences." In *Mahāyāna Buddhism: The Doctrinal Foundations*, 149–71. 2nd ed. London: Routledge, 2009. Originally published 1989 (see pp. 141–66).

Wolf, J. Douglas. "The Lotus Sutra and the Dimension of Time." *Dharma World* 22 (January–February 1995): 53–54; also in *A Buddhist Kaleidoscope: Essays on the Lotus Sutra*, edited by Gene Reeves, 161–64. Tokyo: Kosei Publishing Co., 2002.

————. "Models for Interfaith Dialogue from the Lotus Sutra." *Dharma World* 27 (March–April 2000): 13–15.

Yamada Shōzen. "Poetry and Meaning: Medieval Poets and the Lotus Sutra." In *The Lotus Sutra in Japanese Culture*, edited by George J. Tanabe Jr. and Willa Jane Tanabe, 95–117. Honolulu: University of Hawaii Press, 1989.

Yoshida Kazuhiko. "The Enlightenment of the Dragon King's Daughter in The Lotus Sutra." Translated and adapted by Margaret H. Childs. In *Engendering Faith: Women and Buddhism in Premodern Japan*, edited by Barbara Ruch, 297–324. Ann Arbor: Center for Japanese Studies, University of Michigan, 2002.

Yuyama Akira. "Why Kumārajīva Omited the Latter Half of Chapter V in Translating the Lotus Sutra." In *Festschrift: Dieter Schlingloff*, edited by Friedrich Wilhelm, 325–30. Reinbek: Verlag für Orientalistische Fachpublikationen, 1996.

## Selected Works on the T'ian-t'ai/Tendai Tradition

Abé Ryūichi. "Saichō and Kūkai: A Conflict of Interpretations." *Japanese Journal of Religious Studies* 22, nos. 1–2 (Spring 1995): 103–37.

Chan Chih-wah. "Chih-li (960–1028) and the Crisis of T'ien-t'ai Buddhism in the Early Sung." In *Buddhism in the Sung*, edited by Peter N. Gregory and Daniel A. Getz Jr., 409–41. Honolulu: University of Hawaii Press, 1999.

Chappell, David W., ed. *T'ien-t'ai Buddhism: An Outline of the Fourfold Teachings.* Tokyo: Daiichi-Shobō, 1983. Distributed by the University of Hawaii Press.

———. "Is Tendai Buddhism Relevant to the Modern World?" *Japanese Journal of Religious Studies* 14, nos. 2–3 (June–September 1987): 247–66.

Ch'en, Kenneth K.S. *Buddhism in China: A Historical Survey*, 303–13. Princeton, NJ: Princeton University Press, 1964.

Donner, Neal A. "Chih-i's Meditation on Evil." In *Buddhist and Taoist Practice in Medieval Chinese Society*, edited by David W. Chappell, 49–64. Honolulu: University of Hawaii Press, 1987.

———. "Chih-i." In *The Encyclopedia of Religion* 3, 240–42. New York: Macmillan and Free Press, 1987.

———. "Sudden and Gradual Intimately Conjoined: Chih-i's T'ien-t'ai View." In *Sudden and Gradual Enlightenment: Approaches to Enlightenment in Chinese Thought*, edited by Peter N. Gregory, 201–26. Honolulu: University of Hawaii Press, 1989.

Donner, Neal A., and Daniel B. Stevenson. *The Great Calming and Contemplation: A Study and Annotated Translation of the First Chapter of Chih-i's* Mo-ho chih-kuan. Honolulu: University of Hawaii Press, 1993.

Gishin. *The Collected Teachings of the Tendai School.* Translated by Paul L. Swanson. Berkeley: Numata Center for Buddhist Translation and Research, 1995.

Goddard, Dwight. "Self-cultivation according to the T'ien-t'ai (Tendai) school." In *A Buddhist Bible*, edited by Dwight Goddard. Boston: Beacon Press, 1938.

Grapard, Allan. "Linguistic Cubism—A Singularity of Pluralism in the Sannō Cult." *Japanese Journal of Religious Studies* 14, nos. 2–3 (June–September 1987): 211–34.

———. "Enchin." In *The Encyclopedia of Religion* 5, 105–6. New York: Macmillan and Free Press, 1987.

———. "Honjisuijaku." In *The Encyclopedia of Religion* 6, 455–57. New York: Macmillan and Free Press, 1987.

Groner, Paul. *Saichō: The Establishment of the Japanese Tendai School.* Berkeley: Buddhist Studies Series, 1984.

———. "Saichō." In *The Encyclopedia of Religion* 6, 455–57. New York: Macmillan and Free Press, 1987.

———. "Annen, Tankei, Henjō, and Monastic Discipline in the Tendai School: The Background of the *Futsū jobosatsukai kōshaku.*" *Japanese Journal of Religious Studies* 14, nos. 2–3 (June–September 1987): 129–59.

———. "The Lotus Sutra and Saichō's Interpretation of the Realization of Buddhahood with This Very Body." In *The Lotus Sutra in Japanese Culture*, edited by George J. Tanabe Jr. and Willa Jane Tanabe, 53–74. Honolulu: University of Hawaii Press, 1989.

———. "Shortening the Path: The Interpretation of the Realization of Buddhahood in This Very Existence in the Early Tendai School." In *Paths to Liberation: The Mārga and Its Transformations in Buddhist Thought*, edited by Robert Buswell and Robert Gimello. Honolulu: University of Hawaii Press, 1992.

———. "A Medieval Japanese Reading of the *Mo-ho chih-kuan*: Placing the *Kankō ruijū* in Historical Context." *Japanese Journal of Religious Studies* 22, nos. 1–2 (Spring 1995): 49–81.

———. *Ryogen and Mount Hiei: Japanese Tendai in the Tenth Century.* Honolulu: University of Hawaii Press, 2002.

Habito, Ruben L.F. "Buddha-body Views in Tendai *Hongaku* Writings." *Journal of Indian and Buddhist Studies* 34, no. 2 (1991): 54–60.

———. "The Self as Buddha—in Tendai Hongaku Writings—Orthodoxy and Orthopraxis in Japanese Buddhism." In *Atmajnana—Professor Sengaku Mayeda Felicitation Volume.* Tokyo: Shunjūsha, 1991.

———. "The New Buddhism of Kamakura and the Doctrine of Innate Enlightenment." *The Pacific World* 7 (Fall 1991): 26–35.

———. "The Logic of Nonduality and Absolute Affirmation: Deconstructing Tendai *Hongaku* Writings." *Japanese Journal of Religious Studies* 22, nos. 1–2 (Spring 1995): 83–101.

———. *Originary Enlightenment: Tendai Hongaku Doctrine and Japanese Buddhism.* Studia Philologica Buddhica, Occasional Paper Series XI. Tokyo: The International Institute of Buddhist Studies of ICABS, 1996.

———. *Experiencing Buddhism: Ways of Wisdom and Compassion.* New York: Orbis Books, 2005.

Harrison, Paul M. "Who Gets to Ride in the Great Vehicle? Self-Image and Identity among the Followers of the Early Mahayana." *Journal of the International Association of Buddhist Studies* 10, no. 1 (1987): 67–89.

Hazama Jikō. "The Characteristics of Japanese Tendai." *Japanese Journal of Religious Studies* 14, nos. 2–3 (June–September 1987): 101–12.

Heng-ching. "T'ien-t'ai Chih-i's Theory of Buddha Nature: A Realistic and Humanistic Understanding of the Buddha." In *Buddha Nature: A Festshrift in Honor of Minoru Kiyota*, edited by Paul Griffiths and John Keenan, 153–70. Reno: Buddhist Books International, 1990.

Hurvitz, Leon. "Chih-i (538–597): An Introduction to the Life and Ideas of a Chinese Buddhist Monk." *Mélanges Chinois et Bouddhiques* 12 (1961–62).

———. "The First Systematizations of Buddhist Thought in China." *Journal of Chinese Philosophy* 2 (1975): 361–88.

Hurvitz, Leon, Burton Watson, and Daniel Stevenson. "The Lotus School: The Tiantai Synthesis." In *Sources of Chinese Tradition*, edited by Wm. Theodore de Bary and Irene Bloom, vol. 1, 444–67. 2nd ed. New York: Columbia University Press, 1999.

Kasahara Kazuo. "The Original Development of the Tendai Sect." *Dharma World* 11 (April 1984): 35–38; (May 1984): 40–45; (June 1984): 41–44; (July 1984): 39–42; (August 1984): 40–43; (September 1984): 40–43.

Kiyota Minoru. "The Structure and Meaning of Tendai Thought." *Transactions of the International Conference of Orientalists in Japan* 5 (1960): 69–83.

The Korean Buddhist Research Institute, eds. *Ch'ŏnt'ae Thought in Korean Buddhism*. Seoul: Dongguk University Press, 1999.

Kuroda Toshio. "Historical Consciousness and Hon-jaku Philosophy in the Medieval Period on Mount Hiei." In *The Lotus Sutra in Japanese Culture*, edited by George J. Tanabe Jr. and Willa Jane Tanabe, 143–58. Honolulu: University of Hawaii Press, 1989.

LaFleur, William R. "Saigyō and the Buddhist Value of Nature." *History of Religions* 13, no. 2 (November 1973): 93–128; no. 3 (February 1974): 227–48.

Lai, Whalen. "Faith and Wisdom in the T'ien-t'ai Buddhist tradition: A letter by Ssu-ming Chih-li." *Journal of DHARMA* 6 (1981): 283–98.

———. "A Different Religious Language: The T'ien-t'ai Idea of the Triple Truth." *Ching Feng* 25, no. 2 (1982): 67–78.

Lu K'uan-yü (Charles Luk). "Self-cultivation according to the T'ien-t'ai (Tendai) school: Samath-vipasyana for Beginners." In *The Secrets of Chinese Meditation*, 109–62. New York: Samuel Weiser, 1964, 1994.

Matsunaga Daigan and Alicia. "Tendai." In *Foundation of Japanese Buddhism*, vol. I, chapter 4A, 139–71. Los Angeles: Buddhist Books International, 1974.

McMullin, Neil. "The Sanmon-Jimon Schism in the Tendai School of Buddhism: A Preliminary Analysis." *Journal of the International Association of Buddhist Studies* 7 (1984): 83–105.

———. "The Enryaku-ji and the Gion Shrine-Temple Complex in the Mid-Heian Period." *Japanese Journal of Religious Studies* 14, nos. 2–3 (June–September 1987): 161–84.

———. "The Lotus Sutra and Politics in the Mid-Heian Period." In *The Lotus Sutra in Japanese Culture*, edited by George J. Tanabe Jr. and Willa Jane Tanabe, 119–41. Honolulu: University of Hawaii Press, 1989.

Ng Yu-Kwan. *T'ien-t'ai Buddhism and Early Madhyamika*. Honolulu: University of Hawaii Press, 1993.

Ozaki Makoto. "Saicho's Role and Significance in the Expectation of the Mappo Era." *Studies in Interreligious Dialogue* 1 (1991): 116–28.

Penkower, Linda. "Making and Remaking Tradition: Chan Jan's Strategies toward a T'ang T'ian-t'ai Agenda." In *Tendai Daishi kenkyū*, edited by Tendai Daishi kenkyū henshū iinkai, 1338–1289. Kyoto: Tendai gakkai, 1997.

Petzold, Bruno. *Tendai Buddhism*. Yokohama: International Buddhist Exchange Center, 1979.

Pruden, Leo M. "T'ien-t'ai." In *The Encyclopedia of Religion* 14, 510–19. New York: Macmillan and Free Press, 1987.

Reischauer, Edwin O. *Ennin's Diary: The Record of a Pilgrimage to China in Search of the Law*. New York: Ronald Press, 1955.

———. *Ennin's Travels in T'ang China*. New York: Ronald Press, 1955.

Rhodes, Robert F., translation and introduction. "Saichō's *Mappō Tōmyōki*: The Candle of the Latter Dharma." *Eastern Buddhist* 13, no. 1 (1980): 79–103.

———. "The Four Extensive Vows and Four Noble Truths in T'ien-t'ai Buddhism." *Annual Memoirs of the Otani University Shin Buddhists Comprehensive Research Institute* 2 (1984): 53–91.

———. "Annotated Translation of the *Ssu-chiao-i* (On the Four Teachings), *chüan 1*." *Annual Memoirs of the Otani University Shin Buddhists Comprehensive Research Institute* 3 (1985): 27–101; 4 (1986): 93–141.

———. "The *Kaihōgyō* Practice of Mt. Hiei." *Japanese Journal of Religious Studies* 14, nos. 2–3 (June–September 1987): 185–202.

Saichō. *The Candle of the Latter Dharma*. Translated by Robert Rhodes. Berkeley: Numata Center for Buddhist Translation and Research, 1994.

Saso, Michael, "The Oral Hermeneutics of Tendai Tantric Buddhism." *Japanese Journal of Religious Studies* 14, nos. 2–3 (June–September 1987): 235–46.

Shinohara Koichi. "Quanding's Biography of Zhiyi, the Fourth Chinese Patriarch of the Tiantai Tradition." In *Speaking of Monks: Religious Biography in India and China*, edited by Phyllis Granoff and Koichi Shinohara, 97–232. New York: Mosaic Press, 1992.

———. "From Local History to Universal History." In *Buddhism in the Sung*, edited by Peter N. Gregory and Daniel A. Getz Jr., 524–76. Honolulu: University of Hawaii Press, 1999.

Shirato Waka. "Inherent Enlightenment and Saichō's Acceptance of the Bodhisattva Precepts." *Japanese Journal of Religious Studies* 14, nos. 2–3 (June–September 1987): 113–27.

Sonoda Kōyū. "Saicho." In *Shapers of Japanese Buddhism*, edited by Yūsen Kashiwahara and Kōyū Sonoda, 26–38. Tokyo: Kosei Publishing Co., 1994.

Stevenson, Daniel B. "The Four Kinds of Samadhi in Early T'ien-t'ai Buddhism." In *Traditions of Meditation in Chinese Meditation*, edited by Peter N. Gregory, 45–98. Honolulu: University of Hawaii Press, 1986.

————. *The T'ien-t'ai Four Forms of Samadhi and Late North-South Dynasties, Sui, and Early T'ang Buddhist Devotionalism*. Ann Arbor: University of Michigan Press, 1987.

————. "Protocols of Power: Tz'u-yün Tsun-shih (964–1032) and T'ien-t'ai Lay Buddhist Ritual." In *Buddhism in the Sung*, edited by Peter N. Gregory and Daniel A. Getz Jr., 340–408. Honolulu: University of Hawaii Press, 1999.

Stone, Jacqueline I. "Medieval Tendai Hongaku Thought and the New Kamakura Buddhism: A Reconsideration." *Japanese Journal of Religious Studies* 22, nos. 1–2 (Spring 1995): 17–48.

————. *Original Enlightenment and the Transformation of Medieval Japanese Buddhism*. Honolulu: University of Hawaii Press, 1999.

Sueki Fumihiko. "Two Seemingly Contradictory Aspects of the Teaching of Innate Enlightenment (*hongaku*) in Medieval Japan." *Japanese Journal of Religious Studies* 22, nos. 1–2 (Spring 1995): 3–16.

Swanson, Paul L. "Chih-i's Interpretation of Jneyāvarana: An Application of the Threefold Truth Concept." *Annual Memoirs of the Otani University Shin Buddhists Comprehensive Research Institute* 1 (1983): 51–72.

————. "Chih-i's Interpretation of the Four Noble Truths in the *Fa hua hsüan i.*" *Annual Memoirs of the Otani University Shin Buddhist Comprehensive Research Institute* 1 (1985): 103–31.

————. "T'ien-t'ai Studies in Japan." *Cahiers d'Estrême-Asie* 2 (1986): 219–32.

————, ed. "Tendai Buddhism in Japan" issue of *Japanese Journal of Religious Studies* 14, nos. 2–3. Nagoya: Nanzan Institute for Religion and Culture, 1987.

————. *Foundations of T'ien-t'ai Philosophy: The Flowering of the Two Truths Theory in Chinese Buddhism*. Berkeley: Asian Humanities Press, 1989.

————. "T'ien-t'ai Chih-i's Concept of Threefold Buddha Nature—A Synergy of Reality, Wisdom, and Practice." In *Buddha Nature*. Reno: Buddhist Books International, 1990.

————. "Understanding Chih-i: Through a Glass Darkly?" *Journal of the International Association of Buddhist Studies* 17, no. 2 (1994): 337–60.

————, trans. *The Great Cessation and Contemplation (Mo-ho chih-kuan)*. CD-ROM. Tokyo: Kosei Publishing Co., 2004.

Takakusu Janjirō. "The Tendai School (Phenomenology, Lotus, Saddharma-pundarīka, T'ten-t'ai)." In *The Essentials of Buddhist Philosophy*, 131–47. Bombay: Asia Publishing House, 1956.

Tamura Yoshirō. "Japanese Culture and the Tendai Concept of Original Enlightenment." *Japanese Journal of Religious Studies* 14, nos. 2–3 (June–September 1987): 203–10.

———. "Tendaishū." In *The Encyclopedia of Religion* 14, 396–401. New York: Macmillan and Free Press, 1987.

———. "Japan's Experience of Buddhism: Saicho and Kukai." *Dharma World* 16 (September–October 1989): 32–37.

———. "Japan's Experience of Buddhism: Original Enlightenment and Rebirth in the Pure Land." *Dharma World* 16 (November–December 1989): 30–36.

Unno, Taitetsu. "San-lun, T'ien-t'ai, and Hua-yen." In *Buddhist Spirituality*, edited by Takeuchi Yoshinori, 343–65. New York: Crossroad, 1997.

Weinstein, Stanley. "The Beginnings of Esoteric Buddhism in Japan: The Neglected Tendai Tradition." *Journal of Asian Studies* 34 (1974): 177–91.

Ziporyn, Brook. "What Is the Buddha Looking At? The Importance of Intersubjectivity in the T'ien-t'ai Tradition as Understood by Chih-li." In *Buddhism in the Sung*, edited by Peter N. Gregory and Daniel A. Getz Jr., 442–76. Honolulu: University of Hawaii Press, 1999.

———. *Evil and/or/as the Good: Omnicentrism, Intersubjectivity, and Value Paradox in Tiantai Buddhist Thought.* Cambridge: Harvard University Asia Center, 2002.

———. *Being and Ambiguity: Philosophical Experiments with Tiantai Buddhism.* Chicago: Open Court, 2004.

## SELECTED WORKS ON THE NICHIREN TRADITION

Allam, Cheryl M. "The Nichiren and Catholic Confrontation with Japanese Nationalism." *Buddhist-Christian Studies* 10 (1990): 35–84.

Anesaki Masaharu. *Nichiren, the Buddhist Prophet.* Cambridge: Harvard University Press, 1916.

Asai Endō. "Nichiren Shōnin's View of Humanity: The Final Dharma Age and the Three Thousand Realms in One Thought-Moment." *Japanese Journal of Religious Studies* 26, nos. 3–4 (Fall 1999): 239–59.

Bloom, Alfred. "Observations in the Study of Contemporary Nichiren Buddhism." *Contemporary Religions in Japan* 6, no. 1 (1965): 58–74.

Brinkman, John T. "The Simplicity of Nichiren." *Eastern Buddhist*, n.s., 28, no. 2 (1995): 248–64.

Causton, Richard. *Nichiren Shoshu Buddhism.* London: Rider, 1988.

Christensen, J.A. *Nichiren.* Tokyo: Nichiren-shū, 1981.

Deal, William E. "Nichiren's *Risshō ankoku ron* and Canon Formation." *Japanese Journal of Religious Studies* 26, nos. 3–4 (Fall 1999): 325–48.

Del Campana, Pier P. "*Sandaihihō-shō*: An essay on the three great mysteries by Nichiren." *Monumenta Nipponica* 26, nos. 1–2 (1971): 205–24.

———. "Innovators of Kamakura Buddhism: Shinran and Nichiren." In *Great Historical Figures of Japan*, edited by Hyōe Murakami and Thomas J. Harper, 102–13. Tokyo: Japan Cultural Institute, 1978.

Dolce, Lucia. "Awareness of *mappō*: Soteriological interpretations of time in Nichiren." *The Transactions of the Asiatic Society of Japan*, 4th ser., 7 (1992): 81–106.

———. "Esoteric patterns in Nichiren's thought." *The Japan Foundation Newsletter* 23, no. 5 (1996): 13–16.

———. "Buddhist hermeneutics in medieval Japan: Canonical texts, scholastic tradition and sectarian polemics." In *Canonization and Decanonization*, edited by A. van der Kooij and K. van der Toorn, 229–43. Leiden: Brill, 1998.

———. "Criticism and Appropriation: Nichiren's Attitude toward Esoteric Buddhism." *Japanese Journal of Religious Studies* 26, nos. 3–4 (Fall 1999): 349–82.

———. "Engaged Lotus Buddhism in Medieval Japan." *Dharma World* 34 (January–March 2007): 14–17.

———. *Nichiren and the Lotus Sutra*. Leiden: Brill, 2007.

Dollarhide, Kenneth. "History and time in Nichiren's *Senji-shō*." *Religion* 12 (1982): 233–45.

———. *Nichiren's Senji-shō: An Essay on the Selection of the Proper Time*. New York: Edwin Mellen Press, 1982.

Fujii Manabu. "Nichiren." In *Shapers of Japanese Buddhism*, edited by Yūsen Kashiwahara and Kōyū Sonoda, 123–34. Tokyo: Kosei Publishing Co., 1994.

Fujii Nichidatsu. *Buddhism for World Peace*. Translated by Yumiko Miyazaki. Tokyo: Japan-Bharat Sarvodaya Mitrata Sangha, 1980.

———. *Tranquil Is This Realm of Mine: Dharma Talks and Writings of the Most Venerable Nichidatsu Fujii*. Translated by Yumikio Miyazaki. Atlanta: Nipponzan Myōhōji, 2007.

Gosho Translation Committee, ed. and trans. *The Major Writings of Nichiren Daishonin*. 7 vols. Tokyo: Nichiren Shōshū International Center, 1979–1994.

———. *The Writings of Nichiren Daishonin*. Tokyo: Soka Gakkai, 1999.

Habito, Ruben L.F. "Lotus Buddhism and its Liberational Thrust: A Rereading of the *Lotus Sūtra* by way of Nichiren." *Ching Feng* 35, no. 2 (1992 ): 85–112.

———. "The mystico-prophetic Buddhism of Nichiren: An exploration in comparative theology." In *The Papers of the Henry Luce III Fellows in Theology*, edited by Jonathan Strom, vol. 2, 433–62. Atlanta, GA: Scholars' Press, 1997.

———. "Bodily Reading of the *Lotus Sūtra*: Understanding Nichiren's Buddhism." *Japanese Journal of Religious Studies* 26, nos. 3–4 (Fall 1999): 281–306.

———. "The Uses of Nichiren in Modern Japanese History." *Japanese Journal of Religious Studies* 26, nos. 3–4 (Fall 1999): 424–39.

Habito, Ruben L.F., and Jacqueline I. Stone. "Revisiting Nichiren." *Japanese Journal of Religious Studies* 26, nos. 3–4 (Fall 1999): 223–36.

Hammond, Phillip, and David Machacek. *Soka Gakkai in America.* Oxford: Oxford University Press, 1999.

Hori Kyōtsū, trans. "Nichiren's *Opening the Eyes.*" *Tōkyō risshō joshi tanki daigaku kiyō* 12 (1984): 21–45; 13 (1985): 17–39.

Iida Shotaro. "'A Lotus in the Sun'—An Aspect of the Soka Gakkai in Japan." In *Facets of Buddhism*, 133–43. Delhi: Motilal Banarsidass, 1991.

Ingram, Paul O. "Nichirin's [*sic*] three secrets." *Numen* 24, no. 3 (1977): 207–22.

Itohisa Hōken. "Development of the Nichiren sect in Kyoto: Formation of 'monryū' or sub-sects and their organizational structure." *Ōsaki gakuhō* 140 (1985): 1–8.

Jaffe, Paul D. "Rising from the Lotus: Two bodhisattvas from the Lotus Sutra as a psychodynamic paradigm for Nichiren." *Japanese Journal of Religious Studies* 13, no. 1 (1986): 81–105.

———. "On Nichiren's appropriation of the truth." *Ōsaki gakuhō* 141 (1986): 1–10.

Kadowaki Kakichi. "Nichiren and the Christian Way." *Dharma World* 26 (March–April 1999): 14–18.

———. "What Christians Can Learn from Nichiren." *Dharma World* 26 (May–June 1999): 19–23.

———. "The Future of Humanity as Viewed by Nichiren and Christianity." *Dharma World* 26 (July–August 1999): 22–25.

Kasahara Kazuo. "The Development of the *Daimoku.*" *Dharma World* 14 (July–August 1987): 43–48; (September–October 1987): 44–48; (November–December 1987): 43–47.

Kim, Ha Poong. "Fujii Nichidatsu's *tangyō raihai*: Bodhisattva practice for the nuclear age." *Cross Currents* (1986): 193–202.

Kitagawa Zenchō. "Characteristics of Nichiren's interpretation of the Lotus Sutra." *Ōsaki gakuhō* 138 (1983): 21–28.

Kodera, Takashi James. "Nichiren and his nationalistic eschatology." *Religious Studies* 15 (1979): 41–53.

Lamont, H.G. "Nichiren (1222–1282)." In *Kōdansha Encyclopedia of Japan* 5, 375–76. Tokyo and New York: Kōdansha, 1983.

———. "Nichiren sect." In *Kōdansha Encyclopedia of Japan* 5, 376–77. Tokyo and New York: Kōdansha, 1983.

Large, Stephen S. "Buddhism, socialism and protest in prewar Japan: The career of Seno'o Girō." *Modern Asian Studies* 21, no. 1 (1987): 153–71.

Lee, Edwin B. "Nichiren and nationalism: The religious patriotism of Tanaka Chigaku." *Monumenta Nipponica* 30 (1975): 19–35.

Lloyd, A. "Nichiren" (poem). *Transactions of the Asiatic Society of Japan* 22 (1984): 482–506.

Métraux, Daniel A. *The History and Theology of the Sōka Gakkai.* Lewiston, NY: Edwin Mellen Press, 1988.

———. "The Dispute Between the Sōka Gakkai and the Nichiren Shōshū Priesthood." *Japanese Journal of Religious Studies* 19, no. 4 (December 1992): 325–36.

———. *The Sōka Gakkai Revolution.* New York: University Press of America, 1994.

———. "The Soka Gakkai: Buddhism and the Creation of a Harmonious and Peaceful Society." In *Engaged Buddhism: Buddhist Liberation Movements in Asia*, edited by Christopher S. Queen and Sallie B. King, 365–400. Albany: State University of New York Press, 1996.

Murano Senchū, trans. *Nyorai metsugo go gohyakusai shi kanjin honzon shō* [The true object of worship revealed for the first time in the fifth of five-century periods after the great decease of the Tathāgata]. Tokyo: Young East Association, 1954.

———. "Nichirenshū." In *The Encyclopedia of Religion* 10, 427–31. New York: Macmillan, 1987.

———. *Manual of Nichiren Buddhism.* Tokyo: Nichiren Shu Headquarters, 1995.

Naylor, Christina "Nichiren, imperialism, and the peace movement." *Japanese Journal of Religious Studies* 18, no. 1 (1991): 51–78.

Otani Gyoko. "Nichiren's View of Ethics." In *Buddhist Ethics and Modern Society*, edited by Charles Wei-hsun Fu and Sandra A. Wawrytko. Westport, CT: Greenwood Press, 1991.

Petzold, Bruno. *Buddhist Prophet Nichiren: A Lotus in the Sun.* Edited by Shotaro Iida and Wendy Simmonds. Tokyo: Hokke Jānaru, 1978.

Petzold, Bruno, in collaboration with Shinshō Hanayama. "The Nichiren system." Chapter 27 in *The Classification of Buddhism (Bukkyō Kyōhan)*, edited by Shohei Ichimura, 607–90. Wiesbaden: Harrassowitz, 1995.

Rodd, Laurel Rasplica. "Nichiren and *setsuwa.*" *Japanese Journal of Religious Studies* 5, nos. 2–3 (1978): 159–85.

———. *Nichiren: A Biography.* Occasional paper no. 11. Tempe: Arizona State University, 1978.

———. *Nichiren: Selected Writings.* Asian Studies at Hawaii, no. 26. Honolulu: University of Hawaii Press, 1980.

———. "Nichiren." In *Great Thinkers of the Eastern World*, edited by Ian P. McGreal, 327–29. New York: HarperCollins, 1995.

———. *Nichiren's Teachings to Women.* Selected papers in Asian studies, n.s., no. 5. Western Conference of the Association for Asian Studies, n.d.

Satō Hiroo. "Nichiren's View of Nation and Religion." *Japanese Journal of Religious Studies* 26, nos. 3–4 (Fall 1999): 307–23.

Shinohara Kōichi, "Religion and Political Order in Nichiren's Buddhism." *Japanese Journal of Religious Studies* 8, nos. 3–4 (1981): 225–35.

Shinozaki Michio. "A Buddhist Approach to Ecological Crisis: Rediscovery of the Historical Consciousness in Nichiren." In *A Buddhist Kaleidoscope: Essays on the Lotus Sutra*, edited by Gene Reeves, 395–419. Tokyo: Kosei Publishing Co., 2002.

Stone, Jacqueline I. "How Nichiren saw Chishō Daishi Enchin." In *Chishō Daishi kenkyū*, edited by Chishō Daishi Kenkyū Henshū Iinaki, 55–65. Ōtsu: Tendai Jimonshū, 1989.

———. "Rebuking the enemies of the *Lotus*: Nichirenist exclusivism in historical perspective." *Japanese Journal of Religious Studies* 21, nos. 2–3 (1994): 231–59.

———. "Original enlightenment thought in the Nichiren tradition." In *Buddhism in Practice*, edited by Donald S. Lopez Jr., 228–40. Princeton, NJ: Princeton University Press, 1995.

———. "Chanting the August Title of the *Lotus Sutra: Daimoku* Practices in Classical and Medieval Japan." In *Re-visioning "Kamakura" Buddhism*, edited by Richard K. Payne, 116–66. Honolulu: University of Hawaii Press, 1998.

———. "Priest Nisshin's ordeals." In *Religions of Japan in Practice*, edited by George J. Tanabe Jr., 384–97. Princeton, NJ: Princeton University Press, 1999.

———. "Nichiren and His Successors." Part three of *Original Enlightenment and the Transformation of Medieval Japanese Buddhism*, 237–355. Honolulu: University of Hawaii Press, 1999.

———. "Placing Nichiren in the 'Big Picture': Some Ongoing Issues in Scholarship." *Japanese Journal of Religious Studies* 26, nos. 3–4 (Fall 1999): 383–421.

———. "Biographical Studies of Nichiren." *Japanese Journal of Religious Studies* 26, nos. 3–4 (Fall 1999): 442–58.

———. "Nichiren's Activist Heirs: Sōka Gakkai, Risshō Koseikai, Nipponzan Myōhōji." In *Action Dharma: New Studies in Engaged Buddhism*, edited by Christopher Queen, Charles Prebish, and Damien Keown, 63–94. New York: RoutledgeCurzon, 2003.

Sueki Fumihiko. "Nichiren's Problematic Works." *Japanese Journal of Religious Studies* 26, nos. 3–4 (Fall 1999): 261–80.

Takakusu Janjirō. "The Nichiren School (Lotus-pietism, New Lotus)." In *The Essentials of Buddhist Philosophy*, 186–94. Bombay: Asia Publishing House, 1956.

Tanabe, George J. Jr. "Tanaka Chigaku: The *Lotus Sutra* and the body politic." In

*The Lotus Sutra and Japanese Culture*, edited by George J. Tanabe Jr. and Willa Jane Tanabe, 191–208. Honolulu: University of Hawaii Press, 1989.

———. "The Matsumoto debate." In *Buddhism in Practice*, edited by Donald S. Lopez Jr., 241–48. Princeton, NJ: Princeton University Press, 1995.

Tanaka Chigaku. *What Is Nippon Kokutai?* Translated by Satomi Kishio. Tokyo: Shishi-ō Bunko, 1937.

Uchimura Kanzō. "Saint Nichiren—A Buddhist priest." In *Uchimura Kanzō zenshū* 15 (1933): 288–314. Tokyo: Iwanami Shoten.

Watanabe Hōyō. "Nichiren's thought appearing in the *Risshō ankoku ron* and its acceptance in the modern age." *Ōsaki gakuhō* 138 (1985): 11–20.

———. "Nichiren." In *The Encyclopedia of Religion* 10, 425–27. New York: Macmillan, 1987.

Woodard, William P. "The wartime persecution of Nichiren Buddhism." *The Transactions of the Asiatic Society of Japan*, 3rd ser., 7 (1959): 99–122.

Yampolsky, Philip B., with Burton Watson et al., trans. *Selected Writings of Nichiren*. New York: Columbia University Press, 1990.

———. *Letters of Nichiren*. New York: Columbia University Press, 1996.

# INDEX

The choice of the author to use the terms "Lotus Sutra" and "Dharma Flower Sutra" interchangeably is continued in the index.

# ABOUT THE AUTHOR

GENE REEVES has been studying, teaching, and writing in Japan for twenty years, primarily on Buddhism and interfaith relations. Now an International Advisor at Rissho Kosei-kai, he is retired from the University of Tsukuba, where he taught for eight years. He is a founder of and serves as the Special Minister for the International Buddhist Congregation in Tokyo. He also serves as the International Advisor to the Niwano Peace Foundation and he is the coordinator of an annual International Seminar on the Lotus Sutra. In the spring of 2008 Reeves was a visiting professor at the University of Peking, Beijing, China.

Reeves has been active in interfaith conversations and organizations: he served as Chair of the Planning Committee for the 1987 Congress of the International Association for Religious Freedom (IARF) at Stanford University; he was one of the founders of the Council for a Parliament of the World's Religions; and he is a member of the Board of the Society for Buddhist Christian Studies. In Japan he has been an advisor to the Japan Liaison Committee of the IARF, a participant in the Religious Summit at Mount Hiei, and in various activities of the World Conference of Religions for Peace. As a Buddhist teacher, he travels frequently to China, Singapore, Taiwan, America, and Europe to give talks at universities and churches, mainly on the Lotus Sutra. He is the translator of *The Lotus Sutra: A Contemporary Translation of a Buddhist Classic*.

# ABOUT WISDOM PUBLICATIONS

Wisdom Publications, a nonprofit publisher, is dedicated to making available authentic works relating to Buddhism for the benefit of all. We publish books by ancient and modern masters in all traditions of Buddhism, translations of important texts, and original scholarship. Additionally, we offer books that explore East-West themes unfolding as traditional Buddhism encounters our modern culture in all its aspects. Our titles are published with the appreciation of Buddhism as a living philosophy, and with the special commitment to preserve and transmit important works from Buddhism's many traditions.

To learn more about Wisdom, or to browse books online, visit our website at www.wisdompubs.org.

You may request a copy of our catalog online or by writing to this address:

WISDOM PUBLICATIONS
199 Elm Street
Somerville, Massachusetts 02144 USA
Telephone: 617-776-7416
Fax: 617-776-7841
Email: info@wisdompubs.org
www.wisdompubs.org

# THE WISDOM TRUST